The Boy N

Josie Lloyd's first novel, *It Co*
1997. Emlyn Rees is the author
of Dead Authors and *Undertow*. Together they are the
authors of the top ten bestsellers *Come Together* and *Come
Again*. They live in London.

Also by Josie Lloyd & Emlyn Rees

Come Together
Come Again

The Boy Next Door

Josie Lloyd & Emlyn Rees

ARROW

First published in the United Kingdom in 2002 by
Arrow Books

1 3 5 7 9 10 8 6 4 2

First published in the United Kingdom in 2001 by William Heinemann

Arrow Books
The Random House Group Limited
20 Vauxhall Bridge Road, London SW1V 2SA

Random House Australia (Pty) Limited
20 Alfred Street, Milsons Point, Sydney
New South Wales 2061, Australia

Random House New Zealand Limited
18 Poland Road, Glenfield
Auckland 10, New Zealand

Random House South Africa (Pty) Limited
Endulini, 5a Jubilee Road,
Parktown, 2193, South Africa

The Random House Group Limited Reg. No. 954009

www.randomhouse.co.uk

A CIP catalogue record for this book is available from the British Library

Papers used by Random House are natural, recyclable products made from
wood grown in sustainable forests. The manufacturing processes conform to
the environmental regulations of the country of origin

Printed and bound in Denmark by
Nørhaven Paperback A/S

ISBN 0 09 941482 1

For our Dads, for the sunglasses . . .

Acknowledgements

With thanks to Vivienne, Jonny, Euan, Doug, Carol, Kate, Diana, Emma, Sarah, Gill & Karen at Curtis Brown; Lynne, Andy, Thomas (we'll miss you!), Ron, Dave, Simon, Grainne, Mark, Glenn, Susan & Karen at Random House; Di for her support; Dawn Fozard for the word 'drama'; David and Gwenda and the Savages for the getaways; Gina Ford for the book; and Tallulah for putting up with us.

Chapter I

Fred

'Action,' Eddie calls from outside, and I step through the living-room doorway and out on to the sunlit roof terrace.

Despite being up here on the top floor of what's a four-storey building, there's not a breath of wind. I peer across the undulating cityscape of chimney pots and roof tiles and tower blocks. Shimmering in the distance, the slow-moving traffic snaking over the raised bulk of the Westway sounds strangely muffled, as if I'm observing it from behind a giant Perspex screen. My London: a city where you can be whoever you want to be, a city where thousands of lives are started and finished every day.

Careful not to look at Eddie (he's already told me twice not to), I sit down and face the lens of the camcorder he's holding. 'Hello,' I say, 'my name is Fred Wilson and I am –'

'Cut.'

This time I do look up at Eddie. Like me, he's perched on a white plastic garden chair and is stripped from the waist up. A thin band of shadow cast by a telephone wire rings the biceps of his left arm like a tattoo. He's a few years younger than me and his skin is slick with high-factor sun cream (Eddie doesn't do tans; they'd clash with his black leather jacket).

A gurgle of frustration rises to a growl at the back of my throat. This is the fifth cut I've sustained in as many minutes. Another, I fear, could well prove fatal.

'What now?' I explode, beginning to wish I'd refused his request to help him with this, his inaugural (and consequently slightly cringe-worthy) film-school project.

Eddie screws up his face, embarrassed and trying not to laugh. It's the kind of expression I've seen him use on girls in bars, the kind that melts away their defences and leaves them staring at him with helpless, adoring eyes.

His own eyes are a dark denim blue, although more often than not their wide-awake glory remains concealed behind his scrunched-up eyelids. This is a result of his refusal to wear his prescription glasses for anything other than watching television and this, in turn, is a result of his assumption that he's more attractive to women without them.

'Only if they're into squinty-looking weirdos,' I told him a few months ago, an accusation which (unsurprisingly, in hindsight) he was quick to deny.

And he was right to. Laid-back and sleazy works for Eddie. (Even Rebecca, my own beloved, has admitted as much.) His love life is spectacularly varied – particularly in comparison with my own – leading me to have wondered on several occasions whether it's my general lack of squintiness which has tethered me to a far more stable existence.

'I'm sorry,' he finally says. 'It's just . . .'

'Just *what*?' I demand as his words peter out and this latter-day Lou Reed pushes his dark hair back from his face. 'No, no,' I continue before he has time to speak. 'Let me guess. It's my fingernails, right?' I hold them up before my face. 'They're . . . too long?' I hazard. 'Or too grubby?' But Eddie shakes his head to both suggestions. 'Too *naily*?' I suggest.

He smiles, lopsided and knowing. 'Your nails are just fine.'

'What, then? Still my walk? My posture? My smile? The way I cross my legs?' His brow furrows awkwardly. 'Come on, Mister Scorsese,' I tell him, leaning back in my seat, 'give it to me straight. I can take it.'

Eddie sighs. 'You're being too stilted,' he says. 'It sounds like . . . like you're acting. And it's not meant to.'

This criticism comes as no surprise to me: I hate being scrutinised too closely, have done ever since I was a teenager. 'I warned you I'd be no good,' I say with a shrug.

'You're not . . . no good,' he tells me. 'You're . . .' But his words run out. 'It's just,' he tries again, 'that the words, "*Hello*, my name *is* Fred Wilson and I *am* . . ." . . . they're coming out all wrong.'

'Why?'

'Because people don't talk like that.'

'What people?'

'People like us.'

'People like *us*?'

'Yes. You know, real people . . . people on the street.'

'But we're on a roof terrace,' I point out.

'I was speaking metaphorically.'

'Ah.'

'Just try sounding a little bit less like you're reading the national news on the TV and a little bit more like yourself,' he advises. 'Like, "*Hi*, my *name's* Fred Wilson and I'm . . ." Basically,' he continues, 'relax. It's only a dopey college assignment. No one outside my tutorial group's ever going to see it.'

'Relax?' I counter. 'That's easy enough for you to say. You went to acting school.'

'And my agent hasn't called me for six months,' he reminds me grimly.

Which is why he's working nights as a bar manager at a club called Nitrogene in King's Cross, I remind myself, and why getting something positive out of this film course is so important to him, and why, in turn, I agreed to help him out in the first place. 'OK,' I say. 'I'll give it one more try.'

He mumbles something about adjusting the camcorder's audio mix and I duck back into the living room, and lean idly up against the wall by the door and wait for my cue.

Lime-green curtains are drawn across the two open sash

windows, which face out across the street. To my right, a couple of bookcases stretch from bare-boarded floor to white-plastered ceiling. They're stacked with CDs, books and magazines. Between the bookcases are the wide-screen television, video, DVD, satellite and cable hardware, as well as Sony, Microsoft, Nintendo and Sega's latest offerings. Games, in and out of boxes, lie ensnared in a tangle of wires. The furniture, what little there is, is mostly utilitarian. There's a small pine table and matching chairs over by the kitchen doorway and in the centre of the room is a three-seater sofa, deliberately angled towards the television.

Rebecca doesn't like it here. The air of impermanence bothers her. 'You are where you live,' she once commented, somewhat cryptically, leaving me confused over whether she meant I smelt vaguely of mould and could do with a quick vac, or simply that I lived in a less than salubrious part of town. Not wanting to deal with either possibility, I did what I often do during our exchanges where I know I'm on a hiding to nothing: I kept quiet.

Flat 3, number 9 St Thomas's Gardens is the only property I've ever owned. I've lived here for four years now and, were it not for Rebecca, I'd be planning on sticking with it for another forty. It's big enough for two (Eddie and myself), but too small for three (Eddie, myself and Rebecca). I don't know why I've never made more of an effort with its decor, except that perhaps its very existence as a place to call my own is enough for me and that its appearance could never be anything other than secondary to that.

I moved in here a few months before I started going out with Rebecca and, up until recently, its presence has been tolerated by her in the same way that other people's partners might tolerate their more obnoxious old friends. It's here for now, in other words, but sooner or later it will be nudged aside for the good of the relationship.

I still sleep alone here a couple of nights each week (the rest of the time being spent at Rebecca's altogether more bijou residence over in Maida Vale). This arrangement is a hangover from our early days, a part of the pattern of our fledgling relationship that I've never openly questioned and, up until recently, Rebecca has never seen fit to challenge.

Truth be told, I think it probably suited us both to begin with, having some time and space to ourselves until we fully made up our minds about each other. All that ended with our engagement, of course. Ever since then, who sleeps where and why has been fully up for discussion, and I've found myself fighting an almost continuous rearguard action against Rebecca's repeated attempts to persuade me to sell up and move out, and move in with her.

A part of me, however, in spite of its inevitability, still resists this blending of our two universes into one. This place may not be much, is my reasoning, but it's mine and I worked hard to get it. It's my safety zone, my security and independence rolled into one. Rebecca doesn't see it this way. She sees my flat as an asset, a means – when combined with the sale of her own flat – to a better and brighter future for us both. Her mind is made up and, if there's one thing I've learnt over the past few years, what Rebecca wants she generally gets.

I stare for a moment at my reflection in the mirror on the wall. My eyes are grey and my hair, cropped close against my skull, is hazelnut brown. That I look shattered comes as no surprise. I was up at the crack of dawn, on this my first day off in months, to drop Rebecca at Heathrow Airport.

'Action,' Eddie calls again, and I step outside and take my seat once more. 'Er, hi,' I say to the camera, feeling no less self-conscious than before, 'my name's Fred Wilson and . . . and Eddie here wants me to talk about myself, which has to be a first in all the time I've known him. So . . . so here goes.'

Only it goes precisely nowhere. Instead, I find myself hesitating, pondering the basics of my existence. Explaining myself – the hows and whys of who I am and what made me this way – is hardly my special subject. I'm not into gazing at navels, horizons being more my thing. Give me the future over the past any day.

My gaze falls to my knee and I wave away a wasp that's crawling there.

'I'm a marketing manager for news as it breaks dot.com,' I say, giving the camera a great big marketing grin and slapping on an American accent for effect, as I launch into the rather feeble script that accompanied our last television commercial. 'You've probably heard of us,' I continue. 'If not, you should look us up. We're a twenty-four seven on-line outfit, straight down the wire, into your home or your phone, tailoring up-to-the-minute news and a range of other top-quality services to your needs.' I grin, breathless, and suck in air before concluding, 'Trust me: you'll never read a newspaper again.'

My smiles fades and, leaning forward, I dig out today's edition of *The Times* from where I dropped it beneath my seat earlier. Opening it up before me, I peer conspiratorially over the top at the camera. 'That last statement was, of course, a lie. But the rest of it's pretty true, for an advert. My actual job's not quite as slick and smooth as it sounds either,' I admit. 'Like the hours can be pretty hideous and we're reliant on American investors who might pull out at any time . . . But it's OK, you know? Nothing to write home about, or anything, but it's a job.'

It's actually significantly better than that, but I don't want to harp on about it in front of Eddie, whose own career has recently run into something of a brick wall. Truth be told, I actually enjoy what I do for a living. I mean, sure, the products and services we provide aren't perfect, but that's why it's a challenge working there: to make things better, to make things happen. And that's what they're letting me do, bit by bit: expand our market into the youth sector, by providing access to on-line games and shopping via the site, as well as the news and current affairs that we already do pretty well.

I lower the paper on to my lap. 'Er, what else?' I ask, drumming my fingers absent-mindedly on the paper, as I set about racking my brains for something to say. A few seconds later, still drawing a blank, I shoot Eddie a look of exasperation and he mouths 'Rebecca' at me.

'Oh, yes,' I say, blushing involuntarily over this shocking oversight. 'Rebecca. She's the girl I'm going to marry in a month. Eddie here's going to be my best man. She's in Oslo at the moment on a business trip. She works in marketing as well . . . a magazine publishing company . . . that's where we met . . . and . . . and she's wonderful . . . my best friend and, er, soulmate . . . Soulmate? God, that sounds cheesy . . . Eddie?' I feel the skin on my cheeks burning up. 'Eddie, can we edit that bit?'

But Eddie's ignoring me.

'Thanks a bunch,' I grumble. 'Now where was I? Work . . . Rebecca . . . cheesy comments . . . what next?'

'Cut.'

'What now?' I ask, watching as Eddie lifts his finger from the camcorder's red record switch. 'I thought that was going quite well.'

But Eddie's smiling. 'It wasn't bad,' he says coolly, flicking another switch which causes a shutter to slide smoothly across the camcorder's lens, 'but I need a leak.' He puts the camcorder down and gets to his feet. 'I'll be back in two ticks,' he tells me.

I watch him duck inside, the shady doorway acting like a mystical portal, swallowing him up. Then, tilting back in my chair, I close my eyes against the glare of the sun.

Rebecca . . .

Rebecca's from an incredibly stable, loving and secure background, so different in every way from my own. It's something she takes for granted, of course, but something which I'm drawn towards, with a mixture of envy and desire in my heart.

Thorn House, her parents' country home, stands on the summit of a flat-topped hill overlooking the small Oxfordshire village of Shotbury. It's a vast Georgian mansion, boasting eight bedrooms, a hard tennis court and a converted stable block. In addition to all this there are about forty acres of land, most of which are rented out to a local dairy farmer for pasture, but some of which are taken up by the array of walled gardens and lawns which surround the main house.

I was in the largest of the gardens not so long ago. It's a flat area of at least two acres, surrounded by towering grey stone walls, and was heavy with the scent of lavender. From where I was lying – at the back, on the cool flagstones of the perimeter path – I could see apple and plum trees, runner beans, the glint of greenhouse glass and, perhaps more unusually for the time of year, Rebecca's small bare breasts, pale against the late afternoon sun, moving gently up and down as she sat astride me.

'God, I've been looking forward to this,' she was telling me, scraping her auburn fringe back from her face with one hand. 'I thought lunch was never going to finish.'

'Tell me about it,' I mumbled.

'Did you notice?' she asked, beginning to buck. 'The vicar kept looking at my cleavage. Even', she continued, moving faster now, 'when he was humming the opening bars to "Jerusalem". It – got – me – all – horny,' she grunted.

'But he's about seventy,' I pointed out, picturing the kind, grey-haired old man, nibbling at his biscuits and sipping his tea.

'I – don't –mean – *he* – got – me – horny,' Rebecca explained. 'I – mean – the – thought – of – doing – it –with – a – priest.'

'I see,' I said, although – strictly speaking – I didn't.

Suddenly she slowed and leant forward, until her face was directly above mine. Drops of sweat fell from her brow on to my lips. 'You'd wear a priest's dog collar for me, wouldn't you, if I bought you one?'

'Uh, sure,' I said, not wishing to derail her momentum.

A smile crossed her face, momentarily accentuating her cheekbones. Combined with the emerald-green glint of her eyes, it brought out the feline in her oval-shaped face, leaving me feeling strangely at her mercy.

'I knew you would,' she said.

She closed her eyes and I continued to lie beneath her, watching her enjoy herself. This isn't to say that I wasn't enjoying myself as well. I most certainly was. But still – putting my own pleasure aside for a moment – this was (and, indeed, still is) very much how I saw Rebecca during sex: *her* enjoying *herself*. Wherever her closed eyes had just transported her was somewhere I wasn't invited and somewhere my presence wasn't *required*.

It had taken me a while to realise this. When I'd started having sex with her I'd (rather naively, in retrospect) assumed that I – either through sheer animal magnetism or a fortunate combination of pheromones – had been the catalyst behind her insatiable sexual appetite and ensuing ecstatic delights. It hadn't been until months later that I'd come to understand quite how incidental I was to the whole process. I was a witness to her fantasies, an accessory to the fact of her libido, a personal personal assistant, but nothing more integral than that.

'Oh, God,' she suddenly moaned. 'I – think – I'm – going – to –'

But before she got the chance, a man's voice boomed her name out across the garden.

'Oh, fuck,' she growled through gritted teeth, hurriedly rolling off me. 'Dad.'

A minute later we were sitting peacefully, both now fully dressed, on a cast-iron garden bench, just as her father came into sight.

George Dickenson is a lean man, at least six foot three in height, with a youthful, upright stance and a wide, square jaw. He's always been good to me, ever since the first time we met. He treats me like a son, knowing that I no longer have a father of my own, and I, in turn, am always careful to show him the respect a father should deserve.

'Ah,' he said, putting his arm round Rebecca's shoulders and giving her a hug, 'there you both are. I've been looking for you everywhere.'

Rebecca picked at a thread of cotton hanging from the pocket of his striped, short-sleeved shirt. Like George, she's slim, well-proportioned and, at five foot nine, just a few inches shorter than me.

'I've been showing off the gardens to Fred,' she told him. 'They're so pretty at this time of year.'

'Been over to the pond yet?' George asked me.

'No.'

'I've stocked it up with trout since your last visit,' he went on to announce. He looked up, surveying the state of the sky, before raising a hand to smooth down his thinning grey hair. 'Still plenty of light,' he concluded, smiling first at Rebecca and then at me. 'Mike's feeding them at six thirty. We could go over and watch, if you like . . .' he suggested.

'Sure,' I said.

He turned to Rebecca and asked, 'How about you?'

'Fish,' she said with a grimace. 'Gross. No, I'll head back to the house for a shower.'

'As you like,' George told her, before kissing her on the forehead and setting off with me down the path.

A low stone wall separated the pond from the tennis

court and, following George's lead, I sat down on it. Together we watched Mike, a middle-aged man from the village who helps George around the place, as he threw handfuls of feed into the wide round pond. Rainbow trout broke the surface instantaneously, causing it to boil like a pot of water on a stove.

George had just finished telling me about how he and his sister, Julia (who'd broken her neck falling off a horse when she'd been sixteen), had always come down here to cool off during the summer when they'd been kids. 'Childhood's a magical thing,' he said. 'Everything you learn about the world starts there. It's like being given a blank sheet and being told you can draw anything you want on it. It's up to you.' He looked up at me. 'You and Becky . . .' he probed. 'Children . . . are they something you're considering?'

'Children?' I teased him affectionately. 'Shouldn't we just start with one?'

'You're right, of course,' he conceded with a chuckle, digging out a cigar and lighter from his shirt pocket. 'It's none of my business.' But nevertheless he continued to stare at me as he lit his cigar.

'We've never talked about it,' I told him in deference to the lingering curiosity in his eyes. 'We've both been so busy since we met, you know, what with our careers taking up so much of our time and now the wedding as well.'

He nodded with understanding, but I knew that he wasn't satisfied.

'We're still young,' I added weakly, suddenly seeing how important all this was to him.

'Yes,' he said, finally looking away and drawing reflectively on his cigar, 'and you've got a whole future to build together. Why should you rush?'

We remained in silence for a minute or two and I stared across, over the walls and trees which lay between here and Thorn House.

11

Then George said, 'I was thinking of putting up a marquee on the front lawn for the wedding, if the weather's good.'

'That'd be lovely,' I agreed.

Mike threw a final handful into the pond and called over, 'Till the morning, then, George.'

'Right you are, Mike,' George called back. 'Six weeks,' he then said, turning to face me. 'Not long. It's going to be a good day, eh? When our Becky transforms from Miss Dickenson into Mrs Wilson.'

Even after all these years Wilson, my own surname, still sounded to me like notes played on an out-of-tune piano. 'Yes,' I said, picturing myself out in the marquee, dancing with Rebecca. 'I'm a lucky man.'

'And so am I,' said George. 'I couldn't have chosen a better husband for her myself.'

I nodded my head in appreciation of this comment and George looked away. 'We should get going,' he said, consulting his watch.

Following his lead, I rose and turned to face the house. The gardens were in full bloom and swallows circled above the chimneys. The sun hung low and shadows were beginning to creep across the ground. It was a perfect moment and I made a conscious effort of freeze-framing it, saving it up in its entirety for posterity, fearful, as I always am when anything gets too good, that it might not last, that every moment from here on would be downhill.

I heard George sigh beside me. 'I hope you and Becky will be as happy here one day as Mary and I are now,' he said, starting off down the path. 'I'm very proud, you know, very proud of you both, and very pleased indeed.'

I fell into step alongside him and, saying nothing, walked on, breathing in the smell of his cigar and listening to the sound of our shoes crunching along the gravel path. Maybe George was right and one day Rebecca and I would grow into the vacant roles he and Mary would leave behind. Maybe, I considered, that was where I'd find my comfort and my peace.

That was two weeks ago. Now – here on the roof terrace, waiting for Eddie to reappear – it's just gone one o'clock on a Friday afternoon in the middle of June in the year two thousand – or Y2K, depending on whether or not you bought into the whole millennium marketing deal.

I didn't. This was, I admit, partly due to an aversion on my behalf to commemorative merchandising of any sort – a psychosis which stems largely from being surrounded by the stuff at work. But mainly, my lack of Y2K jingoism can be put down to an innate dread of the actual event itself.

I don't mean the getting drunk and watching fireworks illuminate the recently refurbished London skyline side of it. I was there for that, part of the two-million-strong human concertina that squeezed and cheered its way up and down the banks of the River Thames. I got rained on with the best of them. I ate armpit and swapped sweat. No, I did all that and loved every second of it, and wouldn't have missed it for the world. When I say I'd been dreading the actual event itself, I mean just that. I mean the very moment when the twentieth century slid inexorably into the past.

From across the river I watched as Big Ben, like a referee at a boxing match, counted out the old millennium to the rising cheers of the crowd and introduced the new. And it was then and only then – once I'd seen it with my own eyes and heard it with my own ears – that I finally accepted the horrid truth: the future, *my* future – the part of my life that, up until this moment, had always seemed impossibly distant – had suddenly arrived.

'I love you, sweetie,' Rebecca told me.

'And I love you too,' I replied.

I held her in my drunken arms and kissed her rain-soaked face, and gazed up at the myriad of fireworks bursting across the inky depths of the night sky. Inside me, though, darkness remained. I felt the cold finger of death scraping his jagged fingernails across the sinews of my heart.

Surely, I told myself, this couldn't be true. The year two thousand couldn't really have arrived already, could it? But everywhere I looked, the answer came back 'yes'. In the tiny, almost imperceptible, wrinkles at the corners of Rebecca's eyes as she excitedly reminded me that this was the fourth new year we'd seen in together: yes. In her shoulder-length haircut that I still regarded as new, even though, I now realised, she'd first had the old auburn Rapunzel locks lopped off over two years ago: yes. In the familiar touch of her hands in mine, the segments of our fingers perfectly intertwined, as if they'd grown together that way like vines: yes. And there, in the miniature instamatic picture that Eddie thrust at me: the skin on my face somehow greyer than I remembered, the line of my hair somehow further back than I would have imagined, and the look of the cigarette hanging from my mouth somehow less James Dean than I would have wished for. Yes, yes and yes again.

It was, then, with a heavy heart that I, along with Rebecca, Eddie and the rest of our gang, set out on the slow trudge homewards across Westminster Bridge. Two thousand years of civilisation, I pondered, and what world-trembling contributions had I made? Had I invented the wheel? No, I hadn't. Had I propounded the theory of relativity? Nope, not that either. Had I dreamt up the idea of a World Wide Web. Uh-huh, not me. So what *had* I accomplished with my allotted time? A job I was good at? Yes, I was lucky there. A woman I had fallen in love with and still loved? Yes, I was fortunate there, too.

There was little security in any of this, though. I could get fired from my job. I could get dumped from my relationship. I drank too much . . . I smoked too much . . .

and I could therefore die. Even now, the walls of my blood vessels could be dilating, forming sacs . . . An aneurysm could be but a blink away. And if that was indeed to be my fate, then who would remember me? What epitaph would they carve on my grave? *Here Lies Fred Wilson, Who Never Really Did That Much*? What else *could* they write? I wasn't religious. I wasn't political. I hadn't reproduced. Here I was, ageing by the second, moving closer to death with every breath I took, and what efforts had I made to sink my grip into life? None, came back the answer. None at all. I'd coasted. I'd procrastinated. I'd put off living till later.

Well, now was the time to do something about it. Now was the time for some New Year resolutions. Only this was no ordinary New Year and these would be no ordinary resolutions. These would be New Millennium resolutions, built to last a thousand years and capable of changing the course of a life – *my* life – for ever.

The cigarettes went first. I took one final drag of the Marlboro Light I was smoking, before sending it spinning and sparkling like a miniature Catherine wheel up into the sky. I then pulled the packet from my pocket, crushed it in my fist, and struggled away from Rebecca and the others. Breaking free from the flow of the crowd at the side of the road, I clambered over an unguarded police barrier and dropped down on to a patch of unlit wasteland at the edge of the river bank.

The noise of the crowd diminished immediately and, walking forward, I cast my cigarette packet down into the black and swirling waters of the Thames below. Standing there, with the suitably austere backdrop of the Houses of Parliament before me, I solemnly swore that I would smoke no more. I didn't want another bout of bronchitis like the one that had choked my throat down to the width of a pipe-cleaner the previous November. I'd smoked enough of my future years away already.

'What are you doing?' a voice – Rebecca's – called out.

I spun round from my reverie to see her peering over the police barrier. Her jacket collars were turned up and her ski hat was pulled down low over her brow. I didn't give myself time to think. Now was the time for action. If the cigarettes had been my first resolution, then Rebecca would be my second. 'Come here,' I shouted.

She screwed up her face in distaste. 'But it's filthy.'

I walked over to the barrier and stood beneath her. Reaching out my arms, I told her, 'Drop. I'll catch you. You'll be fine.'

'But why?' she asked, peering at me with suspicion.

'Because.'

'Because what?'

'Because I've got something to say and I need to say it in private.'

She lurched slightly, drunkenly, to the left. 'Can't it wait till we get home?' she asked. 'I'm freezing.'

'No, it can't,' I replied firmly. 'Just trust me. It'll be worth it. You'll see.'

Her eyes narrowed. 'It better be,' she said, unsmiling, before reluctantly climbing over the barrier and swinging down into my arms.

Gently, I lowered her to the ground. 'Don't move,' I told her, quickly taking a couple of steps back.

Her eyes flickered as she scanned the surrounding area for signs of danger. 'Hurry up,' she said. 'This place is giving me the creeps.'

'What I want to know . . .' I began.

But before I could say any more, my voice trailed off like a car radio in a tunnel. I opened my mouth to speak once more, but again with no success. It was like all the saliva had been drained from me, leaving my tongue as rough and as speechless as a cat's.

Rebecca looked me over as she might a collapsed drunk on the doorstep of her favourite designer boutique. 'If this is meant to be some kind of a joke . . .' she warned.

I shook my head furiously, but still I couldn't speak. What was going on? I railed internally. Why had I dried up like this? Was it *me*? I'd made up my mind, hadn't I? This *was* what I wanted, wasn't it? She was my girlfriend of four years. She was beautiful and she was bright. We made each other laugh and the sex was fantastic. And I loved her. Of course I did.

Was it the thought of starting a family of my own, of finally stepping out from the debilitating shadow of my parents, then? No, security was something that I craved. Or was I simply afraid that Rebecca would say no, then? Was that what my tongue-tied state was all about? Of course, this was something I'd considered. God knew I wasn't perfect, and if God knew, then I sincerely doubted that Rebecca was going to be very far behind. But if she declined my offer, she declined. . . . There was nothing I could do about it, and there was certainly no point in letting it put me off asking her in the first place.

I lowered myself to my knees and knelt down on the ground.

Rebecca peered at me through the urban twilight. 'You're not going to puke, are you?' she asked.

Dumbly, I shook my head and watched as she heaved out a sigh of relief. I patted the rough earth before me.

'What?' she queried, cocking her head to one side as she picked at a fleck of dirt on her jeans. 'You don't expect me to get down there with you, do you?'

I nodded my head.

She folded her arms across her chest. 'Forget it. You're pissed. Now get up before you get bitten by a rat.'

I sucked air into my lungs. 'Please,' I hissed. 'Please . . . for me . . .'

'I must be mad,' she said, riffling through her bag and pulling out a curled-up copy of *Time Out*. She leant down and spread it out in front of me, telling me, 'This had better be good,' as she knelt down on top of it.

'It is,' I hissed, seizing her hands in mine. I don't think I'd ever seen anyone looking so beautiful. 'I don't think I've ever seen anyone looking so beautiful,' I told her, tears welling up in my eyes.

'And that's it?' she asked, failing to conceal her disappointment. 'That's what you wanted to tell me?'

Solemnly shaking my head, I took a deep breath. 'I want . . .' I started to croak. Then, sliding my hands down over her thighs, I filled my lungs and blurted out: 'You, Rebecca. I want you . . .'

She stared at me with mounting disbelief. Then she stared down at my hands on her thighs. 'Here?' she queried. 'Now?'

'Yes,' I wheezed at her. 'Right here. Right now.' My God, this was the biggest thing I'd ever said in my life.

I waited with bated breath for her answer and – there – something in my face must have touched her, because suddenly her expression softened.

'Well,' she said, a twinkle in her eyes, 'I must admit . . . the thought of all those people being so close . . .'

'What?'

'. . . and those policemen . . . on their big black stallions . . . who could catch us at any second . . .'

'Sorry?'

But she wasn't listening. 'Not to mention the possibility of arrest and incarceration . . . and . . .' – her eyes rolled momentarily backwards – '. . . mmm . . . handcuffs . . .' Lost, I watched in silence as she bit down on her lip in consideration for a couple of seconds. 'OK,' she finally decided. 'You're on.'

'OK?' I checked. This was hardly the outright embrace or denial of my proposal that I'd been expecting.

'But it'll have to be quick,' she added.

'Quick?' We were talking about a lifetime of commitment here.

Then she stood up. 'Lucky I'm not wearing any

knickers,' she said with a wink, before glancing around excitedly. 'Where do you want me?' she hissed. 'Up against the barrier? Or how about over that mooring post?' Then, catching my expression, she chastised, 'Don't tell me you're going to chicken out now . . .'

Comprehension struck me and, hurriedly, I pulled her back down.

'No,' I blurted out, 'you don't understand. I . . . I don't *want* you . . .'

I felt her whole being tense. 'But –'

'No, I do, but I mean more than that . . . I mean I want *you* . . .' I explained. 'I mean now . . . for ever . . .' I hesitated, desperate. 'Do you understand?'

'I thought . . .' She shoved her face up close to mine, staring hard into my eyes, as what I was saying finally began to dawn on her. 'You don't mean . . . ?'

'Yes,' I whispered. 'Yes, I do. I want you to marry me.'

There! It was out. My eyes locked on hers and I awaited her response.

For a moment she said nothing and instead simply stared at me agog. Then, slowly but surely, a smile spread across her face. 'Oh, my God!' she gasped, looking dizzily about and starting to laugh. 'I thought you wanted to . . .' Her voice pitched upwards. 'Oh, my God!' she shrieked, throwing her arms round my neck. She squeezed me so hard that I thought my ribs would crack. 'Of course I will, Fred.' She sighed, breathing warm air on to the side of my face. 'Of course I'll marry you.'

Opening my eyes now, the first thing they settle on is Eddie's pack of Marlboro reds on the window box beside his empty chair. A momentary pang of envy cuts deep as, above me, the sun continues to beat down. They're the same brand that got me started as a teenager and, on this perfect day, I remember other perfect days from my youth, hours wasted chatting and smoking out in the woods near the village I grew up in, careless of the passing of time.

'OK,' Eddie tells me, re-emerging. He sits down, picks up the camcorder and points it at me. The lens cover slides silently open. 'Give me some background and then we can call it a day.'

'What kind of thing?' I ask, weary now, hoping we're nearly done.

'I don't know.' He ponders before deciding, 'Family. Tell me about them.'

Eddie's heard all this before, of course, but I repeat it anyway, for the camera's sake. 'My father's dead,' I say. 'And my mother lives in Scotland.'

Eddie beckons me with his hand, signalling, I assume, that this is not enough.

'Mum never remarried,' I say, 'but she's got a boyfriend.' I picture Alan, the fifty-five-year-old school-teacher she now lives with. 'She met him through the church. He's nice enough in a quiet sort of way, but I've never really got to know him. He's got grown-up kids of his own.'

I think of Mum and how we grew apart in the years following my father's death, and how, instead of being pushed closer together by our mutual loss, we were driven further apart. And I think about how glad I was when she got it together with Alan, because it meant she was no longer my exclusive responsibility.

'I don't see her as much as I should,' I say. 'You grow up, you grow apart, you know?'

Eddie says nothing; he knows Mum hardly ever phones me.

'I think she's happy,' I conclude, 'and that's what matters . . .'

Eddie still seems to be waiting, so – a little reluctantly – I go on: 'My father died of a heart attack when I was fifteen years old.'

Again, the hand signal from Eddie

I shrug. 'I try not to think about him,' I say. 'It's easier that way.'

I'm not intending to say any more, but then I suddenly remember how my father used to sit on the edge of my bed and sing me to sleep.

'I used to wish that he'd come back,' I admit. 'I used to hope that' – I search the sky for words, then lower my eyes – 'he'd somehow *stop* being dead. I don't know . . . that probably sounds crazy, but I don't mean it that way . . . What I mean is, I had so many questions for him, *about* him, and then, well, then he wasn't there any more and I suddenly realised I'd never get any answers. It's the same for everyone, I suppose,' I say, beginning to wish I hadn't started getting into this and deciding to bring it all to a close. 'There are always going to be regrets.'

There's silence for a second or two, then Eddie switches off the camera and rests it on his thigh. 'Thanks,' he says, 'that's plenty for me to be getting on with.' Leaning forward, he peers at me. 'Are you all right,' he asks.

'Yeah,' I say. 'Why shouldn't I be?'

'Your face,' he explains. 'You look flushed. I think you've caught a bit too much sun.'

I touch my brow with my fingertips and then stare at them: they're shiny with sweat. 'I'm fine,' I say, managing a smile. 'Just dehydrated,' I guess.

In the kitchen, I down a pint of water over the sink, but I still can't shake the heat that's built up inside me. Refilling my glass, I head for my bedroom and pull the door closed behind me. I lie down on the bed and stare up at the ceiling, wishing there were a fan in here to cool my skin.

I close my eyes and try to sleep. But I can't. Instead, memories rise unbidden. Too tired to do otherwise, I succumb to it all, watching as scenes from my childhood and adolescence flicker like a silent movie through my mind. They come as a shuffled chain of facts and scenes to begin with: the games I played with my friends at lunchtimes, the way we used magnifying glasses to write our names on the soles of our shoes in the summers and the cold days we spent pummelling one another with snowballs in the winters. Then come other days, from even further back, days I haven't thought about in years.

My father's Christian name was Miles and I don't remember ever calling him anything else. He was an endless source of mystery to me when I was a child. He was six foot one, the same height as I am now, and his eyes lay narrow and deep in their sockets, like those of a wolf.

Other than that, his appearance was forever changing. Moustaches, beards and sideburns came and went. Trouser widths straightened and flared. One week he was in polka-dots, the next week it was stripes. It seemed to me, growing up, that every time I came close to knowing who he was, he promptly changed into someone else.

Only his absences from home remained a constant. He worked uptown in the West End of London, sometimes for what felt like weeks on end without a break, the same as he had done ever since Mum had given birth to me, his only son.

My mother, Louisa, used to tell me a story about him coming into my room to kiss me goodnight on my seventh birthday. Most of it, though, I remember clearly myself.

He discovered me curled up beneath a pile of jumpers in my wardrobe with a look of abject terror on my face. He was wearing a sky-blue jacket and a bright-pink shirt with sharp-pointed lapels that stretched down past his collarbone. One of his pearly shirt buttons was missing, revealing a knot of belly hair.

When he asked me what I was doing there and why I was pointing a pistol at him – taking my cue from the massive, brass-buckled cowboy belt he was wearing – I shot him clean between the eyes. The black rubber suction dart quivered back and forth on the bridge of his nose, and Miles focused on it in cross-eyed astonishment as I scrambled out between his legs and fled.

It was only ten minutes later, when Mum's distressed cries elicited a wary response from my new hiding place next to the Hoover and mops in the boiler room, that the source of my fear became apparent. I have a memory of her soft brown eyes filling my world as I spoke.

The Miles who'd come to kiss me goodnight, it seemed (in hushed tones), was not my father. The Miles who'd come to kiss me goodnight couldn't be my father, because my father – the *real* Miles – wouldn't have missed my birthday party.

There was, therefore, it seemed, only one possible explanation: the Miles in the house was a fake who'd done away with the real Miles and was now planning to do the same with me. I advised my mother either to call the police or to join me where I was and close the door quietly behind her.

I finally consented to speak to the *fake Miles* some half an hour later. I sat down at the round table in the eating area next to the kitchen. Light rain drummed like fingertips at the windows. It was coal black outside and the only light in the room was the glow of the brass lamp with a shade patterned with Chinese dragons on the small table by the door. Mum was leaning against the brown breakfast bar and Miles was sitting opposite me at the table.

'If you're the real Miles,' I – in accordance with my mother's version of events – asked, 'how old am I?'

Miles shifted uncomfortably in his swivel bucket chair and it creaked beneath his weight. He slurped at his coffee and peered at me over the rim of his mug with bloodshot eyes. 'Seven,' he said.

His voice was gruff, an uneasy mixture of acquired cockney and natural West Country. He put his mug down and his fingers made a noise like ripping Velcro as he scratched at the dark three-day stubble on his jaw. 'Yesterday you were six,' he continued. 'Today you're seven.'

I considered this for a moment, before trying a different tack to expose him for the fake he undoubtedly was. 'What's the code word?' I asked.

His eyes narrowed, his thick eyebrows bunching above his nose. 'What code word?' he queried, wiping his hand across his nose with a noisy squelch.

I pointed the pistol directly at the small red blotch on his face where I'd shot him before. 'If you were the real Miles,' I said with a note of warning, 'you'd know.'

'Ah,' he said, nodding his head in understanding, '*that* code word.' He sat back in his chair and rattled his uneven fingernails on the table. Stifling a yawn, he stared at me impassively. Then his eyes flashed. 'Why do you need me to tell you what it is? Can't you remember yourself?'

'Of course I can.'

'Prove it,' he challenged, folding his arms.

I opened my mouth to speak, then snapped it shut again. I wasn't going to be caught out that easily. 'No,' I said.

He leant forward and wrinkles appeared on his brow as he frowned. 'Why not?'

I frowned back. 'Because it's secret. Because that's the point.'

Miles wagged his finger at me. 'But if you don't tell me what it is, then how do I know that *you're* the real Fred?'

I was outraged. 'Because I *am*,' I spluttered, the pistol wavering in my hand. 'Who else could I be?'

'For all I know,' he pointed out, '*you* could be a fake . . .'

'No!' I gasped. 'That's not fair. *You're* the fake.' I cocked the trigger of my pistol and gritted my teeth. 'And if you don't tell me the code word, I'll –'

Quickly, Miles smiled and his smile fitted my memories of the real Miles: bright but lopsided, disarming and dangerous. 'Sergeant Pepper,' he said.

My mouth fell open in amazement; he'd got it right.

I lowered my pistol and, fighting a sudden wave of tiredness, stretched my legs down, trailing my toes back and forth across the thick cream carpet that looked like it had been sheared off the back of a giant lamb. Pushing my left foot even further down and scrunching up my toes until they gripped the carpet, I asked, 'Why weren't you here for my party?'

Miles glanced at my mother, then back at me. 'I had to meet up with some important people.'

I looked up. I couldn't help myself. 'Government people?' I mouthed at him.

He glanced at my mother again, before covering his mouth so only I could see, and whispering, 'Yes.'

Mum muttered something under her breath, walked to the glass shelving unit and took a cigarette from the silver holder she kept there.

'What did you talk about?' I hissed, pulling my knees up to my chin.

Miles lowered his head conspiratorially, so that it was only inches from the table's surface. A snake of smoke danced up from his knuckles. 'Can I trust you?' he asked. 'Only it's all very hush-hush . . .'

I nodded my head eagerly. 'Of course . . .'

He looked nervously around, as if someone other than my mother might be listening. Then, seemingly satisfied, he raised his forefinger to his lips and told me, 'Captain Carnage has been sighted in London.'

I spun round in my seat, peering into the darkened corners of the room. Captain Carnage was the world's most evil man. He was capable of frightening someone to death with a single stare. As an Extra Special Secret Agent for the Government, Miles was his sworn enemy. I was the only non-spy in the world who knew about Captain Carnage's existence.

Miles blinked heavily as his expression softened.

'Listen, Fred' – he reached across the table and took my hand in his – 'I'm sorry I missed your party.'

I flinched, startled by a tree branch rearing out of the darkness on the other side of the window. 'What if Captain Carnage followed you here?' I asked. 'What if he breaks in while we're asleep?'

Miles hoisted me up on to his shoulder. 'It won't matter, so long as we're all in bed asleep.'

'Why not?' I asked as he carried me towards the stairs.

'Because,' he said, starting to climb, ignoring the squeak of my fingers trailing along the wooden banister, 'when we sleep, we close our eyes and we can't see anything. And that includes evil people. And evil people can't frighten us when we can't see them. The same applies to Captain Carnage. So long as you keep your eyes shut he can't harm you.'

'But what if he gets you? What if he gets you and then wakes me up? What then?'

'Then you've got these to protect you,' Miles said, taking his sunglasses from his shirt pocket. He put them on me and the world grew dark. 'They're Government issue,' he explained. 'One hundred per cent Carnage-proof. Nothing evil can hurt you when you're wearing them.'

I hugged Miles tight and closed my eyes. I loved him. I loved him with all my heart and I knew that what he was saying was true.

Miles's own early years had been less cosseted than my own. He'd dropped out of school in Warminster at the age of fifteen, after running away from his parents' home (neither of whom I ever met). Miles's mother had died in childbirth and his father was a grocer, an ex-Navy war veteran who liked to drink and habitually punished Miles with his fists for the crime he'd unknowingly committed on entering the world.

When he was still alive and I'd grown old enough to

hear, Miles never shied away from telling me the truth about his youth. He viewed himself as an adventurer, a piratical spirit who'd sailed through life making up his own rules as he went along. He was proud of how he'd got to where he was from where he'd come from. If he'd broken laws along the way, it had been because they were wrong, not him.

When he met my mother at the end of the Sixties, he was living in a ramshackle house in the outskirts of Oxford and had established himself a niche market, supplying top-grade hashish to the local student community.

Mum's father, Frederick, was a wealthy lawyer who lived near Aberdeen. Along with my grandmother, he was a strict Presbyterian. He died of bowel cancer when I was eleven and was a kind and generous man who couldn't bear to be in the same room as Miles. My grandmother is still alive, but she suffers from Alzheimer's. Mum lives in the same Scottish village and takes care of her.

When she first met Miles, Mum was reading history at Oxford University. In the two years she'd been away from home she'd fallen in with more curious spirits than she'd encountered during her sheltered upbringing. She'd swapped her Christianity for spirituality and its accompanying hippy ideals (a transition which she'd dramatically reverse in later life). In Miles, a boy so clearly from the wrong side of the tracks, she saw an antidote to what she then regarded as the stultifying and boring years of her youth. He in turn saw beauty and swept her off her feet.

It didn't take him long to persuade her to leave Oxford without taking her finals, but it was a decision that would alienate him from her parents for the rest of his life. Armed with his cash, his stash and his set of weighing scales, they headed off across the country, moving ever onwards from squat to campsite to festival. It was a journey of self-discovery that they both hoped would last for the rest of their lives. But then, in February 1969, the same month that Cambridge scientists successfully fertilised a human egg in a test tube, Miles successfully fertilised an egg inside my mother's womb.

Pregnancy shocked Mum out of her recklessness in one fell swoop. Responsibility reared up inside her. She married Miles in an Aberdeen register office six months later. (Mum's parents refused to attend, although my mother's hopes of a reconciliation had been the reason behind the marriage in the first place.) I was born a few months after that at Charing Cross Hospital. I weighed in at seven pounds and eleven ounces, and had blue eyes that would later turn grey. Mum refers now to the moment of my birth as the moment she rediscovered her faith in Jesus.

In preparation for my arrival, she and Miles had rented a squalid flat in Islington. Mum had also insisted that Miles get a job, and a job he'd got, working as a barman in a trendy Soho bar. Here he continued to subsidise his income with some small-time dealing, and it was here that he fell in with a crowd of similar-minded people, who'd later become his business partners.

My mother, it seems, was never party to this world. Instead, she looked away and, protective of her child, insisted that they move out of London. My father, for whatever reasons of his own, agreed and they bought a house in the village of Rushton, Hertfordshire, and this was where I'd live for the next thirteen years of my life.

Miles, meanwhile, continued to work in Soho, eventually going on to set up a nightclub called Clan in the mid-Seventies. The commute was a long one back then and, as the years rolled by, my mother and I would come to see less and less of him.

Rushton lies in a natural valley within easy driving distance of Woburn Safari Park, Whipsnade Zoo and the Grand Union Canal, and I haven't been there for well over a decade. It has no high street to speak of, though the main Hemel Hempstead road bisects it neatly, running parallel with the fast-flowing River Elo and bridging it at the north end of the village.

An older boy once told me that a razor-toothed troll lived under the bridge and, for years afterwards, I used to run across it as fast as I could on the way back from Cubs, terrified that I'd be plucked from my feet and dragged down into the dank depths below to be devoured.

There are around seventy houses in the village. The majority of them were built in the Fifties and lie on the hill on the west of the river. The east side is dominated by older houses, cottages and an austere Gothic church. The most ancient gravestone I ever found in the graveyard, obscured by a tangle of winter brambles, was dated 1568. It belonged to a man called David Jeremiah Johnson and he haunted my nightmares for weeks to come.

The church is flanked on one side by the Duck and Swan public house. Mum started out frequenting the latter and then, as I approached my teens and her relationship with Miles began to disintegrate, she transferred her emotions into the former, clinging tighter and tighter to its solid foundations in an effort to distract herself from her own world, which was slowly but surely slipping away.

Behind these buildings is the Memorial Hall, built to honour the young men of Rushton and the outlying farms who sacrificed their lives for King and Country in the Great War. Further back are the village green, the Gordon Arms and Rushton Primary, the educational institution where I learnt to name the colours of the rainbow, as well as how to read, write, add and subtract.

On the hill to the west of the Elo runs the Avenue, a long, steep road, lined by towering oaks, which are terrifying in their solidity. I once freewheeled down the hill on a go-cart, with the aim of weaving in and out of every single one of the twenty-two trees on the left-hand side of the road. I made it as far as the twenty-first, before losing my balance and skidding wildly into the tree. I was flung with a crack against the gnarled bark and split the skin on my elbow in a three-inch gash. The cart was left scattered like so much tinder across the side of the road and my scar remains to this day.

I lived in a house called Orchard View, which was sited at the very top of the Avenue on a side road called Hill Drive. It had been built in 1947, the same year Miles had been born (a fact that fascinated me as a child), and had been named after an apple orchard that had once stood there.

Like Miles, the property was in a continuous state of flux. In my mind's eye, roof tiles switched with the seasons, and walls shifted from whitewash to yellow and blue, before reverting back to white again. Extensions, garages and carports rose and fell to accommodate new cars and architectural fashions. Inside was no different. Wallpaper and appliances were altered and updated on what sometimes seemed like a monthly basis. Only the antique furniture which Mum loved remains as a constant in my memory.

Early on in our time there, Miles had the attic converted and that's where my bedroom was. On my first night there I slept on the bottom half of my bunk bed, protected by sheets with soldiers printed on them and a purple candlewick bedspread, which doubled up as a tepee in the summer. My toys were kept in a deep, purpose-built wardrobe, and my ceiling was patterned with luminous stars and planets stickers.

Two windows let in the real night sky. From one, I could look down on to our back garden and across at Mickey's tree house next door. Mickey was the same age as me and was my best friend when I was growing up. Some mornings, bright and early, I'd stare into the highest branches and try to see Jesus, whom Mickey had painted there in a picture she'd won a prize for at nursery school. The other window in my bedroom looked across the five or so feet that separated our houses, directly down into Mickey's own bedroom.

In the summers when we were young, Mickey and I used to open our windows at night and whisper to each other, or launch paper planes across the divide. Other times we'd try to frighten one another, pinching pieces of bamboo from Mickey's dad's allotment at the bottom of the Avenue, strapping them together and tapping at each other's windows in the dead of night.

One evening during a Christmas school holiday, when Mickey and I were both fifteen, I watched unseen through a gap in my curtains while she undressed. As she unfastened her bra and stood in front of her mirror and brushed her hair, I knew that nothing between us would ever be the same again.

Our gardens backed on to a wide and shallow stream, which ran down the hillside to the Elo below. The fields and woods beyond belonged to Jimmy Dughead, a mean-spirited farmer who smoked roll-ups and tied dead crows and rats to his barbed-wire fences.

All the children in the village were terrified of him, mainly as a result of a story told by Tommy Wilmot, a boy a few years older than Mickey and I. Village legend had it that Dughead had once caught Tommy setting rabbit snares in his wood. Instead of handing him over to the police, Dughead had cocked his twelve-bore shotgun and levelled it at Tommy's chest. He'd told Tommy that he'd give him a twenty-second head start, and then teach him a lesson in vermin hunting that he'd never forget. Following a panicked, thorn-torn flight, Tommy had escaped without his backside peppered with shot and had lived to tell the tale. He'd never set foot on Jimmy Dughead's land again and said that only a lunatic would dare do otherwise.

I was with Tommy Wilmot on this one, but Mickey

thought differently. Mickey feared no one, including Jimmy Dughead. She concluded that Dughead's land, for precisely the reason that everyone was afraid to go on it – including her big brother, Scott – was the safest place in the world to hide something. And Mickey and I had something to hide: treasure. And it was because of this that, when I was still nine and Mickey was just ten, we crept across to the middle of the field behind our houses and buried an old used tin of Quality Street chocolates in the earth, using four distant trees to mark the location on our minds. The plan was to leave the tin there until Hallowe'en. Like many of our plans in those days, though, this one contained a hidden flaw.

Two weeks after we'd buried our treasure Jimmy Dughead relocated his prize-winning black bull to the field. Weighing in at over a hundred stone, the bull was a monster, sharp-eyed and capable of crossing the field at a body-crushing gallop in a matter of seconds. It haunted the part of the field where our buried treasure lay and hated children even more than its owner did. Mickey and I attempted on no less than eight separate occasions to get back what was rightly ours, but as if sensing our frustration, the bull wouldn't be budged, and no amount of distractions and diversions proved successful in driving it away long enough for us to achieve our goal.

It was on the afternoon of Hallowe'en itself that Mickey formulated a further recovery plan. This one, she assured me, would work. This day would be the day, she told me, when we'd put one over on Jimmy Dughead and his rotten bull.

It would also turn out to be the day that Mickey Maloney saved my life.

Sitting up on the edge of my bed, I feel sluggish and disorientated, like I've just woken up after falling asleep on a beach. I run my hand down the nape of my neck, only to find it soaked with sweat. Getting up, I cross the room and lean out of the open bedroom window, praying for a breeze, but getting only diesel and petrol fumes instead.

I sigh, angry with myself. I don't like thinking about Miles and about how things used to be. I don't want to miss him. I can't go through all that again. Keeping my mind clear of all that stuff is a habit I forced myself into after his death. It was Mum's idea, the not thinking about him, the same as it was her idea to relocate us to Scotland and for us to change our names and start afresh. Self-protection, that's what it was all about, I suppose. Whatever it was, it certainly wasn't up for discussion. It just happened. It was the way it was, the way it *had* to be. One day I went to bed as Fred Roper, the son of Miles Roper, and the next morning I woke up as Fred Wilson (Mum's maiden name), the son of Louisa Wilson.

The truth about Miles, too, vanished that same night. A new and sanitised version of him came into existence. He became an ordinary man who'd died of an ordinary heart attack, a story which I've stuck to ever since, and one which Eddie, like Rebecca and her family and everyone else I know, accepts without question. Neither my mother nor I ever talk to anyone about how Miles really died, in just the same way that we no longer discuss who he really was.

And as for the fifteen-year-old boy called Fred Roper who grew up in Rushton all those years ago . . . well, he simply no longer exists.

Hearing a distant, dull rumble of thunder, I look up and watch for a moment as a jumbo jet tears a thin white strip across the smoky blue sky. Then I gaze down at the traffic jam four storeys below and listen to the blaring horns and angry shouts. *Phew, what a scorcher!* as they used to say. I wouldn't wish it on anyone, being stuck in a car on a day like today.

Chapter II

Mickey

Joe hates me being late. He also hates my driving. 'We should get a four-wheel drive,' he mutters, glowering as we mount the kerb.

'We've got four wheels already,' I reply reasonably, clunking off the pavement and squeezing into a small space in the stationary traffic. 'This ain't the countryside, sweetheart.'

Joe slouches down in the ripped passenger seat of my dirty white van and doesn't say anything, but then Joe thinks mountain bikes are absolutely essential for modern London living. Call me the odd one out, but I haven't seen any mountains in NW10 recently.

I look out of my window and up at the sky. *Phew, what a scorcher*! as we used to say. It's the kind of one-off Mediterranean-style London day where everyone else starts slapping their foreheads as if they can't believe they haven't installed air-conditioning, while I spend all day fantasising about being at the seaside. In the van, dusty warm air blasts out from the air vents and sticks to the thin slick of sweat on my forehead. I reach for the warm can of Diet Coke from the holder on the dashboard and take a swig. 'Want some?' I try, waggling the can at Joe, but he gives me a haughty look. He's got pale, smooth skin, dark hair and a mole high on his left cheek, which makes him look pretty, beautiful almost.

'Cheer up, it shouldn't be too long.' I sigh, but Joe just folds his arms and looks ahead at the long queue. I reach out to touch his hair, but since he's had it cut he's become all precious and he ducks out of the way.

'You always say that. We're stuck.'

The news comes on and I fiddle with the radio, trying to find something a bit more lively. I generally work on the principle that if something really serious happens I'll hear about it. In the meantime, I try to avoid the mild, local anaesthetic numbness that the news creates by not listening to it every half-hour. It's harder than it sounds. On every station the latest headlines spew out like back issues of a gossip magazine being read out on a tape loop. If it's not some pop star having another baby with a ridiculous name, or a corrupt politician with prostate cancer, it's soundbites of doom and gloom from around the globe, all neatly edited with a funky backing track. *Thousands die in earthquake – one time, one time. Hundreds die in terrorist bombing – koo-koo kerchoo. Global warming out of control – shoutin' out to the Southall posse.* I keep the dial moving until I tune into my favourite country music station and tap my fingers on the steering wheel in time to Hank Williams's slide guitar.

Ahead of us two windscreen cleaners appear through the mirage created by the rows of hot bonnets and idling exhausts. They walk slowly between the cars, bearing their sud-dripping wipers and dirty cloths like weapons as they intimidate their captive audience. Somehow I know they're heading straight for us.

They get to my van, just as the traffic ahead starts to creep forward. I put up my hands in refusal and mouth 'No thanks' through the windscreen, but I've made the fatal mistake of making eye contact. The man, who can't really be more than a teenager, has a dirty bandanna tied round his forehead. He leans over, smacking the soapy washer on my screen. I wind the stiff handle on my door and the driver's window moves down an inch, and I try a different approach, leaning up towards the gap to make myself heard. 'Sorry,' I say, shrugging apologetically. 'No money.'

Oblivious to my polite refusal, the man flicks up my

wipers and pulls his own rubber blade across the glass, leaving a weeping brown streak. A moment later he's holding out his hand, begging. Joe rummages through the sweet wrappers and hair clips in the moulded junk tray between the gear stick and the fan.

I put my hand on his arm. 'Don't,' I warn, but the other man has already seen that Joe's found the emergency pound coin I keep for meters.

'This is all we've got.'

'It's too much,' I whisper. It's our turn to move and I'm running out of time. Both men leer menacingly in at us, almost salivating over the shiny gold coin on our side of the glass.

I take the money from Joe and hastily shove it at the man through the gap at the top of my window. It's an old trick, but he must have had another coin in his hand, because he starts shouting, indignantly showing me a dirty penny piece, pretending that I've given it to him instead. Panicked by his menacing look, I quickly wind up my window, almost trapping his fingers. The man shouts and spits violently on to my windscreen.

'Leave her alone!' yells Joe angrily, twisting in his seat to glare at the man, who shakes his fist at us as we move away.

I pull repeatedly on the windscreen wiper and a jet of water squirts on the glass. The offending spittle is smeared into a thin smudge and eventually disappears, but its effect still lingers. Joe turns back round in his seat and I reach out and touch his shoulder. 'Don't worry, darling. Leave it.'

'But why did he do that?' Joe looks upset and I stroke his cheek, proud of him for sticking up for me. 'You gave him the money.'

'I know,' I say, looking at Joe's sweet face and wondering how the hell I explain to my nine-year-old child that the world can be a very cruel and ugly place.

36

'They're just trying it on,' I pacify, smoothing things over. I glance in the wing mirror and notice that the men have moved on to new victims. I can feel my pulse quicken and all I want to do is get away as fast as possible.

'But why?'

'Because they're poor, I suppose,' I explain, trying to sound calm. 'People do strange things to get money.'

Joe's silent as I swerve across the junction and buck over the bumps in the short-cut road to our street. 'Come on. Let's get the shopping in,' I say, smiling to cheer things up.

I'm very proud of my flower shop. I've had it painted in lilac and the signwriter has done a great job inscribing **MICKEY'S FLOWERS** in silver and white above the windows. It stands out in the parade of shops, looking glossy and inviting between the derelict second-hand furniture place on the corner and the dated red and grey frontage of James Peters Limited next door. I can see Kevin, their chief Brylcreem-slicked estate agent, on the phone through the glass window and wave, but he doesn't respond. He looks like he's melting in his pinstriped suit and he waggles the wide knot of his tie as he churns out his patter.

It was Kevin who did the deal on the flower shop and I don't think he's quite got over the fact that I negotiated a fair whack off the price. He's taken it as a personal slight, especially since he was the one who showed us around the area when we first arrived. 'If you think about it, right,' he said, taking a deep drag on his cigarette, as Joe and I slid around on the leatherette seats of his car, '*Lahn*dan is just, like, a series of villages, all joined together. And this, right,' he shouted above the din of the lorries as he stabbed his cigarette tip towards a scrap of land (the park), 'is no exception. You want village life, you got it. Those posh city types are moving here in droves . . .' Kevin turned round and looked at me in the back seat at this point and blew an impressed whistle. 'Between you and me, love, we're talking boom time.'

Kevin, of course, was talking out of his (no doubt Brylcreemed) posterior and I couldn't help telling him so, which is why he probably ignores me now. I wasn't being unfriendly, it's just that in my experience, 'village life' would not include thousands of strangers crammed into a jumble of converted Victorian houses and concrete high rises all living in fear of burglars, vandals or, for that matter, neighbours who might *speak* to one another. Nor would it include bus lanes, surveillance cameras or residents' parking zones. If this place were even remotely 'villagey', Joe would be able to leave his bike unlocked outside the local shop without it being stolen and I could keep the car running while I popped to the cashpoint. I'd also be able to unload the shopping in comfort.

Instead, I put on the hazard lights and make Joe stand guard by the van.

Lisa opens the door of the shop and the old-fashioned bell I've rigged up chimes as she stands on the doormat. There's a blast of a horn as a car speeds past, and Joe and I both immediately look at Lisa, but she takes no notice. She's twenty-three and by all accounts a total babe, except that it wouldn't occur to her that the long expanse of her sculpted legs, her mane of corkscrew curls or her smooth olive skin would be of interest to anyone else.

'The traffic was terrible,' I groan, as I pant up to her with all the shopping bags.

'Let me give you a hand,' she says. 'You must take a break, Mickey. You'll exhaust yourself.'

Lisa is my life saver. Sometimes I think she's been sent from the heavens, as she appeared like an angel when I opened the shop and has been working with me ever since. She also rents a room from me in our flat upstairs and without her I couldn't make ends meet, or cope with Joe, whom she keeps an eye on when I have to go out. Yet for someone so good-natured she has an incredible capacity for worrying. It's the intangibles of life that set her off. She's fine when it comes to slinging together the funkiest hand-tied bouquet you've ever seen, and ask her to do all the week's ordering and she'll do it with her eyes shut. Yet she'll bite her nails down to the quick worrying about good karma, or combining the right essential oils for her bath. I tease her when such an attack of ying-yang balancing happens, but it always backfires because, when she's run out of things to worry about, she worries about me.

'You must take a rest, honestly,' she repeats, looking after me, as I two-at-a-time the stairs with all the shopping bags up to the flat.

'It saves me going to the gym,' I puff, on my way back down. 'Anything happened?' I ask, ignoring her concerned look.

'We've had our first death,' she replies, plumping up the bunches of Sweet-williams in the bucket by the door. 'Marge took the order.'

I glance over Lisa's shoulder and see Marge, my other assistant, sagged on the stool near the counter at the back of the shop. She licks her thumb and forefinger and turns over the page of the tabloid newspaper, engrossed as usual. A packet of chocolate biscuits is in mid demolition in front of her. 'That's fantastic. When?'

'Tuesday week. They've ordered the full works for the funeral procession. Marge talked them into it.' Lisa sounds disapproving, but then Lisa would do everything for free if she could.

'Great. That'll keep the bank at bay for another week at least.'

Lisa frowns at my tone and I squeeze the top of her arm. 'We'll give the old soul a Mickey's Flowers special send-off. Don't you worry.'

Joe's dug a yo-yo out of his pocket and he plays

disconsolately with it, scuffing his foot on the pavement as he waits by the van. He's wearing long shorts and a baggy T-shirt, and he looks as if he's waiting to grow into his body. 'Don't say anything embarrassing,' he mutters.

'Oh! Well, there's no point in going then,' I tease.

Slyly, he glances at me.

'I'm on your side, remember,' I say more gently. 'OK?'

'OK,' agrees Joe, before pushing me away. 'Go on, you're already late.'

I exchange a look with Lisa and stifle a laugh.

St Luke's is supposed to be the best primary school in the area and I was lucky to get Joe in. There's lots of scary big-hairdo mums who drive large people carriers with shiny bonnets like upturned noses through countless boroughs to deposit their offspring on the double yellow lines outside the school. It takes me five minutes.

When I get there, the school hall is packed and I don't know if it's the late-afternoon sun beating through the wall of windows, or whether it's my natural reaction to being in a school environment, but I immediately feel drowsy and have to combat the urge to duck behind the nearest bike shed and smoke. Instead, I smile at the lady dispatching cups of tea from the canteen hatch and hold my regulation green cup and saucer at chest height, sipping daintily and trying to look responsible, respect-able and all those 'R' words I'm supposed to be.

Ignoring the noisy throng of braying parents, frazzled teachers and the constant scrape of under-sized school chairs on the parquet floor, I slink along the wall, reading the text under a mural depicting, in shades of green paint, tin foil and felt-tip pen, the demise of the rainforest. Since the long ream of paper will undoubtedly go in the bin after parents' evening, it seems to defeat the point, but I've never been one to see the immediate benefits of education. I can't say mine did me any good and I'm not convinced that anything Joe learns at St Luke's will equip him for life.

It's not as if they're interested in teaching the kids anything useful, like how to tile a bathroom, fill in a tax return or change a tyre, for example, but then, I suppose, Joe is only nine.

Joe does a brilliant impression of his teacher, Mr Sastry, which makes him sound like Mick Jagger, so I'm not prepared for such a striking-looking man. I'm also not prepared for the fact that he's clearly younger than me. He has a pointy goatee beard, smooth chocolate skin and smoky green eyes. He stares at me as I finally get to sit down.

There's a small silence.

'Sorry I'm late,' I apologise, smoothing my hair behind my ear.

He waves his hand as if it doesn't matter and proceeds to flick through a folder, looking at rows of marks, before digging out Joe's books from a pile under his desk. It feels odd, as if I'm spying on Joe behind his back. I'm suspicious of most teachers, especially when they're at the end of a long parents' evening. As Mr Sastry chats through most subjects and explains in a reassuring tone that Joe is distinctly average, I'm convinced he doesn't really know what he's talking about. That is, until somewhere after Art and before Maths Mr Sastry pauses and touches the tips of his long fingers together.

'The thing is . . . Joe's . . . how shall I put this?'

'What?' I ask, suddenly alarmed.

'He's very solitary. It's . . . well, he seems such a loner. Is everything OK at home?'

I'm stumped. An image of Joe sitting alone in the corner of a classroom comes to me and I feel panic rising. Joe's fantastic. Why isn't he the most popular kid in the class? 'He's fine,' I bluff. 'Once you get to know him, he's very boisterous. The life and soul, actually.' I smile at Mr Sastry and he nods, although he still looks sceptical.

'I'm not criticising, you understand,' he says. 'Just observing.'

He goes on to show me Joe's Maths book and I find myself squirming on my seat when I see all the mistakes.

'It's genetic,' I say pathetically. 'I don't think he's going to be an accountant. *Thank God*,' I add, trying to be jovial.

Mr Sastry smiles weakly and closes the books. 'Don't worry. We'll get there with Joe. Together we'll get there.'

Once I'm back in the van, a surge of self-pity takes hold of me. I don't feel very together – with or without Mr Sastry. For the first time in ages I find myself wishing I were here with a partner who'd back me up and reassure me. I want someone to tell me that I'm a good parent, that I haven't damaged my child by moving him to a different school in a completely new area. I want them to say that if Joe's quiet it's OK. I want it to be fine that Joe doesn't have a big social life and hasn't made many friends. But, most of all, I want to be enough. And there's a nagging feeling inside me that I'm not.

Sometimes I hate the crushing responsibility of being a single parent. It's so hard knowing that every decision I make affects Joe. Since he was born, it feels as if every word I've said, every move I've made has left an imprint on him and shaped him in some way. And when I think of all the mistakes I've made and what an imperfect parent I've been, it makes me want to rewind and start all over again.

Talking aloud, I give myself a hard stare in the rear-view mirror. The truth is that Joe will be a flawed person no matter how hard I try. He'll make his own way in life with his own mistakes and I can't be responsible for them. All I can do is love him and if he grows up thinking I'm a failure as a parent, I suppose I'll just have to lend him the money for therapy. I smoke two cigarettes by the time I've fully talked myself out of my panic and am halfway through the third when I hit on a plan.

ToyZone is sandwiched in between a large DIY store and a leather furniture warehouse on the North Circular.

They call it paradise for kids; I call it living hell for parents. I almost give up on my mission when I see how far away I have to park and by the time I make it through the turnstiles of the store I've run out of time. I should be home by now, but I'm determined to persevere.

I've decided to buy Joe a kite. It's a kind of solidarity gesture, compensation for being a child and having to put up with school. It's to show him that I care and that I'm not one of those parents who go to parents' evening at school and then come home and have a go at their child.

In theory, it's a simple, impulsive plan, but it takes three green sweat-shirted assistants to point me in the right direction. None of them seems to know what a kite is and I can understand why. Outdoor activities obviously aren't the big thing here. In seconds, I'm lost in a maze of aisles, all lined with computer games, gadgets and consoles. There seem to be thousands of them, of every type and variety. I stop to look at one particularly violent-looking one. I pick up the neat box, shaking my head at the images of exploding aliens. I'm sure this is the one Joe's been on about and I turn over the box to check the price.

There's a man about four feet away along the aisle. He's wearing dark jeans and a casual shirt, and he glances at me, or rather glances at the game in my hand, and I'm about to make a flippant comment about the game being daylight robbery when something in his profile makes my heart thud.

I step nervously towards him. 'Excuse me?'

Quickly he turns and, putting the game he's been looking at back on the shelf, starts to walk away from me.

I take a deep breath and follow him, catching up with him in a few strides. 'Fred? Is it you?' I persist, although I'd bet my life it's him.

Fred stops as I touch him on the back of his arm. Slowly he turns round and, as my eyes meet his, my stomach flips over.

The weirdest sensation takes me over: it feels as if I'm zooming back through time. 'Fred Roper. My God . . . it *is* you,' I say, my voice catching in my throat.

Fred looks panicked for a moment.

'It's me: Mickey,' I go on, flattening my palm on my chest.

Fred looks shiftily around him and scratches the back of his head. Finally he meets my eye and his mouth breaks into a half-grin so familiar, yet so forgotten, it takes my breath away. 'Hi, Mickey,' he says, blinking at me. He says it as if we only saw each other last week, but I still shake my head, astonished. His voice is deeper than I remember, but then I suppose it would be.

'Fred?' I repeat. I still can't believe it's him. There's a pause as we stare at each other. Fred's eyes have creases round them and his face looks thinner, shadowed by a chinful of stubble, but he's undeniably good-looking. He suits being an adult and, as I stare at him more, it seems obvious that this man with trendy cropped hair was always going to emerge from the floppy-haired, shy teenager I last saw. Still, I can't help scanning his face for the features I once knew so well. They're all there, just improved, and the effect astounds me so much that I feel the blood rushing to my cheeks.

'I hardly recognised you. You . . . you look so different,' I say foolishly.

Fred nods, as if he feels the same about me. 'How . . . how are you?' he asks.

'I'm fine, thanks,' I manage, but my legs feel shaky and my palms have started to sweat.

Fred nods slowly, as if taking in my ridiculously inadequate answer.

'And you?'

'Good.' He half laughs with shock. 'Yeah, I'm good.'

A tannoy announcement booms out around us, advertising the special offers in the Sony section of the store, but Fred just continues staring at me and I shift uncomfortably.

I realise now that there's a little part of me that's been expecting this moment for a long, long time, but now that it's come it seems surreal, dreamlike almost. It's so mundane and so calm, when I always imagined that seeing Fred again would be tumultuous and dramatic, but I guess nothing could be as dramatic as the last time we saw each other.

A shudder runs through me at the memory and I look down at my trainers. I'm aware of the unflattering bright lights and how they must highlight the distinctly unhighlighted roots of my hair. It's not like me to be vain, but now I wish I'd made a bit more of an effort and didn't look so dishevelled. I'm sure I'd feel much better if I had some lipstick on. Actually, I'm not certain that's true. I don't think a full mask of make-up would make this any easier.

'I'm buying a present, for my son, Joe,' I blurt, adding, 'He's nine.'

'He'll love that one.' Fred nods at the box in my hand. 'The graphic engine is amazing.'

'No,' I say hastily, putting the game back on the shelf. 'I'm going to get him a kite. I was just looking.'

'Oh,' says Fred.

'I don't really approve of all these,' I admit, nodding at the boxes on the shelves. 'Given half a chance, Joe would just sit in front of the computer all day. Well, you must know what it's like?'

Fred nods, but he doesn't elaborate about his own children.

'I suppose I just want Joe to run around. Like we used to.'

At the mention of our past, Fred bites his lip. There's a pause and I'm aware of the huge bubble separating us. A thousand questions bottleneck on the end of my tongue, but I can't ask any of them. Instead, there's a noisy silence.

'I run a flower shop. Over on Kensal Rise. Here,' I blurt eventually, breaking the tension. I dig out one of my business cards from the breast pocket of my denim jacket and hand it over. Fred looks closely at the type. He holds the rectangle carefully, respectfully, and I point to the address. 'I live in the flat above.'

He looks at me and I know I'm blushing. I half expect him and half want him to hand back the card, but he doesn't.

'Well, you must pop in some time,' I stutter, wondering what to do with my hands, which seem to be out of control on the ends of my wrists. I clasp my fingers together. 'For a coffee or something.'

He puts my card in his pocket.

The trill of my mobile phone makes me jump. I pull it out of my bag and smile apologetically at Fred, turning away to answer. It's Joe.

'Hi, darling, I'm running a bit late,' I say, putting my finger against my other ear to hear properly.

'I'm hungry. Can we have fish fingers?' Joe asks.

'If you like,' I reply, but I'm sounding distracted. 'I'll be home in fifteen minutes or so, OK? Love you.'

I press the red button and smile, turning back to Fred. But he's not there. Ahead of me is an empty aisle. Astounded, I look around, wondering how he can have vanished into thin air. Then I turn round again, feeling my stomach lurch with disappointment as I realise he's gone. For a second I want to burst into tears.

I keep a lookout for him as I make my way to the kite section, but there's no sign. I'm in such a daze that I can't concentrate. The kites are all much more expensive than I thought they'd be and I dither for a while, before plumping for a stunt kite. By the time I get back to the van I'm still shaking, astonished by the enormity and the normality of my encounter with Fred. Of all the people to see again. Fred bloody Roper.

As predicted, Joe's in his bedroom playing on the computer when I get back. The curtains are open and the window is shut. It's stiflingly hot and the bed and tiny floor space are strewn with an assortment of clothes, books and rollerblades. Joe's kneeling on his chair and the paddle jerks in his hands as he presses the buttons. I stand in the doorway, watching him, as the electronic beeping noise reaches a crescendo and he punches the air.

'Ye-ss!'

'Hello, square-eyes,' I say, smiling.

Joe grins at me and clambers off the chair. He stumbles and hops about in agony. 'Ah, ah,' he yelps. 'I've got pins and needles.'

'Serves you right.' I chuckle, turning away as he limps after me. 'Come on.'

Our kitchenette and living room up the hall is a knocked-through room, with floor-to-ceiling windows in one side, leading to a cast-iron balustrade balcony. We never open the windows, mainly because the road outside is so noisy, but also because the balcony is far too unsafe to support a plant pot, let alone a person. Lisa and I have hung up long lengths of different coloured muslin, which makes the place look quite airy, even though there's only space for a sofa, the TV and video stand, and a rickety black plywood desk piled high with all the paperwork I have to do for the shop.

The kitchen is squashed into the far end of the room, the three-foot-square patch of black and white tile-effect lino accessed between the fridge and the end of a long breakfast bar. It's overcrowded with scuffed wooden units, most of which fall apart at the slightest touch. I've vowed that as soon as I have enough money I'm going for a complete make-over. Joe says we should write to one of the DIY programmes on the TV, but I doubt if there's enough space in here for a camera crew and, anyway, having strangers poking around would be far too humiliating.

Joe looks at me, rubbing his foot, as I open the fridge and pull out a can of Diet Coke. 'How was it?' he asks.

'Terrible,' I tease. 'I found out that you're really bad. Disruptive, noisy and –'

'Mum,' he says.

I pinch his cheek. 'They think you're great,' I say. 'But I could have told them that.'

Joe smiles bashfully.

'I got you something,' I say. 'Look.'

I hand over the bag with the kite in it, clasping the cold Coke can under my chin as I wait for Joe's reaction. 'Do you like it?'

'What is it?' asks Joe, taking the long packet out of the bag.

'It's a kite, of course.' I tut.

'Oh,' he says, but he sounds sceptical. 'Thanks.'

'You can fly it in the park,' I enthuse.

'Who with?'

I pause, my heart constricting for a moment. 'Me, if you like.'

Joe puts the kite down on the counter and I have to swallow hard. 'Did you meet Mr Sastry?' he asks, burying his hands in his pockets.

'Uh-huh.'

'What did he say?' Joe sounds suspicious.

I want to tell him exactly what Mr Sastry said. I also want to plead with him to tell me whether he's unhappy and to ask him why he's so quiet at school, but somehow I resist; it would only embarrass him. 'Well,' I say cautiously. 'What do you think he said?'

'He said I was bad at Maths, didn't he?'

'He didn't say you were bad. You're not the best in the class, that's all,' I reply. 'But that doesn't matter. You don't have to be best at everything.'

Joe looks downcast and I can tell I've made a mistake. He knows me too well and he can tell from my tone that I'm not being straight with him. Instead, he's taken this all personally, as a criticism. Just as I did.

'Joe?' I plead. 'Joe. It doesn't matter. I was terrible at Maths . . .'

'I knew he was going to be horrible. I hate him,' says Joe.

He doesn't look at me and turns away, kicking his leg over the back of the sofa and sliding down on to the cushions below. I start towards him and I'm about to explain, when Lisa comes out of her bedroom.

'Have you seen my yoga mat?' she asks, stuffing a water bottle and towel into a small rucksack. She's changed for her class and I notice how fit she looks in her baggy sweatshirt and new exercise pants.

'No, no, I haven't,' I mumble.

'Joe?' she says, ditching her bag next to him on the sofa as she starts looking around the living room, pulling up cushions and peering under the desk. 'Have you seen it? It was here yesterday.'

Joe shrugs and turns on the television, and I withdraw to the kitchen, realising that I've lost my chance to explain.

When I finally get to bed, I can't sleep. I'm surrounded on all sides by noise. Underneath the floorboards the water pipes clank and, on the other side of my bedroom wall, I can hear canned laughter as our unknown neighbours watch TV. Outside, a few feet away, a night bus throbs, making the windows vibrate, and beyond it the pizza delivery mopeds buzz up and down the street like giant mosquitoes.

I get up, throw on my grubby towelling dressing gown and pad into the kitchen. The kite is still on the counter where Joe left it and its packet casts a long shadow on the wall. I know the present hasn't really worked. I should have taken Fred's advice and got Joe a computer game, or maybe I shouldn't have got him anything at all.

Wearily, I crouch down to the broken bottom drawer. This is my junk drawer, stuffed with old hairbrushes, wire freezer tags, a collection of promotional labels that I never sent off, coffee-ring-stained envelopes and a hundred and one other useful items that I can't bring myself to throw away. I root through the contents, looking for the airline passengers' kit that Scott, my brother, gave Joe when he last visited. It's the nearest Joe's going to get to a holiday and he was thrilled with it. Inside the zipper compartment are some nylon socks, face wipes, a miniature toothpaste and toothbrush, a comb, an eye-mask and what I'm looking for: foam earplugs.

Despite the skull-and-crossbones 'Keep Out' sign on Joe's door, I look in on him. He's lying on his back under his camouflage duvet cover, sleeping solidly and noise-lessly, like a mummy. His face is illuminated by the green glow from the light on his computer monitor and I creep into the room to switch it off. He doesn't stir as I crouch down and plant an illegal, tender kiss on his forehead. He looks so serious and for a moment I feel terrified.

I run my fingers through Joe's hair, resisting the urge that I've had since he was little to lean in and check he's still breathing. I want to cry, but I don't. Instead, I sink to my knees by Joe's pillow and stare at his face for a long time, taking in every pore of it, memorising his long eyelashes and the shape of his eyebrows, willing time to stand still for a second in the hope of keeping him just the way he is.

I tiptoe back to my room, even though I know Joe won't wake up, and wedge the foam pads into my ears. As I curl up on my side and listen to the sound of my own breathing whoosh around my head, an orange diagonal of light sweeps up the brown nineteen-fifties wardrobe, across the flaking beige paint on the ceiling and down to the ironing board stacked with a pile of laundry, as another bus passes the window.

Sleep still eludes me, even though I'm exhausted. I lie awake staring at the corner of my pillow. I feel terribly unnerved, as if I've tripped and fallen over, and the world is suddenly at a different angle. I've spent so much time running in the opposite direction from my past and making promises about the future that I feel giddy and a bit lost. I've dismissed everything that happened, shut it out, shunned it, cursed it and pretended that it happened differently, but all the things I haven't resolved are still there. It's hard to admit, but I don't feel like the fearless single mother striding towards a better future, I just feel like a coward.

It's seeing Fred that's made me feel like this. The new Fred, with his adult face, looms in my head, at once obscuring and rekindling my memories with the reality of his presence. As if none of the years between had happened, ancient feelings of betrayal and anguish come rushing back and threaten to choke me. Swallowing hard, I replay our meeting over in my head, over and over again, but this time I stand up to him in the toy shop, flinging down the computer game like a gauntlet and asking him why. That's all I need to know. Why he left so suddenly. Why he didn't phone or write. Why, after everything that happened, he just stopped caring.

I roll over on to my back and try to get comfortable, but the anger sits on my chest like a growling cat. I don't know if I'm more angry with Fred or with myself, for having had such a pathetically polite encounter when, actually, I should have beaten him up. Instead, I babbled on and didn't even let him get a word in edgeways.

But even if I did bump into him again out of the blue, I doubt I'd have the courage to stand up to him. What would I tell him? That I blame him? That in that one defining act of our youth the course of my life changed for ever? Is it really true that everything bad that's happened to me since I last saw him is somehow Fred's fault? Or is it more the case that I'm cross because our childhood should have lasted a little bit longer?

I've spent all this time resenting the fact that it ended so abruptly, that I've forgotten what being young was like. Because, if, like now, I allow myself to think about it, I miss it. I miss it for me, but most of all I miss it for Joe, because once upon a time there was no need for computer games, or hot summer nights alone in a bedroom, because I had Fred. And where there were Fred and me, there was always adventure.

The low grey clouds scudded across the October sky, as I tensed, ready for action. Despite the lack of sunshine I shaded my eyes, squinting up the sharp slope of the field, as I waited for Fred to get into position.

Suddenly I saw him, diagonally opposite, right over the other side of the mud-peaked expanse, his orange cagoule making him stand out against the dark-brown fields beyond. He'd refused to take it off, saying that despite what everyone else said, Miles had told him that bulls were colour blind, and I'd known Fred's stubborn face well enough to realise that there hadn't been any point in arguing.

Feeling sweaty, I unzipped my parka and made the agreed signal – flinging my arm up like Olga Korbut about to perform a triple backflip, but feeling a tingle of fear spread across my hairline as a solitary scrawny magpie plunged from the giant oak tree and landed, squawking, on the fence post in front of me. What was the rhyme? One for sorrow, two for joy . . .

Feeling ominous, I stopped myself looking round for the magpie's mate and concentrated on the task ahead. This was it, then. The time had come at last. This was war.

'Okey-dokey,' I mumbled, rubbing my hands together, kneeling down and pulling at the weak wire patch in the bottom of the fence. It took a lot of wriggling, but finally I was through. Flattening myself against the fence, my heart pounding, I looked up and saw that Fred had clambered on to the stone wall on the other side of the field, holding our weapon aloft against the grey skies. And between us, huge, brutal and hairy, was our enemy: Jimmy Dughead's bull.

For a moment everything was still, our fear suspended in the soggy air. The only sound I could hear was my own heartbeat and a dog barking in the distance. Soon all the kids in the village would be dressing up in their witches and ghost costumes, and the Hallowe'en celebrations would begin. This was our last chance and it had to work.

The night before we'd both sat in my bedroom racking our brains for a plan, as we listened to records and looked up rude words in the dictionary.

'*I* know,' said Fred, his face lighting up with an idea, but as soon as it had come, his shoulder slumped back down into his familiar slouch. 'No. No,' he mumbled.

'What?' I asked, flinging the dictionary aside.

'Nothing. Nothing. It doesn't matter.'

'Fred,' I insisted, swinging my legs off the bed. 'We've got to get the treasure tin. It's got all our money in it. And if we don't get the money, we won't be able to afford any of the tickets for the raffle.'

We'd both been obsessing about the raffle prize which was tickets for the circus in London. Rumour had it that Rushton's only claim to fame, Andy Buckley, the reclusive magician who lived over in the big house, had donated them to his elderly cleaning lady who was putting them in the Hallowe'en raffle as first prize.

'But,' began Fred. Then he sighed heavily. 'No. We can't. Well, we could . . .'

'Come on,' I urged.

Fred looked down at the bean bag. 'Miles has got a –'

But he didn't have a chance to continue, as my mother suddenly opened my bedroom door. Her hair was obviously in giant rollers, as the shiny headscarf looked lumpy on the top of her head. Her eyes were glazed, as they often were in the evening. She was wearing her blue net dressing gown with fluff around the bottom and she clutched at the neck of it as she looked between Fred and me, her expression blank. 'Are you hungry?' she asked unenthusiastically.

I shook my head. 'We had a sandwich, didn't we, Fred?'

I glared at him. The last thing we needed for Mum to start cooking.

'Um, yes,' Fred muttered. 'Thanks anyway, Mrs Maloney.'

She screwed up her mouth, half nodded and, without saying anything else, swung back on the handle and banged the door shut.

'Miles has got a . . .' I hissed excitedly, urging Fred to carry on.

'A starter pistol.'

'A what?'

'You know, like in school. One of those guns they use at the start of a race. They make a huge bang, but they've only got blanks in them.'

'Why has Miles got a starter pistol?' I asked, surprised.

'He used to be an athlete,' Fred said proudly. 'He told me all about it when I saw him putting it away the other day.'

The record had finished and the needle crackled as it undulated in the blank grooves. I thought for a moment before crossing my legs under me and fiddling idly with my Rubik's cube as I worked out a plan. 'I've got it,' I said. 'One of us could go to the bottom of the field and distract the bull while the other one jumps over the wall, runs in and digs up the treasure. If the bull gets nasty, we could fire the starter pistol to give it a shock –'

'Mickey, we can't,' interrupted Fred, leaning over and pulling the needle off the record.

'Why not?'

'Miles would go mad.'

'He wouldn't have to find out. We'll just be borrowing it until we get the treasure back. If we have to use it, we'll just tell everyone it was a firework. Simple.'

But now, looking at Jimmy Dughead's bull, its condensed breath firing out of its quivering, evil nostrils like steam, our plan didn't seem so obviously simple any more. It was far too late to change things, though, so advancing up from the bottom of the muddy field like a matador, I began my distraction routine, yelling out a jumble of words from all the Abba songs I could remember, but Jimmy Dughead's bull didn't share my enthusiasm. 'Come on, come on,' I muttered, before advancing further, continuing in a louder rendition. 'Take a chance on me,' I sang, windmilling my arms and dancing cancan style in my red wellies.

This time I had the bull's full attention. It snorted and scraped its hoof in the dirt as I hopped up and down to 'Dancing Queen'. But it didn't take much more to do the trick. The bull, like a cartoon version of itself, seemed to rear itself up, leaning backwards to give itself more force, then it was off, charging down the field at me.

Behind the bull Fred hopped off the wall and ran into the field, frantically searching for the place where the treasure was buried, trying to align himself in the central spot between the four oak trees.

'Dancing Queeeeeeeeeeen!' I half sang, half yelled, as Jimmy Dughead's bull thundered towards me. Losing my confidence, I ran back to the bottom of the field and threw myself through the gap under the fence.

The bull wasn't pleased and snorted at me, angrily nudging the piece of the fur from my hood that had caught the fence. I jumped back, trying to keep the bull occupied, but with only the thin fence between us it quickly got bored with my timid advances. Which is when it turned round and noticed Fred, who was now slap-bang in the middle of the field, pacing in the gluey mud, staring intently at the ground.

'Fred!' I yelled through cupped hands. 'Fred, watch out!'

Startled, Fred looked up and saw the bull turning up the field towards him. My heart pounded as he tried to pull the starter pistol out of the front pouch of his cagoule.

'Fred! Quick!' I screamed, throwing myself against the fence and watching in horror as the bull hurtled towards him.

Panicked, Fred yanked the starter pistol free. Holding it shakily with both hands, he held it out in front of him and, screwing up his face, turned his head away as he pulled the trigger.

There was a huge, ear-splitting bang.

Open-mouthed, my lungs punched empty, I watched as the bull wobbled for a second, before keeling over on to the ground with a thud. Fred dropped the starter pistol into the mud, his arms hanging by his sides. He stared across the terrifyingly small divide between him and the huge bull.

In a second I was under the fence and squelching through the mud towards him, the echo of the blast ringing in my ears.

'Fred, Fred, are you all right?' I said, catching up with him and shaking his arm. His chest heaved up and down inside his cagoule as first he nodded vigorously and then shook his head from side to side in denial.

I looked down at the bull and advanced slowly towards it. Close up, it was massive and its mottled purple skin was covered with thick hair, spiked up with mud. It stank with a swarming buzz of a smell that made my throat sting. I choked, holding the cuff of my parka over my nose as, tentatively, I extended my foot and prodded the beast with my toe. Its skin rucked slightly over the solid mass of muscle underneath and I jumped away, clinging on to Fred.

We stared in silence for a moment, a fuzz of light rain making us blink as our feet started to sink in the mud.

'It must have had a heart attack,' I said. 'Bloody hell. Just like Doctor Lawson.'

We were experts on heart attacks, following the collapse of Rushton's doctor in the post office a few weeks previously, followed hot on the heels by Mrs Turnball who had collapsed right on to the magazine rack in the local newsagent. At school, we'd all perfected the double-hand-to-chest-knee-buckling death sequence of Rushton's two seemingly sprightly inhabitants and now, it seemed, we'd scored a hat trick: we'd scared Jimmy Dughead's bull to death.

'Come on, quick. Let's get the treasure. You never know, it might wake up,' I said, but Fred didn't move. Still mute with shock, he extended his arm towards the bull and, confused, I followed his trembling finger. Only then did I see what Fred was getting at. In the side of the bull's head, deep-red blood bubbled out of a small, but nevertheless deadly singed hole.

I could see my shocked face reflected in the black curve of the bull's open eye, as slowly I picked up the starter pistol from the mud. But I knew, even before I felt the hot barrel. 'Oh Fred.' I choked, looking from the gun to his pale face. 'It's real. You shot him.'

But neither of us had time to ponder the enormity of what had happened, as the ground started to vibrate like an earthquake. I turned to see Jimmy Dughead careering over the brow of the hill on his huge tractor. When he saw us standing over his prostrate prize bull, he rose up in his seat, shaking his fist in the air like an angry Viking.

'Run!' I screamed, grabbing Fred and jamming the gun into my pocket as we raced down the field, scrambling under the fence and sprinting to the stream that separated it from our houses.

'You little bastards. I'll get you!' Jimmy Dughead yelled, his voice reverberating down the hill after us.

I pushed Fred through the brambles and scrambled after him, wading through the knee-deep stream, forgetting all about the stepping stones. Fred pulled me up the muddy bank on the other side and into the garden of our house. We fell panting on to the patch of earth by Dad's compost heap.

We both knew that Jimmy Dughead had recognised us and we didn't have much time. If he found us, we'd be made into mincemeat. I pulled off my welly and emptied out a gush of water.

'Let's go to the village. He'll never find us there,' I said and Fred nodded. Hopping up the path as I pulled my welly back on, I watched Fred race ahead to where my Raleigh Chopper was lying on its side and pull it upright.

'Quick. Go, Fred,' I urged, climbing on to the long seat behind him and clinging on.

But Jimmy Dughead must have realised our plan, because the gate to the farm at the top of the road was already open as we wobbled down the gap by Dad's car. And as we screeched out of the drive, we could hear the tractor bumping over the cattle grid.

'He's going to run us down,' shouted Fred, finding his voice, at last, as he looked over his shoulder. We flew down the centre of the Avenue, whizzing past all the neighbours' gates, straight over all the potholes we usually avoided, our cheeks pinned back, our teeth clattering as we gathered speed down the steepest hill in the world and our voices rattled in our chests as the tractor came thundering after us.

As we hurtled into the village, Fred's feet couldn't keep up with the pedals and we shouted in unison as they whipped round without us. Like an escaped roller coaster car, the chopper careered over the stone bridge, making us lose our stomachs over the bump. Still faster we went, unable to stop, torn between imminent death and Jimmy Dughead. Out of control, we weaved in and out of parked cars on the high street, flew over the crossing by the school, bounced up on to the grass verge and then, flying through the air, landed in the Memorial Hall car park and smashed head first into the bins, where, finally, we came to a noisy halt.

Groaning and rubbing our heads, we both sat upright. Fred flicked away some chicken bones caught up in his cagoule and rubbed his back, but otherwise we both seemed miraculously unscathed. When we'd untangled ourselves from the tin lids, we salvaged the chopper and leant it up against the wall, before peeking round the corner to have a look at the road. There was no sign of Jimmy Dughead, who must've taken the long way round to avoid the narrow stone bridge, but our hearts were still pounding.

'Let's get to the pub,' whispered Fred, still out of breath. 'Pretend that nothing's happened. There'll be loads of people there.'

I nodded and, sticking close, we sneaked along the back wall of the Memorial Hall to the green. Then, squeezing ourselves flat against the pink plaster of the Gordon Arms, we skulked along the wall and, with a quick 'sh' to Elsie, the pub's lame sheepdog, slipped in through the dark wooden doors of the saloon bar.

Inside, the air was warm and smoky, and the crackle of the fire was only just audible over the shunting of furniture, as the ladies from the Memorial Hall set out the tables for the evening's festivities, covering them with long paper cloths and foil-wrapped dishes.

Fred and I were just sneaking along under the dart-board, when the back door of the pub swung open and a draft blew right through us.

'Where are those bleedin' kids?' yelled Jimmy Dughead.

Quick as lightening, Fred yanked me down by my sleeve and we dived under the end table. Through the crack between the long paper tablecloths we watched as Eric, the landlord of the Gordon Arms, puffed out his barrel chest.

'There's no children in here, Jim.'

'They've done in Hercules,' raged Jimmy Dughead. 'My prize bull,' he added, striding into the pub. 'I'm going to skin the little sods alive,' he boomed and even the faces on the toby jugs hanging on the beam above the bar seemed to grimace with terror. 'They've shot him.'

The atmosphere seemed to freeze for a second as the happy burble of voices cut abruptly. We were trapped. We couldn't go back out the way we'd come in without being seen. The only way was forward.

'Shot him? With a gun?' asked the landlady, Sue, coming out from behind the bar.

'Come on!' hissed Fred, and I followed him, as we crawled on our hands and knees under the long line of tables.

'Don't be ridiculous, Jimmy.'

I heard Miles's familiar laugh above me. Sure enough, next to me were Miles's fashionable tasselled shoes. For a second I froze, but then I yanked his trouser leg and he lifted up the tablecloth. Silently, I raised the gun so that Miles could see it. For a split second I thought he was going to pull me out by my ear and expose me to the wrath of Jimmy Dughead, but instead his face remained blank as, without a word, he took the gun from me and tucked it inside his coat as if nothing had happened. The flick of his head was barely perceptible as he ordered me to go and I felt the firm force of his shoe on my bum as I scampered after Fred.

I could see Jimmy Dughead's thick legs striding towards the table.

'It was your nipper, Roper. I swear it. And yer neighbours'.'

'Now, how would kids get hold of a gun, Jim?' I heard Miles say calmly, as I raced after Fred, my hands and knees scraping on the joins between the brown carpet and the maroon tiles as we reached the end of the line of tables where I bumped into Fred's behind.

Spotting our opportunity, as Two Ton Teresa, the school dinner lady, swung through the kitchen door with a tray full of hot dog buns, I pushed Fred up and in a second we'd dodged through into the pub kitchen. Crouching down, we scampered under the level of the stainless-steel unit and bundled out of the back door into the garden, darting under a line of damp tea towels blowing on the line.

We were back on the bridge before we stopped for breath, folding over double.

Fred looked up at me, his hands on his knees. 'What shall we do with the gun?'

'I gave it back to Miles, in the pub,' I panted, my heart hammering with a mixture of fear and exhilaration.

Fred looked truly shocked at this. 'Oh, Mickey. We're going to get into so much trouble. Miles made me promise never to touch it.'

I stood up and took a deep breath, pushing my hair back from my face with both hands. 'Well, he shouldn't have a gun in the first place,' I said. 'Guns are illegal.'

'Do you think he'll get in trouble with the police?' asked Fred.

I shrugged my shoulders.

Fred sniffed loudly, wiping his nose on his cagoule sleeve. His pale cheeks had bright-red blotches on them. 'What are we going to do?'

'We'll have to run away,' I said.

Running away was a situation I'd often imagined, except that every time I thought about doing it, I spent so long composing my goodbye note and planning which essentials to take, that by the time I got round to contemplating the small leather suitcase on top of my wardrobe I'd usually gone off the idea. Either that, or got hungry.

I'd certainly never considered what it would be like to run away on the spur of the moment, like this. But now, with no treasure, being wanted for the murder of Hercules by Jimmy Dughead, and being in so much trouble with Miles and my parents, who'd banish me to my room for a whole year once they found out, going away suddenly seemed like a brilliant idea.

'A car will be along,' I said, squiggling my toes against the wet ends of my socks inside my wellies.

'But it could be ages,' Fred protested, his face solemn as he realised how serious I was.

'Well, we'll just have to wait,' I said, jumping up so I was sitting on the wall, feeling the cold stones press into the back of my thighs. I folded my arms round me, but I couldn't help shivering.

We were silent for a long time.

Kicking our heels and feeling bored, we both stared at the river. I'd never seen it this high. Usually, in the summer, clear water trickled over the moss-covered stones on the river bed, and you could see the little black fish as they battled against the current. Today, though, the water was at least five feet deep and flowing fast, leaves and twigs caught up in the murky swill so that it looked like chocolate milkshake.

'Saved your life,' Fred said eventually, catching my arm with a jolt, as he jumped up on the wall next to me, but we could barely smile at each other. He'd picked up a stick from somewhere and made it clatter against the shiny stones. Then, nudging me, he threw the stick behind him into the river.

'I'll race you,' he challenged, already flipping himself

off the wall, pelting across the bridge to see the stick come under the other side.

'Not fair,' I said, skipping after him and catching up, relieved to have something to do as we both stretched over the wide bridge wall and looked down into the water. A second later Fred's twig came out from under the bridge, darting in the mini-waves.

'More!' I demanded, allowing Fred to cheer me up with our old childhood game.

We dashed down to the side of the bridge and collected twigs. Then we went back to the right spot on the bridge and stood with one twig each.

'Ready . . . steady . . .' teased Fred. 'Go!' he added suddenly and we both hurled our twigs into the water, before darting back across the road to the other side of the bridge and peering down.

'I can't see them,' said Fred, hoisting himself over the wall to get a better look, his feet lifting off the road as he looked down into the water.

I looked too, but I still couldn't see, so Fred wriggled further over and made a funny noise that echoed on the underside of the bridge.

'Saved your life,' I laughed, pushing him playfully. But this time, I didn't catch him. I meant to, but maybe I pushed too hard. Maybe I wasn't quick enough, because it had been an exhausting day, and maybe Fred couldn't hold on for the same reason but, like a sack of potatoes, he overbalanced and, in a blink, was gone with a huge splash.

'Fred!' I screamed, throwing myself on to the wall to see over the edge. 'Fred?'

But he'd already been carried downstream, his head bobbing in the water, his arm shooting up as he tried to hold on to something – anything – in the swirling torrent, his orange cagoule rising up round his chest.

I looked around me frantically, my heart pounding with a new kind of terror. 'Help! Help! Someone help me!' I shouted, but no one was in sight. It was getting dark and they would all be in the village already. I rushed to the other side of the bridge and back again, panic overwhelming me.

Running across the bridge and scrambling down the river bank, I scanned the water, knowing that with each precious second Fred was in more and more danger. He was a terrible swimmer. He's come last in the fifty-metres breaststroke at school, while I had already done my bronze survival badge.

'Help!' he screamed, with a strangled gurgle.

'Hang on, hang on, I'm coming,' I yelled, spotting him and trying to keep up with his tumbling form, as his head disappeared below the water.

Kicking off my wellies and pulling off my parka, I launched myself from the bank into the brown foam. Immediately, I felt heavy as the water seeped into my clothes, freezing my skin. I yelped as the river dragged my feet from under me and whipped me away from the bank. Blinking and spluttering with the cold, I tried to clear the water from my eyes and called out for Fred.

I felt like I'd been carried along for ages before I saw an orange flash of Fred's cagoule. I launched myself at it, grabbing it and clinging on for dear life, as I dragged him towards me. Thankfully, the weight of us both hindered our progress in the fast flow. Coughing, I ducked under a tree branch and a second later, dragging Fred under his chin and swimming for my life, I had my footing.

'Fred . . . No . . .' I screamed, pushing him roughly against the river bank and watching in horror as his head lolled to one side. Keeping hold of his hood, I pulled myself on to the sloping grass verge, before kneeling down and grabbing him under his arms to pull him out. I could barely lift him. He was so heavy with his clothes bogged down with water. I was crying and breathless, slipping on the bank, my teeth chattering with cold and fright. Eventually I pulled Fred up as far as I could and cradled him in my arms.

'Fred,' I sobbed, slapping his face with my blue fingers, before remembering the thing we'd learnt in the survival course. Making my hands into one fist, I put them on Fred's stomach and pulled up towards his ribs. 'Fred, come on . . . Fred . . . it's going to be all right.'

Suddenly, he lurched on to his side and threw up a great stomach-load of river water, before convulsing into a coughing fit. I didn't mind, though. I was so relieved he was alive and I hadn't killed him.

'Oh, Fred, oh, Fred,' I cried, rubbing his back as he coughed.

Eventually he stopped and fell back exhausted on my lap, his hair plastered to his pale face as he looked up at me. 'Did my stick win?' he asked in a small voice.

And then I collapsed next to him, laughing as we clung on to each other.

'Yes, Fred, you won, this time,' I said, 'You won, you won.' And above us, over the village, a firework exploded in a bright green shower of sparkles.

The bin men wake me up. Joe's sitting next to me on my bed, his legs stretched out. He's fully dressed and is riffling through a pack of cards. I dig the earplugs out of my ears.

'You were giggling in your sleep,' he says.

'Hm. Was I?' I sit up and rub my eyes. 'What time is it?'

'Seven thirty. You didn't hear the alarm. Can I have breakfast?'

I nod and pat Joe on the leg. He slips off my bed, still engrossed in the cards, and goes through to the kitchen. I hear him opening the fridge and I yawn and sit up. The duvet is on the floor and I pull it back up on the bed, before heading for the bathroom.

It's only since I've been single that I sleep like a mad

woman, flailing my arms around, kicking and (according to Joe) muttering and grunting. When I was married to Martin I didn't stir in the night, but then I didn't sleep much, either. I just lay on my side of the bed and looked at the clock.

I still find it spooky that I was ever married, but then I was pretty much as close as you can get to being clinically brain-dead without anyone noticing. By twenty-one I'd made lots of decisions based on flawed logic, rather than logical feelings, but even I had to admit that my betrothal to a man I wasn't in love with in return for his promise to be a father to Joe and provide a home away from the suffocation of Rushton was one of the worst. Yet, despite my sense of foreboding, I plunged into my wedlock-up, only to realise that no amount of new carpeting or self-assembly furniture could make up for the fact that Martin's hairy back made my toenails itch underneath. I also learnt that there's nothing as lonely as sleeping next to someone you don't love.

I shower quickly, brush my teeth and join Joe in the kitchen. He's looking at the instructions for the kite. I think he feels guilty about yesterday. I, on the other hand, feel guilty about today. It's Saturday and I'm going to have to help Lisa since Marge has a hospital appointment. It's something to do her varicose veins and she did start to tell me, but I'd rather not know. Marge gets a kick out of all things medical and if she could have more operations, she would. The gorier and more personal, the better.

The upshot is that Joe will be on his own, at least until mid-afternoon. He doesn't seem as bothered as I am and I make promises about taking him out to the park later, but I think he's relieved that he can play on the computer in peace.

The morning passes in a blur and I'm pleased that the shop is so busy. It's just gone one o'clock when Fred walks in.

'Hi,' he says bashfully, pointing at the door. 'I was just passing, so I thought . . .'

He's wearing shorts and sunglasses on a thick rubber strap round his neck. I realise that I'm staring at him with my mouth open. 'Hi,' I say stupidly, feeling shocked and unprepared. I'm also embarrassed. After thinking about him last night, I feel somehow caught out and exposed.

Lisa is looking between us, but I can't look at her. I feel too flustered to explain.

'It's a great shop,' says Fred.

'Thanks,' I mumble.

'Are you busy? Only I can come back . . .'

'No. No. Not at all,' I gush, remembering my manners. 'Come up to the flat for a coffee. You don't mind, do you?' I ask Lisa, turning my head away from Fred and widening my eyes at her.

She raises her eyebrows mischievously in reply. 'No problem,' she says.

Jittery with nerves, I walk past her and Fred follows me up the stairs. I'm conscious of the scuffed carpet, flaking paint and exposed pipes. For some reason I want to make a good impression. I want to prove that I've made it as an adult.

Fred follows me into the living room and, with difficulty, I open the window to let some air in. In the kitchen, the sink is full of washing up and the side is covered with smears of butter, Marmite and a jumble of bread crusts where Joe must have made a sandwich earlier.

'Sorry about the mess, I'm not used to having visitors. In fact, you're the first person to drop by,' I say sheepishly as I fill up the kettle. 'Kids, eh?' I joke, ripping off a piece of kitchen roll and wiping the kitchen counter. 'Are yours as bad as this?'

'I don't have any,' says Fred, looking confused.

'I thought . . . well, last night at ToyZone? You were buying games . . .'

Fred scratches the back of his neck. 'I was looking at them for me. For me and my flatmate, Eddie . . .'

'Oh, I see,' I say, except that I don't. The way he says it makes it sound like such a normal thing to do that it occurs to me that Fred might be gay.

I watch as he cranes his neck and looks between the kitchen and living room. Suddenly, seeing it through his eyes, it seems incredibly small and poky.

'It's nice,' he says. 'You live here on your own?'

'No. Lisa lodges here, but apart from her it's just Joe and me. I was married, but um . . . well, it didn't work out. I don't think marriage was really my thing. You . . . ?'

'Engaged.'

'Oh,' I say, folding my arms. I can't seem to stop putting my foot in it. Thank God I've only got two, otherwise who knows what damage I might cause. 'Well, congratulations.'

Fred nods. 'Thanks.'

'When's the big day?'

'A month.'

'Oh.' I nod. 'Soon.'

There's a pause as Fred stares at me and I feel myself flushing. We both laugh nervously.

'Mum?' It's Joe, calling from his bedroom.

'Come and meet Joe,' I say, trying to sound breezy and normal, but feeling anything but.

I hate introducing Joe to men. The few times I've seen people, it's been a disaster. The last one was Tom, about a year ago. He was very nice, in a kind of laddish way, but he couldn't accept that I had a child. Instead, he tried his best to ignore it and then he got angry when any weekend plans we made needed to include Joe. Unsurprisingly, he and Joe hated each other on sight and I had to finish it almost as soon as it had started.

'Joe, this is Fred,' I begin, as Fred and I stand at his bedroom door. 'He's an old friend of mine.' I sound

Victorian and prissy, even to myself. 'We once knew each other in Rushton . . .'

Joe and Fred both ignore me. Instead, they nod at each other and both say, 'All right,' in the same tone. Maybe it's a boy thing, but they seem very cool and easy with the situation. They turn their attention to the computer.

'What are you playing?' asks Fred, before I get the chance to explain things further.

Joe mumbles the name of the game and Fred nods.

'I've got that,' he says, walking into the room as if he's known Joe for ever. 'What level are you on?'

'I'm stuck on three,' says Joe nonchalantly, as if a total stranger walking towards him across the sacred carpet of his private space is a normal, everyday occurrence. I practically have to get a papal dispensation signed just to vacuum in here.

'I can get to the mutants, but then the skateboarders get me,' says Joe, as if it's no big deal.

I can't believe what I'm hearing. Joe's been tearing his hair out for a week now, unable to move on with the game. How come he's suddenly so calm?

'I know what you mean,' says Fred. 'It's a bummer, isn't it? It took me ages to suss it, but it's easy once you know how. Do you want me to show you?'

Joe nods.

'Budge up, then,' says Fred and Joe slides along the end of his bed, where he's sitting, to make room, before handing Fred the paddle as he sits down. Within seconds they're both staring at the screen and Fred is patiently explaining to Joe what he's doing.

I retreat, feeling redundant and perplexed. In the kitchen I clear things up a bit, but I'm being extra quiet, trying to earwig on what's going on in Joe's room. It's odd having Fred in our flat. It feels like the most natural thing in the world, but at the same time I'm aware that I hardly know anything about him. For all I know he could have spent the last fifteen years being a child molester. He could be anyone but the Fred Roper I used to know.

The kettle boils.

'Fred?' I call, looking up at the ceiling. It feels as if I'm calling for Joe, but when I get no response I sneak back to Joe's room to check on progress.

Joe's enraptured. 'That's brilliant,' he gushes. He turns to me. 'Mum, I'm on to the next level. It's easy.'

Fred stands up, handing the paddle back to Joe.

Joe smiles up at him. 'Thanks,' he says, his eyes shining with gratitude. 'Can I go down the shop for some crisps?' he asks me and I nod.

'Don't be long, though, we're going to the park in a bit, remember.'

Putting the game on pause, Joe scoots past us, the most excited I've seen him for a long while.

'He's great,' says Fred, as he follows me back to the kitchen.

'Well, you've certainly made his day.'

I stare after Joe for a moment, before busying myself making instant coffee.

'How do you take it?' I ask.

'Black, no sugar. Thanks.'

'Right.' I nod, turning my back on Fred. I feel as if I should know this fact about him. It's weird not knowing how this stranger likes his coffee, but knowing that he takes his Slush Puppies blue. Come to think of it, I'm probably one of the few people on the planet who could identify Fred in a line-up by the dagger-shaped scar he has on his left elbow where we fell off a go-cart, and yet I haven't got a clue where he lives or, for that matter, what he does for a living. As I punch a hole in the top of a new jar of instant coffee the coffee grains jump and I must admit that I feel similarly jangled, as if Fred has punched a hole in the vacuum seal of my life, too.

'So,' says Fred, when I hand him his coffee. 'Where do we start?'

I blow a nervous breath on the steam spiralling from my mug. 'I'm not sure.'

We chat for a while and swap bits of information. I feel like we're reading out soundbites from our respective CVs, but somehow none of it seems as if it's particularly relevant. He tells me about his job in computers and I tell him about the move away from Kent.

'Joe and I stayed there for a while after the divorce, but I didn't like it much. I kept having to sneak around, avoiding Martin's friends. I'd already trained as a florist, but I went back to college to do a business course. I always fancied living in London and when this place came up, I applied for a bank loan and thought, what the hell.' I wave my hand flippantly.

'That's you, Mickey. You were always so brave.'

'Brave,' I snort. 'I'm not brave.'

'Yes, you are.'

I shake my head. 'Come off it. You don't know me. I was a teenager the last time you saw me. Since then, I've been complete chicken shit.'

'I don't believe you. You were never afraid of new things. New adventures. I used to be jealous.'

'Well, I'm different now.'

'Are you?'

'Yes,' I say. 'Of course I am. Completely different.'

Fred looks at me and then looks down, and we're silent for a long moment. Our conversation was bound to run out sooner rather than later. It's as if there's a giant skip full of junk from the past and we can't see past it or over it until it's cleared away. Fred rubs the handle of his coffee cup and sighs.

I decide to pop the bubble. 'Why didn't you write?' I ask, putting my mug down. I put my hands on my hips and stare at him, but he still looks away. 'Why didn't you phone, or anything?' Even though I'm trying to sound like it doesn't matter, I can hear the churlish tone in my voice.

Fred looks up at me. 'I did write,' he says, but I shake my head to stop him.

'Don't lie to me,' I say, biting my lips together. 'There's no need. I mean . . . not that it matters any more, but . . .' I clear my throat. 'I was so shaken up when you went. OK, so I got that scribbled postcard with your address, but then . . . nothing. I couldn't believe you didn't want to stay in touch,' I admit, feeling the raw truth sting my eyes. 'It was such a shitty way to end what we had. I was so upset. Actually, upset doesn't come close. I was angry . . .'

'You were angry? *You* were angry?' Fred sounds indignant. 'I wrote and wrote to you. I was miserable. Christ, Mickey, you have no idea . . .'

'I never got your letters. And I wrote to *you* nearly every day. For ages, as it happens.' Suddenly I blurt out a laugh, remembering my outpourings, trying desperately to keep Fred close to me, even though he was miles away. 'Actually, it's just as well. What I wrote was pretty embarrassing.'

'Not as bad as my bad poetry, surely?'

'You sent poetry?'

Fred nods. 'Well, poetry is going a bit far. It was terrible doggerel nonsense,' he admits. 'Roses are red, violets are blue . . . that kind of thing.'

'Violets aren't blue.' I smile. 'They're purple.'

'I knew you wouldn't appreciate it.'

'That's nothing,' I confess. 'I sent you Brut aftershave.'

Fred laughs. 'Oh, gross.'

And looking at him, I can't help smiling too. 'You never said thank you.'

'I expect my mother intercepted your letters. She was desperate for me not to have any contact. Any reminders . . . you know . . .' Fred sighs. 'I'm so sorry.'

'Mine must have done the same. Interfering old bag. I'd

72

never do that,' I say distractedly, stunned by the magnitude of our parents' intervention, but nevertheless feeling the words 'I'm so sorry' somehow dissipate my anger.

'You wouldn't have to. We'd have e-mail and mobile phones. It would be so easy to stay in touch now. Despite parents. Despite everything.'

'I guess.'

Fred reaches out and covers my hand with his. 'For what it's worth,' he says, 'I missed you.'

A shudder runs through me and for a moment I feel paralysed. I look down, alarmed at the warmth of his touch. He's got blond hairs on the backs of his fingers, and I'm aware of how tanned and strong his hands are.

'Me too.' I smile, slipping my hand out from under his grasp.

Lisa's serving a customer and someone is waiting, so I'm busy for a moment when we get back down to the shop. I watch Fred out of the corner of my eye. He stands in the corner, looking around.

'So tell me about this fiancée of yours,' I ask when I've finished serving. 'I take it she has a name?'

'Rebecca,' he says.

'Rebecca,' I repeat. 'What's she like?'

Fred blows out his cheeks and looks a bit perplexed. 'She's . . .'

'Come on, you must be able to describe the lucky woman you're going to marry,' I tease.

Fred puts his hands in his pockets and lifts his shoulder to his ears. 'I don't know how you'd describe her. She's in marketing. She's just got back from Oslo. I'm going over to see her now.' He trails off.

'Take some flowers for her. On me.'

'No, it's not necessary . . . really.'

'Come on, take some roses. This lot will mostly have had it by Monday. Someone might as well enjoy them.'

I stoop down and pick up a large bunch of long-stemmed roses out of the black bucket by the till. I handle them carefully on account of their wickedly sharp thorns. Personally, I don't like them. I prefer fresh spring flowers; somehow, red roses are so clichéd. Still, they're expensive and it sounds like this Rebecca has expensive taste, so I'm not going to disappoint her.

'Mickey. You don't have to. Not that many. One or two will do . . .'

'You've got to take a decent bunch,' I say, generously adding a whole lot more. I wrap the roses in cellophane and brown paper, and tie a large raffia string bow round them. 'Where's your sense of romance? There,' I say, handing them over.

Fred takes them reluctantly. 'You're very kind.'

'It's nothing. I hope she likes them.' I clasp my hands behind my back, all too aware of my unladylike finger-nails.

Fred looks hesitant and shuffles his feet. He's almost obscured by the roses.

'We should meet up again,' he says and I nod.

'You know where to find me.'

I walk with Fred to the door and open it. The bell tinkles.

'It's good seeing you, Mickey,' he says.

'You too,' I reply. I feel very strange, as if an old emotion has shifted, or lifted. I can't tell.

Fred stares at me for a moment. We're so close that I almost wonder whether he can see my heart hammering against my T-shirt. He looks as if he half expects me to kiss him on the cheek, or shake his hand. Instead, I smile and stand against the open door. The large bunch of roses crunches between us as he goes past.

I close the door after him and Lisa comes to join me. We both stare through the gap between the stickers on the glass, as Fred walks away.

'Who was that?' she asks.

'That was Fred Roper.' I sigh wistfully. 'My old next-door neighbour.'

'He's very dishy, isn't he?'

'Tell me about it,' I reply. 'Tell me about it.'

Chapter III

Fred

Pink blossom is scattered along the pavement outside Mickey's shop, reminding me of the wallpaper that patterned my parents' hallway in the mid-Seventies. As I start to walk, the petals flutter away from my feet, and I find myself feeling self-conscious in a way I haven't done since my early teens. In true growth-spurt fashion, my body seems alien, and I'm convinced that even the most regular of my movements must appear exaggerated and jerky, like the limbs of a broken puppet.

The cause of all this is, of course, Mickey. I can't help wondering if she's watching me and, if she is, whom she sees. Do traces of the Fred Roper she used to know still remain? Or has whatever bond we once shared been lost to her for ever, severed that same grim teenage day that I moved up to Scotland to live with Mum?

I resist the urge to glance over my shoulder. What would I actually be looking for? Confirmation that Mickey still cares for me? Is that why, in spite of my better judgement, I felt compelled to take her up on her offer to call in on her just now? Was it reassurance I was seeking? Was I measuring myself up against the man I once was, so that I could feel I'd done the right thing by leaving him behind? Is that why, after all these years of actively keeping my past at bay, I decided to dig it up? Or rather, was it that seeing Mickey in ToyZone made me realise how much I'd missed her?

It might have been her clothes, the lack of recognisable labels on her jacket and trainers, contrasting with all those

carefully displayed marketing slogans and flashy pack-
ages in the store, but something about the woman
standing beside me in the ToyZone games department
made me look.

Even in profile, even though she was undeniably older,
I knew immediately that she was Mickey Maloney. Her
pretty, tomboyish face – although slightly rounder, perhaps, than it had once been – was still as familiar as my
own. How could it have been otherwise? I'd watched her
develop from childhood, her cheekbones rising in line
with her small, slightly upturned nose, her jawline
straightening, growing strong and self-assured, and her
short curved lips turning tender and full. Shiny brown
hair was tied up on the top of her head and loose curls
hung down, longer than I remembered, brushing against
the pale, exposed skin of her neck above her jacket collar.
I found myself staring helplessly at her, astounded that
she could be so close and yet be completely unaware of my
presence.

Her jeans were scruffy, the same as they'd always been
when we were children. She looked fit and there was the
same easy confidence as of old about her whole stance, as
if her body were something she'd never bothered about
too much or concerned herself with for too long. She was
– what? – four or five inches shorter than me. It was hard
to be certain with her stretching over, as she was now, to
take a console game from the rack. Five inches would
make sense. That was certainly the way I remembered her,
with my chin resting on the crown of her head as we'd
danced.

I looked back up at her face, suddenly swamped again
by how much it meant to me. It was a thousand snapshots
rolled into one. It was a history of us both. Then she turned
her head towards me and the moment vanished as quickly
as it had arrived.

Denial and, if that failed, flight. These two had always

been my preferred tactics on the (grand total of two) previous occasions when people from my youth had sprung uninvited into my here and now. The first time had been almost a decade before at Manchester University, when I'd convincingly denied my old self to a fellow History undergraduate who'd correctly identified me as the Fred Roper who'd lived up the Avenue from him in Rushton during the early Eighties, the same Fred Roper whose father had . . . The second occasion – and certainly the more dangerous of the two as far as the risk of exposure had been concerned – had involved a dramatic and pragmatic attack of nausea on my behalf at a house party I'd been at with Rebecca some years later, when I'd spotted a man peering at me in drunken astonishment across the living room and recognised him as Jonny Phipps, a boy with whom I'd been at Greenaway College during my early teens and one who, again, would have known all about me and all about Miles.

And now, here I was being presented with a third occasion, and this woman turning towards me wasn't just any old person from my past but, rather, the one person, with the possible exception of my mother, who knew more about who I'd once been than anyone else on the planet.

I should have continued to walk, of course, on past the queuing customers, the tills and the bored-looking cashiers, on through the glass swing doors and beyond, out into the evening sunshine and the crowded car park and its safe anonymity. The last thing I should have done was stopped. But I did. And we spoke.

Even afterwards, out in the car park, the pride I should have felt over finally having done the sensible thing, by quietly slipping away when she'd answered her phone, was absent. Instead, an inverted reaction was taking place and I found myself drilled with a shame I couldn't shake.

For the first time in my life it occurred to me that perhaps what I'd been doing, rather than moving on, had been running away. Surely, I couldn't help thinking, I owed Mickey more than that. Surely, after everything we'd been through together, I owed her an opportunity to explain. And surely I owed it to myself as well to discover why exactly it was that she'd taken it upon herself to break my heart.

Here, a day later, on the street outside Mickey's shop, I round the corner and come to a halt. Well, one thing is for certain: if my purpose in calling round was to satisfy my curiosity, then I've failed. *She never got my letters.* My God. Suddenly I see a parallel world of possibilities out there that's been denied to me. Instead of giving up on us the way I did (assuming that Mickey had already done the same), what if her replies had reached me? What if they'd given me the strength to fight for the life I'd had, rather than letting it be erased? What if I'd guessed – it seems so obvious now – that her parents would have got to my letters first? How different would my life be today? Would Mickey and I have made a go of it together? Would we be making a go of it together still?

Without warning, an overwhelming surge of affection for her races through me, and I smile. With my heart beating loudly in my ears, I'm seized by this crazy desire to spin on my heels and run back to the shop. There's so much more left to discuss – about our parents and everything that happened, about Joe, about so much stuff over so many years.

The world flares brightly as I remove my shades and wipe the back of my arm across my face. A bead of sweat trickles slowly down my brow and runs along the bridge of my nose before splashing on to one of the roses I'm holding. I stand and stare at it, shining there like dew. Then I gaze at the flowers: a gift from Mickey to me, which I, in turn, am about to transform into a gift from myself to Rebecca.

Rebecca.

What am I thinking of? I can't go barging back into Mickey's life on a whim like this, not when I no longer have room for her in mine. And that is how it is, isn't it? My life is already a fulfilling place to be. That's what my New Year's resolutions were all about – ensuring that this would indeed be the case.

OK, so Mickey was once my best friend and, all right, when our lives went their separate ways I did miss her desperately. But now? After all this time? No, too much has changed between us for us to go back to being anything like we were. She has a son, a new business, a new life and, in four weeks' time, I'll be married, settled, content. All I'm doing now is chasing old dreams, searching for closure on a chapter of my life that no longer exists. Mickey doesn't know the first thing about me any more, not even my name. These are old emotions I'm feeling, echoes from my adolescence. They'll fade. I know they will, given time. As with Miles, eventually she will disappear.

I replace my shades and walk on in the direction of my home. I have a life here, with Rebecca, today, I forcibly remind myself, and it's that in which I must immerse myself once more; not in what was, or in what might have been, but in what *is*. Mickey Maloney is someone I must forget all about. I must see her for what she is: another piece of my past that I've buried before and can bury again.

The first thing I do when I get home is open the bin in the kitchen and stuff the roses deep down inside, burying them beneath last night's pizza box and this morning's breakfast slops.

Later that afternoon I drive down past the brickwork Victorian railway workers' cottages on the Queen's Park estate, and promptly get caught in a heavy and slow-moving tailback on the Harrow Road. During the half-hour journey that it takes me to cover the two miles between here and Rebecca's flat, I make one phone call, receive one phone call and lose about five litres of body fluids in sweat to the car seat's leather upholstery.

I've owned my car, an early-Eighties red Renault 5, for six years. Rebecca, who drives a customised, deep-sea-blue Saab convertible, hates my Renault with a vengeance, and has, on more than one occasion, proposed trading it in for a more reliable and sophisticated mode of transport ('Like a donkey,' she suggested – rather unkindly, I thought). Cars are important to Rebecca and that's why she refuses to ride in mine. This isn't something that bothers me. In my otherwise technophile existence, my Renault is the one thing I'm sentimental about. We share history. It's lasted me through eight mobile phone tariffs, four jobs, two girlfriends and one motorway pile-up. So long as it continues to look after me, I shall continue to do the same for it.

The phone call I make is to Susan, who's in the office working on the prospect profiles and current sales dollars stats we're due to present on Thursday to our Virginian finance director, Michael. He's flying over Stateside to the east coast next weekend for his monthly meeting with our American investors and, as always, needs ammunition in the form of optimistic graphware to demonstrate that our income streams are turning into rivers and that – yes, indeed – we will be out of the red by the end of the year (which, hopefully, we will).

The call I make is to check that Susan, a good friend as well as my long-time colleague, isn't going stir crazy in there with only the web-development team and customer support staff for company. This isn't as selfless as it sounds. Like Susan, I'm incapable of logging into the office from home and working via the extranet (too many distractions: television, Sony and Eddie, to name but three), and I'll be sitting exactly where she is now tomorrow, relying on her to break up my Sunday graveyard shift with a similar phone call of her own.

'I'm melting, Dorothy!' she screeches down the phone at me. 'Get me out of here!'

I laugh, picturing the scene of the dastardly Wicked Witch of the West's demise at the end of *The Wizard of Oz*.

'To wish today away,' I reply, 'all you have to do is click the heels of your shoes together three times.'

'I can't.'

'What's the matter?' I tease. 'You can't count that high?'

'Actually, Einstein,' she corrects me, 'it's because, in order to have shoe heels to click with, you need to be wearing shoes . . .'

'And you're not?'

'No.'

'Why not?'

'Because they're in the fridge.'

'The fridge?' I check.

'Uh-huh,' she confirms. 'Cooling down.'

'Cooling *down*?'

'Along with my knickers . . .'

'Your knick—'

'Well,' she asks, aggrieved, 'what do you expect a girl to do? The air-conditioner's broken and my thighs are dripping like a couple of spit roasts. Anyway,' she adds in a slightly more conciliatory tone, 'Germaine Greer says women shouldn't have to wear knickers if they don't want to.'

'Down with knickers,' I agree. 'Good for her.'

I hear the flick and hiss of Susan lighting a cigarette (Silk Cut) and taking a deep drag. Although it's sadly no longer applicable to me, smoking at your desk is the only perk of working weekends. (Weekdays you're restricted to Cancer Corner, a patch of flagstones beneath an artificial palm tree in the main atrium down in reception.)

'Why don't you call the service company and get them to send an engineer in to fix it,' I suggest. 'Their emergency number should be on Jimmy's ROM –'

'Been there, done that,' she interrupts.

'And?'

Her voice drops down a notch. 'They're not answering. Or they are, but I'm not getting anywhere with them. I keep getting stuck in this labyrinthine voicemail system of theirs,' she goes on.

'How about e-mail –'

'Their response times are a joke.' She pauses as she sighs. 'You know what? I probably would have more luck asking the Wizard of Oz for help.'

She sniffs and I picture the drama queen pout she's no doubt deploying right now, her white-blonde hair falling in wavy strands across her angular, elf-like face. I thank my lucky stars I'm not there to see it in person. It would involve, at the very least, a meltdown-stemming ice-cream run to the company café on my behalf; I'm helpless with her that way.

'Forget it,' I tell her, drawing level with a grumbling refrigerator van parked outside a butcher's shop. 'He's a quack. Little guy behind a big screen. Everybody knows that.'

'Thanks for sharing,' she says; then, 'Where are you, by the way? No, no, don't tell me,' she hurries on. 'Let me guess. Sitting on a secluded beach somewhere on the Cornish coast, with a fishing rod wedged into the sand between your feet and an ice-cold bottle of beer in your hand?'

I smile. Susan – a walk-up-a-mountain-and-contemplate-your-life-once-in-a-while kind of a gal – is always throwing updated Arcadian idylls like this at me. It's part of her campaign to get me to overcome what she regards as an almost pathological reluctance on Rebecca's behalf to leave the confines of the city for anywhere geographically closer and less Condé Nast *Traveller* than, say, Tuscany.

I'm about to make the point that, only two weeks ago, Rebecca whisked me off to her parents' place . . . when an articulated lorry blocking the crossroads up ahead sets off a deafening chorus of car horns. During this enforced hiatus in our conversation, I find my response changing. Rebecca doesn't think of Thorn House as a real place, not really, I consider, remembering what she said to me the first time I went with her to meet George and Mary: 'It's like Kew Gardens: very pretty and great for a day out, but let's face it, the shops are crap.'

'Or then again,' Susan cuts back a half-minute later, when the noise of the car horns has diminished to a level where communication without the aid of carrier pigeons is once again possible, 'you could just be doing your usual and flogging that clapped-out, hunk of junk around town, *un*impressing the women and getting burnt off by bath-chair-bound octogenarians at the traffic lights . . .'

'Hey,' I tell her, backing up my indignation with a Cosa Nostra accent, 'show some *goddamned respect*, huh? Another fifty years and this *clapped-out hunk of junk*, as you call it, will be officially classified as a vintage vehicle.'

'In fifty years, Don Corleone,' she snaps back, 'it'll be landfill.'

Smiling and surrendering at the same time, I stick my nose out of the window like a dog and inhale a lung-load of one part oxygen, ten parts toxins. With the thought of the countryside still fresh in my mind, before I know it I've managed inadvertently to free-associate my way from London, to Thorn House, to Rebecca, to Rushton, and suddenly I'm picturing myself walking away from Mickey's shop once more.

Only this time, I turn after no more than four steps and walk quickly back. There, in the window, I think I see her face for a second, pressed up against the glass . . . Then the sun breaks from behind a building across the street and the window-pane blazes fierce white at me, flashing like a camera, so that I can't see anything any more.

Was she watching me? I find myself wondering once more. *Was she*?

'How's everything else going?' I hurriedly ask, cutting the image, and refocusing my attention back on the road ahead and the sound of Susan's voice.

Aside from the hangover she's still sweating off from a product launch we went to on Wednesday night in Soho (when Susan somehow contrived not to go to bed at all), she tells me in jaded tones, she's fine. She asks me whether I remember the conversation we ended up having just before I went home in the booth at Jay's Shakedown around 2 a.m., but I don't. All I remember is being exhausted and a few vodka and tonics worse for wear. Susan says she's glad, making me immediately wonder if I'm missing something. A vague, drunken memory surfaces – something maudlin on my behalf about marriage and settling down and growing up – but then its gone again, dispersing into the ether, like smoke.

It's too late to check any of this with Susan, anyway; she's already switched the subject back to work. She tells me that she's chatted with the event organisers for the launch party we're throwing next Saturday for newsasitbreaks.com's new games channel in a warehouse in Brick Lane. Getting awareness up and running for the site's games channel is what Susan and I have been working on for the last six months. We're hoping it's going to attract a lot of younger clients and visitors to the site and, because of this, it's vital that the party goes off with a bang.

From the look of it, she says, it is. Most of the clients, prospects and service providers we've invited have accepted. The skate ramp we've commissioned is ready to go, as are the giant games screens, where we'll get to watch hotshot pro-gamers and newbie kids from all over the planet battling it out live on new demos. Most important of all, the timings for the simultaneous event have been finalised with New York and Tokyo and – with the GMT evening slot confirmed – we're not going to be the ones doing the antisocial hours.

'In other words,' Susan wraps up, 'it's going to be an awesome event and, touch wood, we shouldn't have anything more harrowing to worry about than choosing what to wear.'

'Imports a go-go, for you, then, my friend,' I surmise. (Susan orders all her weird and wonderful teen labels fresh from Japanese and US web outfits.)

We say our goodbyes and I click off, telling her I'll speak to her tomorrow. Then, at that precise moment – just as I'm reversing into a parking space opposite the imposing grey mansion block which houses Rebecca's flat – my phone rings again and I glance down at the LCD screen and see Rebecca's name winking up at me. 'Hi,' I say, answering. 'Where are you?'

'Up here, daar-leeng,' she replies, her voice coming over all husky and Marlene Dietrich.

Glancing across at her building, I see her standing there, framed by her kitchen window on the fourth floor. In the background, even though it's only a blur of silver and green from this distance, my brain fills in the familiar array of Clifton Nurseries plants and Harvey Nichols pots and pans behind her. Rebecca's wearing what looks like a white dress and has her neck crooked to one side, holding the phone there, as she pulls the sash window open. I'm pleased to see her and I'm relieved that this is indeed the case: maybe all those weird thoughts concerning Mickey were just a result of too many sunny summer vibes.

'How was Oslo?' I ask.

By way of a response, Rebecca leans forward, hands on hips, and shimmies at me provocatively. 'I wanna be loved by you,' she sings down the phone at me, ditching Marlene for Marilyn, continuing to shimmy and running her hands over her hips.

A smile spreads across my lips and now, sincerely, my attention is one hundred per cent Rebecca's. It's not the first time I've witnessed this act, not by a long way, but still, the sense of anticipation it inspires gets me every time. Not taking my eyes from her for a second, I switch off the engine and pull the key free from the ignition. I give myself up, to her and to the moment.

'Just you, and nobody else but you,' she continues sweetly into my ear, her arms now wrapped round her bare shoulders. 'I wanna be loved by you . . .'

Slowly she rotates until her back is to me. Her fingers, appearing like another person's from this angle, wander sensuously up and down the sides of her back. I release my seat belt and shift around in my seat so that I can get a better view.

An exhibitionist fiancée was never something I actively sought in life, but hell, we've all got to make sacrifices from time to time. And if the source of my sacrifice happens to be five feet nine and a perfect eight, then surely it would be churlish of me to complain.

Her hips flick from side to side as she continues to work it. 'Al-ow-oo-own . . .'

Then her hands pull swiftly at the corners of her dress (which I now see for what it is: a huge white bath towel), opening it out into a rectangle that screens everything bar her head and neck. No, I think to myself, turning away would be wrong. I have a responsibility to Rebecca here. If she has a psychological need to tease and taunt me from time to time with these lewd and lascivious displays of naked flesh, then the very least I, as her fiancé, can do is support her. It's a care in the community issue, as simple as that.

'Boop-oop-ee-do!'

She releases the towel and I watch it drop to the floor. Then, before another word can be spoken between us, or her buttocks can wiggle another millimetre, the phone cuts dead and, without so much as a backwards glance or a stitch on, she strides out of sight. I wait a few seconds for her return, but the window remains empty.

Then I'm moving, scrabbling out of the car and locking the door behind me (naturally more out of habit than any real fear of theft). I hurry across the street and let myself in to what I've come to regard as my second home.

There's a stack of mail on the small table in the communal hall downstairs – takeaway menus and bills (one for the gas in both mine and Rebecca's names) – but there's no time for such trivia now. Upstairs is a naked and brazenly wanton woman who's mine for the taking. I bound up the four flights of stairs, pausing only to catch my breath briefly on the fourth-floor landing, before reaching out for the handle of the front door of Rebecca's flat.

I find Rebecca in her African-slated, sandalwood-scented bathroom. Mirrors cover two of the four walls from floor to ceiling, and the whole place is alive with the flickering light of aromatherapy candles and their accompanying dancing shadows. Rebecca is down on all fours on the rug next to the bath. Her skin is golden in this light, and her bottom is pointing in my direction, quivering expectantly. She turns her head to one side and stares at my reflection in the mirror. 'Come here and fuck me,' she tells me. 'Hard.'

Two minutes later and I'm walking dejectedly through to the bedroom. I flop down in the middle of Rebecca's continent-sized continental bed. It's wooden and French and, according to the Chelsea dealer who swapped it with Rebecca for a month's salary, an antique. I avoid Rebecca's eyes as she comes in and lies down beside me. Instead, I stare deliberately at her body. Away from the kind light of her bathroom of sin, her skin is creamy white and flawless. I stare at her nipples, as small and as brown and as hard as hazelnuts, but still my body refuses to respond. Finally, I pluck up the courage to look her in the face. 'I'm sorry,' I mumble. 'I don't know what –'

Rebecca presses her finger to my lips. 'No need,' she whispers.

She stares at me for a second or two, before shuffling a little closer and peering at me sidelong through narrowed, sultry eyes. As she blinks, her painted eyelids blaze momentarily, as perfectly varied and designed as a peacock's feather. 'Are you sure you don't want me to . . .?' she softly asks. 'You never know,' she continues, brushing her hand across my thigh, 'I might be able to' – her eyebrows arch – 'help you rise to the occasion . . .?'

If only, I think. But at the same time I know that she'd be wasting her time. The numbness that filled my loins in the bathroom is as lasting, I'm certain, as any dentist's injection. It's like my genitals no longer exist. 'No,' I say. 'I'd really rather we didn't.'

I gaze up at the minimalist chrome and brushed cotton lampshade hanging from the simple plaster rose at the centre of the bedroom ceiling. Rebecca traces her finger along the arc of my shoulder, but I don't react. If I'm feeling this wretched now, having failed to rise to the occasion once, imagine how much worse it'll be if it happens again.

Slowly, I roll over on to my side and push my nose up close to her neck and breathe in the double nasal whammy of Vidal Sassoon Hair Wash and Clarins Body Lift. It's a combination that's always provided nothing but entice-ment in the past, but today it just smells like soap. I roll away again.

'I'm sure it happens to everyone from time to time,' Rebecca says comfortingly.

She watches me for a reaction to this. This is something she's always doing, as if one of my main duties in our relationship is to provide confirmation of what she thinks she already knows about me. Then, as soon as my face has betrayed whatever it is that she's looking for (in this case, abject gratitude over her understanding nature) and I'm about to speak myself, she quickly carries on. 'Not with me, though,' she adds. 'This is definitely a first for me.'

I groan and, grabbing a couple of pillows, prop myself up in a sitting position at the head of the bed. 'God,' I say, 'I feel so embarrassed.'

'*You* feel embarrassed. How do you think *I* feel?' she asks, visibly put out. 'It's hardly the kind of behaviour you hope for when you set out to seduce the man you're going to marry . . .'

It's at times of spiritual isolation like this that I do wonder about the sheer sexual nature of our relationship. Not that I'm against having sex with Rebecca. She's exceptionally gifted at it and, physically, is exactly the kind of girl I always fantasised about ending up with. But if we were unable to . . . what then? What would we be left with? What would be left of *us*? What would we talk about and what would we do?

'Is it me?' she asks. 'Don't you find me attractive any more?'

'You're incredible,' I react. 'This has got nothing to do with you. It's me.'

I mean this one hundred per cent. Her bits are all in exactly the same places they were when we bade one another a fond and frisky pre-Oslo farewell on Thursday night. Nothing about her has altered, or looks different in any way.

She looks at me expectantly, as if this explanation in itself is not sufficient.

'I don't know,' I begin. 'It's probably stress. Work's been tough and, well, you know, there's the wedding coming up, too – not', I hurriedly add, 'that I've got any doubts or anything, but still, it all adds up, doesn't it?'

Rebecca doesn't reply. She doesn't need to; I already know what she's thinking. She's thinking that she works hard, too, and she's getting married, too, and she's still capable of having sex. 'It'll be all right,' she says.

'It *is* all right,' I reply, suddenly wanting to terminate this conversation. 'It's a blip, that's all.'

'There's nothing else on your mind?' she enquires after an awkward silence. 'Nothing you want to tell me?'

'Like what?' I ask. This comes out as a challenge, but only, I reason immediately afterwards, because her question sounded like one, too.

'I don't know,' she says innocently. 'You tell me.'

I do have an answer for her, but it's not one I'm prepared to voice. I hardly even dare acknowledge it to myself. At the same time, though, it is difficult to avoid. She was there in the bathroom. *Mickey* was there. Not in the flesh, obviously, but here, in my mind. I was looking at Rebecca, but I was thinking about Mickey, and not even thinking about having sex with Mickey, but thinking about how euphoric I felt after seeing her today. And I was thinking, too, of another night, years ago, when Mickey and I had lain side by side on the floor of a deserted building, surrounded by candles and in love. And then I was looking at Rebecca and I realised where I was and the guilt kicked in. Loyalty, I suppose that's the answer I should give to Rebecca now. Emotionally, I've been disloyal to her. Emotionally, I've allowed myself to be mugged by a loyalty to another woman that should have become redundant years ago.

'What if it happens again?' I ask her, considering that I might be wrong about this and that I might actually be suffering from a genuine medical ailment.

'It won't.'

'But what if it does?'

'There's always Viagra,' she suggests, only half joking.

'That might not work, either,' I say. 'And then what? We

won't be able to have sex . . . we won't be able to have children . . . it'll affect everything . . .'

She pouts at me reprovingly. 'Children?' she asks.

'Yes,' I say, 'you know, little people.'

'Since when did children become a part of the plan?' she asks.

'What do you mean?'

Propping herself up on her elbow, she questions me back: 'What do you mean, what do I mean? What do *you* mean?'

'Nothing.'

She cocks her head to one side, unconvinced. 'Nothing?'

'Nothing.'

'You must have meant something,' she says, sensibly enough, 'or you wouldn't have said it, would you?'

'OK,' I concede, 'it's something I thought I might like to do one day, something I thought *we* might like to do . . .'

'When?'

'Well, I hadn't thought about it that hard. After we're married, I suppose . . .'

'No, I mean when did you think about it?'

'Oh, I don't know,' I bluster. 'I can't name a date or anything. I just did. You know, looking at other people.'

'What other people?'

'People with children,' I say vaguely. 'You know, friends of ours with children.'

'We don't have any friends with children,' Rebecca points out. And she's right. It occurs to me for the first time: we don't. Only now, of course, an image of Mickey this afternoon springs out at me and my earlier pledge not to think about her falls by the wayside again.

'Yes,' I equivocate, 'well, maybe we should question that.' I'm confused, confused by all these questions, and confused because the easy answers in my head are the ones about Mickey and Joe and how happy they looked

92

and how happy looking at them made me feel – answers that I can't give to Rebecca.

'Question it?' Rebecca mocks. 'What do you want to do, Fred? Head up to the Queen's Park playground and round some of them up? Stick them in your phone under P for parents? Have them round once a month to discuss nappy rash and school selection procedures?'

'No,' I say, trying to sound as reasonable as possible before this tirade. 'I'm simply saying that it's a normal thing. And . . . and it's an important thing,' I add, gathering impetus, '. . . and –'

Rebecca snorts dismissively. 'The reason', she interrupts, 'we don't have any friends with children, Fred, is because people with children are boring. What?' she says, her eyes shining, obviously having read the indignation in my face and throwing some back in response. 'Just because it sounds callous doesn't mean it isn't true.'

'They're not boring,' I object.

She shakes her head, a look of bemusement on her face. 'I can't believe you're getting broody.'

'I'm not.'

'Well, it sure sounds that way from here . . .' She gives me a patient smile, before rolling languidly over to the side of the bed, and kneeling up as she pulls on a shirt.

'Think about it,' she tells me, flopping back down on to the bed. 'Parents, by definition, are responsible. And being responsible', she goes on, 'means being dull. They don't drink,' she informs me, 'and they don't party. What they do do is sit at home and vegetate. And do you want to know why?' she asks, before filibustering on before I get a chance to intervene. 'Because they've opted out. Because they've poured all their energies into their offspring and they've emptied themselves out in the process. Because they're no longer out there competing with the rest of us. And, fine, one day I might be ready for that. One day, I might need the rest and might decide to hand the baton over. But not now. For fuck's sake, Fred,' she says, giving me this wild grin. 'I'm too young.' She leans over and kisses me on the cheek. 'And so', she adds pointedly, 'are you.'

'That's what I told your father,' I say.

She looks surprised by this information and, somehow, this cheers me up. 'What?' she asks.

'I told him that we were too young to have children.'

Her look of surprise remains. 'He asked you about that?'

'Yes.'

'When?'

'The week before last. That day the vicar came over.'

Rebecca shakes her head, grinning. 'The cheeky old sod,' she says affectionately. 'How did he react?'

'He agreed.'

'Well,' she says, 'there you go, then.'

Again, I find myself objecting. 'Well, nothing. What's our age got to do with anything? Plenty of people younger than us have children. You know, ten years younger than us . . . more, even . . . I bet if you asked them they wouldn't say that they were bored or *opting out*.'

'Probably not, but they wouldn't know any better, would they? If that's what they've been doing with their lives since they left school, then they'd have no idea about what they've been missing out on.' She shrugs, perching her right ankle over her knee and starting to pick at the nail on her big toe. 'Young mums. Yeuch,' she groans. 'Personally, I can't think of anything worse than being trapped looking after some brat when you should be out there having fun. Talk about wasting your life.'

I'm about to reply, but then I stop myself. I close my mouth and I stop listening, too. There's no point in taking this argument any further. It's not like either of us has been drinking. It's not like Rebecca doesn't mean what she's been saying, any more than me. But even though I know she's entitled to her opinion, I can't shake the feeling of disgust she's dredged up inside me. I have this wonderful projection of Mickey and Joe in my mind. They're walking through a park, hand in hand, chattering busily and laughing. And then I have Rebecca's words, tearing the whole scene to shreds.

I look around Rebecca's room and take it all in: the vast imported Balinese wardrobe, the aluminium-finish television, the Virgin Select dressing gown on the peg on the back of the reclaimed wooden door, the Philip Stark lamp on the dressing table and the Lloyd Loom chair, neatly positioned in front of the spot-lit Portobello Road boutique mirror. Then I look at Rebecca herself. She's side on to me now, reaching out for the television remote control, oblivious to the sudden importance of this conversation to me. I run my eyes over her beautiful features before staring at my own reflection in the mirror.

'Oh, Fred?' she says, turning back to me as the television flickers into life.

'What?' I ask, unmoving.

'Is it all right if you move your car?'

'Sorry?'

She gives me a pained look. 'It's just that it makes the street look so terribly shabby,' she explains, 'and I've got an estate agent coming round later to do an evaluation so that we can get this place on the market and start looking for somewhere to move into together after the wedding.' She smiles at me and blows me a kiss before focusing her attention back on the TV. 'Thanks, sweetie,' she adds, finding a quiz show and turning up the volume.

With still a whole stack of last-minute loose ends left to tie up for Saturday's games channel publicity bash, I leave work early on Thursday (around 7 p.m.) and take the tube over to Knightsbridge.

It's Phil's twenty-seventh birthday and he's asked us all

along for a picnic. He was my flatmate for the first couple of years after I moved to London and he's now going out with Katie, Rebecca's best friend from college.

It's a warm evening and there are plenty of other groups of people scattered around Hyde Park, playing football, cuddling in the long grass, or simply sitting under trees reading books and newspapers. But still, Phil's gang of fifteen or so of our friends aren't difficult to spot, their noise and animation easily giving them away. Even from fifty yards off you can tell that they're drunk. Akash is chasing a squealing Michelle around a bench at the edge of the lake, and some of the others are clustered round a sturdy old beech, heaving down on the lower branches, trying to dislodge what I guess must be a frisbee. I see Rebecca and Eddie, sitting on a rug at the hub of all this action. They haven't spotted me and I watch them for a couple of seconds, laughing together, before going over to join them.

'You look shattered,' Rebecca tells me. 'How did the meeting go?' She's wearing a smart grey business skirt and a white silk top. Her shoes and jacket are by her side and her feet are bare.

I think back to this afternoon, to the lengthy sales stats meeting with Susan and Michael. I gaze across at the shimmering gold of the Albert Memorial and my eyelids weigh down. 'Exhausting,' I reply, reaching for a beer.

'Want some?' Eddie asks, his grin set and his eyes unfocused, as he offers me the joint he's been smoking.

I shake my head. 'Better not,' I say. 'It'll just knock me out.'

He passes the joint to Rebecca, who inhales deeply, before lying down on her back and staring up at the sky, continuing to smoke.

Over the next hour or so I do my best to join in. I play frisbee for a while and then drink a few beers with Phil and Chas, who quiz me about what we're doing for my stag night, which is taking place in two weeks' time. Somehow, though, the beer fails to take effect, or raise me up from my low in any way. Instead, it has the same result that gin always has on me, pushing me down deeper into myself.

Getting Mickey out of my head is proving harder than I could ever have imagined. It's as if the burst of latent emotion I felt for her outside her shop planted roots there and has grown ever since, so that now I can feel it stretching, groaning inside me like a tree in the wind.

'Listen,' I tell Rebecca, walking over to where she and Eddie are sitting, giggling on the rug. I crouch down in front of her. 'I think I'm going to head home,' I say.

Rebecca stares at me through uncomprehending, stoned eyes. 'But why?' she asks. 'We're having a nice, chilled time . . .'

'Yeah,' Eddie adds, 'stay.'

'I've got a whole stack of stuff to do before Saturday,' I say.

'What's Saturday?' Eddie asks.

'His big games launch,' Rebecca fills in for me.

'Oh,' Eddie says, cracking open another can of beer.

I look Rebecca up and down. Things have been a little awkward between us since Saturday's bathroom episode. We made love on Tuesday morning before work, but it was a sleepy and forgetful affair, which failed to clear the air between us. 'Are you going to come or not?' I ask her.

'What?' she queries. 'Now, or to the launch?'

'Both.'

I watch her brow knit in concentration as she lights a cigarette. 'Saturday's out,' she eventually says. 'I'm going round to see the dressmaker.' She pauses, as she inhales on her cigarette. 'And now . . . I think I'll hang around here a while,' she decides. She smiles at me apologetically. 'Is that all right, baby?' she enquires. 'Only I'm probably a bit too stoned to be much company for you . . . I'll head back to mine later . . . let you get some rest.'

'Fine,' I say. I don't blame her. It's a beautiful evening and, in any other mood, I'd be staying put, too. 'Are you going to be all right for getting home?' I check.

'Yeah,' she says, 'sure.'

'Don't worry,' Eddie reassures me, giving me a Boy Scout salute. 'I'll make sure she gets in a cab.'

Leaning forward, I kiss Rebecca. 'I'll speak to you tomorrow, then,' I say. 'Give me a call.'

Back home, I sit down at the desk in my bedroom and unlock the second drawer down. Inside is a shoebox full of family photos that I rescued from the bin after I caught my mother throwing them out soon after we moved to Scotland. It's travelled with me from flat to flat ever since, but this is the first time I've ever flipped through its contents. Finally, I find the photograph I'm looking for.

It's in black and white, and captures a moment from the first day that Mickey and I spent in one another's company. In it, we're lying side by side on a tartan-patterned rug in Mickey's parents' back garden. Our fingers are intertwined and we're gazing up at the sky. Mum is sitting on the rug beside us, smiling for the camera. In the background, half obscured by a giant porcupine of pampas, is Mickey's mother, Marie. She's wearing a wide-brimmed hat and an extravagant sarong, and is talking to Miles. You can just about make out Scott, Mickey's elder brother, sitting on the back doorstep. Mickey's father, Geoff, is nowhere to be seen, making me think that it must have been him who operated the camera. A shadow stretches across the garden from the faded, creosoted wooden fence that formed the boundary between our two homes.

The photo was taken on Mickey's first birthday. I was eight months old. Sitting here now, I realise that from that frozen moment on, the clocks of our lives started ticking again, and anything and everything was possible.

*

'I hate him.'

I was lying on the flat asphalt roof of Dave Kirby's garage over on the other side of Rushton from my house and I was talking about Miles. The sound of David Bowie singing 'Ashes to Ashes' drifted up from a radio playing in the garden next door, along with the hot sizzle and smell of barbecued chicken. It was the day before term started at Bowley Comprehensive and a week before I'd join the fifth form of Rathborne Preparatory School for boys.

Two months before, at the end of the summer term, Mickey and I had walked together out of the gates of Rushton Primary School, and across the bridge and up the Avenue to our homes for the last time. Miles was pulling me out of state education and putting me into the private, fee-paying system instead. After two years at Rathborne I would sit my Common Entrance exams and be sent off to a boarding school. Mickey and I would never sit in the same class again.

Dave, long-legged and lanky, the captain of our football team at Rushton Primary and one of my best friends, was stretched out on his stomach next to me, training a pair of battered binoculars across the road. The burnt backs of his knees blinked like bloodshot eyes as he bounced his heels on his navy-blue shorts and the newly grown black hairs on his shins glistened with sweat. It was a hot and humid Sunday, two months before my eleventh birthday.

Dave's gaze was fixed on Sam Johnson's house, the last in Fern Road. The stone walls of its back garden were six feet high and, from our elevated position, you could look down into the back left-hand corner of the garden. Two red beach towels lay there, unoccupied, on the yellowed grass next to a sprawling, blooming rhododendron bush. Miles was at the front of my mind, so much so that he might have been lying there himself, repeating time and time again what he'd told me the day before: 'You're a chatty kid, Fred. You'll adapt.'

'You can't *hate* him,' Pippa said, 'he's your dad.'

I turned on to my side so I could face her. Pippa was dark-haired and gawky, and her spectacles flashed in the sun, making me shield my eyes with my hand. She was wearing tight green shorts and a yellow crop top, and her feet were bare.

Mickey had become firm friends with Pippa over the last six months. They caught the bus into Bowley sometimes to go shopping for clothes in Miss Selfridge and Dorothy Perkins, and to try on make-up in Brown's department store. Being a boy, I was automatically excluded from going with Mickey on these adventures, ending up hanging out with Dave instead down at the video arcades in Houndsfield Street, spending our pocket money on rubbing out each other's names from the Space Invaders' Hall of Fame.

I glanced over at Mickey, who lay next to Pippa in chopped-off jeans and her brother Scott's Blondie T-shirt. Her face, brown as a hazelnut from eight weeks of mucking about out of doors, was turned up to the cloudless sky and her eyes were hidden by a pair of her mum's sunglasses, so big that they made her face look like a fly's. She hadn't stirred a muscle for the last half-hour and didn't do so now.

'So what?' I challenged Pippa.

'So . . .' Pippa's voice trailed off for a moment and I raised my eyebrows at her. 'So . . .' she continued, thinking some more, '. . . so without him you wouldn't even be here.'

The sheer logic of what she'd just said momentarily stumped me, but it didn't prevent me from snapping back, 'Well, maybe I'd prefer it that way.'

Pippa looked at me sidelong, her expression a mixture of suspicion and amusement. She nudged Mickey in the ribs. 'Did you hear that, Mickey?' she asked. 'Fred wishes he was dead.'

'I never said that.'

'You might as well have,' Pippa pointed out.

'I never,' I insisted. 'You're twisting my words. I said I hated Miles. I never said anything about wanting to die.'

Mickey slowly rolled over, dropped her mum's sunglasses down on to the tip of her nose and peered over the top of them at Pippa. 'It won't make any difference,' she said.

'What won't?' Pippa asked.

'Fred having to go the posh kids' school. Just because he goes there doesn't mean he has to turn into a posh kid himself.' Mickey grinned at me. 'Don't worry about it,' she reassured me. 'Nothing's going to change. You wait and see.'

Looking into Mickey's eyes, I almost believed her. She was right about most things she said. Still, the thought of sitting in a strange new class, surrounded by strange new faces, filled me with fear. It didn't have to be this way and it wouldn't be if it weren't for Miles.

I'd been with Miles the day before, walking with him through Chinatown in Soho, London. The day had been hot, the streets crowded, and the exotic smells of roasting meat and simmering sauces had clogged the air. Chicken and duck carcasses had hung in the windows of the restaurants like alien babies, and Miles had been late for something or other and had been in a stinking mood.

The cause of all this had had something to do with his business partner, Carl, who'd gone abroad a couple of months before and had failed to return. 'Nervous breakdown,' I'd overheard Miles telling Mum. 'Probably in a rehab clinic somewhere trying to remember his own name.'

There'd been some trouble following Carl's vanishing act, involving lawyers and the club's ownership, which I hadn't understood, but which had cost Miles a lot of money to get fixed in his favour. It had been this, according to Mum, that had been making him so grumpy.

Once we'd reached Clan, Miles had left me downstairs for eight hours with a cheese sandwich and a bottle of lemonade for company. I'd sat there, bored, cursing him for every minute that had passed.

Looking away from Mickey, I grimaced, wishing I could stay up here on Dave's roof for ever. Home was a real problem by now. An atmosphere of permanent tension had gathered there. It felt as if a thunderstorm were about to break in the living room and send forks of lightning crackling out through the kitchen and bedrooms. It had been that way since Christmas, when Mum and Miles had argued late into the night about a photograph of Miles that had appeared in a magazine.

I'd seen the photo myself, over at Dave's house. It had shown a grinning Miles with another man, both of them with their arms round two women, much younger and, even to my eyes then, even prettier than my mother. The byline beneath the picture had read: 'I'm In With the In Crowd: nightclub owner, Miles Roper, shows the girls a good time with East End boxing promoter Richie Smith'. The photo hadn't conveyed any sense of celebrity on to my shoulders. I'd been embarrassed, because Mum had been embarrassed and because Miles was my father.

In the wake of this scandal, Mum had started to spend her nights in the spare room. This development in their marriage had come as no surprise to me. Miles and she had never been close in my eyes. They'd always inhabited such different worlds. She'd always been stoical and sensible, and had involved herself in the church and the local community. And Miles, well, he'd never set foot in a church in his life, and had a continual look of amusement whenever the friends she'd made in Rushton through her interests and activities had visited.

I couldn't understand how it was that they hadn't already got a divorce. 'Because having us in his life makes him feel a better man and maybe he has a point,' Mum had told Grandma one Christmas when Miles had failed to show up until Boxing Day. 'Because they must still love each other,' Mickey had said, 'in some weird way that we can't understand.' 'And because Mum thinks divorce is sinful,' I'd countered, remembering a conversation I'd heard her having once with Steven Kent's mother, after his father had run off with his secretary.

Whatever their reasons for staying together, though, what remained of their relationship now seemed to operate around the principle of politeness. They talked about practicalities, but never anything to do with their emotions. I was their link. It was impossible to avoid. When I wasn't in the room with them, I wondered if they even talked at all.

'I still hate him,' I said to Pippa, ignoring her rolling eyes and staring her out until she stopped.

'OK,' said Pippa, '*why* do you hate him? He's probably only doing what he thinks best. My mum said she'd send me to a private school if she had the money. She went to a grammar school and that's the same sort of thing, and she reckons they're much better than comps.'

I didn't know what a grammar school was then, just like I didn't then know that Miles had in fact dropped out of one eighteen years before without a single academic qualification to his name. Miles thought Bowley Comp was rubbish and that was all there was to it. I was going to get the best education money could buy – whether I liked it or not. And nothing – not even my mother, who thought Bowley perfectly adequate – was going to mess with his reasoning.

Miles was already talking about revamping the club, so cash wasn't a problem. Nor was politics. From being a rebel in his youth, he'd moved on, working hard and growing rich. Now he aimed to stay that way. He'd even voted Tory for the first time in his life in the general election the year before, handing his entrepreneurial allegiance to the offspring of another grocer, one Margaret Thatcher, in return for a promised drop in taxes.

Aged ten, I knew not and cared less what Miles's reasoning was. Margaret Thatcher reminded me of my grandma when she'd been at the sherry and my only experiences of mismanaged socialism had been the power cuts and the stink of rubbish on the streets during strikes. All I cared about was that Miles had unilaterally decided to split me up from my friends. And all I knew was that I didn't want to go.

'Well?' Pippa asked.

'Well what?'

'*Why* do you hate Miles?'

A bee buzzed by and I waved it away with my hand, using its appearance as an excuse for cutting off my conversation with Pippa as I followed its progress through the air. Turning my head, I stared at the dark-red brick-work on the side of the house next door. The dusty grey cement between the individual bricks was like a maze and my eyes followed its path while my mind followed another equally complicated route.

Why *did* I hate Miles? It was a question that – despite what Pippa might think to the contrary – I had already addressed. The loathsomeness of Miles was, in fact, a subject that had occupied my mind repeatedly over the last few weeks as the end of the summer holiday (and all that had signified to me) had approached.

On the surface there were some simple enough answers. I hated him because he made my mother sad and some-times angry. I hated him because he was hardly ever at home during the daylight hours and he spent most of his weekends in London. And I hated him because, in my mind's eye, he was no different from my teachers: on the rare occasions that his path did cross mine, all he did was ask me questions about my life without telling me any-thing of his. Above all of these reasons, though, I hated

Miles because I loved him and I didn't think he loved me back.

'You could refuse to go,' Mickey said. 'If you do that, then he can't stop you, can he? It's like with my dad and him telling me not to get my ears pierced.' She pinched the very tip of her earlobe between her forefinger and thumb, and waggled it at me demonstrably. A tiny silver star sparkled. 'It didn't stop me. I did it anyway.'

'It's different,' I said, wishing it really were that easy. 'You can take your earrings out when your dad's around.'

'You could always run away,' she said.

We both laughed. Running away was Mickey's ultimate solution to everything and I hadn't yet seen her do it once.

'Or get expelled,' she continued. 'That could be fun and he couldn't send you back if they wouldn't have you.'

'It's no good,' I moaned. 'He'd only send me somewhere else.'

'Shut up, you two,' Dave suddenly hissed. 'They're back.'

Our group reaction to Dave's words was both frantic and immediate. Mickey's sunglasses were off in a flash and the three of us were huddling around Dave, jockeying for position, elbows at the ready to claim the right to have the binoculars next. Like Red Indian scouts, we then froze and stared across the ground between ourselves and Sam Johnson's back garden. Two people in swimming costumes were now visible in the corner by the towels, and Dave hadn't been lying when he'd rung us an hour before: one of them, wearing a black and white polka-dot bikini, was without doubt Miss McKilroy, the plump, blonde-haired teacher who'd joined the staff at Rushton Primary the previous September.

'What's going on?' Pippa asked. I glanced quickly at her. She was rubbing furiously at her glasses before putting them back on and squinting across the divide in frustration. 'Is it her?'

'Yes,' Mickey, Dave and I said simultaneously.

I looked back across the road. Sam Johnson and Miss McKilroy were now sitting down on the towels.

'*And* Sam Johnson?' Pippa enquired, starting to snigger.

'Yes,' we all replied.

Sam Johnson worked as a building contractor in and around Bowley, and did the Sunday evening hospital radio slot at the Whispering Glades old people's home. He was as old as my parents and was in charge of the Rushton Players, the local amateur dramatics group that put on plays twice yearly at the Memorial Hall. I'd seen him in *The Importance of Being Earnest* the month before, which my mum, as part of the Church Sewing Circle, had helped to make the costumes for. At the end of the play he'd kissed Miss McKilroy on stage and every boy and girl from Rushton Primary in the audience had gasped and looked at each other with wide eyes and open mouths. Mickey's elder brother, Scott, who up until this point had been sitting next to me in the dark, trying (and failing) to grope his new girlfriend, Alison Rawiing, had grumbled loudly in Alison's ear, 'At least someone around here's getting some action.'

'Give us a go,' I said to Dave, tugging at the binocular strap.

'In a minute.'

'What's going on?' Pippa asked again.

'They're just lying there,' Mickey said.

'Very close,' I added.

'Very, very close,' Dave confirmed.

I watched as Sam Johnson stood up and disappeared from view for a few seconds, before returning and proceeding to sit astride the prostrate Miss McKilroy. By now, the atmosphere on the top of Dave's garage was electric. Mickey giggled nervously.

'Suntan lotion,' Dave relayed. 'He's rubbing it all over her back.'

'Minute's up,' I said, tapping Dave on the shoulder.

Reluctantly, he surrendered the binoculars.

'Me next,' Mickey chimed, squeezing up close to me.

I raised the binoculars to my eyes and slowly panned across the top of the brick wall and down, until the lenses were filled with flesh. I adjusted the dial that controlled the focus until I could see both Sam Johnson and Miss McKilroy clearly, right down to her puffy cheeks and sharp nose. She rolled over so that she was lying on her back and . . . and . . . and I could hardly believe my eyes: her bikini top was no longer there. 'I can see her tits!' I squeaked.

'What?' Dave gasped.

'I can!' I gasped back, focusing in on them. 'I can see Miss McKilroy's tits!'

'Give me the binoculars,' Dave said.

'No,' Mickey interrupted, 'it's me next.'

I didn't care whose turn it was next. All I cared about in the world right then was the sight before me: Miss McKilroy's blotchy, blubbery boobs. Their nipples were like great blobs of chewed-up strawberry bubble gum and each separate, sweaty tit must have weighed in at over a ton. 'They're horrible!' I gasped in delight.

'My turn,' Mickey said and, before I could do anything to stop her, she'd snatched the binoculars away from me and was staring through them herself.

I raised my hand to my eyes to shield them from the sun. Without the aid of the binoculars, though, it was no good: Miss McKilroy's body had reverted to being nothing more than a pink blur.

'The dirty old sod,' Mickey said a couple of seconds later. 'He's rubbing sun cream into them.'

'Into what?' Dave demanded.

'Her tits, of course.'

'Let me see,' Pippa begged, tugging at the binoculars.

'No, they're mine,' Dave snapped.

Mickey held firm, shaking them both off. 'They're

snogging,' she told us. 'He's lying on top of her and they're snogging.'

'Please, Mickey,' Pippa implored.

Mickey carried on looking for a couple more seconds, then handed the binoculars to Pippa.

Dave scowled. 'I wish we had a camera,' he said. 'You know, one of those big ones that can zoom in. We could stick photos up at the bus stop.' He shook his head. 'Imagine what everyone's parents would say.'

Pippa shrieked, 'Yeuch! Tongues!'

The moment we heard Pippa's voice, we knew she'd blown it. With or without binoculars, the flurry of motion in Sam Johnson's garden meant only one thing: we'd been rumbled. Within seconds, Sam Johnson was on his feet, looking around, while below him, Miss McKilroy scrambled around frantically for her bikini top.

'Leg it!' Dave said and was gone, swinging over the side of the garage roof and down the drainpipe in one easy, fluid motion.

Pippa, frozen to the spot, stared on in dismay as Mickey and I followed suit. We slithered down after Dave, collapsing in a heap of limbs at the bottom, breathless with exertion and exhilaration.

'Pippa Carrier!' a voice – unmistakably that of Miss McKilroy – called out. 'Pippa Carrier! You stay exactly where you are.'

Mickey, Dave and I exchanged looks. 'What are we going to do?' Mickey asked. 'She's going to have our guts for garters.'

Mickey was right. Within weeks of her arrival at Rushton Primary, Miss McKilroy had established herself a reputation for strictness and discipline which none of us had witnessed before. Everyone had dreaded the days when she was on playground duty, as they would invariably result in extra homework or detention for one of us. Even though we'd now all left her school, we didn't believe for an instant that her influence over us and, more particularly, over our parents, had vanished.

'You two go,' Dave said. 'I'll stay here with Pippa.'

'We'll all stay,' Mickey said.

'No.' Dave was adamant. 'There's no point. She'll get me because it's my house and she'll get Pippa because she's seen her.'

'What do you think she'll do?' I asked.

Dave shrugged uncertainly. 'So long as we hide the binoculars, there's not a lot she can do, is there?'

'Suppose not,' I said.

Mickey smirked. 'She's hardly going to tell anyone else anyway, is she? Not after what we saw Sam Johnson doing to her . . .'

The sound of the doorbell buzzing reached us from inside Dave's house.

Mickey grimaced. 'Then again . . .'

'Go on,' Dave told us, glancing up at Pippa who was now standing at the top of the drainpipe with the binoculars hanging limply round her neck. 'Scram.'

Mickey and I had learnt a long time ago that the telephone lines linking our parents' homes were more than capable of outrunning any Rushton child. It was because of this that, about half an hour after we'd vaulted Dave Kirby's garden fence and sneaked away from the scene of the crime, we found ourselves sitting on the chipped marble step of Alexander Woolfstone's tomb at the back of the cemetery on the other side of the River Elo. Mickey had hardly spoken since we'd crossed the bridge and was now staring moodily at the numbers 1765 engraved in the door of the tomb behind us as she traced them with a finger. I turned back to the tiny ant hole in the loose, dry earth by my feet and waggled the twig that I'd stuck down it, watching the ants rise up angrily.

'Do you think Miss McKilroy's told our mums?' I asked.

Mickey didn't look round. 'Dunno.'

'What do you think they'll do if she has?'

'Dunno.'

I broke the twig off in the hole and kicked earth over it, sealing it off. The ants circled round the new terrain in confusion, before stopping as if scenting the air like dogs for a clue as to what to do next.

'My mum knows Miss McKilroy from doing the costumes for the play.' I turned round to see that Mickey was now facing me. Her hair lay flat against her brow. 'Your mum doesn't know her, does she?'

'Only from school. She told Mum that I talked too much.'

'She says that about everyone,' I started. 'She told –'

'You've never kissed anyone, have you, Fred?' Mickey interrupted.

'Well,' I said, after a moment's thought, 'my mum and my grandma kiss me all the time, and –'

'They don't count.'

'Why not?'

'They just don't.'

'In that case,' I said, 'no, I haven't.' I looked down at my shoes. The ants had started clearing out the hole. 'What about you?' I asked.

'I kissed Simon Cory once. In the playground,' she added. 'For a bet.' I was about to ask her what it was like when she added, 'But it wasn't a proper kiss.'

I swivelled round on the marble to face her. 'What do you mean?'

'With tongues.'

I remembered what Pippa had said up on Dave's roof and repeated it now: 'Yeuch.'

Mickey bowed her head so that her fringe hid her eyes. 'I wouldn't listen to Pippa,' she mumbled. 'She's never kissed anyone either.' She flicked her hair back. 'It might not be yeuchy at all.'

I studied Mickey's lips. They were dry from the sun, but

110

I liked their curvy shape. I wondered if she might be right and Pippa wrong. I'd watched Mickey's lips smile a thousand times and I'd watched her blow spit bubbles on the end of her tongue, but I'd never once thought of either parts of her body in kissing terms. I wondered what it would feel like. My eyes met Mickey's for a second and I felt myself blush.

'It looks pukey on the television,' I said quickly. 'Especially when it goes on and on, and they play soppy music.'

Mickey's eyes flashed suddenly and she snorted at me, 'Fine, then. Don't.'

'Don't what?' I asked.

'Don't kiss me.' She scrambled to her feet and looked across the valley.

I jumped up, so that my eyes drew level with hers. She sucked her lower lip angrily into her mouth.

'You want me to kiss you?' I asked, amazed.

She looked me up and down uncertainly, then her expression hardened. 'Forget it,' she told me, spinning on her heels and stomping off down the path. 'I've changed my mind.'

I stayed where I was, watching her go, completely at a loss for what to do next. I felt the warm air closing in around me and a drop of sweat running down the side of my face. Then I started to run.

I caught up with her just before she reached the church-yard gate and skipped around her so that I stood between her and it. 'Wait,' I said breathlessly.

She glared at me, her face the colour of a sunset, and reached out to push me aside. It was then that I did it. I put my hands on her shoulders, stepped forward and pressed my lips up against hers.

We stared into each other's eyes, the tips of our noses squashed together. Warm breath funnelled from her nostrils on to my cheeks, tickling me, and I blinked,

111

wanting to laugh. But Mickey looked so serious that I didn't dare. So instead, I waited, and then I watched as she closed her eyes. This is it, then, I thought. She's really going to do it. She's actually going to kiss me with her –

And then, without warning, she did. With the speed of a striking snake, her tongue darted out from her own mouth and pushed inside mine. Slimy as a slug and wriggly as a worm, it brushed over my own tongue. I froze. I couldn't move and I couldn't breathe. This was the most extraordinary thing I'd ever known. But now that our tongues were touching, what next?

I stared at her eyelids and prayed for a sign.

Then came a shriek and we pulled apart, simultaneously looking up into the sky as a starling broke from the cover of the bushes. When I looked down again, past Mickey's shining eyes, I was amazed to see that the ground still lay beneath my feet.

'That was . . .' I began. But I didn't know what it was, only that it was new.

'Don't tell anyone,' Mickey said.

'Why not?'

'Just because,' she said, smiling. She stepped away from me and walked to the churchyard gate. When she got there she turned back to me. 'We should go home,' she said. 'It's getting late.'

I nodded my head and followed her out of the gate, across the Elo and up the Avenue. We didn't speak the whole way, both of us lost in our own thoughts. I don't know what Mickey was thinking, but my memory of the walk is still as clear as it was when I said goodbye to her outside my house. I didn't care about whether Miss McKilroy had been round to see my mum. Nor did I did care that tomorrow Mickey would be going to her new school without me at her side. I didn't even care about Miles. In my mind right then, there was only Mickey.

I put the photo back in the shoebox and return it to the drawer. Then I take Mickey's business card from my wallet and key her number into my phone. Without giving myself time to hesitate, I press OK. Then I count the rings: one, two, three, four, five, six –

'Hello,' she answers.

I take a deep breath. 'Hi, Mickey,' I say, 'it's me, Fred. Sorry to be calling you so late, only there's something I want to ask you.'

Chapter IV

Mickey

Joe's grinning from ear to ear, as he turns away from the giant screen. Thousands of miles away, the pixilated and slightly time-lapsed face of his opponent, a Japanese boy who looks about thirteen, breaks into a begrudging smile. His gazes shift nervously around the bottom of the screen like a novice TV reporter, before he goes fuzzy and disappears. After the digital surround sound of the intergalactic game, my ears are ringing and, as the lights come on, I can't help swallowing a yawn.

Fred, who's been running around for the last hour, appears by my side. He applauds along with the crowd of blinking kids and adults who've all been staring up at the screens, as Joe and his Japanese opponent battled it out. He leans in close to me as Joe scrambles off his stool and accepts his prize: a trendy rubber courier bag presented by Nina, the promotions-girl-come-chaperone. She looks a bit out of her depth, with the kind of toothy radar smile and incessantly posing limbs that would make her a natural at holding a number board in a bikini contest rather than looking after an unruly mob of adrenalised kids.

'I can't believe Joe did it,' says Fred, clapping proudly as Joe wrestles the bag away from Nina, who's busy posing for photos. 'I couldn't have done that.'

'All those hours in front of the computer have paid off at last,' I reply, waving to Joe, who pushes towards us through the crowd of kids, all swarming the other way towards the bank of computer consoles. Behind him, an American advert for another game explodes on to the giant screen and a clubby soundtrack booms out around us.

'Long ago, in another world . . .' begins the dramatic voice-over.

'Blimey. It doesn't stop, does it?'

'Non-stop adventure. That's the idea,' replies Fred, who is clearly chuffed with the progress of the launch, although I have to say that, so far, most of it has gone over my head . . . and straight to Joe's, by the looks of things.

'So, what did you think?' shouts Fred over the din, but one look at Joe's face and it's not difficult to tell that being one of the heroes of an international game launch is possibly the most exciting thing that has ever happened to him.

'Lush,' he replies.

Fred and I smile at each other as Joe drops to his knees in front of us and, in a frenzy of excitement, unzips his bag. Inside are a black designer T-shirt with the name of Fred's computer company in discreet yellow lettering, two of the latest games and some cinema tickets.

Joe looks up at me, his mouth open with the sheer brilliance of all his exclusive freebies.

Nina catches up with Joe and flicks her sleek brown hair over her shoulder. 'How about a lesson on the ramp?' she suggests in her high-pitched sales squeak. She has absurdly long pink nails with very white tips that scrape down the list on her clipboard.

'There's a slot with Zack,' she says. 'Or you could blade with Quark, if you like?' She gestures to the skateboarding ramp which dominates the floor, before glancing nervously at Fred.

'You're doing a great job, Nina, thanks,' he says, not missing his obvious cue.

Nina melts at his compliment. She giggles deferentially and snorts unattractively down her nose. 'Thanks.' She nods, as another of the kids, a boy of Joe's age, slips through the crowd and joins us.

'Are these your parents?' he asks Joe.

Joe nods and points up at me. 'That's my mum,' he says, standing, and then cocks his head. 'And Fred. Our . . . friend.' Joe grins up at us both. 'Tyler,' he says, by way of explanation. 'He lives up the road from us.'

'Hi,' I say, astonished at Joe. Usually he's so shy.

I catch Fred smiling. I can tell that he's pleased at being described as 'our friend'.

Tyler mumbles a greeting and turns his full attention back to Joe. 'That was epic, man, you on the game. Are you going to blade with Quark?' he asks. 'I've seen him on this video . . .'

Joe and Tyler stomp off down the shiny metal ramp together to where the skateboard and rollerblading demonstrations are being held.

Nina's super-thin eyebrows knit together. She places her hand flat on her clipboard and looks at us sincerely. 'Don't worry, I'll find you,' she says, before turning away and hurrying after the boys.

'Looks like we're off the hook,' says Fred, rubbing his ear bashfully.

Joe's goodie bag remains exploded at my feet and I crouch down to pick up all the contents.

Fred holds my elbow as I stand up. 'Come on, let's go and get a drink.' He smiles, leading the way down the other walkway to the juice bar.

I dawdle behind him, fiddling with the zip on Joe's bag, my attention caught by the skateboarders who flip up over the rim of the giant ramp and perform gravity-defying spins and turns, their twisting bodies caught in the sweeping searchlights.

Although we're in a warehouse in East London, you'd never know. The party planners have transformed the large open space into an urban jungle, with walkways between different areas, so that it's impossible to tell the shape of the place, or how big it is. I've never been to somewhere so trendy and state-of-the-art and, so far, it's been quite a struggle to stop myself from gushing to Fred, like an awe-struck kid.

Below us, down an industrial metal ladder, the party is in full swing in the juice bar. A light show illuminates giant screens above the bar, the light moving in time to the ambient music, accompanied by the bubble of conversation and clink of glasses from the crowd below.

'Mum?'

I look up and see Joe hanging over a scaffolding bar above me. He's fastening a silver crash helmet under his chin.

'This is fantastic,' he yells, and I grin up at him and wave. I can tell by his smile that he's forgiven me at last.

When Fred called a few days ago to invite us tonight, I was half asleep and in such shock that he'd rung that I agreed without thinking. Yet the second I put the phone down an all-consuming forty-eight-hour bout of worrying engulfed me, culminating in a full-scale panic before we left.

'Why don't you ring up and ask what to wear?' suggested Lisa, as I huffed and puffed around the shop.

'I can't,' I whined. 'Besides, I'd look . . .'

'Look what?'

'Oh, nothing,' I bleated, totally demoralised.

Upstairs, Joe was equally unhelpful, as I riffled through every possible combination of outfits.

'Chill, Mum,' he advised. 'I don't see why you don't wear what you normally wear.'

'What I normally wear?' I snapped, throwing my hands up and growling with frustration. 'It's a launch party. I'm not going to wear jeans and trainers, am I, stupid? It's Fred's business do.'

'He's not going to care what you wear,' Joe countered, with his usual nine-year-old wisdom, even though he was clearly offended that I'd called him stupid.

117

'Oh . . . just . . . go and wash your face,' I snarled unfairly. 'And clean your teeth.'

Joe pulled a snotty face and stalked out of my bedroom, slamming the door behind him. I jolted, guilt overwhelming me.

Once alone, I scrutinised my face in the wardrobe mirror, feeling unbearably frumpy and neglected. The last time I went to a business function it was Martin's mobile phone company's and I hated every minute of it. At Martin's request, and against my better judgement, I wore an evening dress and spent most of the time with a napkin over my cleavage to protect it from the scrutiny of Martin's leery colleagues. I doubted Fred's company would be anything like it, judging from Fred, but I still felt nervous about being on show.

But it was Rebecca who was making my stomach turn with panic. Part of me wanted to ring Fred up and cancel seeing him, but I couldn't let Joe down, so instead, I started rehearsing. Holding my hair up at the back of my head, I gave the mirror my most confident look. 'Hi, Rebecca,' I mimed, smiling as widely as possible. 'I'm Mickey.' Sticking out my tongue at myself, I tried again. 'Hi, I'm Mickey Maloney. Fred and me . . .'

I let my hair and my face drop, before slumping on the bed, my confidence deserting me as a barrage of questions racked up in my head. Was Rebecca going to be at the launch? Would she know about Fred and me? What would Fred have said to her after our last meeting? How would Fred have described me? Were we all going to be friends and hang out together? Why, after all, had Fred invited us? What did he want?

Now, I glance at Fred and I'm still hopelessly in the dark. Rather than having any answers, I've just got a load more questions.

'What?' he says, smiling as he stops on the ladder and looks up at me. His face is caught in the swoop of light and his eyes seem to sparkle. He's wearing a charcoal-grey T-shirt that complements his lightly tanned face and, for a second, my heart is in my throat.

'Nothing,' I reply, but part of me wants to stop and say, *Exactly, Fred. What? What's all this about? Where's Rebecca? What's going on? And . . . and when did you get to be so bloody good-looking*?

'Give me that,' he says, smiling at me as he reaches out for Joe's goodie bag and I hand it over, glad that he can't read my mind.

Of course, Joe was right all along. I shouldn't have dressed up. I feel ridiculous in my pinstriped trouser suit, which is the trendiest item I could find in my wardrobe, but is still hopelessly out of fashion. All the girls here are in funky urban gear, all of which looks scruffy in an expensive, designer kind of way and, apart from the odd slick of lip-gloss, seem entirely au naturel.

By comparison, I feel like I've had a head-on collision with the supermarket cosmetics display stand, the badly co-ordinated contents of which I'm currently lugging round in my huge mummy bag, along with a whole load of other personal clobber. It serves me right for being so vain. I thought that having the usual essentials like a hairbrush and a sweatshirt for Joe, not to mention my bulging appointments book stuffed with junk mail and held together with elastic bands, would make me feel prepared and grown-up. Instead, I just feel old.

'Listen, Mickey, there's one thing,' whispers Fred, as we're about to make our way through the crowd to the bar. He sounds serious.

'Yes?'

'I use Wilson now, as my surname.'

'*Wilson*?'

Fred looks shiftily around him to make sure no one has heard. 'Mum decided after . . . you know. We took her maiden name.' Fred smiles at me for encouragement, but I can only stare at him in shock. 'Mickey, it's no big deal. It's just probably better if you don't mention me as Roper, if anyone asks. Because I'm not. Not any more . . .'

'OK,' I mumble, scanning Fred's face, but he just nods as if he's made some sort of insignificant little pact with me and, before I have a chance to say anything, he heads into the crowd.

People keep coming up to him to say hello and I get the impression that he must be good at his job, as they all seem respectful and heap praise on him about his company, but Fred just politely bats them out of the way and ushers me towards the bar. He seems so confident and in control, this Fred Wilson. It's like seeing a new person. Yet a part of me wants to hold up my hand, draw the attention of the crowd and say, 'Sorry, folks, just a small mistake. This is Fred *Roper*.'

It shouldn't make a difference, but it does. Fred Wilson isn't a part of me and I'm not a part of Fred Wilson and, childishly, I feel that in denying his past, Fred has denied me something, too. Because I was a part of Fred Roper. The shared experience that linked us may have stretched over the years like a cobweb, but it was still there. Now I realise that in spite of every promise we made, Fred made a clean break and, for all those years when we were apart, he was happy being a different person all along.

But then again, why shouldn't he have changed his name? What happened to him was so awful that I can hardly blame him for putting it behind him. People reinvent themselves all the time for much smaller reasons and, if I'd been in Fred's shoes, I'd have probably done the same. To be honest, it would have been nice to have had that luxury. At least Fred didn't see what happened, like I did. He wasn't there. He didn't smell that dreadful smell that haunted me for years.

'I'll just pop to the loo,' I whisper as Fred is greeted by yet another colleague.

'I'll be right here, OK?' he says and I nod, feeling absurdly flattered. I'm so used to looking after Joe and the shop that I'd forgotten how nice it feels for someone else to take care of me.

After carefully scrutinising the weird symbols on one of the doors, I decide that it must be the Ladies and push against the heavy door. For a moment I look back in dismay, wondering where I've gone wrong, as a wall of stainless steel panels faces me. Hopelessly, I prod at them, but nothing happens. Even the loos are too sophisticated for me.

A girl with blonde hair appears behind me and comes to the rescue. She pushes hard on one of the panels and it swings back to reveal a stainless-steel toilet cubicle, complete with space-age-looking toilet. 'Bloody obvious, right.' She smiles, sympathising with me.

'Thanks.'

She's waiting when I come out, washing her hands in the water fountain round the corner. 'You're with Fred, aren't you?' she asks.

'Yes.' I smile back, taking a thick white hand towel from a pile by the sink.

'I'm Susan,' she says, pushing her fringe behind her ear and leaning one hip against the sink, as she looks at me. She takes a packet of cigarettes from the pocket of her funky trousers and lights one. 'Fred's my boss,' she explains. 'Although, to be honest, I'm the bossy one.'

'I'm Mickey.'

There's a pause, as she smokes contemplatively, looking at me. 'I like the retro look,' she says, nodding at my suit.

I stare at her for a moment, wondering whether she's being rude.

She catches my look. 'No, honestly,' she says. 'You look great.'

I scan her wide, honest face once more and decide that she's being serious. 'You mean I've finally got to that stage where I'm so unfashionable, I'm actually fashionable?'

'Honey, it *woiks*,' says Susan in a phoney American accent and we both laugh.

'I feel like a walking Accessorize store,' I confide, pulling a face at my huge handbag.

Susan reaches out for it. 'I'll put it with Fred's stuff.'

Gratefully, I hand it over and follow her to the door, although how she knows where it is, is a mystery.

'Have you known Fred long?' she asks.

I nod. 'For ever, but I haven't seen him for a while.'

'Well, it's nice that you're here. It means he can enjoy himself and stop being such a boring workaholic, like he is at these dos.'

'Oh?' I say curiously, unable to stop myself. 'Doesn't Rebecca usually come?'

'Rebecca?' says Susan, as if I'm joking, then she clocks my look. 'I take it you haven't met Rebecca?'

'No.'

'Well, let's just say this isn't her scene.' Susan pulls a face as she holds open the door. 'Not Gucci enough, darling,' she adds in a confidential whisper, 'if you know what I mean.'

I find Fred chatting by the bar. He smiles at me and hands me a drink, but he's mid conversation with two men. They're talking what I assume is e-business speak, but could well be Martian. Astounded, I make wide eyes at Fred over the rim of my glass.

'Sorry,' says Fred, interrupting. He gives me a re-assuring look. 'Let me translate. This is Peter and Tim. They *are* home shopping. All you could want from lipstick to lampshades. This is Mickey.'

'So are you another one of Fred's mob?' Peter asks, in a florid cockney accent. He's short, bald and he taps his thick platinum ring on his glass with frenetic energy.

'No, no,' I stutter, feeling like an impostor. 'I'm . . . I'm a florist.'

'A florist,' says Peter. He nods his head for a moment.

'You could be just the person we're looking for. Don't you reckon, Tim?'

Tim, who's clearly Peter's assistant, nods eagerly.

'Oh, no, really . . . I've only got a little shop. It's nothing –' I start.

'It's great,' interrupts Fred, discreetly sliding his foot towards mine and pressing against it. 'It's in Kensal Rise near your offices.'

'Yeah, we're down on the canal.' Peter sniffs and looks at me. 'I don't suppose you could come in and cheer the place up, could you? I don't go in for all that floral basket shit. But our New York office has these wicked flowers all over the place. All modern . . .'

I look between Peter and Fred and back at Peter. 'Well . . . I *could* have a look . . .' I say, taking my cue from Fred, who nods encouragingly.

'You'd be brilliant,' he says, before turning to Peter. 'Believe me, she's excellent.'

'Fix it, Tim.' Peter nods, turning away. 'Later, Fred. Mickey . . .'

'Can I have your number?' asks Tim, pulling out an electronic pocket organiser.

I smile at Fred, as I tell Tim my details.

'I'll call you on Monday to arrange an appointment.' Tim says decisively as he snaps his organiser shut.

Fred clinks glasses with me after he's gone. 'See, that wasn't so hard. You never know. Peter's company's huge. If you get in there, you'll be laughing.'

'Hm, well, we'll see.' I smile, not wanting to be optimistic. I can't believe Fred has done me such a favour and made it seem so effortless. I feel like a complete amateur by comparison. I've spent the last few months tied up in knots over the copy for an advert I put in the local paper and here's Fred casually doing mega deals over a few drinks. Compared with my little flower business, this all seems like a different world.

'Don't you have to . . . you know . . . mingle?' I ask, as Fred draws me over to the bar and huddles up next to me.

'I should, but I'm not going to.' He grins as he pushes another cocktail towards me.

'I warn you,' I say, taking a sip of the heady fruit concoction. 'I'm not used to drinking. These taste lethal.'

'I think we should go and check out the virtual reality game in the jungle section. What do you say?' He smiles.

'Ah, I see,' I tease. 'Trying to get me pissed, so that you can beat me. That old chestnut. Well, you can't get round me that easily.'

I reach out to try and jab Fred in the ribs, as the alcohol hits my brain, but he's too quick and ducks out of the way.

'Come on.' He grins. 'Let's see how those old reflexes of yours are.'

'Huh!' I snort. 'Still razor. Just you wait.'

But as I follow Fred, I don't feel razor sharp, I feel fuzzy and happy in a floppy sort of way. I'm glad Rebecca isn't here. It's wonderful having the most popular and important man in the room all to myself, even though I know it won't last. And as we scurry past all the attractive, fashionable girls, I want to stop, point at Fred and say in a very loud voice. 'See him? He was mine, once. *I had him.*'

The next day I'm felled by the worst hangover I've experienced in years. I'm not really with it as I try and throw together a Sunday lunch and my mood isn't improved when Joe comes through from his bedroom with the telephone.

'It's Grandma,' he says, passing me the phone. I wipe my hands on a tea towel and take it. There's no greeting from my mother.

'I can't get over it. After all this time and I thought you'd got that out of your system ages ago. Fred Roper!' she says, sounding genuinely shocked. 'Joe's been telling me all about him.'

'Hello, Mum,' I say, ignoring her outrage, feeling an unusual double whammy of old and new heckles rising.

'It's taken me right back. When I think of his father! Oh!' She takes a sharp intake of breath and I picture her on the stairs in her house in Rushton, dramatically putting her hand to her chest.

Immediately I feel my defences spring up like spikes in a fortress. 'What exactly is the problem?' I ask through gritted teeth, wishing I had the nerve to say 'your problem' instead.

'Well, you know, I've always said –'

'Mum!' I interrupt, my patience snapping. 'Can you just drop it. That was a long time ago. Fred's got a completely new life now. He's responsible and kind and, for your information, it's wonderful seeing him again. He isn't anything like Miles . . .' I stop myself, angry that I'm doing the thing I always do and justifying myself to her. I know it never works.

'But what about Joe? Think of him –'

'Mum!' I take a deep breath. 'Please. This has got nothing to do with you.'

'I'm just concerned for my grandson, darling. Someone's got to look out for him,' she says in a peeved voice and I have to stop myself from growling. Ever since Joe was born, she's always managed to imply that I'm a terrible mother. I have to prevent myself from rising. I'm not even going to *start* on her faults. I'm incredibly tempted to let rip and challenge her about the letters and for ruining Fred and me all those years ago. But there's no point. She thinks she's in the right. She always thought she was in the right. There's no sense in explaining to her all the damage she's done, because she'd simply deny it.

'Did you ring for any particular reason?' I ask pointedly.

'We're going to your father's cousin's wake the weekend after next weekend,' she says. 'I was wondering whether you could come over and feed Oscar while we're away.'

Oscar is my parents' ancient cat.

'Only everyone around here seems to be *on holiday* at the moment,' she continues and I can tell this is for my father's benefit who must be nearby.

'Sure,' I say and ring off as soon as possible.

As the week progresses, I don't stop feeling out of sorts and on edge. But it's not the business that's worrying me, or Joe, or any of the things that usually preoccupy my mind. No, my problem is that, despite my mother's best efforts to put me off, I've got Fred head. Or, more specifically, Fred in the head.

He keeps popping into my thoughts and I find myself having imaginary conversations with him. As the days go by and I don't hear from him, I crave communication. On Thursday, I'm up at dawn buying from the market and, by the time I'm back at the shop refreshing all the stock, Lisa has had enough.

As usual, we're in the back of the shop, behind the till. There's not much room, only just enough for a wide table and an old porcelain sink. I've fixed up a couple of shelves, which are haphazardly stacked with ribbons, the credit card machine, a kettle and jar of coffee and, the most essential item of the lot, the radio, which plays a morning pop show. Between Lisa and me, the table is stacked with heaps of foliage, including all types of variegated ferns and fern. On top is a bundle of flowers, their stems all pointing towards us and we work through them, one by one, snipping the bottoms of their stems and rinsing them, before arranging them in the black buckets.

To an untrained eye it looks completely chaotic, but one of the most satisfying things about my job is that by nine o'clock, when I open the doors, the flowers will look their best and the shop serene and ordered. Well, that's the plan, anyway.

'Mickey?' Lisa clicks her fingers in front of my face.

'Huh?'

'Come back.'

I shake my head and smile at her.

'You haven't heard a word I've said, have you?'

I shift uncomfortably. 'Wasn't it something about the oasis order?'

'Yes. About *five minutes* ago.' She looks exasperated.

'Sorry.'

Lisa puts down her secateurs. 'I know you're thinking about him.'

'Who?' I ask innocently, but I know I've been rumbled.

Lisa puts one hand on her hip and raises her eyebrows at me. 'I don't know what it is between you and Fred,' she says. 'But it's obviously unfinished business. When are you seeing him again?'

'I don't know.' I sigh heavily, jabbing a length of wire into the head of an orange gerbera and winding it down around the stem. 'That's just the problem. I don't know anything. We had such a great time the other night, but it was all left so open-ended.'

'Do you want to see him?'

'Of course I do, but it's too complicated. He's about to get married for starters.'

'So why did he invite you to that launch party the other night?'

I shrug hopelessly.

'Look, you were going to tell him about Peter, from the launch. Why don't you just go round and see him?' she continues.

'What? Now?'

'Why not? You're always the one telling *me* to be impulsive.'

'But it's first thing in the morning.'

127

'So? When was time ever important in these things?'

It takes a further half-hour to convince myself that Lisa has a point. By the time I get into the van, I feel giddy with nerves and excitement, as if I'm about to do something incredibly naughty. It's crazy, really, because if I'm trying to prove a point, I'm only proving it to myself. There's no one else around whom this matters to, yet I still have a full-blown conversation trying to persuade prim Mickey that this is a good idea.

When I find it, Fred's street isn't what I'd expected. I'd imagined it would be somewhere plush and posh, but it's an average scruffy London thoroughfare with budding plane trees and a potholed bus lane. I double-check it in my battered *A-Z* against the address I scrawled in eyeliner in my book when Fred dropped me and Joe off in a cab after the party, and park on a yellow line outside the dilapidated town house. I must have driven down this road countless times and it strikes me now how incredible it is that Fred was here all the time and I never knew.

I turn off the engine and get out of the van as a jogger comes out from a house two doors down and starts panting up the street towards me. I nod and say hello, but the middle-aged man looks at me suspiciously and gives me a wide berth.

There's obviously a tag war going on in the neighbourhood, because every spare bit of wall is sprayed with layers of colourful graffiti. I push my sunglasses to the top of my head and look up at the assortment of flaking windows of Fred's building, wondering which is his flat. There seems no sign of life in any of them, except for a fat ginger cat who sits in the front bay window on the ground floor, slowly blinking in the sunshine.

There's a loud clatter as over the road the owner of a café pulls up the metal shutters and I decide to bide a bit of time and psych myself up before I intrude on Fred. Inside the café the owner pulls down a plastic chair from the chipped Formica table so that I can sit down. He winks at me and whistles along to the radio as he sweeps the floor, and it occurs to me, as I fiddle with the sugar shaker, that I haven't had time just to sit like this on my own for as long as I can remember. I rest my chin on my fist and relish the moment, letting my nostrils fill with the aroma of fresh coffee as my eyes relax against the sun which streams through the windows, illuminating a shimmering spotlight of dust. On the other side of the window is Fred's house and I realise I'm experiencing an emotion so ridiculously familiar to me that it almost makes me laugh.

Despite all our fears, when we finished at Rushton Primary and I started at Bowley Comp after the hot summer, the fact that Fred was at a different school hardly made any impact on our lives at all. We adapted to the way things were, as children do. He had new friends and so did I, but we still had each other when other friends had gone home and during the long Sunday evening slog between TV no man's land and bedtime.

At the time I was jealous. His posh prep school sounded interesting, with its big sports fields, language laboratory and swanky art department. That said, I wouldn't have swapped my Saturday mornings when Dad cooked a fry-up for Fred's unreasonable weekend lessons, but at least Fred appeared to be learning. As far as I could see, my own long-haul journey through the education system at Bowley Comprehensive seemed boring and fairly pointless by comparison.

When anything major happened – there was a fight or falling out – I told Fred, but mostly by the time I got home each evening the experience of school had washed over me and left me feeling pretty much as I had done the evening before. Apart from the fact that the loos smelt more than Rushton Primary and there was more puss on the mirrors, the only real differences I could discern at

Bowley Comprehensive was that the chairs were bigger, the detentions longer and we had to walk further between lessons.

In class, as in Rushton Primary, I was constantly told off for daydreaming or chattering at the back and the only thing that inspired me was the large faded map of the world that covered one wall of our classroom. I would gaze up at the contoured pastel land masses, rolling the names of foreign cities around on my tongue, and childishly fantasise about zooming round them in a souped-up red car with a go-faster stripe on a mission to find cunningly disguised 00Fred, who had the local lingo sussed, and was at the ready to shoot the baddies and restore order.

Back in reality, it was instalments of *Dallas* and the extra-curricular details of school life that kept me interested on a day-to-day basis. I smoked cigarettes at the bottom of the sports field, did derogatory impressions of all the teachers and scratched rude words on the school desks with a compass at every available opportunity. I only avoided getting into serious trouble because Pippa, my old primary school stooge, let me copy her neat homework on the bus each morning, in return for my reassurance that she could be the deputy leader of our gang.

As gang leader, I busied myself by being the meddling expert on who was friends with whom, who preferred which male singer out of which pop band and who had the latest hairstyle courtesy of Crops and Bobbers, the hairdressers in Bowley High Street. And the most consuming topic of the lot – boys.

Needless to say, the ones we came into contact with at school were revolting and worthy of our scorn, but secretly we were all fascinated. To prove my superiority, I let slip to the girls in my class that I'd *French-kissed a boy* and made up facial expressions, that gave each one of them a very different impression of the experience I'd actually had. Mickey's Secret Snog became a whispered talking point and, for want of any better gossip, my fame as a kisser was so exaggerated and so many contenders were put forward as to the identity of the kissee, that it grew impossible to own up to the fact that it had only been Fred.

At first I was amazed that I wasn't exposed as the liar I was, but as time went on and the fabrication of my advanced state of secret sexual enlightenment continued, I revelled in my notoriety. Not to be outdone by Tracey Hitchin, my rival in 2C, I spread it about that I had 'come on' first. Not even Pippa knew the truth. Amazingly, no one ever sussed that I stuffed toilet paper down the tiny cups of my trainer bra. Nor did they twig that the swollen abdomen I displayed once a month, like a pregnant woman, was a combination of cheese and onion crisps and clever muscle control. While everyone clucked around whispering 'poor Mickey', I milked my so-called woman-hood to such an extent that I almost believed I had actually written the letter that was printed in the problem page of *Jackie* magazine about a tampon that had become stuck . . . *up there*.

In truth, I had no idea what to expect from *up there*. I avoided any conversation with my mum on the subject, assuming that I was deeply dysfunctional and weird. In private, I studied my flat chest and childish body impatiently, and prayed hard for something, anything, to start happening for real.

Then, when I was thirteen, Fred finished at Rathborne Prep School and went away to boarding school. Even though we'd been warned and were expecting it, the fact that he was now going to be away permanently came as a terrible shock. To me, it seemed as if he was going to the other side of the planet. As he drove away from Hill Drive in Miles's Porsche, I knew that an era had ended and, despite making Fred swear on his life that he'd correspond every week and give me all the glamorous details of life away from home, he didn't.

In his absence, the world went crazy as puberty kicked in. Out went the toilet paper from my bra and in its place my breasts grew and grew, as did the battles I had with my parents over the various tempestuous and always short-lived love affairs I embarked on with a motley selection of spotty youths. When Fred came home, I hardly saw him, such was my preoccupation with my dramatic and, what I considered to be extremely fulfilled, life. I had records to buy, hair to dye, parties to attend and Fred was just the boy next door. The posh boy at that.

So nothing prepared me for the shock of Fred's home-coming in the Christmas holidays two years later. All of a sudden he was different: not only taller and broader, but with real stubble and a fashionable haircut. As I peeked through the gap in the net curtains in our dining room and saw him embracing Louisa, his mother, on the drive next door, swamping her in the folds of a second-hand, yet incredibly trendy, khaki army coat, there was no doubt in my mind that Fred had turned into a man. Even through steamed-up glass, I was smitten.

I wasn't the only one. With a desperate need for fresh blood of the male variety in Rushton, especially with the Christmas disco coming up, nearly every one of my female rivals earmarked Fred as slow-dance snog material. Even Annabel Roberts, the prettiest girl in my class and target of all my bitching, decided to befriend me when she found out that Fred and I were next-door neighbours.

I doubt very much whether Fred was aware of his soaring social status, or just how many girls in Rushton fancied him, but I decided that I was going to win. As I saw it, Fred rightfully belonged to me. I knew him best, I lived closest and I had the greatest chance of seducing him. So the night before the disco, just to make sure Fred knew what was on offer, I deliberately left the curtains open as I undressed.

At the back of the Memorial Hall the mud had frozen into hard ridges and the puddles were glazed with ice, but I still felt in a warm, cheery mood. After several hours of preening around at Pippa's house I felt prepared: my eyelashes bowing with an extra-thick slick of electric-blue mascara, my lips lined and glossed in strawberry and everywhere else perfumed with half a can of Impulse body spray. Not only that, I had booze and cigarettes.

'What's that?' asked Pippa, as I proudly unscrewed the top of an orange squash bottle and breathed in the pungent vapours of the murky brown concoction I'd surreptitiously siphoned off from the bottles in my dad's drinks cabinet.

'Gin, Martini, Cinzano Rosso . . . and something green.'

Pippa wrinkled up her nose when I proffered the bottle. 'Won't we get smashed?'

'That's the general idea,' I said with a grin.

'But it's freezing, Mickey, can't we drink it inside?' begged Pippa, stamping from one foot to the other, the Father Christmas dangly earrings she'd bought for tonight swinging in time. There was no reason why she should be cold, what with her sensible shoes and the mohair scarf which peeked out of her warm school coat.

'No,' I insisted. As I'd already explained, it would be seriously uncool to arrive before Fred. There was no way I was going to be a groupie. Pippa and I would make our entrance when it was guaranteed we'd be noticed.

'Drink it. It'll warm you up,' I suggested.

Pippa took a swig, winced and slapped her chest, before handing it back. I ground the end of my cigarette under the toe of my new black patent stilettos and peeked round the corner to get a look inside.

Through the open doors it was clear that the Memorial

Hall had been transformed. The home-made straw nativity scene had been obscured by the Terry's Disco, hired all the way from Bowley. Red, blue and green lights pulsed from the bar across the loud disco, while the large mirror ball suspended from the ceiling cast shadows around the walls like a shoal of darting silver fish and turned the scuffed old floorboards below into a magical whirlpool. Above it, streamers hung down from a net of pink balloons, which bobbed in the draft as everyone arrived.

A shiver of excitement rushed through me as I pressed myself up against the wall out of sight and took a hefty swig from the bottle.

'You're getting frost on your fringe,' said Pippa.

'Am I?' I asked, carefully dabbing my crimped and back-combed fringe, which was sprayed solid with glitter spray. 'Will you go and look, then?' I asked anxiously.

Pippa rolled her eyes. This was the twentieth time I'd asked her in as many minutes.

'Go on,' I pleaded.

With a bored scowl, Pippa left our hiding place and went to look inside.

'Yes, he's there,' she reported a minute later.

I clapped my hands with glee. Tonight was going to be a good one. 'How do I look?' I asked, pulling down the hem of my pencil skirt towards my knees, the skin of which had gone a mottled blue.

'Fine,' said Pippa.

Paranoid, I smelt my armpits. 'I don't have BO, do I?' I checked, gripping my batwing top and shoving it towards Pippa.

She coughed and waved in front of her nose. 'No,' she said, squinting.

'Come on, then, let the party begin.' I smiled as I sashayed towards the door.

Inside, as the music pumped out, I could feel the

anticipation building, as the tables around the dark edges of the hall filled up.

'There he is,' I said, nudging Pippa, looking over to see Fred talking to Dave and a gang of our old mates from Rushton Primary. Fred looked far more sophisticated than the lot of them in a blue stripy shirt, and he swept his long fringe out of his eyes as he talked.

Squeezing my lips together, I wrapped my thin satin jacket over the orange juice bottle to smuggle our illegal booze in and walked my best walk across the hall to a table in the corner.

'Is he looking?' I asked Pippa through gritted teeth.

'Mickey,' she grumbled.

'Is he?' I insisted.

Pippa turned round and looked directly over to Fred. 'Yes,' she said, raising her hand to wave.

I grabbed it. 'Don't.' I eyeballed Pippa menacingly.

'What?' she asked, exasperated.

'The whole point is to play hard to get,' I said, quickly sitting down at the table, pretending to be completely oblivious to the boys. I waved to Annabel, Lucy and Claire, and before long our table was chocka-block full of Bowley Comp girls.

We didn't have to wait long before the disco was in full swing. With a midnight curfew only four precious hours away, and the limitations of orange juice and Coca-Cola being served from the Memorial Hall kitchen, everyone had brought their own alcohol and was determined to get stuck in as quickly as possible.

'So is there anyone you fancy, Mickey?' shouted Annabel over the music, as she surreptitiously divvied up her bottle of Cinzano and lemonade.

'Maybe,' I replied. 'What about you?'

She nodded, looking meaningfully in Fred's direction. 'But I'm not telling.'

Feeling cross, I got up and started a tireless campaign on

135

the dance floor. I wasn't going to play her game. I wasn't going to be that obvious. Instead, I made it clear that I didn't have a care in the world, leading our new dance routines, as I stood in line with Claire, Maria and Denise. By eleven o'clock, Fred hadn't had the chance to get near me.

'Relax!' I sang, in time to Frankie Goes To Hollywood's hit, flicking out my foot, my hands on my waist as I jumped round ninety degrees in line with the others.

'Mickey!' It was Lisa shouting in my ear.

'What?'

'It's Pippa. She wants you. She's in the loos.'

Lisa thumbed over her shoulder towards the toilet door at the back of the hall.

Pushing my way to the front of the queue, I knocked loudly and called out for Pippa. I heard the bolt being moved inside and pushed open the door. Pippa was kneeling on the speckled maroon lino, hugging the toilet bowl. She looked up at me, her eyes bloodshot and her hair clumped into puke-soaked rat's tails.

'Oh no, Pippa!' I pulled the cubicle door shut behind me.

'Ugh,' she managed in greeting, before throwing up her guts. I turned away, gagging at the smell of regurgitated alcohol and half-chewed peanuts.

Pippa groaned and I rubbed her back, hearing the muffled sound of the disco.

'Grab your partners, ladies. We're slowing things down,' Terry crooned, the microphone squeaking with feedback as he changed the record. It was Wham!, 'Last Christmas', my favourite record. I couldn't miss this one.

Panicked, I bent down. 'Are you OK?' I asked. 'Only it's the –'

Pippa interrupted with a violent gush of vomit. Spitting and coughing, she let out a whimper. 'Don't go, Mickey,' she begged, looking up at me. Even in the dim light of the toilet I could tell she was pale green.

'It's going to be OK,' I said, as kindly as I could, crouching down beside her, and trying unsuccessfully to mop up with the shiny paper loo roll, as I listened with a sinking heart to my favourite lyrics going on without me.

'Who's in there?' It was Mrs Bevan-Jones, Rushton's Youth Club Manager, who was running the drinks stall from the kitchen. 'There's a queue out here.'

Gingerly I opened the door of the cubicle and slipped out. 'It's Pippa. She's not feeling very well.'

'Oh?'

'I think she's got food poisoning,' I lied. 'She's puke—' I caught sight of Mrs Bevan-Jones's scowl. 'She's terribly sick.'

'Oh, dear,' tutted Mrs Bevan-Jones. 'She'll have to move out of here. Perhaps the vicar will take her home.'

Behind us I could hear Pippa straining as she threw up get again. 'Mickey?' she bleated.

'Hang on,' I called.

I looked at Mrs Bevan-Jones. 'I think it's best if I go and get some water,' I said with a grimace. Mrs Bevan-Jones nodded and pushed me aside, rapping on the toilet door. Guiltily, I slunk away. I knew Pippa would be furious, but Mrs Bevan-Jones was the authority on first aid. What she didn't know about giving mouth-to-mouth resuscitation to a Tiny Tears doll wasn't worth knowing and, when she finally sobered up, Pippa would thank me for leaving her in such capable hands.

Already, the dance floor was a seething mass of swaying couples and I searched frantically for Fred, ducking round the edge of the room to try to see him. It didn't take me long. In the middle of the crowd, Annabel had her arms wrapped tightly round Fred's neck. Even with her eyes closed it was clear that she was steering him straight for the dangling bunch of mistletoe. I stopped, rooted to the spot in the shadows, my throat constricting as I watched them sway to the dance I'd planned for myself. Then Terry released the string and the net full of balloons fell from the ceiling and everyone looked up, their faces delighted as the balloons cascaded romantically among them. Turning on my heels, blinded by tears, I marched through the door and out into the night.

Outside, it had started to snow. I turned up my thin collar, shivering as thick flakes wafted down around me, settling in a fine layer on the steps of the Memorial Hall. Ahead, the road was deserted, the white stillness only broken by the frenetic circuit of coloured lights in the plastic Santa Claus frieze in the Spar window. I trudged out, my hopes shattered, as George Michael crooned on in the warmth behind me.

What was I thinking of? Of course Fred was going to go with Annabel. What chance did I possibly stand? Why would he think of us as anything other than old friends?

'Mickey! Wait.' I heard Fred's voice shouting out behind me and stopped, not turning back. Quickly I wiped my face and dug my hands deep into my pockets.

'Where are you going?' he asked, out of breath as he caught up with me. He looked cold in his shirtsleeves, his cheeks pink as he pointed back at the Memorial Hall.

I shrugged and looked down at my feet. They'd been fine when I was dancing in the disco, but now they were killing me. 'Home,' I mumbled, avoiding Fred's concerned look. The last thing I wanted was for him to see how upset I was.

'Don't you want to stay till the end?' he asked, looking back at the disco.

I screwed up my nose. 'It was getting boring,' I said, walking on and trying to stop myself limping.

'I thought we were going to dance,' said Fred and I could hear the disappointment in his voice.

I turned round. I could see plumes of white vapour coming from Fred's mouth, as the snow started settling in his hair. 'Did you?' I said, managing to sound casual. 'You looked busy to me.'

'Don't be like that,' he implored. 'Come on, I've hardly seen you since I came home. Come back inside.'

Stubbornly, I shook my head.

'But it's Christmas.' He took a step towards me.

'So?' I grouched, refusing to be cajoled by his friendly tone.

Fred rolled his eyes at me and smiled. 'So, if you're not going to dance with me inside, Mickey Maloney, I'll just have to dance with you out here,' he said, laughing as he grabbed me and pulled me into the middle of the road.

'Fred!' I protested, but I was smiling as he put his arm round my waist and held my hand in his. Inside the Memorial Hall the muffled strains of Tina Turner singing 'What's Love Got To Do with It' seeped out from under the door as Fred swung me round in the road.

'Hello, stranger,' he said, smiling down at me. 'What do you want for Christmas?'

You, you idiot, I felt like shouting. Instead, I shrugged and adopted my friendliest 'old mates' tone. 'Nothing much. It'll probably be jumpers as usual. Grandma Ritchie is coming and you know how mad she is. What about you?'

'We're not talking about Christmas at ours. Miles hasn't turned up yet.'

'What? You mean you haven't seen him?'

'Nope. Mum's in a filthy mood about it. If he doesn't show, I expect Christmas will be cancelled.'

'I'm sure it'd be all right if you come to ours,' I said. 'We'll just be watching telly and stuff. I think there's a James Bond on . . .' My voice trailed away as my eyes melted into Fred's.

'Mickey?' He wiped a snowflake from the end of my nose.

'What?'

'Shut up,' he said, pulling me towards him and wrapping his arms tightly round me. And then, as the soft snow fell around us and covered our footprints, he kissed me.

The café owner wipes some spilt sugar off my table, interrupting my reverie. Smiling, I pay for my coffee and take the breakfast I've ordered over the road to Fred's house. I'm convinced that my visit can't be interpreted as anything other than a friendly drop-by and that Fred will be happy to see me. Yet as soon as my trembling finger leaves the bell, my courage deserts me.

In the vital moments as I wait to see Fred's shadow on the other side of the glass panels in the door, doubts crash into my head. Fred, or the concept of Fred, is just in my imagination and pursuing these feeling is like attempting to sail off into the sunset in a much loved, but nevertheless punctured, rubber dinghy. I'm being ridiculous; seeking out friendship from a man I haven't seen or heard from in fifteen years. Surely it's just fluke that we still get on and make each other laugh? I'm simply being sentimental for old times' sake, because once he was a boy I had such overwhelming feelings for that I thought I'd die without him. But now? Now he's a man and he's probably safely cuddled up in bed with the woman he's going to marry.

Every impulse in my body tells me to run and the longer I stand glued to the doorstep the longer I feel like I'm back in Rushton playing rat-a-tat ginger. I'm about to bolt for it at the last minute when the door opens, making me start.

'Mickey?' says Fred, sounding and looking confused as he holds on to the latch. His face has crease marks on it, and his hair is all rumpled and sticks up at the back. He's wearing a pair of cotton pyjama bottoms and his chest is bare. It's tanned and muscular, and I can see the outline of his ribs as he yawns. Since I'm on the doorstep and therefore lower than Fred, his chest fills my entire field of vision. Immediately, I feel blood rushing to my face.

I haven't been this close to a half-naked man for a very

long time and up until this moment, and for as long as I can remember, my sex drive has been well and truly parked. Parked, that is, in a forgotten lock-up in a dingy part of town. At the sight of Fred, however, the dusty doors are flung open and it bursts into action. Before I know what's hit me, hormones are revving around parts of me that I'd forgotten were parts.

'What time is it?' asks Fred, scratching the fluff of hair on his belly. The last time I saw Fred's belly it was hairless and smooth, and I have to make my hand into a fist to stop myself touching it and claiming it as mine again.

'Eight-ish,' I stutter, keeping my eyes locked with Fred's so that I don't look down again. 'Sorry, I didn't think. It's the middle of the day for me. I'll leave you to it.'

'No, no,' says Fred, opening the door wider. 'Come in, come in.'

'Forget it,' I squeak, feeling choked with confusion and panic. 'I'm disturbing you. If Rebecca's here . . .'

'Rebecca?' snorts Fred, shaking his head. 'Don't worry. Rebecca never stays and Eddie didn't come back last night. I'm home alone. Come on in.'

He stoops down and picks up a pile of takeaway menus and cab cards from the doormat, before straightening up. I follow him into the house and up the stairs.

I can do this, I tell myself, as I tread carefully up the threadbare carpet, willing myself not to look up at Fred's bum. I'm here as a . . . as a . . . what? A friend. That's it. A neighbourly friend. But as quickly as I think this, I know that it's the concept of being Fred's friend that confuses me. Joe seemed perfectly happy to describe Fred as 'our friend', but what kind of friend am I really?

Fred and I certainly aren't best friends, as we were when we were kids, but does that make us ex-friends? Or are we new friends? And if we are, then why should the past matter? If we're new friends, should I feel less pleased that we're alone? Would a friend of any description have the words 'Rebecca never stays' excitedly chiming round and round her head with each step she takes nearer to being home alone with Fred?

I'll stick to being a neighbour. You're always safe being defined as a neighbour – even if I am the curtain-twitching, nosy kind. The truth is that for the past few days I've been longing to see where Fred lives. I've wanted to see him in context and I've imagined his place to be all designer, full of trendy couches and minimalist furniture. So I'm quite shocked when he prods the door open with his foot and I follow him into his flat.

The living room has a fusty smell of stale cigarettes and the sofa is covered with newspapers. Fred picks up a T-shirt from the back of it and puts it on, inside out. I feel intrepid and nervous as I peek at the stacks of videos and CDs. It's been ages since I was last in a bloke's flat and I'm not quite sure what to do with myself.

I'm wondering just why it is that Rebecca never stays, when I glance through a doorway to the bathroom and see one of the possible reasons. There's a Game Boy on the toilet cistern and the toilet seat is up. A neglected brown spider plant sits on the windowsill and the ridged opaque glass is cracked. It's not exactly what I'd call girl-friendly and certainly nowhere near 'Gucci enough' for Rebecca, as Susan, Fred's colleague, implied.

'I'll put the kettle on,' Fred says, walking into the kitchen.

'No need,' I trill, but I know I'm sounding skittish and nervous. 'I brought some breakfast.' I hold up the paper bag from across the road. 'Coffee and sausage sandwiches.'

Fred ruffles his hair and sort of yawns down his nose.

'You do eat breakfast?' I check.

Fred smiles, breaking his yawn. 'Of course. Sorry, I'm just not very awake yet.'

'Oh,' I say. 'Late night?'

'Hm. I had to go out with a whole load of people from

work. We ended up at some bar. I bailed out at about four this morning, I think.'

'Very glam,' I say, smiling, but inside I feel deflated. I've spent most of the last few days thinking about all the things we still have in common, but I've just been kidding myself. The reality is that Fred's life is completely different from mine. At four o'clock this morning I was thinking about getting up, not going to bed.

I look around the kitchen, but there doesn't seem to be a space on which to put my bag. There's a laptop open on the pine table, surrounded by piles of papers, while the work surface is stacked with a couple of dirty plates, next to an Indian-takeaway bag. I peek out through the dirty glass door in the living room, wishing I could open it and let some fresh air in.

'What's out there?' I ask.

'It's nothing much. Just a roof terrace. I'll show you, if you like.'

I nod and Fred walks over and opens the doors.

The view is amazing and I breathe in deeply. 'It's lovely,' I say, wandering over the wooden decking to look between the chimney pots. 'You could make it a complete haven up here with a bit of work. Look at all this light; it's wonderful.'

'Is it? I'd never really thought about it.' Fred squints in the sunshine. 'I've certainly never been up here at this time before.'

'You're so lucky to have this space. I'd be out here every day if I were you,' I say, sitting on one of the plastic chairs, and taking the coffee cups out of the paper carrier bag and placing them on the disused window box.

Fred flops down in the other chair and crosses his foot over his knee. He blinks heavily as I hand him the sandwich, bound in greaseproof paper. He unwraps it, checking its contents. 'Drowning in ketchup. I'm amazed you remembered.'

'Just like Miles used to make . . .' I stop abruptly, tripped up by my insensitivity. We stare at each other for a moment and I put my hand to my mouth.

'Sorry . . . I didn't mean –' I begin.

Fred shakes his head and smiles. 'It's OK. I can handle it.'

I pass over his coffee. 'Breakfast is the least I can do to say thank you for the other night,' I say with a smile. 'You have a new, adoring fan.'

'Really? That's very nice of you. I didn't know you still cared.'

'Not me,' I tut, smiling. 'Joe. He thinks you're chocolate. Actually, I think he wants to *be* you.'

'I hope you've put him off.'

'I tried, but it wasn't easy.'

Fred grins. 'Well, I'm glad he enjoyed himself.' He pauses and squints through one eye, against the sun. 'What about you?'

'Me?' I ask. 'I thought it was incredible. Actually, that's why I'm here. I am the bearer of fantastic news and I couldn't keep it to myself any longer.' I smile at Fred and he raises his eyebrows at me. 'Peter. Your Peter from the other night,' I explain. 'He's come up trumps. More than trumps. I went to his offices and he's given me a contract to do their flowers every week.'

Fred shuffles up in his seat. 'Mickey, that's great.'

'You're telling me. What he's proposing to pay me is enough to cover my rates. It's all thanks to you.'

Fred holds his sandwich. 'Let's call it quits. This is just what I need.'

'Joe's happier as well,' I continue. 'You wouldn't recognise him; he's a different person since the other night. He's been bragging to everyone about it and he's even made arrangements with the boy he met there, Tyler, for the weekend.' I take a bite out of my sandwich.

Fred smiles as he finishes a mouthful. 'You know,' he says. 'Joe's so . . . *cool*, isn't he? I've never really known a child before. I mean, not since I was one myself. I assumed they'd be a bit of a . . . burden. But . . . he's –' Fred pauses and gropes for the word. '*Interesting*.'

I can't help snorting with laughter, as I lever the plastic lid off my coffee cup. 'Don't sound so shocked,' I tell him. 'Children aren't aliens. You were a kid once, remember. And I seem to recall you were . . . moderately *interesting*.'

Fred pulls a face at me. 'I suppose. I guess I'd forgotten.'

'Anyway. Joe's had good parenting,' I tease modestly. 'Of course he's *cool*.'

Fred nods and glances down at his sandwich, then back at me. He looks as if he's about to say something.

'What?' I ask, still smiling.

'Nothing. It's nothing.'

'What?'

'It's . . . It doesn't matter, it's just . . .' Fred shifts nervously in his seat. 'I know it's none of my business, but when we were at the launch, I mentioned Martin to Joe when we were at the sushi stand . . .'

'And?'

'I thought Martin was Joe's father, but Joe said he wasn't. He seemed a bit embarrassed. It took me by surprise, that's all.'

'Oh, I see.'

I look down at my lap. There's a part of me that always feels defensive when I hear Joe talking about his father or Martin to anyone. I spend so much time trying my best to be two parents that when Joe mentions his confused upbringing it trips me up. I never think it's an issue, but I suppose for Joe it must be. I'm surprised he talked to Fred about it.

Fred looks embarrassed. 'Sorry, I shouldn't have said anything –'

'Don't be silly,' I interrupt. 'I don't mind. It's just a long story, that's all.'

Continuing to munch, Fred sweeps out his arm, as if we

have all the time in the world and I feel like I do owe him an explanation for Joe's sake. Joe hates explaining things himself, so I guess it's up to me. I'm about to do my usual jaunty gloss over the details, when it occurs to me that I haven't trusted anyone enough to tell them my story for a very long time. I look at Fred's expectant face and suddenly it feels right to tell him, as if he should know it all anyway. As the facts tumble out, I feel relieved.

I met Dan at a gig in Camden when I was nineteen. At the time I'd hardly ever been to London, certainly on my own. Even so, I was at my most cocky and confident as I strode into the bar and clapped eyes on him. He was two years older than me, played in a band and had more wild dreams than I'd ever imagined possible. I was intoxicated by him, hooked on his dark good looks and, from the first night, I hardly strayed out of his sight. Within a month I'd left home and moved in with him to a tiny bedsit in Brixton.

I loved London and, coming from Rushton, was totally seduced by the anonymity of it all. I loved the fact that every time I met someone new and introduced myself they didn't look at me knowingly and say, 'Oh, so you're *that* Mickey Maloney.' It was as if I'd shed a skin and was starting again as a new person.

Then there was Dan. I spent all my time hanging out with him, swooning around and generally being in love with the idea of being in love. I felt as if he adored me, but in reality he only threw me titbits of attention when I flattered him, or bolstered the enormous expectations he had of the successful, glittering future that was always going to happen at any moment.

Looking back, the two years we spent together were like a giant holiday. Far from the grown-up idyll I thought I was living, we both behaved like carefree and irresponsible teenagers left to their own devices. Every week we drew the dole, drank cheap cans of beer and behaved like sex-starved rabbits. Our love shack, as we called it, was grotty and damp, but it seemed like paradise to me. For the first time since Fred, with Dan I thought that anything was possible. He called me his muse and, even though I couldn't afford to eat anything other than pot noodles, it didn't seem to matter. We were being creative and nothing could stand in our way.

That was, until I got pregnant.

At first, Dan was over the moon and made a thousand promises about our future. It seemed as if having a family was the most natural thing in the world. Dan would write poems to his unborn child, boast about me to his friends and kiss my stomach over and over again.

But then Joe was born and everything changed. Suddenly there were three of us instead of two and it all started to fall apart. Dan got angry that I couldn't go out with him, or stay up all night like I used to, and he couldn't deal with it when Joe cried.

When Joe was two months old I came back from the shops one day and there was a tear-stained note. Dan had written every predictable cliché about loving me for ever, but he couldn't give up on his dream of making it with his band. As if a light suddenly went on, I realised I'd been dumped good and proper. I had no choice but to go back to Rushton with my tail between my legs.

'Shit, Mickey, I'm sorry,' Fred mutters, when I've finished telling him all this.

He frowns sympathetically at me, but I wave my hand. 'Don't be, it's ancient history,' I say, meaning it. Actually, I feel rather happy talking about Dan. My usual 'things didn't work out' explanation is designed to keep people from knowing the truth, but it feels refreshing to let Fred in. It's kind of liberating for once to tell the facts as they were, and not to heap all the blame conveniently on myself, just to avoid talking about it.

'Aren't you bitter?' asks Fred. 'I would be.'

'No, I've got Joe. He makes up for everything.'

'And have you seen Dan since?'

I shake my head and shrug. 'Vanished into thin air. I doubt he'll show his face. He owes me nine years of child support. Anyway, I don't want to see him and it'd be terrible for Joe. I think he's got a certain idea of his father, which I doubt Dan could ever live up to.'

'And Martin? How does he fit in?'

'Martin came along just when I thought living at home with Mum and a small baby was going to drive me insane. When he asked me to marry him, I said yes more out of some crazy notion that Joe needed a father figure in his life than anything else.'

Fred leans back in his chair. He makes a good listener. 'What was Martin like?' he asks.

'Dull,' I reply. 'Fine on paper and I did try really hard to fall in love with him, but all the time I was with him I felt like I was doing life, rather than living it. He was the absolute opposite of Dan. It only took about two months before I realised that I'd shrunk into Martin's never-ending routine. Drinks with the boys on a Friday, football on Saturdays, washing the car on Sundays and so it went on . . . and on.'

'It doesn't sound very you.'

'I tried to make it me, but in the end I just couldn't. All the time, I felt like a spectator watching myself from the corner of the room, until I finally came to my senses.'

'When did it end?'

'Just over three years ago. Ever since I'd gone back to Rushton after living with Dan, I'd wanted to come back to London. When I realised I was perfectly capable of standing on my own two feet I left. I felt determined to make a go of things myself. Poor old Martin. I think I hurt him quite a bit and it wasn't exactly fair on Joe.'

Fred's silent for a long moment. When I look up at him,

he's staring right at me and there's something in his eyes that makes my heart start pounding.

'Do you think you could ever fall in love again, Mickey?'

'I don't know,' I say, shrugging, my voice hoarse. Coughing, I break eye contact and try to laugh off the moment. 'Anything's possible. Anyway, what is love? You're the expert. You tell me. You're the one about to get married.'

Fred stretches and looks at his toes. He smiles wryly to himself. 'Ah, Rebecca,' he says, but he almost sounds wistful, as if he's reluctant to speak her name.

'Yes, Rebecca,' I say pointedly, feeling like we've said far too much and gone much too long without mentioning her. 'How is the future Mrs Roper?'

'Wilson.'

'Sorry!' I flap my hand, embarrassed. 'Wilson. Well, when do I get to meet her?'

Fred stares out across the rooftops and doesn't answer.

'She . . . she does know about me?' I check.

Fred sighs a heavy sigh and rubs his eyes before he looks up at me. His face is serious. 'Not exactly. Not at the moment,' he admits. 'It's tricky –'

'Tricky?' I interrupt. 'What's so tricky?'

'She doesn't know.'

'What do you mean?'

Fred takes a deep breath. 'She doesn't know about Miles.'

I'm so shocked by this that for a moment I can't say anything. 'You mean –'

Fred nods. 'She knows that I lived in Rushton, but she doesn't know that I was ever called Roper, or what happened to Miles.'

I'm dumbfounded. 'I see,' I manage.

'There seemed to be no point in telling her. Nobody knows, really, except you.' He exhales guiltily when he sees my look of disbelief. 'I . . . I can't really mention it now. It's too late. And anyway, I don't want to. I'm happy with the way things are. The past is the past.'

'Oh. And I suppose that includes me?'

Fred shakes his head. 'No, of course it doesn't.'

'Are you sure?'

'Yes, it's great seeing you again. I really mean that. And I will tell Rebecca about you and everything apart from the stuff about Miles. I was going to anyway. I –'

'All of it? About you taking me and Joe to the launch the other night?'

Fred nods.

'I'm not going to see you again if it means sneaking around behind her back. It's not fair.'

'I know . . .'

'Please don't be flaky,' I insist. 'I can't stand flaky men.'

Fred looks sheepishly at me and I glance sideways at him, giving him a beady scowl. 'Promise me?' I insist.

'I promise.'

'Hm,' I reply, standing up to stretch my legs, smoothing down my jeans. Folding my arms, I walk around the roof terrace and finally sit down on the low wall.

Fred stands and comes to sit next to me. Behind us, four storeys below, traffic is starting to build along the street and I can see people walking towards the tube. It seems like a different world from up here.

'I suppose I should think about going to work,' says Fred, sighing after a while.

'Don't sound so enthusiastic.' I chuckle.

'You always did make me want to skive. Being up here makes it all seem a bit pointless and frantic. I wish we could just spend the day doing nothing.'

'So do I,' I say, meaning it more than ever.

We both look at the view.

'Hey. Saved your life.' He laughs, suddenly jolting me. He pulls me upright by my arm and we both giggle. Then, for a second, my eyes lock with his, our faces just inches apart, and I hold my breath.

Chapter V

Fred

1985, the worst year of my life, began as the best.

I remember my time with Mickey as one long embrace. We started kissing in the snow outside Rushton Memorial Hall in December 1984 and hardly came up for air before I was sent back to boarding school in the new year. I don't know if what grew between us during those first few months was love, but it was powerful enough to leave me breathless with tears some nights as I lay in my dormitory bed and thought of Mickey back home. She seemed so far away and all I wanted to do was reach out and touch her hand.

As the year progressed and one school term passed into another, I'd dream at nights of being in Rushton. I'd float through the rooms of my house like a ghost, passing Miles in corridors and on landings, watching him talking in whispers to shadowy, wraithlike figures, retreating behind closed doors whenever he noticed me. Drifting onwards, I'd listen to Mum as she worked in the kitchen, or spoke on the phone, or sorted out clothes for charity jumble sales, and the familiar sound of her voice always filled me with peace. Invariably, though, I'd end up tramping the roads and lanes of the village, hand in hand with Mickey, as a summer sun blazed down and threw our shadows like grotesque giants against the walls and hedges. Each journey would end with that moment of five summers before, with the two of us standing by the churchyard gate, gazing up at the starling as it broke across the rust-red sky and my heart split open for the very first time.

With morning, these dreams would collapse. Summoned by the high-pitched rattle of electric bells, I'd find myself back in my dormitory, listening to the alien noise of twenty other fifteen-year-old boys waking, farting and squabbling over basins, toothbrushes, spot creams and deodorants. I'd rise and wash and dress, and join the chattering stream of my fellow pupils, which flowed up to the dining room in Main School, for breakfast and the start of another day.

Sited on a hundred-acre estate in the heart of the Cotswolds, Greenaway College was – and, as far as I know, still is – home to around three hundred boys, ranging in age from thirteen to eighteen. Originally a Norman manor house, it had grown over the years into a sprawling collection of honey-coloured buildings the size of a small village. At some point (I forget the date), a Victorian industrialist called Endicot Greenaway had bought the lot and founded a feeder school for the governing ranks of the British Empire. I remember how the names of the school's glorious dead were carved into the backs of chairs in dormitories and classrooms, next to the battles and foreign campaigns which had claimed their lives.

I was in the fifth form, halfway through my allotted time here. Unless I succeeded in persuading Miles and Mum to let me go to a sixth-form college nearer home, two and a half more years stretched ahead of me before I'd be done with this place. Everything I took for granted in Rushton – buses, shops, freedom of movement and, most important of all, Mickey – was now either inaccessible or prohibited. They belonged to the outside world and I was no longer in it. I was fifteen years old and five foot ten, and the only thing I knew about life was that it existed outside these buildings and fields.

Ever since I'd first come here when I'd been thirteen, I'd lived for the holidays when I'd be back home. Now that

Mickey was my girlfriend, this longing had become more intense still. I wanted her back, beside me, for real. I wanted so much more than her voice at the end of a telephone, or the scent of her perfume on a letter.

I received at least one letter from Mickey each week. Her envelopes came in strange shapes and sizes and colours and patterns. She'd adorn them with stickers and drawings, or write on them with metallic inks in lurid greens and purples and silvers and golds. Sometimes she'd send small parcels, enclosing taped copies of the new albums she'd bought, as well as trinkets and sweets and flattened cigarettes.

At the start of summer term 1985, the term I was to take my O-level examinations, rereading her words in the dormitory at night, I grew first to recognise and then silently to glory in the fact that somewhere over the last few months I'd fallen in love.

Mickey's communications served another purpose, too. Through a news service that would have rivalled Reuters, Mickey Maloney brought the real world back into my life. There was nothing, I think, that went on in Rushton in the first five months of that year that I didn't get to know about.

Miles's sporadic visits home, for example, had ceased abruptly at the end of the Easter holidays when I'd gone back to Greenaway. Mum had started holding Christian Fellowship meetings on Wednesday evenings and had tried (and failed) on several occasions to cajole Mickey into attending. Miss McKilroy (she of the blotchy, blubbery boobs) had become pregnant and Sam Johnson, the purported father, had put his house in Rushton up for sale and moved to North Wales. Dave had been suspended from Bowley Comprehensive for pulling a moony out of the back of the school bus at a passing Rolls-Royce (the driver of which had been a humourless High Court judge). Mickey's older brother, Scott, had achieved even greater notoriety by dumping Alison Rawling on the night of her seventeenth birthday, thereby causing her to scratch his initials into her forearm with a penknife in a fit of Gothic pique ('an example to us all of why we should put our faith in Jesus and not our fellow man,' according to Mum; and, 'an example of the tragic effect of listening to too many of Scott's Cure records,' according to Mickey).

Some news, though, you couldn't communicate in letters. Some news you had to see to believe.

'*Our father . . .*'

'Pass it on . . .' Rob Oldfield hissed into my ear.

'*Who art in heaven . . .*'

'Check out the spiv with the ponytail and the cheesy grin,' Oldfield hissed again.

'*Hallowed be thy name . . .*'

I nudged Luke Davidson, the boy on my left, and hissed, 'Pass it on . . .'

'*Thy kingdom come . . .*'

I looked across the flagstoned aisle of the school chapel at the block of wooden pews opposite, which was reserved for parents. It was the second Sunday of term and, as a result of some mad Victorian educator's weaning theory, it had been deigned the first day that the boys' parents should be allowed to visit them. Mum was meant to have been coming, but she'd gone down with an unseasonable dose of flu a few days before, and Miles had never come, not once in the two and half years I'd been here. I'd therefore resigned myself to a day of wandering the school grounds alone, while the rest of my year disappeared off for lunch. Anything right now was a welcome distraction from this miserable thought and I scanned the faces for the ponytailed spiv.

'*Thy will be done . . .*'

And saw him sitting two rows back.

'*On earth as it is in heaven . . .*'

Grinning like the winner of a Bee Gees look-a-like contest.

'*Give us this day our daily bread . . .*'

Directly at me.

'*And forgive us our trespasses . . .*'

With a mahogany tan and white eye sockets from wearing shades in the sun.

'*As we forgive those who trespass against us . . .*'

Dressed in a bright red shirt and a shiny grey suit.

'*And lead us not into temptation, but deliver us from evil . . .*'

With a fat gold Rolex on one wrist.

'*For thine is the kingdom . . .*'

And a fat copper bangle on the other.

'*The power and the glory . . .*'

'Pass what on?' Luke asked, following my stare.

'*For ever and ever . . .*'

'Nothing,' I replied.

'*Amen.*'

'I bet you a million he's wearing white socks and grey slip-ons,' Oldfield whispered from my right as the chaplain began on some announcements.

'What?' I mumbled, still staring across the aisle.

'Pikey grey slip-ons,' Oldfield reiterated a little too loudly for the chaplain's liking, causing him to glance irritably in our direction. Oldfield fell silent for a couple of seconds, before whispering again, 'What do you think his name is?'

'The chaplain?'

'No, you arse, the spiv.'

I considered this for a moment, before whispering back, 'Miles.'

Oldfield sniggered. 'Miles is good. I was going to say Trevor or Warren, or something really naff like Randy, but Miles really is rather good –'

'No,' I said, twisting my neck round to look straight into Oldfield's bespectacled eyes. 'I mean his name *is* Miles.' I set my face into what I hoped was a vague approximation of the expression Clint Eastwood had employed in the

155

graveyard shootout scene at the end of *The Good, the Bad and the Ugly* and then I spat it out, knowing that it was only a matter of time before the genetic connection became apparent. 'He's my father.'

Oldfield's jaw dropped, leaving his mouth an O of disbelief. He said nothing for a second and glanced from me to Miles. Then he played Lee Van Cleef to my Eastwood, staring as hard into my eyes as I had into his, waiting for me to crack. But I didn't, because what I'd told him had been the truth: the man with the tan was indeed my father. Oldfield's mouth clamped shut and I watched as, slowly but surely, his face turned from pink to red. Then his shoulders shuddered and great bubbles of snot burst from his nostrils on to his upper lip.

Luke jabbed me in the ribs and mouthed, 'What's up with him?'

I didn't reply and instead stared down between my shoes at the wooden base of the pew. I pictured Miles and wished him dead. What was he doing here? Why had he come? Then I remembered my mother and where I was, and hurriedly apologised to God for the death wish and merely wished Miles elsewhere instead. After all, he *was* meant to be somewhere else. In Malaga, to be precise, with his secretary, Janine, looking for a site for a new nightclub to invest in. That's what Mum had told me, anyway.

'It's Roper's . . .' I heard Oldfield gasp to whoever sat to his right, his shoulders still shaking uncontrollably. 'The spiv. It's Roper's father . . . the spiv's his dad . . .'

Oldfield twisted round to face me, his eyes slick with laughter and, in that instant, my embarrassment died and in its place burnt anger. Who the hell did Oldfield think he was? Or any of these people, come to think of it? So what if Miles dressed like a spiv? What did that mean to me? I hadn't even known what a spiv was before I'd come to this school.

I'd been taught it, just the same as I'd been taught about

plebs and proles and Kevs and Sharons and white socks and pikey accents and all the other delineators of class that I didn't care about, but which seemed so important to most people here.

And – what? – Oldfield and all the rest of them, their parents looked better, did they, in their boring middle-aged tweeds and scarves and old school ties? Not to me, they didn't. I thought of Mickey and Mum and Pippa and Dave, and everyone else back home whom Oldfield probably considered beneath him. I glared deep into the whites of his eyes and told him, 'Go to hell, you stuck-up twat!'

The effect was immediate. Oldfield's silent hysteria vanished as instantly as it had arrived. His mouth reverted to a stunned O. He gaped. He gawked. He hardly seemed to breathe. Never before had I seen someone so affected by the power of language.

It was then that a strange prickle of electricity began to shiver down my neck and spine. I didn't move. Instead, I listened: nothing. Then I heard it, faint but unmistakable: the dying echo of my voice reverberating through the weighty chapel air. When I looked up, my bowels turned to water. Every single face in the congregation was directed towards mine and each mirrored the slack-jawed amazement of Oldfield's. Then, like a crowd at a Wimbledon tennis final following a well-struck ball, they turned in unison and stared down the aisle towards the pulpit.

The chaplain, a formidable Scotsman in his late forties, had eyes the colour of wet slate. His forearms were the size of Sunday roasts and one rumour had it that he'd won prizes in his youth at the Highland Games for tossing the caber, while another claimed he trawled the local village pubs at weekends, seeking out atheists and alcoholics to pick fights with.

Whether there was any truth in either of these rumours became instantly irrelevant to me, as I realised that the only thing he was currently considering throwing anywhere, or picking a fight with, was me. His surplice ruffled up around his arms as he reared forward and his hooked nose drew level with the beak of the lectern's carved wooden eagle. 'Frederick Roper!' he barked, his flashing eyes offering up the promise of certain doom and eternal hellfire. 'See me in the cloister after the service.'

Miles was waiting for me outside, leaning against the side of his white Porsche 928, his slick jacket flapping in the breeze, its sleeves rolled up over his shirt to his elbows like someone out of *Miami Vice*. It's an image of him which remains perfectly clear in my mind to this day. I don't know what film he imagined he was acting in, but looking back now, I suspect it probably co-starred Burt Reynolds and featured a plot involving drinking, driving and rescuing topless girls from corrupt Texan cops.

I started my walk towards him. My explanation for my swearing hadn't washed with the chaplain and, on top of a half-hour lecture on the Nature of Sin, I'd been instructed to pay penance by spending two hours before breakfast on Monday morning picking weeds from the chapel flowerbeds. Miles flicked his cigarette away when I was a few feet from him and I watched it land and cartwheel across the tarmac.

He gripped my hand and shook it, staring over at the chaplain who was watching us from the crypt doorway. Up close, Miles looked rough. It wasn't that he was unshaven or anything as superficial as that. His roughness ran deeper. It was in his eyes, in the dark folds of his skin. They spoke of sleepless nights and worries and fears. He reminded me of the new boys who arrived at school each September, the ones who wore brave faces all day, only to wet their beds and cry themselves to sleep at night. His voice, however, belied all this. It remained as cocky as ever. 'What did the frock have to say?' he asked.

'Why are you here?' I replied. 'Mum said you were looking for a new site . . .'

'What?'

'A new site. In Spain. She said –'

'Oh, yeah,' he mumbled, 'that. It didn't work out. Come on,' he went on, opening the car door, 'let's go and get a drink.'

I didn't talk to Miles as the Porsche purred down the long school drive. Instead, I gazed out of the passenger window at the woods, the bright sunlight occasionally picking out various temples and other long-since abandoned architectural follies which lay scattered about the school grounds.

We drove to a pub about ten miles away from Greenaway and Miles deposited me in the beer garden, out of the landlord's sight, while he went inside to get us both a pint. There were plenty of kids my age, I'm sure, who would have loved to have had a father like Miles, someone who'd break the law for them like this, but I wasn't one of them. Miles's bonding moments made me awkward. They contained an underlying shallowness. Any childhood illusions I'd still entertained about him being a loving family man had finally been dispelled for good when I'd worked for him during the Easter holiday as a way of saving up some cash.

I'd visited Clan before, of course, but always during the daytime, when Mum had been otherwise occupied and Miles had been forced into looking after me. On these days his nightclub had always struck me as a depressing place, as disconnected from life and laughter as a tomb. Miles would disappear and talk business upstairs, leaving me to my own devices down in the ghostly twilight of the deserted club floor. Over the years I'd watched a succession of sallow-skinned cleaners sweeping the floors free of cigarette butts and broken glass, and mopping the beer stains off the bar. I'd wondered what all the fuss had been about and had tried to imagine the small dance floor packed with glamorous couples, their moods and movements orchestrated by singers and bands.

The first few nights I worked there blew my mind. It was everything that photo of Miles and the models from a few years previously had hinted at, but which I'd always denied to myself. Miles *was* that man in the newspaper. The Miles from home, the one who lay in bed late, or slouched by the new pool in the summer, endlessly smoking cigarettes and shouting at people down the phone, fitted in here. It was where he'd been moulded and it was where he belonged. Home, I quickly realised, wasn't the centre of his universe; this was. So where did that leave me?

Miles had given me the job partly because I was tall for my age and partly because he worried that being away at school might somehow have been making me soft. He'd shoved Mum's objections roughly aside. 'You keep saying I should show more interest in him,' I'd heard him telling her. 'So let me. It's not like he's going to be working at the bar or anything, just collecting glasses . . .'

Mum had fallen silent and Miles had read this as her giving her assent.

'I'll get Tony to keep him on the straight and narrow,' he'd added by way of a sweetener.

Tony Hall, or Tony the Crony, as I'd always secretly thought of him, had been with Miles for ten years or more. Five years younger than Miles, he was a silent and brooding figure, with a neck like a bull and alert blue eyes, which never missed a trick. I'd known him from as far back as I could remember, but in all this time he'd rarely spoken to me, always preferring to acknowledge me with a nod, rather than ask me how I was. He scared me a little, to be truthful. He seemed to be perpetually waiting for something bad to happen, knowing that he was the man to sort it out when it did. Miles trusted him implicitly. They'd always been together whenever I'd visited Clan, inseparable, the brains and brawn behind the club.

Miles had been in the business since he'd been a teenager and the sooner I got stuck in myself, he felt, the better. It was my business too, he'd told me. His old partner, Carl, had never returned from his trip abroad four years before and Miles had readjusted his opinion that Carl was in a rehab clinic somewhere to saying that he'd probably got mixed up with someone even nastier than him who'd sorted him out for good. Wherever Carl was, though, Miles didn't care. The ownership of Clan had long since successfully been transferred into Miles's name and, one day, he'd implied before in public, it would be handed on to me.

Miles worked the door himself every night for a couple of hours after Clan opened. He'd meet the guests and shake their hands, and guide anyone famous, or – in the case of women – good-looking, over to tables near his at the left-hand side of the stage. He and Tony would join them at around nine and sit there, Tony evenly surveying the dance floor, with Miles next to him, smoking and joking and getting drunk.

I met a lot of people the first few nights I worked there. Many of their names meant nothing to me, but there were footballers, and the occasional rock star and television personality as well, and it was exciting to be close to them, to observe Miles with them, knowing that he was my father and that he commanded their respect – not that I'd ever have given him the pleasure of letting him know that this was how I felt. Instead, I found myself visualising Mum in Rushton, waiting in disapproval for me to get home, climb out of the cab and step back into her world. Showing Miles that I liked working for him would only, I felt, have been a betrayal of her. And perhaps myself, too. I just didn't know.

The truth was that Miles's attitude towards me

confused me. In public, he always grinned when he introduced me to people, as if I were the most important person in his life. Yet in private we hardly communicated at all and, on the rare occasions when we did, he didn't seem remotely interested in what I had to say. Maybe he was trying to hurt Mum. That was the one possible explanation for his ambivalent attitude towards me. Maybe having me here, away from her, gave him some kind of a kick. Or perhaps having me around just made him feel less guilty.

One night – the last night, as it turned out, that I'd ever work for Miles – I went up to his office at the end of my shift to find the door locked. This in itself was nothing unusual. Miles conducted clandestine meetings up there most nights, with various men whose names I didn't know and to whom he had never introduced me. They were hard-looking men, invariably well-dressed and accompanied by men even bigger than Tony. That night, though, as I reached out to knock on Miles's door, it wasn't the sound of men talking that I was clearly able to hear. Instead, I heard a woman panting and crying out in pleasure, then Miles, speaking to her in a low voice, telling her what he wanted to do to her next.

The first job I ever quit was the one my own father had given me. I told him by phone the next day, but I never told him why, or ever set foot in Clan again.

Now, sitting out in the beer garden of the pub near school, I watched Miles walking towards me, a fresh cigarette in his mouth and a pint glass of frothy beer in either hand. He sat down opposite me, pulled his pack of cigarettes from his pocket and shoved them across the table at me.

'I don't,' I said, lying, but not wanting to give him the pleasure of seeing me light up, when he knew that it would upset Mum if she knew. It would be one more secret between us, one more reason for him to count on me as his.

'You want to tell me what the hell all that crap in the church was about?' he asked.

I didn't reply. In the light of what he'd just said, there seemed little point in discussing the nature of blasphemy with him. Besides, I'd already given up justifying my actions to Miles. His suddenly showing an interest in me, even being here at all, made me wary enough as it was.

'Well?' he asked.

'What do you care?' I muttered without looking up from the table.

I'd expected a rebuke, but instead he simply said, 'I'm here, aren't I?' He rubbed at his nose with the back of his hand. 'That speccy kid next to you was giving you grief about something, wasn't he?'

I nodded my head.

'Do you want to tell me about it?' he asked after a moment's silence.

'No.'

'Want me to have a word with him?'

'I can deal with it myself. Look,' I continued, 'let's just drop it, all right? It's not important.'

'If that's the way you want it . . .'

Again, I said nothing.

'How are your lessons going?' he asked.

I picked up the pint of bitter that Miles had bought me and took a sip, noticing that he was already halfway through his own drink, even though he'd only just sat down. Mine tasted acrid and yo-yoed in my stomach, but I managed to hold it down. I cleared my throat and tried to look like I could handle it all right. 'OK,' I replied.

'You working hard?'

'Yes.' I screwed up my face, searching my mind for small talk. 'Sometimes. History is hard, you know. And the Latin . . . I get confused . . . Some of the other boys in my year, they've been studying it since they were seven . . .'

Miles nodded his head in what I took to be

understanding. 'You've got O levels coming up, haven't you?'

'Yeah. In a month.'

'Don't worry about them too much.'

'I'm not.'

His mouth cracked into a half-grin. 'But don't worry about them too little either,' he said. 'I pay good money to send you here.'

'I know.'

'Seriously, though, son, if you fail them, you fail them. I never got any qualifications and it's not held me back.'

I stared at him impassively. This was nothing I hadn't heard before.

'You can always come and work for me,' he added.

I took another swig of my beer.

'What about the rest of it?' he asked.

'The rest of what?'

'School. You know, what you get up to when you're not working . . . How's all that?'

What do you want to know? I thought. That I'm sick to death of this place and the end of term seems a century away? That I'm planning (whether you like it or not) on refusing to attend sixth form anywhere other than at home with Mickey? Or that I'm terrified about messing my exams up before then? No, I thought. You don't want to know any of that stuff, any more than I want to tell you. You'd rather ignore it, in exactly the same way you've ignored everything to do with Mum and me that hasn't suited you.

And even if I did tell you the truth, you wouldn't be able to handle it, would you? You wouldn't understand about the exams, about how important they are to me, about me wanting to make something decent of myself. You wouldn't understand because you think exams are for jerks and your idea of decent is hanging out with cheap crooks and fucking cheap whores behind your wife's back.

164

He lit another cigarette and smiled at me uncertainly, waiting for me to speak.

I shrugged. 'It's all right.'

'Are you still seeing Mickey?'

I shifted awkwardly on my seat. 'We write,' I told him, and then, 'We're going to go on holiday together in the summer.'

This last sentence had slipped out, because going away with Mickey, just the two of us, had been occupying my mind all term. I hadn't wanted Miles to know it, in case he objected and said we were too young. I'd wanted to spring it on him and Mum as Mickey and I were walking out of the house with our bags already packed. My heart stepped up a beat, as I waited for his objection, but it never came.

'She's a beautiful girl,' he said, smiling gently. 'Are you in love with her?'

I didn't answer. My emotions were my own. I didn't want Miles – this man who I considered had got selfishness down to a fine art – sneering at them, undermining me with his own scepticism.

'You'd know if you were . . .' he told me, his eyes glinting.

'Oh, right,' I snapped, 'and you're the expert on love now, are you?'

'I never said that.'

'What do you care what I think about her?'

I watched him scratch at the stubble under his chin, lost in deliberation. He said nothing and looked away from me, across the pub garden to the open fields beyond.

'You don't like me much, do you, Fred?' he eventually asked, turning and levelling his stare at me.

'No,' I said, 'I don't.'

'I'm sorry for that.'

His eyes flickered, searching my face for a reaction. He didn't get one. I swallowed down the hurt I felt. I loved Miles, but no, I didn't like him. To tell him that I did would be a betrayal of myself and I didn't want to give him my forgiveness; he'd done nothing to deserve it. Everything in his life was so easy for him and so difficult for the people around him. I wanted him to suffer now, as I'd suffered because of him. I wasn't going to lie to him about who he was, or what I thought about him.

'Yeah,' I said, 'well, maybe you should've thought of that before.'

'Maybe I should,' he conceded, but with a roughness in his voice. 'But maybe that's what I'm doing right now.'

He lifted his glass and drank, lowering it from his lips when only a centimetre of liquid remained. Contemplatively, he swilled it round the glass. 'There's something I've got to tell you,' he finally said. I studied his face. The insecurity I'd noticed outside the chapel was back. *Go on*, I thought. *Say it. Say you're going to leave Mum.* 'There's been some trouble at the club,' he went on.

Miles never talked business with me. 'What's happened?' I asked.

'It's Tony. He's walked out and I don't think he's going to be coming back.'

This made no sense to me. 'But –'

Miles lifted his hand to silence me. 'He made some threats before he left. I'm not going to burden you with the details, because it might not come to anything.'

'But if it does?' I asked.

'If it does, then . . . I don't know. I don't know yet, Fred . . . but everything,' – he stressed the word again, almost, it seemed, for his own benefit – '*everything* might change.' His face twitched in awkward sincerity.

'I don't understand,' I said.

'What I told you before,' he continued, 'about being sorry . . . I want you to know that I meant it. I never planned things to be this way between us. I always thought that when you were a little older, I'd . . . we'd . . .' He pulled a Zippo lighter from his pocket. 'Listen to

166

me,' he growled at himself. 'I can't even make myself heard.'

As he leant forward to light a cigarette, I stared at the hair on the top of his head and noticed for the first time that it had started to thin. I wanted to know what thoughts were rushing through his brain beneath. Tony had threatened him. Was Miles frightened, or angry, or both? Was he in danger? Was he going to lose the club? What was he going to do about it and why was he speaking to me in riddles? Any other son, I think, would have asked his father these questions, but I couldn't bring myself to. All I saw was an opportunity to reject him, to take strength from his weakness and to throw his love back in his face. I wouldn't feel pity for him. I wouldn't have him turning my view of him round on a whim like this. He was going to have to work a lot harder than that. 'I should be getting back,' I said. 'I've got work to do.'

He looked up at me and I ignored the sadness in his eyes, my face already set like stone.

Three years ago I became addicted to an intricate and violent computer game called Quake. It was a shoot 'em up, and Eddie and I would spend hours battling it out with each other in the flat, or pooling our resources against other combatants on-line. Whenever I paused or actually quit the game, I'd find myself suffering immediate pangs of withdrawal over the beautifully designed virtual world I'd just abandoned. My real environment would appear lacklustre and monochrome in comparison, and all I'd want to do was to slip straight back on-line again.

It's the same with Mickey now: one fix leaves me craving another. The low-level angst, melancholy and depression that invariably accompanied my first few slices of Quake cold turkey are all present and correct here today. (Hence my leaning up against the empty and unused filing cabinet in my office, staring out of the window, like some lovesick Fifties teenager slumped up against a Wurlitzer.) So, too, are the retinal flashes I used to suffer – only this time they feature snapshots and memories of a childhood spent in Rushton during the last century, rather than (thankfully) virtual machine-guns carving virtual enemies in half.

I feel so relaxed with Mickey, so . . . *accepted* for who I really am. It's like having all the pressure of the last fifteen years since Miles's death lifted from me. It's like dropping my mask and smiling with my own mouth for the first time. Mickey was there. She knows how it was. She sees me warts and all and she doesn't judge me for it. And if she can do that – if *I* can be that way with her – where does that leave Rebecca and Eddie and everyone else? Do we really know each other at all?

Behind me, my laptop belches – one of Susan's little innovations which signals that my lunch hour is over and it's time to hit the grindstone once more. With a deep sigh, I peel myself off the filing cabinet and walk back to my desk and sit down. I wipe my hand across my forehead and, staring at the glaze of sweat on my palm, curse the air-conditioning company and global warming in general for what must be the fiftieth time today. Then my laptop barks at me and starts to pant (another of Susan's gimmicks), and I click on to check my mail:

`Hey, there, Mr Romantic-Faraway-Look-In-His-Eyes. Dreaming about your wedding day?`

Twisting in my chair, I peer through the gap on the glass front of my office, between the flashy silver and red graphics of a couple of newsasitbreaks.com posters left over from last year's Tech Spin trade fair.

Sure enough, across the open-plan desks of the perpetually animated sales team, Susan is staring back at me from her own glass pen, smiling while fanning her face with a fluorescent orange flip-flop. I shake my head at her in reply and she holds eye contact with me as she touch-types a further communication. My screen barks once more and I read:

Rebecca?

Again, I look round at Susan and again I shake my head. Another text message pops into my inbox:

Well, I certainly hope it's no one else . . .

Without thinking – about Rebecca, about the wedding, about the sheer bloody *consequences* of this kind of banter – I rattle back:

It is . . .

It takes roughly the length of a blink between the moment I hit SEND and my reply reaching Susan's screen. And it takes me roughly the same amount of time to realise quite how public I've just allowed the confusion within me to become.

My attempt to ascertain Susan's reaction is frustrated by one of the sales team, Jim, who's now up on his feet and pitching between us, phone clamped between his shoulder and jaw, waving his arms around like he's guiding a chopper on to an oil rig during a tempest.

My frustration, though, is temporary; Susan's back to me within seconds:

For real?

The forefinger of my right hand gets as far as the Y of my intended YES, when my fingers freeze above the keyboard.

I *can't* tell Susan – even though the urge to set free the mess of emotions inside me and confide in someone is so strong. Actually speaking about my feelings, I know will start some terrible ball rolling down a steep, steep slope, gathering up all before it and changing the appearance of my world for ever. I mean, that's how it happens, isn't it? It's like when you're a kid. You confide in someone about something and they tell someone else, and the next thing you realise everybody knows what you've said and you have to stand by it. It's no longer a possibility you're simply mulling over in your mind but an intent upon which you're suddenly expected to act.

And I can't act, can I? I can't see Mickey again, not without telling Rebecca about her first. Mickey was insistent about it. No flakiness, she said. But how can I introduce Mickey to Rebecca as a friend when there's still a risk that Mickey might let something slip about Miles, and when . . . when the truth of it is that yesterday, sitting up there on the roof terrace with her, I was thinking about her as much more than that?

Reaching out for the keyboard once more, I delete the Y I've already typed and settle, instead, for:

Forget about it.

Susan's back at me in a flash:

OK, but if you ever want to talk, you know where to find me.

I type her OK and glance over at the bacon and avocado sandwich I picked up at lunchtime, still in its plastic triangle on the windowsill. I know I should probably eat something, but my appetite's shot to bits and, instead, I grab my can of Diet Coke and take a swig.

I gaze around my office, at the squared-off polystyrene ceiling, the Velcro dartboard on the wall, the bright white target chart with its magnetic red and black flags (fallout from some strictly analogue management guru drafted in by Personnel last year). Then, so distracted and simultaneously buzzed am I by what I nearly let slip to Susan that I do what I've been avoiding doing all morning: I survey my desk.

I like to think of myself as a 'paperless office' kind of a person, but the evidence before me is way off. Normally, my work is as portable as my laptop and phone, but today, today I have something the size of the *Sunday Times* print run on my desk. To the right of my laptop is a stack of sponsorship initiatives and their correlating content suggestions that Susan's been working on with Graham and that now need wheat-chaffing by me. There are also some queried invoices from the Brick Lane launch that Accounts want clarifyed. None of this, though, is what's bothering me.

No, it's the significantly larger pile of paperwork to the left of my laptop that's responsible for my uncharacteristic recalcitrance in relation to my desk. Rising up from the Wonder Woman mouse mat that forms its foundations (part of Michael's Thanksgiving jollity towards his British team), it teeters perilously out across the edge of the desk like a condemned factory chimney. I try to look away, but it's no use: the same as with a particularly nasty horror film at a particularly nasty juncture, it has me hooked.

There it stands: the Wedding: To Do pile.

The worrying thing is that I can't bring myself to connect to what any of this means, let alone do anything about it. And it frightens me. I'm getting married in just over two weeks' time. I should be excited and nervous, but I'm not. I'm detached and distant from the whole event. My certainty has vanished and there doesn't seem to be a thing I can do about it.

Instead, all I can do is picture myself at the altar of Shotbury church before Rebecca arrives on our wedding day, turning round and surveying the people in the pews behind me, searching, ever searching for the one face I want to see, but the one face that I know isn't and can't be there.

Love. What's that? What I have with Rebecca? What I *thought* I had with Rebecca? What I *think* I can have with Mickey once more? I haven't been head-over-heels in love with anyone since I was a teenager. Perhaps head-over-heels in love is an option *only* available to teenagers, and other people who are fortunate enough never to have had their hearts broken and hardened. Perhaps I'm crazy wanting more than I already have.

*

171

'Honestly, these people don't half get on my tits,' Rebecca observes. 'Three bed with garden. That's what I told them. Not one bed with conservatory, or three bed with balcony. It can't be that difficult, can it? And the rot they come out with. The market's this, the market's that. What do they know about markets and marketing? I've done more marketing diplomas than they've had hot dinners, or kebabs – or whatever it is that that they shovel into their sweaty bellies. And do you know what else, Fred? Fred?'

'Wuh?' The road ahead comes sharply into focus and I turn to Rebecca, who's in the driving seat next to me.

'Fred, are you listening?'

The last thing I remember is getting into the car after a disappointing viewing of a cramped basement flat over on Carlton Vale. 'What?'

'Are you –'

'Sure,' I say, fumbling around in my memory for Rebecca's last words and hazarding a wild guess: 'Shovelling stuff into Betty's wellies, right?'

Rebecca rolls her eyes at me, muttering, 'Estate agents, darling. I was talking about estate agents,' before turning her attention back to the road.

The blood-red cherry of her lips suddenly shrinks as she sticks her foot down on the accelerator, slams her palm on to the horn and swerves to the left. The car horn blares long and loud, and I drop my shades and stare up out of Rebecca's convertible at the wide blue sky.

'Up yours, Grandpa,' Rebecca shouts through the open window at an angry-looking man in a rusty old Mini Metro that she's just cut up. 'Now, then,' she continues, winking at me and pushing back a rogue auburn curl from her forehead, 'who's next?'

'Next?'

'On the list.'

I look down at the folder marked SATURDAY on my lap.

SUNDAY, along with folders equating to several other blocked-out days before our wedding, are back at Rebecca's flat, which we left at just gone eight this morning, 'To give us a jump on everyone else and a good ten hours in which to get stuff done'.

'Which list?' I ask, because the SATURDAY folder contains several of them, each neatly typed up and colour-coded by Rebecca's assistant, Paul.

'Let's stick with estate agents for now,' Rebecca says. 'We can move on to travel agents after lunch.' She reaches across and squeezes my thigh, all peace and love once more, taking her eyes off the road for a second and flashing me a smile. 'Had any more thoughts on where you'd like to take me?' she asks.

Rather meanly, the answer 'Siberian salt mine' pops into my head, but I fail to voice it. Failing to voice a variety of things has been my saving grace this morning. I've failed to voice my increasing discomfort at flat-hunting when my own flat still suits me just fine. And I've failed to voice my concern over my inability to look Rebecca in the eye whenever she mentions anything to do with the wedding. And, of course, I've failed yet again to mention Mickey. My silence on these matters has, I think, saved me from being physically ejected from Rebecca's Saab and simultaneously dumped and reversed over – a fate which, admittedly, I might well deserve.

'Well,' I answer, stalling for time as we pull to a halt at some lights. The truth is that, seeing as neither of us can get time off from work immediately after the wedding, I haven't given the matter of booking a honeymoon much thought. 'I was thinking that maybe –'

'Virgins,' Rebecca interrupts.

Confused, I check out the pavements on either side of us, but the only people I see are a woman pushing a pram and a couple of men in paint-spattered overalls standing outside a café. 'Where?' I ask.

173

'The British Virgin Islands,' Rebecca elaborates. 'Eddie says the American ones are overdeveloped, and –'

'Eddie?' I ask, surprised by this unlikely source of honeymoon information.

The lights change and Rebecca guns the engine and we accelerate down the twenty yards of clear road ahead, before screeching to a halt at the tail end of another traffic jam. The acrid stench of burning rubber fills the air.

'He was telling me in Hyde Park that he sailed all round there when he was crewing that yacht when he left school and that it's totally gorgeous.' Rebecca glances across at me. 'I mean, totally.'

'Sounds great,' I say.

Looking forward again, she sharply taps my knee. 'List,' she reminds me.

I open the SATURDAY folder and pull out the estate agents sheet, scanning down over the ones we've already visited. (Rebecca: 'Phoning up's a waste of time. You've got to get in there and show some face. It's like everything in life: you've got to prove you want it.') Well, we've proved our want in no less than twelve agencies so far, covering most of Maida Vale, and now we're branching out into my neck of the woods around Queen's Park.

I read off the one at the top of the list, 'James Peters Limited', and give Rebecca the address and, the moment I do this, an alarm bell starts to shrill at the back of my mind and it doesn't take me long to work out why. 'Maybe we should give that one a miss,' I say.

'Why?'

'I don't know,' I fumble, trying to sound casual. 'I've walked past it before. It looks a bit shoddy.'

'They might have lower commission rates, in that case,' she counters. 'Anyway, we're going to be driving right past them, so we might as well stop. Look,' she adds before I can raise any further objections, pointing up ahead, 'that's it there.'

The strictly early-Eighties paintwork of an estate agency – spookily reminiscent of a red and grey duvet cover I once possessed in my early teens – draws closer and closer by the second, as do the peeling fly posters on the window of the disused corner shop two doors along. Neither of these grabs my attention, though. That's reserved for the shop sandwiched between these two, the tasteful yet eye-catching sign of which I'm now fixated upon, as it slowly yet inexorably comes into focus, silver letter by silver letter.

'Perfect!' Rebecca chimes.

The indicator of Rebecca's Saab tick-tacks on and off as we wait for the Volvo estate in front of us to pull away from the kerb. Desolate, I glare up at the heavens, before lowering my gaze earthwards once more to the sign reading MICKEY'S FLOWERS, less than five yards away.

Beaming at me, Rebecca smoothly steers the Saab into the parking space that the Volvo's just vacated. My return smile is weak and wobbly, a nigh on perfect approximation of how I feel. But then, as my peripheral vision makes me suddenly aware of movement in the doorway of Mickey's shop, I stop smiling altogether. Feeling sick, I hunker down in the car seat, folding my legs as far down beneath me as they'll go.

'What a sweet little shop,' Rebecca says, switching off the engine, unfastening her seat belt and perching her shades like an Alice band on the top of her head.

'Yeah,' I grunt non-committally, staring resolutely ahead, wondering if I can risk a quick peep through Mickey's window to ascertain precisely how much peril I'm in.

But no sooner do I try, than I discover that I can't. Mickey Maloney's there all right, standing a couple of yards back in the open doorway, with her hair tied up with a red polka-dot handkerchief, talking to a tall man who's holding a giant plastic-wrapped bouquet. I watch as he steps to one side, temporarily blocking Mickey from my view.

'Do we really need to do this today?' I try. 'I mean, haven't we got enough on our plate at the moment without getting involved with estate agents?'

She pouts. 'It's not my fault my flat went so quickly,' she chastises me. It's true. The agent's sign only went up on her flat a couple of days ago and she's had two offers for the asking price already. 'Now stop being so grumpy,' she continues. 'The sooner we start, the sooner it'll be over.'

'Come on,' I say to Rebecca, hurriedly unfolding myself and getting out of the car.

For the first time today, Rebecca appears to be slowing down. She checks her face in the rear-view mirror and then waits for a lorry to pass, before leisurely getting out herself and walking round the front of the car to join me.

I nod encouragingly at the doorway to James Peters Limited. 'Let's get in there and show them some face,' I remind her with an enthusiastic smile. 'Show them that we want it . . .'

In the time it takes Rebecca to smooth down the sides of her rib-hugging pink top and black moleskin micro skirt, the human genome is mapped from start to finish. 'Why's that woman staring at us?' she then asks.

'What woman?' I reply, suddenly finding myself absolutely fascinated by a loose piece of thread on the pocket of my jeans.

'The flower girl.'

I stare up the street and start to walk that way, too. 'What flower girl?'

Rebecca places a hand on my shoulder, forcing me to a stop. 'Not there,' she says. 'Here. Behind you.'

'No idea,' I reply without looking. 'Anyway, we'd better be –'

'She's waving at us.'

'She is?' I ask.

'Yes,' Rebecca tells me.

'Oh.'

'And walking towards us,' Rebecca adds.

'Ah.'

'And reaching out to tap you on the shoulder.'

'I see.'

As I feel Mickey's finger on my shoulder and hear her voice gently enquiring 'Fred?' from behind me, I turn slowly to face her.

Even since yesterday morning, when we sat on my roof and sipped our coffee, she's caught the sun and tiny freckles now pattern her cheeks, and I want nothing more than to reach out and brush my fingers across them. It makes me sad, knowing that these changes only seem big to me because I haven't been there to see them happening. I find myself staring at her lips, remembering kissing her in the snow that Christmas, so long ago. 'Mickey,' I say, my voice coming over hopelessly inadequate. 'Fancy seeing you here.'

She looks at me curiously. 'Er, yeah,' she says, half smiling. 'Right outside my shop . . . fancy that.'

I hear Rebecca clearing her throat by my side and I find myself nodding my head and grinning at Mickey inanely. I can't think what to say. What *do* you say in circumstances like these? All I know is how I feel: crass, shallow and treacherous, as if by not acknowledging Mickey as I truly see her I'm rewinding time, erasing everything that's happened between us since we met up that evening in ToyZone. Rebecca clears her throat again, but I can't stop looking at Mickey, bewitched as I am by actually being here with her again.

'And . . . are . . . you . . . well?' I ask.

Mickey's still trying to read my face. 'Yes,' she replies, bemused, no doubt, by my formality, 'and yourself?'

Beside me, Rebecca practically launches herself into a coughing fit and I finally turn to face her. 'This is . . .

Mickey,' I tell her. 'She's an old friend. We grew up together.'

Rebecca gives Mickey the once-over. 'That would explain it, then.'

'Explain what?' Mickey asks.

'Why Fred's never mentioned you before . . . He's always been a bit of a dark horse when it comes to his past . . .'

Mickey cocks her head to one side and briefly, almost imperceptibly, looks up into my eyes. But then, before I can shake my head, or mouth her 'Sorry', or in any other way communicate quite how bad I feel, she's smiling pleasantly back at Rebecca. 'Well, he's certainly told me all about you,' Mickey says, wiping her hand on her trousers. 'Rebecca, isn't it?'

'Yes.' Rebecca seems slightly surprised by this information, no doubt having just calculated that for Mickey to know her name I must have seen her more recently than childhood.

I take a deep breath, deciding here and now to try and make it up to Mickey on the flakiness front by filling Rebecca in on what's been going on. It's going to come out anyway and I'd rather it came from me. That way, at least, I'll have completed my bargain with Mickey. And, perversely, this suddenly seems much more important than whatever suspicions it might raise in Rebecca's mind. 'We bumped into each other in ToyZone a few weeks ago,' I begin, 'and then I thought it would be a nice idea, what with the games channel launch coming up, if –'

But that's as far as I get with the recent history of my friendship with Mickey. Rebecca's not listening; she's speaking instead. 'ToyZone,' she says to Mickey. 'Don't tell me you're a computer games nerd as well?'

'Er, no,' Mickey explains. 'I was buying a present for Joe, actually.'

'Joe?'

'My son.'

Rebecca merely nods her head at this information, but her whole demeanour seems to shift. She smiles properly at Mickey for the first time, the killer smile, the one I remember from the night I first met her. Everything else about her relaxes too, from her shoulders right on down to her crossed arms, one of which she now hooks proprietarily round my waist.

I watch Rebecca looking Mickey up and down, and I wonder what it is she sees that makes her so at ease. A flower girl, an unimportant Eliza Doolittle, shorter than her and worse dressed? Someone who works with her hands for a living? Someone who's pretty, but really doesn't know the first thing about make-up and fashion? She sees all these things, perhaps, but above them all, I think, she sees a mother, someone who's nothing like Rebecca and therefore, by definition, of no interest to me.

Just then, Joe comes hurtling round the corner on a skateboard, closely followed by the boy he met at the games channel launch. They're both dressed in Blue Room baggies and, in spite of the heat of the day, woollen hats. The other boy whips past and clatters on up the street.

'Wotcha, Mum,' Joe says, jumping off his board by Mickey's feet and flipping it up so that it rests against his leg.

'You must be Joe,' Rebecca says, giving it the big grin again.

Joe nods at her, unconvinced, staring at where her hip is pressed up against mine.

'And how old are you, then?' Rebecca asks.

Joe screws up his face and scrutinises hers. 'Forty-seven,' he finally says. 'I'm a dwarf. Didn't Mum tell you?' He then smiles shyly at me. 'Hi, Fred,' he says. 'How ya doing?'

'Good,' I tell him, stifling a chuckle and unfastening Rebecca's hand from my waist as I step forward. 'You?'

179

'All right,' he says with a laid-back shrug.

'Got anything good lined up?' I ask.

He shakes his head. 'Nah.' Then he changes his mind. 'We're going over to Granny and Grandpa's house next Saturday,' he confides. 'In Rushton. Mum says you used to live there . . .'

'I did. A long time ago.' I risk a quick glance at Mickey, but she's staring down at Joe. 'I've got great memories of it.'

Joe tucks his fringe contemplatively under his hat. 'Mum said you moved away when you were a teenager,' he says, looking at me sidelong. 'You ever been back?'

'No,' I say, looking at him sadly.

He nods in understanding. 'Why don't you come with us, then?' he suggests. 'Granny and Grandpa are going to be away, and we could –'

'Joe!' Mickey puts her arm over his shoulder and gives him a squeeze. She's blushing. 'Sorry,' she apologises to Rebecca. 'He gets a little carried away sometimes.'

Joe's eyes flash with embarrassment. He bows his head moodily, spinning the bottom wheel of his board around with his foot. 'I was only saying . . .' he mumbles.

'I'd love to,' I intervene, trying to smooth the situation over. 'And under any other circumstances I would. But I can't right now . . .'

'Why not?' he asks, staring up at me.

'Because . . .' I begin, before trailing off. 'I can't because I'm getting married in two weeks' time,' I eventually say.

Joe's eyes dart to Rebecca, then back. 'To her?' he asks.

'Yes,' I tell him, 'to Rebecca.'

Joe pulls free from Mickey and drops his board to the pavement, speeding off up the street towards his waiting friend without looking back.

Mickey stares after him, dumbstruck. 'I'm so sorry,' she starts to say. 'He's . . .'

'Forget about it,' I tell her.

180

Rebecca checks her watch meaningfully and smiles at Mickey. 'He's really sweet,' she says and extends her arm. 'Nice meeting you,' she continues as they shake hands. 'But we'd better get going now, hadn't we, Fred?' she adds.

My eyes lock with Mickey's. Her whole face is a question, but I have no answer for her, not with Rebecca here at my side. I lean forward and kiss her lightly on the cheek. Her hair smells of flowers. 'Goodbye,' I tell her, pulling back.

'Goodbye,' she says and there's an instant, as her eyes search my face, when I find myself daring to hope that the word is as difficult for her to say as it is for me to hear.

On Sunday morning I pick up my mother from King's Cross Station and drive her over to Rebecca's flat for lunch. Rebecca's parents are there as well and the occasion is something of a meet and greet, as their only previous contact has consisted of a single conversation on the telephone following the announcement of our engagement. Mum keeps herself to herself in Scotland. This trip to London is the result of months of persuasion.

George, as expected, is the outward personification of charm and good humour throughout the meal, but deep down, I suspect that both he and Mary find Mum a little too puritanical for their taste. That's certainly how she presents herself: a drab and dour Scottish matron, so different from how I remember her from when I was a small child. What little conversation she makes revolves around polite enquiries about Shotbury church and the form the religious service is to take.

When she kisses me goodbye on the railway platform the following morning the relief on her face is impossible to miss; she's glad she's going home. 'She's a lovely girl,' she tells me. 'Look after her. Build your world around her. That's what I've done with Alan.'

'Mum . . .' But my words run out. I want to be able to tell her all the doubts that are assailing me. I want her to be my mother again and make everything simple for me, to explain the world to me and show me where and how I fit into it. I don't want this isolation any more. 'Say hi to Alan,' is all I can manage before the guard blows his whistle and Mum climbs aboard.

As she waves goodbye, I think I see tears in her eyes, but then she's gone and I'm no longer sure. I walk away, wondering if sometimes she sees Miles in me and whether it's this that keeps us so much further apart than the hundreds of miles between our homes.

The next few days are packed with so many distractions that I barely have a moment's contemplation to myself. It's like my feet are staple-gunned to a wedding day conveyor belt and nothing, but nothing is going to stop me from getting there.

Thursday evening arrives and I drive with Eddie out past Kingston-on-Thames, to a pub called the Rose and Thorn, arriving around seven thirty. It's a tawdry little place with 'olde worlde' county inn pretensions, in spite of the fact that the high-rise tower blocks of London's sprawling suburbia lie only a half-mile down the road.

Inside, English Civil War helmets, reproduction muskets and other antique market paraphernalia clutter the ornamental wooden ceiling rafters. A couple of locals are perched at the bar and against the wall a jukebox regurgitates soft rock anthems at a volume so low that it wouldn't disturb a baby. We're not here for the atmosphere, though, but because this is where my stag weekend begins.

I say weekend, but thankfully (owing to adverse boat-booking conditions encountered by Eddie), it's only set to last until Saturday. I say thankfully because, quite frankly, I'm not really in the mood for it at all. It soon becomes apparent that I'm the only one who feels this way, though.

As the other members of our party (nine in all) arrive over the next hour or so, the pace of the drinking quickens and soon enough my gloomy mood dissipates, browbeaten into remission by the general high spirits. I play pool with Andrew and John, two of my old house mates from Manchester University, and I have a long chat with Will, the only person I'm still in touch with from Kemble's, the sixth-form college I ended up in after Mum moved us to Scotland.

At nine thirty we grab our bags and follow Eddie round to the back of the pub. Here, several narrow boats are moored on a couple of rickety pontoons against the Thames river bank. We climb aboard *Naseby*, our temporary home for the next two nights, and the evening slides into a drunken fog.

I continue to use alcohol as an anaesthetic the next day, as we head haphazardly down the Thames, stopping off at riverside pubs on the way, throwing each other overboard, sunbathing on the deck and generally forgetting about everything in the world apart from what is here and what is now. By nightfall, however, when we're moored up outside our fourth pub of the day and we've just finished eating, the anaesthetic has worn off. It's like I've drunk myself sober and, even among my friends, I feel terribly alone.

Leaving the others below in the cabin, I make my way up on to the deck and forward to the prow of the boat. Once there, I sit down with my legs dangling over the side and light a cigarette that I surreptitiously lifted from Eddie's pack earlier. In spite of the amount of alcohol I've consumed, I'm still aware of the nicotine kicking in. My lungs suck it up into my bloodstream like water into a desiccated sponge and, for the first time this week, the tension drops from my shoulders and in that moment – as soon as my guard is dropped – I pine, like a homesick child, knowing that I don't belong here any more and that everything has changed.

I stare down at the starry sky, reflected in the calm black water. The river looks bottomless from here, like if you fell in you'd just keep on falling, flailing through the darkness, spinning further and further away from the light and air above. I picture Miles. It's impossible not to whenever the thought of death crosses my mind. Was that what it was like for him? I wonder. Did he know it was final, the moment it happened? Did he experience the same combination of powerlessness and hopelessness that filled my heart when he left me behind?

What would he make of all this now? Of Mickey? And me? And the way I feel? 'She's a beautiful girl,' he said. I can see him now, there in that pub, smiling before asking me, 'Are you in love with her?' I swallow, biting down on my lip, trying not to think about him. But it's no good. I can't help wishing now that I'd answered him, that I could have let him a little into my life before he left it for good. He would have been pleased, I think. In spite of the way things got between him and Mum, he still would have wanted me to be happy, wouldn't he?

'Why aren't you here?' I whisper, my voice rough and my throat dry. 'Why couldn't you be here to tell me yourself?'

A solitary tear runs down my cheek. I lift my beer bottle and drink, before taking another drag on my cigarette. I won't cry. I won't cry for him after all this time. It doesn't matter what he would have thought, I tell myself. He's dead. That's all that matters. Everything I think I know about him is meaningless. It's make-believe. He doesn't even exist.

I hear the sound of footsteps on the deck behind me and turn to see Eddie swaying towards me, camera still in hand. 'Naughty boy,' he chastises, nodding at my cigarette, before sitting down next to me.

'Turn it off.'

He doesn't. Instead, he asks, 'Why?'

'Because you can't live life like that,' I tell him, 'in front of a camera . . . like an actor. Because it doesn't work.'

He relents and switches off the camera. 'Are you all right?' he asks.

'Yes,' I reply, but automatically I find I'm justifying myself, covering up what's inside like I always do: 'I'm just feeling a little maudlin, that's all. It's probably the booze.'

'Nervous about next weekend?'

'Something like that.'

'Big change, huh?'

I nod my head.

'It's what it's all about,' he says. 'No point in standing still too long, you just get bored.'

'I suppose so.'

'Beautiful here, isn't it?' Eddie comments, lying on his back and gazing up. 'You don't get skies like this in London. Too many lights. You need to get away from electricity altogether to appreciate this.'

'Thanks', I tell him, 'for organising everything.'

'Have you enjoyed yourself?'

'Yes.'

'Good, because . . .'

'Because what?' I ask when he fails to continue.

'I don't know.' He trails off again, no doubt taking some time out to organise his stoned thoughts. 'It's hard,' he eventually says. 'Sometimes it's hard being a friend to someone. Sometimes it's hard to get it right.'

'What do you mean?' I ask, flicking the cigarette into the river and watching the stars shimmer and blur.

'So long as you had a good time, that's all . . .'

'I did. What about tomorrow?' I enquire, turning to him. His face is dark with shadow. 'What time do you think we'll get back?'

'Around lunchtime. Why?'

'No reason,' I say, standing up. 'Come on. Let's go and check in with the others.'

As we walk back to the cockpit and cabin entrance, I think of my car, parked outside the Rose and Thorn back in Kingston, and about getting into it, and I think, too, about the many directions in which I can drive.

Chapter VI

Mickey

Of course, I should've known that she was going to be beautiful. It was obvious that Fred was bound to marry someone as fashionable and obviously successful as himself, but somehow I'd managed to block it out. I'd taken the one bit of information I had about Rebecca and invented the least threatening vision of her I could. So when Susan said that Fred's business events weren't 'Gucci enough' for Rebecca, I took it to mean that she was some lifeless, limp-haired snob, only good for designer shoe shopping and rustling up the odd gourmet canapé. And when I found out that she never stayed at Fred's flat she'd become even more disembodied. I'd assumed that she was tucked away in some Chelsea pad, slipping into the background, being submissive and dull, while Fred shone. I'd even gone as far as allowing myself to believe that she'd inveigled herself into Fred's affections until he'd been bamboozled into proposing.

What I hadn't considered was that she'd be real. Not only real, but beautiful, street-wise, ultra-trendy, sexy, intelligent and, worst of all, that she and Fred would look so good together. And it's their togetherness that sticks in my throat. I've spent all this time seeing the past existing in Fred, so that seeing him existing in the present feels like a slap round the face. Because Rebecca is nice; so nice, in fact, that she's the kind of person that maybe, in a different lifetime, with a whole new wardrobe of clothes, a complete hair, make-up and CD collection make-over, I could be friends with. And I feel hopelessly foolish – foolish because I didn't ask Fred enough questions about her, foolish because he should have told me he was engaged to an absolutely stunning woman and foolish because it matters.

These thoughts have been consuming me ever since I saw her outside my shop a week ago, but this morning, for the sake of my own sanity and for the sake of Joe, who's been bearing the brunt of my bad mood, I'm trying very hard to remove Rebecca, or more specifically Rebecca and Fred, from my head. As Joe and I drive over to my parents' house in Rushton, I reason that the only sensible thing is to let Fred go. I need to sever the loose strands that tie us together, rather than weave more. Fred has his own life and I have mine. To think that the two overlap in any way is nonsense.

I've been so busy setting up the shop that I haven't been back to Rushton for almost six months. Each time I come back, I notice that still more of the rolling hills, streams and woods that the school bus used to rumble past have been chewed up. This time I spot a sprawling business estate, full of low-level breeze-block buildings that seem eerily deserted. As I take the old route, I find myself on a pristine new bypass, punctuated by so many roundabouts that I feel like I'm driving on a board game. I'm in for a bigger shock as I make my way into the village itself. The Gordon Arms has been taken over by a pub-restaurant chain and a plastic banner advertising Sunday Lunch for £4.99 flaps over the doorway, while the Memorial Hall car park has been turned into an adventure playground complete with a sagging bouncy castle.

That's not all. At the bottom of Hill Drive there's a large hoarding with a watercolour-effect artist's impression of a cul-de-sac full of mock Tudor houses, complete with latticed windows, cobbled driveways and a frisky-looking terrier. The blurb advertises 'desirable secluded family cottages in the heart of the countryside'. It appears that

Jimmy Dughead has sold out to property developers and the 'desirable cottages' have swallowed the very fields that made up the countryside round here. Sure enough, up the road from our house in the entrance to the farm, there are huge tyre tracks imprinted in the spill of sand on the road and an abandoned JCB stands where the gate used to be.

The spare keys to my parents' house are under the back doormat, where they've been since I was a teenager. I've often told Mum to devise a more ingenious hiding place, but she's always insisted that she knows everyone around here, so security isn't an issue. Not for much longer, by the looks of things. I glance up from the back doorstep, across the small rectangle of lawn, past the whirligig with its limp plastic bag full of pegs, to the trees at the bottom of our garden. In the field beyond, the imposing timber frames of the new houses creep like skeletons over the skyline.

Inside, the house smells of my parents: a curious, dusty mixture of pot pourri, brewing tea and hairspray. It's strange being here without them, as if the house is infused with the low-frequency sound of them, like a familiar radio station turned down low. I push the switch by the kitchen door and the long fluorescent lighting strip hanging from the ceiling buzzes, then flickers several times before lighting up.

There's a note from Mum on the flowery plastic table-cloth, directing us to a pie that she's left in the fridge for lunch. Joe and I glance at each other. My mother's never been famous for her culinary skills and intrepidly Joe opens the fridge and pulls out a glass dish with a sunken slab of overcooked brown pastry on top. He looks under the dish to ascertain its contents. 'Corned beef,' he says and I turn up my nose in unison with him. 'Yuk.'

'There's eggs. I'll make an omelette or something,' I suggest, gesturing to the basket-effect china dish on the side.

189

Joe passes it over, a disdainful look on his face. 'They look funny,' he says, picking up one of the eggs. 'This one's got poo on it.'

'That's because they're from the farm down the road,' I tut. 'They're free-range.'

'I don't want any,' he says. 'There's no sell-by date on them.'

'Joe, they won't kill you.' I laugh. 'Where do you think eggs come from?'

'The supermarket,' he replies, bending down to stroke Oscar, the cat, who mews around his legs.

I decide to deal with the cat first, since that's the reason we're here. There's a small utility room off the kitchen with a door into the garage. An ancient washing machine takes up most of the space, along with a concertina peg rack stuffed full of coats. On top of the slatted pine unit there's a row of jars filled with murky pickled objects and plastic buckets full of muddy potatoes and marrows from Dad's allotment. There's also a pile of old Sunday papers and a few ancient gardening manuals. Oscar weaves in and out of the clutter, nudging my hand as I open a tin of cat food, hardly giving me time to get the globular brown chunks out into his bowl. I tickle him, trying to push him out of the way, but he still manages to knock the fork out of my hand and I curse, crouching down to pick up it up, which is when I see a mark with the word '*Scott*' written next to it.

Under the coats by the door leading to the garage, the wall is covered in a haphazard ruler with faded felt-tip marks, recording the various stages of our growth as children. Forgetting Oscar, who has tipped the can on to its side and is scooping out the food with his paw, I put my finger to the wall. Low down is a mark, with '*Mickey, 6*', and an inch below it, '*Fred, 5¾*', written in green ink. I trace our growth pattern up the wall, past the garage door handle, until Fred overtakes me at the age of twelve. Smiling, I rest my hand on the wall, feeling the space where he used to be. Since I found out that Fred changed his surname I've been feeling as if our childhood was like a pencil drawing defaced by a grubby eraser, but seeing these marks brings it all back into focus again and makes it real.

I glance through the doorway at Joe who's doing up his rollerblades and it hits me that my own mother once took the time to record our heights. It seems so strange to think about it, when she always appeared to dislike children. But then I only think that because I know I was never her favourite child. That privilege was reserved for Scott who, with his surly detachment from the family, always had my mother clamouring for his attention. It's not really surprising that he ended up as an airline pilot and spends his life as far away as possible.

When it came to me, though, I think Mum realised pretty early on that she'd been cruelly short-changed on her tutu-wearing, peaches-and-cream little girl fantasy and instead got a gobby, grubby tomboy, who always took her father's side. And while I think she's proud of me now, it still doesn't change the fact that I've spent most of my adult years deliberately trying to be the opposite of her. Up until now I've always resented this house and everything it stands for, yet I suddenly feel happy that my parents still live here and that this wall still bears the scars of my passage through time.

Joe seems to have a sixth sense and looks up to find me grinning. 'What?' he asks.

'Nothing. I just found something, that's all.'

He does a wobbly comedy walk towards me, as he only has one of his rollerblades on, and I show him the marks on the wall. 'Am I taller than Fred was?' he asks, looking at Fred's height when he was nine.

'I don't know. Let's see.'

I clear the coats out of the way and Joe stands with his back flat against the wall.

'Uh-huh.' I grin. 'That's cheating. You have to take your rollerblades off.'

Joe obliges, kicking off his boot. I put the gardening manual on top of his head and hold it against the wall, and he ducks out from under it. 'I'm shorter,' he says, disappointed.

'You should eat some eggs.' I laugh. 'Then you'll grow.'

Right through my childhood I assumed that the whole purpose of religious holidays was to make it OK to eat a lot. Oblivious to any significance, I happily tucked into pancakes, hot cross buns, turkey with all the trimmings and harvest bread with extra butter as appropriate. It wasn't until it dawned on me, some time during a Religious Studies exam in 1984, that Easter had a religious purpose (and wasn't just a race to see who could consume the most chocolate), that I decided to ask my parents about their own beliefs. They skilfully batted away my enquiries.

The issue of religion was treated with equal measures of superstition and suspicion in our household. That was until I fell pregnant and then, all of a sudden all hell broke loose. But until that fateful day, when I was made to feel like the original sinner, both parents had maintained a pursed-lipped pact of silence on all moral issues. Instinctively, I knew that below it was a seething torrent of resentment on both sides.

This was probably due to the fact that, previous to my existence, there'd been a humdinger of a barney between the Irish Catholic Maloney side of the family and the Richie grandparents, who'd laid out their stall with their daughter's intended by declaring that the Pope was Satan, all priests were child molesters and the only thing fit for Ireland was a bomb. The Maloneys had retaliated by informing the Richies (in public) that they were *common*, a gasp-inducing accusation that, while probably true, set

Mum on a firm course of compensatory snobbism for the rest of her married life.

In order to spite Dad and his so-called highbrow roots, the new Mrs Maloney set about borrowing certain religious scare-mongering tactics from her mother, mad Grandma Richie who, since Grandpa Richie got squashed by a bus, resided with a vicious bull-terrier in a pebble-dashed bungalow in Dartford. Like Grandma Richie, Mum used to ban pocket money if we used the Lord's name in vain: oh God, bloody, hell, damn or any combination of the above, were particular no-nos although, weirdly, Jesus Christ as an expletive somehow slipped through her censorious net. She also crossed herself any time she bumped into anyone Jewish, Muslim or Baptist, but claimed to admire the Mormons – not that there were any in Rushton. In addition, she tried and failed every year to give up cigarettes for Lent and became positively sniffy if anyone attempted to buy condoms from the chemist in Bowley, where she worked three days a week.

This idiosyncratically Catholic attitude to birth control was probably responsible for her two self-confessed 'mistakes': Scott, me. It remains a constant source of amazement that my mum and dad actually had sex – twice. How ever Marie Richie, she of the brassy beehive with just-so rhinestone shoes and a handbag to match, hooked up with painfully shy Geoffrey Maloney, second-generation Irish boy, was a mystery. They were married in Hemel Hempstead and honeymooned near my paternal ancestral territory in Derry. The story goes that Dad fished every day in the tranquil waters of the nearby lake, while Mum sat hunched up in his old Ford car in a fake fur coat and cried her heart out for the glamorous life that would never be hers.

Eighteen months later, when Scott was born, the young Mr and Mrs Maloney moved here, to Hill Drive, and set about decorating in various shades of purple and orange.

Even as newly-weds they disagreed on more or less everything, but Mum, with her ability to turn on the tears like a skilled movie diva, mostly got her own way. For this she regarded Dad as something of a drip and said so, pretty constantly, until the rare occasions when he would snap and disappear to his allotment for hours. When that happened she patted her latest hairdo, squeezed her brightly coloured lips together and uttered, in her best hard-done-by tone, 'Just look at that, children. Underneath it all, your father is a cruel, cruel man.'

Yet this was another of her dramatic fantasies, fed by years of secret soap opera addiction. She would've liked nothing more than to have had grand, passionate fights, but Dad didn't have a cruel bone in his body. Instead, he tortured her with his patience. To this day he remains as long-suffering and loyal as an abused dog, having nursed Mum through various bouts of aerobic-video fanaticism, tranquilliser addiction, Tupperware purchasing, pyramid selling (including saucy underwear franchising), depression, an ill-fated flirtation with a Peugeot car salesman and, most recently, several phantom cancer scares.

For all this Mum has remained steadfastly ungrateful, although nobody would be able to tell, since her whole purpose in life seems to be to keep up appearances to the good people of Rushton, who – as I've pointed out on many occasions – probably don't give a damn. In public, she always bragged in an offhand way, claiming that Dad was 'in the oil business', while in private she railed at her would be JR Ewing husband for not being entrepreneurial and for lacking what she called 'oomph'. To my mind, if Dad lacked ambition and sparkle it wasn't surprising, considering she trod on any ideas he ever had. She never once appreciated that her husband's uninspiring daily toil as an overseer of the rapidly expanding petrol station business of Hertfordshire kept food on our table and paid her mail-order-catalogue accounts.

But as much as the uncelebrated Geoffrey Maloney kept his wife on the tracks of normality and did his best to make up for her lack of parenting skills, his wife complained bitterly that she was holding him back. Probably the worst thing that could have happened was that Miles and Louisa Roper moved into the big house next door. They fed into every lifestyle aspiration Mum had and, since she spent her life trying to point out the things she had in common with all the people around her, finding her identity in the illusion she had of her role in her community, she felt undermined by her fashionable neighbours, comparing her lot relentlessly and ruthlessly with theirs, and finding hers lacking.

For a while, until the cracks started to show, I think she liked the fact that she lived next door to the Ropers, perhaps feeling a frisson of excitement that, in being so close, maybe a bit of Miles's glamour, or Louisa's beauty and grace, had rubbed off on her.

I've always held Mum in some way responsible for driving Fred away but, if I think about it charitably, it must have come as a terrible shock to her when she realised just how different the Ropers were. When everything exploded she reacted with the loudest voice, feeling shame at her proximity to the one-time friends and decrying them with instant tabloid-like condemnation. And so it was that while my mother didn't even pause for breath in her tirade of outrage, Louisa and Fred slipped away and, in the blink of an eye, the Ropers had gone from Rushton for ever.

Up in my old bedroom I look out of the window across to Fred's old house. I don't know who lives there now, but the house has been painted yet again. It looks garish, like a pantomime dame disguised in stage make-up and a wig, but for anyone in the know it's still possible to see that the paint is thicker on the front porch, where spray paint once defaced the house. I lean on the windowsill, looking across to Fred's old room, but the window is obscured by one of those baby-friendly black-out blinds and I focus instead on my own window, picking at the edge of the rainbow sticker that's been stuck to the glass for over twenty years and hides a small crack where Fred once threw a stone too hard.

I was never any good at biology, but I find myself wondering if butterflies ever visit their old cocoons. If they do, I wonder if they feel any of the strangeness I feel standing in my old bedroom. It's like coming back after years to a prison cell, somehow feeling unnerved by the intimacy of four walls that have witnessed such vast emotions, yet knowing that what remains of me here is no more than a dusty fingerprint.

When I was a teenager I always assumed that I'd live in a house much bigger than my parents'. I took it as a basic right, a natural path through evolution, that I would be more affluent than them and that my lifestyle would, one day, be grand and lavish. It hasn't really worked out like that though and, now that I live in a small flat, I envy my parents the fact that their junk is only enough to fill Scott's room and they have the space to leave mine alone.

I sit on the low stool in front of my old dressing table, feeling the frill of faded flower-patterned material that sticks out from under the glass top, and look at my reflection in three angled oblongs of mirror. Tucked into the top mirror clip is a curled-up photograph of me with Joe when he was a baby. I'm holding him so that his back is against my stomach and we both stare at the camera with the same impatient expression. It's the kind of photograph my mother likes, but I think it's a terrible likeness of both me and Joe.

I put the photo back and turn away to the cupboard behind me. Inside, there are several winter coats and suits of my mother's draped in dry-cleaner's plastic. On the end of the gold hanging rail there's a china pomander on a frayed ribbon. I reach up and sniff the small holes in the top, but I can't tell if I'm just conjuring up a memory, or if the scent is real.

I sigh and close the cupboard door. There's no point in being in here; it makes me feel depressed. I walk on to the landing to the window at the top of the stairs, my feet instinctively treading a silent path across the beige carpet that avoids the creaking floorboards underneath. From the landing window I look down into the back garden.

Joe looks bored and a bit fed up. He leans on the fence near the back door, scuffing his rollerblades on the rough stony path that runs from the front drive down the side of the house and along the garden fence. I'm about to knock on the window and wave, when Joe's expression changes. I watch as his face breaks into a wide grin and he eagerly jumps away from the fence and starts clomping off along the path to the front of the house. I strain my head, trying to see what has caught his attention, but I can't.

By the time I get to the bottom of the stairs I can hear voices out on the drive and, with a sinking heart, assume that my parents have returned prematurely. Quickly, I root around in the array of china figurines on the shelf by the mirror to find the front door key. When finally I get the front door open, however, I'm astounded by what I see.

On the drive there's an old red Renault 5, parked behind my van. Joe's sitting behind the steering wheel looking delighted. Beside him, Fred stands by the open driver's door, smiling patiently as Joe plays with the steering wheel and various levers.

I feel blood rushing to my cheeks as Fred looks up at me bashfully and waves, before ushering Joe out of the car.

'Look Mum,' says Joe, tripping towards me. 'Fred came after all.' He looks up eagerly at Fred, who approaches, jiggling his keys in his hand.

'Hello, Mickey,' he says, almost apologetically.

I can't believe he's here. He was absolutely the last

person I was expecting to see. I cock my head to one side, trying to find answers in Fred's eyes, but he avoids my questioning gaze.

'I'm glad you're here,' continues Joe. 'I was getting really bored.'

I pull a face at my son, then look at Fred, but he turns his attention to Joe.

'You can't be bored. This is Rushton. There's loads to do.' He laughs.

'You look terrible,' I say, standing to one side and holding the door open for Fred to come in. As he steps towards me, I can see that his eyes are bloodshot and he looks as if he hasn't slept. Instinctively, I want to reach out and stroke his cheek and ask him what's happened, but I can't and anyway, Fred doesn't give me the chance.

'Thanks.' He steps into the house, wiping his feet on the mat.

'Mum!' admonishes Joe. 'Don't be mean. Come on, Fred.' He shoots past me and up the corridor into the kitchen, before I have time to tell him to take off his rollerblades.

I close the door and, while Fred's back is turned, hastily check my reflection in the hall mirror. I grab my ponytail and roughly yank it tight, not that it makes any difference: I still look a mess. 'Aren't you supposed to be on your stag do?' I ask, walking into the kitchen as casually as I can. I lean against the unit and fold my arms, but I can feel my heart hammering.

'I was. I got back this morning,' says Fred.

'What's a stag do?' asks Joe, sitting on one of the kitchen chairs and pulling off his rollerblades.

'It's where a whole bunch of men go away somewhere, drink too much, feel sick and wonder why the hell they're bothering,' Fred says, looking at me.

'Why?' asks Joe.

'Good question,' says Fred, smiling, before breaking eye

contact. 'You'll find out about it when you're older. Anyway, I remembered you were here, so I thought I'd come and surprise you. I hoped the fresh air might do me some good.'

Joe seems perfectly satisfied with this explanation and jumps up. 'I found you on the wall. Come and see,' he says, sliding across the kitchen lino in his socks. Fred follows him into the utility room.

I swipe my hand over my mouth and press my lips, willing my heart rate to slow down. How can this all seem so normal? How can Fred walk into this house and be so natural, when there's a million reasons why this is anything but? I can hear him laughing with Joe and there's a part of me that wants to laugh too, but there's also another that wants to tell him to leave. He can't make friends with Joe; it's not fair. But then, Joe's just a kid and Fred's made his day by turning up. Is it worth upsetting Joe when, if I'm honest, Fred has made my day, too?

I can't look at Fred when he comes back into the kitchen.

'It's all changed around here, hasn't it?' he says.

I nod mutely.

He ducks his head and looks out of the kitchen window up to the back field. 'Can you believe it? They've built on the field. I wonder if those people will be haunted by the bull.'

'What bull?' asks Joe.

Fred raises his eyebrows. 'Didn't your mum ever tell you about the bull?'

'Fred,' I caution, but I can't help smiling.

'Go on, Fred, tell us,' begs Joe enthusiastically.

'A long time ago,' Fred begins. He looks at Joe, then back at me, as if something has occurred to him. 'Actually, we were probably your age. We buried a tin of treasure in the field over there.'

'What was in it? What was the treasure?'

'I can't remember,' says Fred, 'but it was important at

the time. Anyway, Jimmy Dughead – he's the scary farmer who used to own the land – put his prize bull, Hercules, in that back field and we couldn't get our stuff.'

'So I came up with a plan to distract the bull, only it didn't work,' I add, gazing at Fred.

'What happened?' asks Joe, looking between us.

'I shot it,' Fred says, scratching behind his ear.

Joe's mouth opens with this revelation. 'You *shot* it?'

'Uh-huh.' Fred nods. 'Killed it outright.'

'With a gun?' gasps Joe.

'I thought it was a pretend one, like they use at school sports days to start the races with, only it wasn't. I only meant to scare the damn thing.'

'What happened?' asks Joe.

'To cut a very long story short,' I say deliberately, staring at Fred, willing him not to go into details. 'We got away with it.'

Fred looks at me, his eyes telling me that he's colluding with me, but that he's also having fun.

'Well, *sort* of,' he corrects me. He turns to Joe. 'I got a right telling off from my dad and wasn't allowed to go out for ages, but Mickey got away with it. She always had that knack, your mother.'

I can tell this is fun for Joe. He's never had anyone who's had old history with me and hearing about my youth from Fred is making him look on me in a different light. He stares at me with new eyes, as if he's seeing me as a person, rather than just his boring old mum. I shift uncomfortably, feeling strangely shy. I love remembering this stuff for myself, but I feel odd over Joe knowing about it, as if somehow he'll stop respecting me.

'What happened to the treasure?' he asks Fred.

Fred shrugs. 'I don't know. I guess it's still there.'

'Can we go and get it?' demands Joe, clearly caught up in the adventure. He looks between Fred and me.

'It won't be there, darling.' I laugh. 'They're building

200

new houses up there. It's bound to have been dug up already.'

'It might not have,' says Fred mischievously.

'Fred! Don't even think about it. It's trespassing.'

'Oh.' He grins. 'And when did that ever stop you?'

The sun comes out as Fred, Joe and I pick our way through the piles of bricks and concrete mixers up on Jimmy Dughead's old field. Up close the new houses look feeble. Their timber frames seem to be stapled together like badly made scenery and it's doubtful whether they're going to survive against even the lightest of winds.

As we tramp through the deserted building site, Fred entertains Joe with a ridiculous monologue about the future inhabitants. 'Whoops! There's Mr Jones on the loo. Sorry!' he says, pulling a face at Joe and waving his hand in front of his face at a pretend smell. 'Good morning, Mrs Jones,' he continues, stepping out through a future back doorway into a future garden and doffing a pretend hat. 'Your garden's looking marvellous. What a view!'

Joe's in fits of giggles and I'm laughing too, as Fred stops and breathes in deeply, looking out over the trees to the rooftops of Rushton. I try to read his face, but I can't tell what he's feeling, whether it's nostalgia, regret, or just plain denial. He seems to be on a mission not to let me get a serious word in, or ask any questions. His policy is a great hit with Joe and I have to admit that his good humour is infectious.

'It's about here, isn't it?' he asks suddenly, turning to me and making my heart jump with his bright smile.

I shrug. 'It all looks so different. I can't remember.' I look around me. We're standing in a plot marked out by wooden posts connected by lengths of string.

'You must be able to,' tuts Fred. 'It was your idea. You said to bury the treasure in the middle of the four oak trees.' Fred points to the trees. 'So it must be here.'

Joe's eyes light up with excitement. 'Shall we start digging?' he asks, looking down at the flattened earth.

'I think it's better if we prod around first. Why don't we borrow some of these posts?' Fred suggests.

Joe and Fred tramp off to a corner of the plot, dislodging the wooden post in that, before doing the same with another. I watch them, feeling the weight of time that has passed since Fred and I were last here. I shade my eyes against the sun and smile as Joe waves his post at me.

'Here,' Fred says, 'make yourself useful.' He passes me one of the posts and for a second his fingers cover mine. I look up at him, wondering what he's trying to communicate, but in another second the moment is broken and he turns away to help Joe with the other post. We must look ridiculous, all three of us, walking around in circles jabbing the ground.

After a while Fred leaves Joe and comes over to me. 'I hope you don't mind me showing up like this,' he says.

I turn my head to look at him, wiping my hair out of my face. With the sun behind him, his short hair is made into a halo and I'm amazed by how strong and tall he looks. I feel myself blushing. 'I could do without these hare-brained schemes of yours.' I laugh.

I face Fred. I think the fresh air has done him good. He has colour in his cheeks again and he grins happily at me.

'You know, I feel so liberated,' he says, then he drops his voice. 'You'll never guess what I've done?' He bites his lip and for a second my heart skips a beat.

I stare at him, wide-eyed, waiting for him to tell me that he's changed everything. 'What's that?' I manage.

'I've left my phone *and* my watch in the car,' he says, stretching his arms out wide and laughing. I nod, not knowing what to say. I feel almost choked by the realisation of what I wanted to hear.

'I've found it!' Joe yells and Fred rushes over.

I stab my post into the ground with unnecessary force, telling myself to let go of my ridiculous fantasy.

Sure enough Joe's post has been stopped by an object beneath the surface.

Fred looks at me, his eyes glittering in the sun. 'Could be it,' he says.

'It's probably just a rock,' I say, but I'm excited too.

Joe's already on his hands and knees digging at the earth with his hands. It's strange to see him get so filthy. Usually he's very prissy when it comes to keeping his clothes clean. Fred squats down next to him and I join in, until all three of us are laughing and scrabbling at the hole.

'There it is! There it is!' squeals Joe.

Fred leans down, levering his hand around the hole. Eventually he pulls out the round tin box.

'My God!' I laugh, clapping my hands with glee. 'I can't believe it! Open it, Fred, go on.'

Fred's laughing too, as he struggles with the lid, but it's rusty and won't budge. 'I can't. It's jammed on tight. We'll have to take it back to the house. Come on Joe, help me put these posts back.'

I shovel the earth back into the hole we've made, scraping more round to even out the surface. Then I jump on it to flatten it down, lifting my knees up and pounding my feet down. I don't know whether it's frustration, or exuberance, or both, but as I jump, it's strangely therapeutic. I'm going to play along with Fred and enjoy today, just for today. If I try and read signs into everything he does, I'm going to go crazy.

'Come on, Mum, let's go!' Joe yells.

'OK.' I smile, catching my breath and smoothing down my jeans.

'I think we should go the traditional route, don't you, Mickey?' Fred winks at me.

'After you,' I say, curtseying and sweeping my arm out down the hill to the trees and the stream beyond.

The undergrowth is a lot more tangled than I remember it. I'm covered in briars as we make it through to the ditch at the back of our garden. The stream runs at a trickle and the sun glints through the canopy of trees, dappling the water.

'The trick is to get a good run at it,' instructs Fred, pointing to the steep bank the other side.

'It won't work.' I laugh. 'The stepping stones have gone and look how muddy it is.'

'Stand back, stand back,' Fred says, handing me the tin. He looks at Joe. 'I've done this a thousand times before. Watch and learn . . .'

He pretends to spit on his hands before rubbing them together. Joe giggles.

In a second, Fred runs down the bank, into the stream, his foot sinking with a squelch into the mud at the bottom. With a huge effort, he pulls his foot out and heads up the bank, but his momentum has gone and he loses his footing, laughing as he lands spreadeagled on the slope. He slides back down into the stream, as Joe and I fall about with laughter. 'Very funny,' says Fred, smiling as he flicks off mud from his fingers. He stands in the stream and looks at us. He's soaked through and runs his hand over his hair, leaving a large dollop of mud.

With a giant whoopee, Joe makes a run for it, trying to jump over the stream and up the bank the other side, but Fred catches him with a growl, and in a second the two of them have toppled over and are rolling around in the stream chucking water at each other.

I hold the tin against my stomach, laughing as I watch them horsing around. Joe's soaked, but I don't care. I can't remember the last time I saw him being so uninhibited and as I watch Fred and him lunging at each other, I look up at the sky through the trees and smell the cool air, hearing nothing but the birds and shouts of delight. I want to hold on to this moment for ever.

When we finally get into my parents' garden, Joe and Fred are both out of breath. I unlock the door and make them take their shoes off. They both stand on the doorstep looking naughty, shivering pathetically as they clasp their hands in front of them, like extras from *Oliver Twist*.

'I'll get you some dry things,' I say, smiling. 'Stay there! Both of you.'

I come back down bearing towels and some old clothes of mine for Joe. 'These are all I could find for you,' I tell Fred, holding up a pair of my dad's old pyjamas and a brown cardigan with leather pads at the elbows. Joe giggles as Fred pulls a face and takes them from me.

'Serves you right, Fred Roper.' I laugh. 'Strip off and I'll put your clothes in the machine.'

'What here? Now?' asks Fred.

'I'll turn my back,' I tease. I catch Joe looking between Fred and me. He's smiling and I turn to him to cover my embarrassment. 'And you too. Come on. Get those things off.'

Joe looks bashful and I relent.

'OK, OK, you big pair of girls.'

I turn away back into the kitchen and leave them to it. But I do look. I watch out of the kitchen window as Fred takes off his T-shirt, feeling my abdomen tense as I see his chest and the way his stomach creases as he bends over. I turn away, biting my lips together as I get some newspaper from the utility room and cover the kitchen table, before placing the tin on it.

Fred and Joe eventually come through the back door.

'Sexy,' I tease, looking Fred up and down, as he hands me his clothes. It's meant to be sarcastic, but actually he does look sexy, even with mud smeared on his face.

'Come on, Fred, open the tin,' says Joe, sitting up at the table.

'You'll need this.' I pull open the kitchen drawer and hand Fred a screwdriver.

I pick up Joe's clothes, walk into the utility room and open the washing machine. I throw them in, then check the washing instructions on the labels on Fred's clothes, feeling strangely exhilarated as I hold his designer T-shirt for a second. Knowing that I'm out of sight, I pull it to my face, breathing in his scent.

'Mickey?' calls Fred.

Flustered, I hurry back to the table.

Fred has already levered the screwdriver under the lid. He looks between Joe and me. 'OK. One . . . two –'

'Go on, go on,' urges Joe, unable to bear the suspense any longer.

Fred puts his hand on top of the tin, teasing him. 'I don't know if I can be bothered,' he says, puffing out his cheeks.

Joe bangs his hand on the table. 'Fred!'

Fred slides the tin towards him. 'You do it.'

He sits back, looking at me, as Joe stands up and pulls up the lid of the tin. It feels exciting watching, as if Joe is our child and he's opening a Christmas present.

'Er!' he exclaims. 'What's that?' he asks, pulling out a soggy packet.

'Ah.' Fred sighs, taking the packet from him by its corner. 'That, Joe, is our space dust.'

I lean forward. 'What else is in there?'

Joe pulls out two crumpled one-pound notes. 'What are these?' He flattens them out on the table.

'Old pound notes. They were worth a fortune,' says Fred.

'We were going to try and buy tickets for the circus.' I pick one of them up, amazed by the vivid greenness of the paper and how young the queen looks. 'Do you remember?'

'What was the name of that magician from the big house on the way to Bowley?' Fred laughs, clicking his fingers, as he tries to remember.

'Andy . . . Andy Buckley!' he says in unison with me. 'My God! Do you remember, Mickey?'

Of course I remember. As Joe unloads the tin, pulling out our cards, gun caps, bubble gum, cigarettes, old notes, keys, plastic skips, Fred's penknife and magnifying glass, and various pilfered miniature bottles of Grant's whisky and Gordon's gin, it's like unloading a time capsule.

The last item out is a pair of sunglasses. I see Fred's face change as Joe holds them up.

He pulls the stems apart and puts them on. The glasses are far too big and slip down his nose. 'Whose are these?' he asks.

'They belonged to my father,' Fred says slowly.

Joe, picking up on Fred's tone, takes them off and hands them over guiltily. 'Oh,' he says.

Fred holds the glasses in his hand for a second, looking at the lenses. 'These were the magic glasses he gave me. To keep the baddies away.'

I glance up at Fred, feeling an overwhelming urge to hug him.

'What was your dad like?' asks Joe, but I can tell Fred doesn't want to answer.

'Sadly, Fred's dad died before his time,' I say.

'Sorry,' says Joe, staring at Fred.

Breaking the moment, I look down at the items on the table. 'Quite a stash, eh?' I raise my eyebrows at Joe, but he obviously doesn't agree.

'Is that it?' he asks, picking up the empty tin and looking inside.

'What do you mean, "is that it?",' Fred says, resuming his jolly mood. He puts the glasses to one side, then picks up his old penknife and feels the blade with his thumb and forefinger. 'This is our youth we're talking about.'

I look at the items spread before us and I can see that Joe has a point. I want to weep for the innocence we had then, the happy times all these things represent. But more than that, I want to weep because I'm seeing Fred being Fred, my Fred, the Fred I used to know.

'What shall we do with it now?' asks Joe.

Fred shrugs. 'I don't know. You can have this, if you like.' He gives Joe the penknife.

'Are you sure?'

'Yes, I'd forgotten about it anyway.' Fred is watching Joe with the knife.

'It doesn't matter,' says Joe. 'Just because you'd forgotten about it, it doesn't stop it belonging to you.'

I smile at Fred and he grins back.

'I know,' says Joe suddenly. 'We should bury more treasure that we can dig up one day.'

And as Joe and Fred discuss the millennium capsule that they buried at Joe's old school, all I can think is that if I had something to keep safe it would be today.

At Joe's insistence, with little resistance from either Fred or me, Fred stays for dinner. Between us we cook up a mountain of sausages and mash, and I open a bottle of wine. As darkness falls, I put Fred's and Joe's clothes on the radiator and dig out the candle set I gave Mum last Christmas. Before long the kitchen windows have steamed up and everything is cosy as Fred and I reminisce about our childhood, remembering all our friends from Rushton Primary and reliving our old adventures.

Eventually, Joe starts yawning. I chuckle, reaching out to touch his face. 'Come on, you. Time for bed.'

'Do I have to?' he moans, not wanting to miss out.

'Yes,' I insist. 'Now off you go. I haven't made up the bed in my old room yet, so go into Grandma's room. OK?'

Reluctantly, he agrees. He kisses me on the cheek and then stands by Fred's chair.

Fred punches him playfully on the shoulder. 'See you, then,' he says. Joe punches him back and there's a pause. I can tell he wants to know when he's going to see Fred again, or whether he'll be here in the morning. I know what Joe's like for trying to pin things down and I will him not to say anything. I can't think about the next five minutes, let alone the next five hours. But then Joe darts forward and kisses Fred on the cheek, before running out of the kitchen and up the stairs.

Fred gazes after him and then looks at the table. There's silence for a moment. After being so intimate and playing happy families all day, I feel nervous. I don't want to break the spell. Not yet, anyway. 'Cigarette?' I ask and Fred nods.

We huddle up together on the back doorstep and it feels like we're teenagers again. We smoke in silence for ages, contemplating the bright canopy of stars above us.

'I've had such a great day,' says Fred softly.

'You were brilliant with Joe,' I say, meaning it. 'You know, you'd be a great father –' I stop myself and fold my arms. That sounded dreadful and there's an awkward pause. 'I mean . . . one day . . . you and . . .' I trail off, stubbing my cigarette out, angry for making such a blunder, not wanting to say her name.

We're silent for a while and as much as I love talking about the past, the present has to overtake sooner or later. I steel myself to ask the questions I need to ask. Eventually I pluck up the courage to speak. 'She doesn't know you're here, does she? Rebecca, I mean?' I ask quietly.

Fred exhales and flicks his cigarette down the drain. 'No.' He sighs. 'No, of course she doesn't. She's down in Brighton on her hen weekend.'

There's no apology in his voice and as he turns to face me I know, finally, that this is about me.

'I had to come,' he says and I nod.

'I'm glad you did.'

'I thought it would be scary being here, but there are so many happy memories.' Fred sighs deeply and looks up at the sky. Then he looks over his shoulder at me. 'I remember what it was like to spy on you from my bedroom window.'

'I used to spy on *you*. It was the other way round.'

'No, actually.' He chuckles. 'I caught you undressing once.'

'Oh, that. I know.' I grin back smugly.

Fred shifts on the doorstep to face me. 'You *know*?'

'Christmas nineteen eighty-four. The night before the disco at the Memorial Hall. I did it on purpose . . . *actually*.'

Fred looks shocked for a moment, then puts his head back and roars with laughter. 'Oh, Mickey,' he says eventually and sighs. 'We were going to go on holiday, weren't we?'

'There were lots of things we nearly did . . .'

My sentence hangs between us in the night air. I've brought up our past, right up to now, this moment, and Fred knows it. It could be for a second or a year that we stare at each other. However long it is, it's enough time to know that whatever we started all those years ago isn't finished. Not by a long way.

The world seems to go silent and it's as if I'm melting into Fred's gaze. Without even knowing it, I'm leaning in towards him.

At the last moment I panic, quickly jerking back and breaking eye contact. Startled, I look down into my lap, fiddling with the edge of my cardigan. *What am I doing? What am I* –

I don't have time to think any more. In a split second Fred grasps me hard behind my neck and pulls me towards him. I don't even have time to see his face before our lips crash together in a kiss so out of control that it's almost violent.

Gasping for breath, I grab his face, our mouths clashing with insatiable hunger, our bodies pressed together so tightly it's as if they're magnetised. I can feel my blood rushing through me, my heart pounding with exquisite relief. It feels as though I've been let out of captivity and I'm being me again for the first time in years. Fred pushes out my hairband and runs his fingers through my hair, setting it free. I slide my hands up inside his pyjama top, feeling the bare skin of his back, wanting him so much it's hurting. It's only then that I realise I'm shaking uncontrollably.

Fred pulls away and cups my cheeks in his hands. He leans his forehead against mine. 'Are you cold?' he whispers.

'No.' I giggle. 'Just –'

But I can't say what it is, or describe the excitement I'm feeling and Fred doesn't need an answer. He finds my lips again, locking his to mine as he pulls me up, holding me tight as we push through the back door and stumble towards the table. Still kissing me, he lays me down and I pull him on top of me. I grab his hair as we cling to each other and it's as if there's only us in the whole universe. I pull up my legs, sliding them up his body as we grind against each other and I'm gasping, kissing him deeply, and all I can think about is that I've been storing this up for nearly half my life and it feels like such a huge relief. As I feel his hands slide against my skin, I want him, more than I've ever wanted anything or anyone.

It's the stairs that give Joe away. Knowing the anatomy of this house like my own body, I hear the middle stair creak and the sound hits me like a bullet. I push Fred away, gulping for air and smoothing down my shirt. 'Joe?' I squeak, eyeballing Fred, who blushes, staggering backwards into the chair.

I rush out to the hall and intercept Joe on the bottom stair. I can't meet his inquisitive stare.

'Can I have a glass of water?' he asks.

'Of course you can,' I say, suddenly wanting to cry, as reality punches me in the face. 'I'll bring it up, OK?'

I shake my head, telling Fred not to speak as I go to the sink and fill up a glass. Like a zombie, I walk upstairs.

Joe's sitting up in my parents' bed. I hand the water to him. 'Sleep tight.'

211

'Mum?' he says, as I'm halfway to the door. 'Is Fred staying?'

I turn stiffly. 'I don't know, darling.' I feel the wave of passion I felt only moments ago crash and trickle away as I look at his face. 'I don't think so.'

Back in the kitchen, Fred's collected our wineglasses from outside and is filling them up. He looks ridiculous, trying to maintain his dignity in a pair of pyjamas. He hands me my glass. 'I'm sorry. Christ, Mickey –'

He steps towards me, but I put my hand on his chest. 'I can't do this, Fred,' I say, willing myself not to cry. 'I want to, but I can't. I can't be . . .'

'Be what?' he asks, holding my shoulder.

'I can't be some . . . I don't know . . .' I say shakily, looking at the kitchen floor. 'You're getting married next week.'

Fred moves away. 'I didn't mean it like that –'

'Today has just been a nostalgia trip and we got carried away.' My voice is firm. 'It's probably the wine.' I try to laugh, before taking a glug from the wineglass, but it doesn't help my bravado. When I look up at Fred, I feel tears stinging the inside of my nose.

'You don't mean that,' he says. 'You know it's more than that. I –'

And I don't know where it comes from, what happens next, because I know that Fred is about to say the words I've been desperate to hear. And although inside me there's a sixteen-year-old girl wanting this romantic moment with every fibre of her being, there's me here and now, filled with another lifetime of experience. Too much has happened and too much is at stake. I hold up my hand. 'Don't. Just don't.'

Fred's eyebrows knit together. 'But . . . but don't you –'

'Of course I do.' I choke. 'But that's not the point. The point is that we're not sixteen any more. We hardly know each other now.'

212

'But Mickey –' he begins, but I shake my head desperately.

'Even if we did see this through, I can't tell you that just because we've met again we're going to have a happy ending and rush off into the sunset. It would mean starting from scratch and seeing how it goes. Rebecca's a beautiful girl and she loves you. I can't tell you to throw away your marriage for something that might not work. I've got a family now. There's Joe . . . there's everything.'

I slump down on to a chair, fighting my tears.

'Can't we? . . . I don't know.' Fred exhales. He sits down opposite me and shakes his head, reaching out to me across the table with both hands, but I can't touch him.

'It's hopeless. It won't work . . . us seeing each other again.' I swallow hard. I look up at Fred, my eyes brimming with tears. 'What we had once was real. Let's not spoil that.'

I was in love. I was more in love than anyone had ever been. But I wasn't going to tell anyone before I'd told Fred. In the meantime it was the biggest, best, most fabulous secret in the world. A secret that was obviously driving my friends crazy and, as I looked around the expectant faces of Pippa, Lisa and Annabel, sitting in our booth in the new McDonald's opposite Bowley bus station, I felt infinitely, fantastically superior.

'So are you, Mickey?' Lisa repeated.

I shrugged smugly, putting my folders back into my school bag. Every one had been turned into a reminder of Fred. Fr4MM was my favourite so far. It adorned my Geography folder, the letters formed out of a loopy daisy-chain doodle. On the front of my French book, J'AIME FR, this time in pencil with a three-dimensional arrow around it. I'd only gone the whole hog on the inside of my English notebook where it said, in capitals, I LOVE FRED ROPER – a fact that had not escaped Pippa.

'She is,' said Pippa. 'Look at her English book.'

'Let's see.' Lucy lunged towards it.

'No,' I said, slapping my hand down on it.

'For another milkshake,' bribed Annabel.

'No! I said no!' I giggled. 'It's private.'

'But I saw it in English,' Pippa protested. 'I saw you write it.'

'So?'

'What does it say?' begged Lucy, who always hated to be left out.

'Nothing,' I teased, flashing open the book in a nano-second, closing it again and stuffing it deep into my school bag.

'Oh, Mickey!' Annabel and Pippa moaned together.

I tapped the side of my nose to tell them to mind their own business. Taking up my milkshake cup, I stirred the straw around the bottom.

'It was nothing, anyway,' said Pippa, put out. 'Fred Roper . . .' She let out a long, fake yawn. 'Boring.'

'*Boring*?' I flushed.

'It is boring. You won't tell us anything,' Annabel confirmed.

'That's because there's nothing *to* tell,' said Pippa.

'You don't know that,' I said defensively.

Pippa grinned in her sly way. 'Ah. So you have?'

'Have you, Mickey?' asked Lucy eagerly. 'Have you done it with him?'

I looked at them all, exasperated but secretly pleased they were so interested.

I let their expectation hang in the air for a moment. 'No,' I said eventually. 'But I'm going to –'

'Tara Anson's done it,' chirped Annabel.

'With who?' I asked sceptically.

'Paul White in the sixth form.'

'Paul White and Tara Anson?' I scoffed. 'I don't think so.'

'She has,' confirmed Lucy. 'She told Catherine after our Biology mock exam. And Catherine told Lorna, who told Annabel.'

Annabel nodded. This was exactly the reason I was keeping quiet about Fred.

'But she wasn't even going out with him,' said Pippa.

'Yeah. Slag,' I told them spitefully.

'At least she's not a tease,' said Annabel, who quite admired Tara. 'You've been going out with Fred for ages and you haven't done it.'

'We've done most other things, though,' I rebuffed.

'Fingers and tops?' asked Lucy.

I dipped my chip into the dollop of ketchup on the paper carton. 'And other things,' I hinted.

'Have you seen it, then?' asked Pippa.

'Felt it.'

'What was it like?'

'Nice.' I shrugged, not wanting to go into details. Pippa and Lucy crowded together, giggling at this information. Annabel leant in close too.

'Tara said that Paul White's was horrible,' she confided.

'Well, Fred's isn't,' I said, spotting the bus across the road and standing up. 'It's the best.'

Intrigued, Pippa followed me on to the bus and we sat in our usual seats at the back. Once the ritual of insult shouting, paper throwing and cigarette trading had died down and the bus chugged out of Bowley, she sighed heavily. 'Have you done much revision for Maths?' she asked. I shook my head. 'Neither have I,' she continued.

'I bet you have. You always do,' I said. 'You don't have to lie to me.'

'You don't have to lie to me, either.' She sounded offended.

I turned to her. 'I don't,' I said. Surely she knew by now that she was my best friend.

'So? Are you really going to do it with Fred?' she asked.

I nodded. 'I would have done before, but I want it to be perfect. I've got it all planned out.'

'Really? When?'

'Can you keep a secret?' I'd been bursting to tell someone our plan. Pippa nodded. 'You promise you won't tell the others?'

'Of course I won't.'

I leant towards her, keeping my voice down. 'We're going on holiday after the exams.'

'Wow! Where?'

'France.'

'With parents?'

'No. That's the best bit, we're going on our own.'

'You're so lucky. I'd never be allowed to do that. What did your mum say?'

'She doesn't know. That's why it's a secret. We're not going to tell anyone. We're just going to do it. We'll tell our parents as we're leaving and they won't be able to do anything.'

Pippa looked at me, her face a mixture of admiration and worry. 'But –'

'Don't say anything. It's going to be brilliant.'

Of course it was going to be brilliant. Everything was brilliant. Being in love with Fred was like having a big bubble inside me. Sometimes I wanted to burst it, spill the beans and tell everyone, but most of the time, like now, I was pleased I'd kept it to myself and had only told Pippa a little bit of our plan.

As I said goodbye to her at the bus stop by the church in Rushton and dawdled up the footpath along the Avenue, reaching out to swing around each of the oak trees, I wanted to kiss each one, knowing that I would soon be saying goodbye to them. Fred and I were on our way and everything, everything was about to kick off. Of course there was the small matter of O levels, but with a bit of luck I'd pass and Fred was bound to pass his. Then everything would start.

Fred had told me all about the sixth-form college we were both going to apply to. It was on the other side of Bowley and once we got our grades through it shouldn't be too difficult to persuade our parents to let us go there. If they got worried about the money, I'd get a Saturday job or something. They were bound to relent once they understood how miserable I'd be if I stayed at Bowley Comp. I was ready to meet new friends and if Fred and I were there together we'd be a proper couple. We might even find a flat nearby and we could get a dog.

But then, maybe a dog wasn't such a wise idea, because after our A levels in two years' time we were going to go travelling. Fred said he wanted to go to Australia and we'd both looked at Louisa's atlas the last time he was home. We'd taken it in turns to flick through the giant pages and the other one would shout 'stop'. The plan was wherever the atlas fell open we'd visit. That was how we came up with the trip to France.

It was going to be wonderful, lazing in the sun, cooking sausages on a campfire, snuggling up in our sleeping bags at night. But France was just the start. In a couple of years we'd have saved enough money to go on our world trip. We'd probably spend two years, we reckoned, stopping in various countries. There was so much of Africa to see and Fred reckoned that if we were any good at camping we could go right out into the jungle.

To be honest, that sounded a bit dangerous – I was more into going to America. We hadn't decided yet whether we'd fly there before or after Africa, but I reckoned if we got to New York, then Fred could get a job on a big newspaper since he was so good at English and I could work for a radio station or something.

One thing was for sure: neither of us was ever going to come back and live smelly old Rushton . . . ever. If we returned to England at all, we were going to live in a big house right out in the country with the sea at the end of the garden. Fred had promised that he'd buy me a donkey, and there would be sheep and pet pigs, oh, and babies. Fred wanted two, but I said the more the merrier. I reckoned on five at least.

I sighed happily, thinking of our family. We weren't going to be anything like his parents, or mine, for that matter. We were always going to love each other and go out all the time. And when our kids grew up, we were always going to be on their side and they'd be able to do whatever they wanted. We weren't going to stifle them with rules, or make them stay in. But that was years and years away. Anyway, we had to have sex first. A lot.

I couldn't wait until next year: I'd be sixteen and could go on the pill. Then, when we went to college, everything would be easy. I had it all planned. Dawdling up the hill, I tried to imagine what it would be like the first time we made love. I bit my lip, wondering whether we'd be nervous, or whether it would hurt. No, it would be magical, just like everything else about Fred. God, I missed him.

Behind me I heard the low rumble of a car. I turn to see Miles's Porsche stealthily heading up the hill. Miles sat behind the wheel, his face set in a grim, unsmiling expression. I saw him look in his rear-view mirror and turn to me. For a second our eyes met and I smiled, waving, but Miles ignored me, concentrating his attention on the road. I stopped, feeling riled. I knew Fred had his differences with Miles, but he'd always been nice to me. Besides, I hadn't seen him for ages. The least he could do was wave. After all, I was going out with his son.

Miles brought the car to a halt outside Fred's house, not bothering to pull into the drive. I continued up the hill towards the car, watching him quickly getting out, slamming the driver's door, before rushing into his house.

I dawdled up towards ours wondering what was going on, but nothing seemed to stir behind the Ropers' windows and slowly I walked on.

'Hi!' I called, turning my key in the front door. Inside I could hear the theme tune of the six o'clock news.

Dad was home early. He sat in the armchair in front of the television, stroking the cat, and I dumped my school bag by the door, before kissing him on the cheek.

'Good day at school?' he asked.

'All right,' I replied, walking over to the window and pulling our net curtains aside to have a look at next door.

Talking about Fred at home wasn't proving easy. Since everyone was used us hanging out together, the fact that we were officially going out didn't make as much impact as I'd hoped. My mother infuriated me by being dismissive and admitted that she was relieved I wasn't going out with Doug, my last boyfriend from Bowley Comp. Whenever I mentioned Fred she'd wave her hand abstractedly, as if she thought the whole thing was transient. When I overheard her telling Rita, the receptionist at the doctors' surgery, that Fred was my latest 'beau', describing our relationship as 'sweet', I was furious. Fred and I weren't 'sweet', we were real. To prove my point I put the silver ring I had on my engagement finger, hoping to wake her up to the reality of my feelings, but she either didn't notice, or just ignored me.

I took off my jacket and threw it on the sofa, as my mother came in with a cup of tea. She put it down on the arm of Dad's chair. 'You can hang that up for a start,' she said, nodding to my jacket. 'And don't get too comfortable. If I were you, I'd make a start on your revision. You can put in a good couple of hours before dinner.'

'Give her a break, Marie,' said Dad. 'She doesn't have to begin right this minute.'

'Her exams are in a few weeks!' Mum replied. 'If you want her to fail, then fine.'

Ignoring them both, I looked back out of the window.

'What are you staring at?' asked Dad.

'Miles is back,' I said distractedly, watching as the front door opened.

'Come away from there,' said Mum, bustling over, but not able to resist having a peek herself.

Through the window I could see Miles coming out of the house next door. Behind him Louisa, who usually looked so serene and calm, was distraught as she clung on to his arm. I watched Miles angrily shake off her grip, as he marched to the drive. He was carrying a large holdall in one hand and a pile of papers in the other. As he hurried towards the car, I could see him trying to stuff the papers in the bag.

Louisa put her hands to her mouth in anguish, as she called something out to Miles, but he ignored her.

'Really!' Mum tutted. 'They're arguing –' But she didn't get any further, her attention caught by an approaching police car.

'What's going on?' asked Dad, stirring from his chair, as blue light flashed in our front room. I felt a horrible sense of foreboding as the police car slowed, the siren cutting abruptly.

Quickly, I ran from the front room to the front door, pulling it open.

'Come back here, Mickey!' I could hear my mum shouting, but I didn't care, I had to see what was happening.

The police car pulled up on the kerb on the far side of Miles's Porsche and the doors opened quickly. I could hear the radio in the car, as a policemen from the passenger's seat stepped out into the road. The driver put on his hat, as he emerged on to the pavement. They both looked towards Miles.

There were more sirens in the distance. I looked over at Louisa, whose face seemed to crumple as she shouted 'No!' and put her hand out to Miles, but Miles, who was near the door of his Porsche, didn't stop. He didn't even look back at her, or at the policemen. Instead, with lightening speed, he yanked open the door of his car. I could see the panicked look on his face, as he threw the bag into the passenger's seat, and papers flying everywhere. He didn't stop to pick them up. Jumping into the driver's seat and barely having time to close the door, Miles turned on the engine. I ran out into our drive, as the Porsche reversed away from the police car towards me. It swung round before, with a screech of tyres, it sped away down the hill.

'Miles!' screamed Louisa.

The policemen looked flustered, as they jumped back into their patrol car. I couldn't believe the noise as the siren burst back into life and within seconds the police car had set off in hot pursuit of Miles's Porsche.

Without stopping, I raced out into Hill Drive. I could see the Porsche speeding away down the Avenue, the police car racing after it. At the bottom of the Avenue a second police car was coming up the other way. It swerved round, blocking the road. Meanwhile, the first car was gaining ground on Miles's Porsche, but even though there was no way he was going to make it round the second stationary car Miles didn't slow down.

Instead, he swerved his Porsche at the last minute, up on to the path at the side of the Avenue, trying to slip through. But he didn't make it. Instead, there was an almighty crash.

The Porsche concertinaed into the last large oak at the bottom of the Avenue.

As I ran forward, sprinting down the hill, a large plume of smoke rushed up from the crumpled bonnet of Miles's Porsche and, a split-second later, there was a huge explosion and flames leapt upwards.

There was noise everywhere. People were coming out of their houses. A policeman was yelling for everyone to

221

keep back. I ducked, putting my forearm up to my face as the heat of the blaze hit me. Then I felt a pair of arms go round me, yanking me back, and I only had a second to realise it was my father, before he buried my face in his jumper, forcing me away from the choking smoke, hugging me tightly, as I started to scream.

Chapter VII

Fred

Less than a month before my O-level examinations were due to commence it fell to Mr Pearce, the master of my boarding house at Greenaway College, to tell me that my father had died.

I was called out of my last class before tea by a prefect and asked to accompany him to my housemaster's study. Here, Mr Pearce sat me down and repeated what my mother had told him: that Miles had been killed outright in a car accident near my home, that there were complications and that the police had been involved. I was to meet my mother at King's Cross Station in London at eleven o'clock the following morning and I was to pack a bag, as I might be gone some time. 'It's going to be difficult,' he told me, 'but try to be brave for her as well as yourself.'

Apart from refusing his suggestion of a glass of whisky and thanking him for offering to write to the examination board concerning my circumstances, I said nothing.

Later that night, in bed, I stared at the dormitory ceiling until morning broke, with tears of mourning and guilt streaming silently down my face. It had only been the week before that Miles had come to visit me and I'd sat with him in the pub garden, drinking my pint and refusing to listen to what he'd had to say.

A second blow struck me the following morning as I rode the train up to London. It caught me punch-drunk, reeling as I still was from the news I'd received the night before. Not only was Miles's death headline news in the papers, but so, too, were the circumstances surrounding it. The police had been trying to find him in order to question him, when he'd lost control of his car and crashed. What they'd wanted to question him about and why he'd chosen to run were as yet unclear.

When I joined my mother she explained that the police were going through Miles's possessions both at home and at Clan. Although she'd already been interviewed by them herself, and would be so again, all they'd told her was that they were working on a tip-off they'd received concerning a serious crime that Miles might or might not have been involved with. They would let us know, they'd said, any further details as and when they arose.

I remember little of the next few days. We caught a train to Aberdeen and moved into my grandmother's house. My mother spent her days in the drawing room beside the telephone, staring at the wall and muttering prayers. I sat next to her, drinking the endless cups of tea which my grandmother provided, determined that Mum wouldn't see me cry. I listened to the grandfather clock recording the slow passing of time, barely capable of holding a thought in my head for more than a second.

The information we'd been waiting for came with the morning newspaper a week later. The police had dug up a body in the basement of Clan. To begin with, this information failed to evolve from newspaper copy in my mind. It remained detached in every way from reality, as impossible to assimilate as the horrors that had unfolded in the football stadium at Heysel some weeks earlier.

The body belonged to Miles's ex-business partner, Carl. It had been unearthed by the police down there in the concrete in the days which had followed Miles's death. Before I'd read it in the lead article on the front page of *The Times*, Carl's name had meant little more to me other than any of those of the various other people who'd come in and out of Miles's and Mum's lives over the years. I'd been eleven when he'd gone abroad and never come back. But now, after I'd read his name afresh and seen the grainy photograph of the man I half remembered, a million unanswerable questions had been launched. It had been an execution-style killing, the cause of death being a single bullet through the back of the head.

Three weeks later, with the police investigation ongoing, the inquest into Miles' death still looming and my mother still in Scotland, I returned to school to complete my revision and sit my exams. Miles's funeral, attended only by my mother and myself, and conducted with the minimum of attention and the maximum of speed, had taken place at a crematorium near Miles's birthplace in Warminster a few days before. It had left me numb.

Sitting there in the school library, looking out of the window at the chapel, I couldn't stop myself thinking about just what there'd been left of Miles to cremate. It had been this way for days. Flashes of what had happened to Miles kept bursting through to the front of my mind. Everything in my life suddenly seemed connected to his death, from the smell of burning toast in the dining room at breakfast to the sound of a car's engine. There was no escape.

At a desk opposite me an older boy stared. During examination time the school library was meant to be the exclusive preserve of sixth-formers, with members of the junior years working in the communal studies in the boarding houses. My presence here was unusual, a privilege which had been extended to me as a result of my current exceptional circumstances. This wasn't, however, the reason why the boy was staring.

Like every other student here, he *knew* who I was and he *knew* what my father had done – or he thought he did, anyway. I stared back at him until he returned his attention to his work. Miles's involvement in the 'Clan Killing', as the newspapers had taken to calling it, had yet to be proven. But the press and public had convicted him in his absence on the circumstances surrounding his death. If he hadn't done it, the argument had gone, why would he have tried to run? They'd vilified him as an archetypal gangster, the assumption being that he must have known something of the body uncovered in his club and had probably orchestrated its burial himself.

Staring was something I'd grown used to these last two days at Greenaway. I'd expected nothing less from the majority of the school who didn't know me. What I'd dreaded, and what had indeed happened, was that my friends effectively had ostracised me. It wasn't that they'd stopped talking to me, more that when they'd tried, they'd been unable to find anything to say. Our conversations had run out quickly on my first night back and, by the next morning, they'd dried up altogether. It had been as if the common ground on which we'd stood had been ripped as a carpet from beneath our feet, sending us toppling in different directions. I'd landed somewhere new, somewhere that they couldn't follow, even if they'd wanted to.

I looked down at my revision spread out on the desk before me. Picking up one of the sheets of paper, I attempted to read my own handwriting, but again I failed. What I saw reminded me of a video about dyslexia that I'd watched during a General Studies class the term before. The letters of the alphabet appeared animated, jiggling around and blurring into one another each time I attempted to order and make sense of them. No matter how hard I stared, their meaning remained beyond my grasp, as indecipherable to me as hieroglyphics.

I didn't have a hope in hell of passing any of my exams. I'd known as much the moment my mother had broached the topic of my returning here to sit them. I'd argued against it at the time, knowing full well the kind of reception I could expect. The argument itself, however –

the fact that my mother had finally found a subject to break her silence over – was something I'd welcomed. Watching her take charge, and finding myself subjugated to her will, had reminded me of my practical, problem-solving mother of old. And no sooner had I witnessed this resurrection than I'd known that I would do as she wished, because that way, at least, lay movement and an escape from the stasis into which we'd collapsed.

More important to me, being at Greenaway would also take me closer to Mickey and it had been this desire to see her that had finally dispelled any misgivings on my behalf concerning my return.

The only other option available had been to stay in Scotland. Any move back to Rushton had, thanks to my mother, ceased to exist as a possibility. Without consulting me first, she'd put our house there up for sale. My reaction had been one of horror. Rushton, to me, meant Mickey – and Mickey, to me, meant everything. How dare Mum have torn me away from her? Didn't I have a say in where we lived as well? She'd stone-walled me in response. We would never be going back and that had been her final word on the topic. I'd get over Mickey, was, I think, how she'd seen it. That was certainly how she'd conduct her own life from now on, by getting over people and moving on.

I'd attempted to ring Mickey three times from Scotland. On the first two occasions her mother, Marie, had answered the phone and had told me that Mickey was out. On the third attempt, again it had been Marie who'd answered, but this time she'd put me on to Geoff, Mickey's dad. With sadness in his voice, but resolution in his words, he'd told me what I think Marie had been trying to tell me all along: they didn't want me either to see, call or write to their daughter again.

I checked the clock on the library wall: it was just gone nine. Lights-out time back at my boarding house was at ten and I wanted to take a shower before then. I felt grubby, as I had done every minute of these last three weeks. With the pressure of claustrophobia suddenly bearing down on me, I gathered up the useless clutter of pens and books and notes from the table. I had to get out of here, away from the silence and the ranks of musty books. But even as I thought this, I knew that there was nowhere I could go that would make me feel better. The misery I held inside was not something I could outrun. Miles was dead, and Mickey was far away and I had no means of contacting her.

Outside, it was starting to get dark and I lit a cigarette, carelessly passing the teachers' common room on my right. It didn't bother me if I got caught smoking. I could be fined, or suspended, but so what? None of this meant anything to me any more. Like the school itself, these rules had become insignificant. They belonged to another, gentler world. I passed the chapel and sat down beneath a tree, looking out across the school sports fields, where a group of boys my age were kicking a football around. Then I stood up and ground out my cigarette beneath my shoe, setting off along the path which led back to my boarding house.

Not long later, the sound of my name reached me through the heat and hiss of the shower: 'Roper!'

'What?' I mumbled without moving, the water running down my face turning my voice into a growl.

'Roper!'

The unbroken voice came as a shrill bark this time, and I rubbed the shampoo from my eyes and swivelled round on the tiled floor of the communal shower.

'I said, *what*?' I snapped through the steam at the silhouette of a boy who was standing in the doorway.

'Telephone,' he answered with sudden contrition in his voice.

'Payphone?'

'Yes.'

'Did they say who it was?' I asked, stepping out of the shower's range and turning off the tap, before reaching for my towel. I'd learnt to be wary of the public payphone provided for the use of the boys in the house, since a journalist had tried talking to me, asking me sick and stupid questions about Miles and how I'd felt. My mother always called via Mr Pearce's private line, so I already knew that it couldn't be her.

'I don't know,' the boy muttered. 'Sorry,' he went on, scratching his knee. 'I didn't ask.'

'Tell them I'll be there in a minute.'

'OK, Roper.'

'And thanks,' I added.

I dried myself off, wrapped my towel round my waist and walked from the changing rooms, along the corridor and down to the payphones, which were located outside the games room in the basement. Oldfield, whom I'd yet to speak to after the incident in the chapel where he'd called Miles a spiv, was using one phone and the receiver of the other was off the hook, resting on top of the cash box, which was bolted to the wall. The clack of a snooker ball being hit and someone cursing his bad luck came from behind the closed games room door, against which a prefect called Clarkson, wearing a kaftan round his shoulders and neck, was slouched.

'Hurry up, Roper,' he drawled, glowering across at me as he languidly pushed his long fringe back. 'Some of us have got important calls to make.'

There had been a time when I would have taken this comment for what it was: a command. Clarkson, the captain of the school rugby team, was a good two stone heavier than me and was used to getting what he wanted when he wanted it.

'Go fuck yourself,' I told him, turning my back on him, and picking up the receiver and lifting it to my ear. 'Hello,' I said, ignoring the sounds of outrage behind me.

'Fred?'

'Mickey?' I asked in disbelief.

'Fred!'

'I –' we both said together.

'No, you –' we both said in unison again.

I felt the skin on my face stretching, suddenly remembering what it was like to smile. I cradled the receiver closer to my ear. 'Thank God,' I said, enveloped by her presence, feeling as warm and comforted by it as if it had been a blanket. 'Thank God you've called.'

'How –' she started to say. Then she paused and I heard her squeal.

I closed my eyes and I could see her, my wonderful, beautiful Mickey, smiling for me. 'Talk to me,' I said.

Her voice became grave. 'How are you?'

'I'm . . .' I shook my head. How was I? What a question. 'I'm . . .' I tried again. 'I'm so bloody glad it's you.'

'I've missed you.'

'I tried calling,' I blurted out. 'I spoke to your mum and your dad and they . . . they told me not to . . .' I suddenly had so much to say that I didn't know where to begin. 'Where are you?' I asked. 'They're not there, are they? Because they'll –'

'I'm going to kill them.'

'Don't,' I told her, remembering how I'd felt after her dad had put the phone down on me. 'They're only doing it to . . . How did you know I'd be here?' I asked.

'Because even if she is in Scotland, your mother's still Louisa and you've still got exams to do . . .'

'God, I want to see you.'

'Really?'

'Of course, really. What do you –'

'OK, then,' she interrupted.

'OK?' I laughed. 'But your parents . . .'

'Forget about them.'

'What about my mum, then? She wants me back in

Scotland at half-term. There's no way she's going to let me –'

'I don't mean then,' she told me. 'I mean now.'

'What?'

There was a pause, then: 'I'm at the station.'

'What station?'

I heard her laughing at the other end of the phone. 'The one that – according to Dad's road map – is about ten miles from your school.'

'But how?'

'Does it matter?'

'Of course not,' I said, suddenly filled with hope.

'Can you get away?'

'I don't know. I mean, yes. I'll find a way.' I thought quickly. 'Lights-out is in half an hour. I'll be able to sneak out after that.' I suddenly remembered the presence of Clarkson and started to whisper. 'Do you want me to come to the station?' I asked.

'Is someone there?' Mickey guessed.

'Yes,' I confirmed, 'but it doesn't matter. Tell me.'

'Why don't I come to you?' she asked. 'I've got enough money for a taxi. I can be there by the time you sneak out. Is there somewhere safe I can meet you?'

Oldfield finished his call on the phone next to me, and Clarkson took his place and started to dial. He turned and stared at me with blackened, malevolent eyes, and I looked away.

'Hang on a moment,' I told Mickey and I waited a couple of seconds for Clarkson to begin his call. 'OK,' I continued once he was speaking. 'There are some disused buildings in the grounds. We could break into one of them. I'll meet you at the bottom of the school drive in an hour . . .'

'I'll bring some candles,' she said. 'And I can pick up some food and something to drink . . .'

'And cigarettes,' I said. 'I'm out.'

231

'And cigarettes . . .'

'The end of the drive, then?' I checked. 'At eleven. Are you sure you'll be able to find it?'

'Don't worry,' she reassured me. 'I'll be there.' The line crackled and I didn't speak. I couldn't bring myself to say goodbye. It was Mickey who broke the silence. 'Fred . . .' she said.

'What?'

'I love you.'

Half an hour later, upstairs in my dormitory, lying on my bed with the taste of toothpaste still fresh in my mouth, I stared through the blackness with wide-open eyes. Around me the silence was disturbed by the familiar sounds of dormitory life. People whispered and bed springs creaked. These were noises I'd grown used to over the last three years. They'd long since stopped bothering me or keeping me from my sleep. But I didn't want to sleep now. My body and mind were as alert as if I'd just been flung into an ice-cold plunge pool. I wanted the voices to stop and the movements to subside. The moment they did I'd be out of here.

Sitting in my car outside the crematorium near Warminster, I lean forward over the steering wheel and wipe a space in the steamed-up windscreen. Peering up, I watch the sodden grey sky wringing itself out. Rain drums down on to the car, as heavy as hail, and I pull my coat from the passenger seat and struggle into it. Taking an old baseball cap from the glove compartment, I tug it tight on to my head and reach for the door handle.

Even though I know this is something I have to do alone, I wish that Mickey were here. This bridging of my present and my past, I know, would be so much easier with her by my side, showing me the way. But she isn't here. And she doesn't know I am either. I haven't seen her since Sunday morning when I woke up on my own on the sofa in her parents' living room, and dressed and let myself out of the house.

Releasing my fingers from the door handle, I sink back into my seat, pull the pack of cigarettes from the dashboard and light one up. Smoke billows before my face and, winding the window down a fraction, I watch it curl out.

Mickey was right in what she said after Joe had interrupted us in her parents' kitchen. She was right, too, in preventing matters from going any further between us. Yet still I won't surrender the precious scent of her skin as we sat on the doorstep, and I cupped her face in my hands and pressed my lips up against hers. I can't do it, any more than I can relinquish the feel of her hands on my body, or the look of longing in her eyes as she blamed what had happened between us on our having drunk too much wine. The passion I'd felt only moments before had been intoxicating, but it had had nothing to do with alcohol. The passion I'd felt as we'd kissed had been something that I'd only felt once before in my lifetime and that time it had been with Mickey, too.

I'm in love with her. There's no question about it. She floats through my dreams and I wake with her face imprinted on my mind. My days are spent aching for her. I'm in love with her and I'm no longer in love with Rebecca. I've fallen out of love with Rebecca and in love with Mickey. It doesn't matter which way I choose to look at it, one fact remains: on Saturday, in three days' time, I'm marrying a woman I no longer love, a woman to whom I've been unfaithful in my head for many weeks now and to whom, just a few days ago, I would have been unfaithful with my body, if I'd only been allowed.

But Mickey was right. What I wanted to do – what *we* almost did *together* – was wrong. We're not sixteen any more. Our lives are bigger now than what we desire. There are too many other considerations to be taken into account, too many other people's lives which intertwine with our own. The baggage we've accumulated over the years is too significant for us to jettison and start afresh. We've become too grown-up for that.

Grinding out my half-smoked cigarette in the ashtray, wishing I'd never lit it in the first place, I open the car door and step outside. Then, slamming it behind me and holding my arm up to shield my face against the driving rain, I dash across the car park to the crematorium. It's a long, low concrete building and, on reaching it, I duck beneath its pouring eaves and walk round to the entrance. Forty or so people are gathered here, talking in low whispers and, as I come in, some of them turn to look me over, a collective, calm inquisitiveness in their faces.

A dark-haired man around my age steps forward. There's a tear-swollen puffiness to his gaunt cheekbones and dark circles beneath his eyes. 'Were you a friend of Bill's?' he asks me. 'I'm Roger, his eldest son.'

I shake my head. 'No,' I tell him, suddenly taken aback by the number of people here to commemorate one man's life. 'I'm just here to . . .' I clear my throat. 'Do you know who's in charge of the crematorium?' I ask. 'Is there someone who manages everything?'

'Hang on a second,' he tells me, turning his back on me. 'Jonathan?' he calls and I watch a short, square-shouldered clergyman walk over towards us.

'I need to find a . . .' I begin, before my mind becomes clouded with confusion and my words trail off. 'Grave,' I continue. 'I was about to say grave, only obviously . . .' I nod upwards at the crematorium's roof, towards where the chimneys probably are.

'Mrs Philips should be able to help you,' the clergyman tells me. 'She keeps all the records and she should be back from lunch by now.' He points away from the crematorium, over the road and across a well-kept lawn, to a small red-brick house. 'You'll find her there.'

I thank him and set out across the road, looking up

towards the distant gates, where a hearse is slowly leading a procession of accompanying cars towards the waiting crowd of mourners behind me. I think back to the last time I was here, when a burning, unforgiving sun filled the sky, and there were no people here other than my mother and myself.

Mrs Philips is in her early forties and has an open and enquiring manner, smiling at me as I walk into her office and approach the wooden counter behind which she works. 'How can I help you?' she asks.

'Miles . . .' I begin, before correcting myself. 'My father', I try again, 'was cremated here in nineteen eighty-five and I've driven down from London today, because I wanted to see where he was buried, only now I'm here I've realised how stupid I'm being, because obviously, there wouldn't have been any remains left to bury after he was bur— after he was cremated.' I realise from her expression that I'm speaking too quickly and I take a breath before continuing, 'I was wondering if you could tell me what happened to his ashes. I know my mother hasn't got them. We didn't take anything back with us after the service, and . . .'

But there my steam runs out. My head drops and I find myself staring at my darkened, blurred reflection in the varnished wooden counter. Internally, I kick myself for being so short-sighted. I should have known there was nothing for me here.

'We have a garden of remembrance,' Mrs Philips explains. 'Some of our clients opt to have their relatives' ashes placed there. Do you know if your mother –'

'No,' I tell her. 'I doubt Mum would have . . .'

'In that case . . .' Mrs Philips says a little awkwardly. 'If we receive no instructions to the contrary, it's our policy to scatter the ashes in the woods behind the crematorium. It's a very peaceful place,' she adds with a kindly smile.

'Thank you,' I say, turning to leave. 'I'll go there.'

'Before you do,' Mrs Philips says, causing me to turn

235

back to face her. 'Why don't you let me just check?' She gets to her feet.

'Really,' I say, 'there's no need. I'll just . . .'

But she's insistent. 'You never know,' she tells me, 'your father might be in the garden after all and it would be a shame not to see him after travelling all this way.'

I'm about to thank her for her offer, but decline her help. (I can't imagine Mum having wanted Miles remembered by anyone.) But it's too late. Mrs Philips is already disappearing through the swing doors that separate this room from whatever lies behind. I gaze down at my wet shoes and become uncomfortably aware of the glow of sweat permeating my rain-spattered face. There's a swishing of doors and, looking up, I see Mrs Philips returning with a heavy, leather-bound ledger in her hands.

She places it on the counter between us and opens it up. 'Nineteen eighty-five, you say . . .'

'June,' I confirm, suddenly nervous of the question that I know will come next.

'And the name?' she duly asks.

'Roper,' I tell her. 'Miles Roper.'

I watch her intently, but she doesn't display even a trace of reaction to my words. Quite the contrary, I hear her muttering them as she flicks over the pages, running her finger down the columns of the deceased as she reads.

'Here we are,' she says brightly, turning the ledger round to face me and pointing at Miles's name next to a grid reference. 'Aren't you glad we looked now?'

'You mean he has got a place in the garden?' I ask, looking up from the ledger in disbelief.

'Absolutely,' she states. 'Row twenty-seven, plot sixteen.'

'Thank you, Mrs Philips,' I tell her.

'My pleasure, Mr Roper,' she says and then, no doubt registering the consternation in my face, she asks, 'Is everything all right?'

'Yes,' I tell her, feeling my facial muscles relaxing. 'I think it really is.'

Outside, the rain has diminished somewhat and now drifts noiselessly down, like dust. As I walk back past the crematorium, I can hear from within the swell of an organ and the sound of muffled voices singing along to the tune of 'The Lord's my shepherd'. As instructed by Mrs Philips, I follow the white metal signs to the Garden of Remembrance, which lies to the right of the crematorium. It covers a couple of acres, no more, and as I navigate my way through the rows of plots I wonder at how little we all come to in the end.

Row twenty-seven is down near the woods. Walking along it with my head bowed low, I feel weak with apprehension, almost as if I'm about to see Miles in person. What would I say to him, I wonder, if I were to find him now, sitting there on one of these meagre plots of earth, smoking a cigarette and looking up at me with those cool, assessing eyes? Would I read repentance in them, or innocence? Not, of course, that he'd be anything like how I remember him. Fifteen years have passed since his death, which would make him fifty-three years old now, instead of the thirty-eight at which he lies frozen in my mind. He was only thirty-eight, less than ten years older than I am now.

I keep walking, concentrating on the tiny brass plates in the ground at my side, and the plastic and fresh flowers that have been placed beside them. As I pass plot fifteen, I feel my guts lurch and then, as I reach plot seventeen, I come to a halt. I knew Mum wouldn't have done this. I knew she'd have rather had Miles scattered to the winds. Mrs Philips's ledger must have been mistaken.

But then, just as I'm about to leave, something catches my eye and I stare down at the tangle of weeds between the two plots. Kneeling down, careless of the cold and wet which filters through my trousers to my skin, I claw at the dock leaves and thistles, and there I see a lacklustre brass plate which reads:

Miles Stanley Roper
1947–1985

O Saviour Christ, our woes dispel;
For some are sick, and some are sad,
And some have never loved thee well,
And some have lost the love they had.

I run through these words, chosen by my mother, over and over again, and then I stare up at the bleak sky.

No, Miles never did love Christ, or God for that matter, either. Miles always lived by his own rules and, somehow, I doubt he's been bent towards anyone else's, even now. The brass plate has the dull glow of a distant fire and I trace my finger over his name, but there's no warmth to be felt there on this cold day.

So much of Miles's life and, indeed, his death remains veiled in mystery. Was he involved in Carl's murder? And if so, did he pull the trigger himself? The police certainly believed that the answer to both these questions was an emphatic yes, although of course he'd never gone to trial, or even been interviewed by them.

Tony Hall had been the one who'd told them all this, just like, after his falling out with Miles, he'd been the one who'd told them where to find the body. Miles had never had an opportunity to give his side of the story. Tony had told the police that Miles had boasted to him about killing Carl after an argument over the signing of some papers concerning Clan's ownership. That had been enough for them and, following Miles's death, the case of Carl's murder had been left officially open, but unofficially all lines of further enquiry had ceased.

Tony the Crony, whatever his own involvement might

have been, had never been charged, and Clan itself had closed and never reopened. All the proceeds from the sale of the building and its contents had gone towards paying off the debts which Miles had left behind.

As for me, I don't think Miles was guilty of murder. This was my gut reaction at the time as his son, but over the years it's something I've stuck with, not for my self-protection so much, as because I just don't think murder was something he was capable of. He was a rogue. I don't deny that. He wasn't a good man, in the same way that he wasn't a good husband or a good father. But he wasn't evil. He was ambitious and greedy and, at times, uncaring and selfish, but never evil. I don't think he had the necessary callousness to put a gun to the back of someone's head and pull the trigger. That was always far more Tony's style. That said, I do believe Miles might have known; there was nothing, I don't think, that went on in Clan that he didn't know about. It's possible that he might have persuaded Tony to do it for him. That would have been far more his style and would have explained why it was he'd then chosen to run.

Or maybe . . . maybe I'm wrong . . . maybe Miles did do it. Maybe he shot Carl with the same pistol I shot Jimmy Dughead's bull. Because that's the other thing I still believe about Miles: with him, anything and everything was always possible.

I gaze across the garden at the crematorium. It reminds me of the nuclear bunkers I used cut out of magazines in the Seventies, to show Miles in the hope that he'd build us a shelter in our back garden. 'Rushton isn't a military target,' I remember him telling me. 'But you're Britain's best secret agent,' I told him back. 'Of course the Russians are going to want to kill you first,' I explained. 'You're the one who knows all the secrets.'

And nothing there, at least, has changed. Whatever secrets he had are with him now.

I reach inside my coat pocket and take out the sunglasses that Mickey and I buried with the rest of our treasure in the field on Jimmy Dughead's land. I think back to almost a quarter of a century ago, to the night of my seventh birthday, when Miles first slipped them on to my face as he carried me up the stairs to bed. 'They're Government issue,' I remember him explaining. 'One hundred per cent Carnage-proof. Nothing evil can hurt you when you're wearing them.' Unfolding the sunglasses' arms, I lean forward and push them into the soft earth, so that the dark lenses stare up at me from below the brass plate. 'Goodbye, Dad,' I say, getting to my feet, and turning and heading back to the car.

On Friday afternoon I leave work early and go back to the flat and collect my bags, before driving to Shotbury, where I book myself into my accommodation above the bar in the King's Head Hotel.

It consists of a low-beamed spacious bedroom, with an en suite bathroom. The bedroom contains two single beds, one for my best man, Eddie, and one for myself. Eddie, who discovered yesterday afternoon that he'd have to cover for someone tonight at Nitrogene, will be unable to join me until much later. His plan is to drive here direct from the club after his shift ends, which means that it's unlikely he'll arrive much before four in the morning. His much-vaunted evening of drinking and reminiscing over the end of my bachelor days will therefore, I'm relieved to say, not be happening.

Checking the time, I work out that Rebecca will be flying back from Oslo, landing any minute now, and probably won't reach Thorn House for another couple of hours. George called me at work this morning to check that everything was OK and to suggest meeting up with myself and Eddie for a couple of beers this evening. Thorn House, it seemed, had become too overrun with Rebecca's bridesmaids and florists for George's liking and any opportunity of restoring a balance of masculinity to the house was one he would have welcomed.

It was something I would have arranged anyway, a visit to Thorn House this evening, but when I told him about Eddie's difficulties with Nitrogene, George insisted on my joining himself, Mary, Rebecca and the others for dinner later on. Either that, he said, or he could come down to meet me in the King's Head bar. I told him dinner would be fine. Going to visit them was what I wanted. Besides, I knew it would be impossible for me to talk to him one on one right now.

Not bothering to hang up any of my clothes in the wardrobe or place my trousers in the press provided, I throw my bag on to Eddie's empty bed and flop down on my own. Propping myself up with pillows and scanning through the TV channels with the remote control, I settle on a cartoon and watch a series of brightly coloured creatures cracking jokes in shrill voices and chasing one another endlessly around. Closing my eyes, I think of my mother, with Alan no doubt at her side, boarding the sleeper train in Scotland, in order that she'll arrive here tomorrow morning in time to witness the marriage of her only son.

Thorn House is a whirl of activity by the time I pull into the driveway at just gone eight. Men and women in jeans and bright-red T-shirts are unloading boxes from a van into one of the outbuildings. As discussed with George less than two months ago, a fine-looking white marquee now stands on the front lawn, contrasting more heavily by the second with the crepuscular backdrop of the house itself. As I park my car in the drive alongside it and get out, I see Rebecca rushing out of the front door and across the grass to greet me. She reaches me and hugs me, and I stare over her shoulder and wonder how long this night will last.

'Are you all right?' she enquires, pulling back and resting her hands on my shoulders.

'What makes you ask?'

'You look . . .' She peers searchingly into my eyes and I'm unable to hold her stare. 'Fred,' she says, her voice earnest, 'are you OK? Nothing awful's happened, has it?'

'No,' I tell her truthfully, 'nothing awful at all.'

'But something must . . . you seem so sad . . .'

I rack my brains for something to say. 'Eddie . . .' I begin as the thought occurs to me.

'What?' she interrupts.

'He's not going to be here till early in the morning,' I continue.

'Oh,' she says, looking away from me, up towards the house, distracted by something I cannot see. I'm aware of her hands relaxing on my shoulders. 'Is that all?' she asks, turning back to me.

'Yes.'

She smiles and slips her hand into mine, saying, 'I've got so much to show you, darling. Mum and Dad have been organising stuff all week and it all looks . . .' She tugs at my hand and starts to lead me across the lawn. 'Come and see for yourself,' she says.

Katie and Susan, Rebecca's bridesmaids, are already inside the marquee and, together, the three of them excitedly explain the layout of the tables, pointing out where our various groups of guests will be sitting during the meal and speeches.

'It's going to be fabulous,' Katie says, waving her arm across the vast space. 'Imagine it once everyone's here, with all the flower arrangements in place and the candles lit . . .'

'You wait till you see Rebecca in her dress,' Susan teases.

I look at my bride-to-be, beautiful and gazing serenely at the top table where tomorrow she'll be sitting as a wedded woman, next to me, a married man.

'Forget the dress.' Susan laughs. 'He's more interested in the underwear – aren't you, Fred?'

I nod my head in agreement, but my face remains impassive. I like Katie and Susan, but I wish they weren't here. I need to speak to Rebecca and I need to do it alone.

The evening doesn't play out that way, though. After the marquee come the kitchens, and a half-hour discussion with Mary and George about the order in which the food, champagne and wine are to be served. The more I hear, the more distant I feel myself becoming. I crave simplicity and normality over this. The money they've spent sickens me to my core. I can't help thinking of where Mum lives in Scotland and how she's my only relative invited to this event, and how different I really am from Rebecca's family. And, of course, I think of Mickey and what happened at her parents' house last weekend, and how right her reaction was, but still, how intrinsically wrong everything here still feels. Mary's and George's voices fade further and further out in my mind until I'm barely listening to them at all. I observe them, as detached as if I were watching a silent movie. But I can't change the channel. I can't turn it off and walk away.

It's not until after dinner that I get an opportunity to speak to Rebecca alone.

'I know you're not meant to on the night before your wedding,' she whispers into my ear as we're walking between the dining room and the sitting room, 'but I've never really been one for believing in luck . . .'

'What?' I ask her, stopping where I am, and watching George, Mary and the girls disappearing one by one through the sitting-room door.

'Just a quickie,' she says, pulling me towards the stairs. 'No one will notice. They're all drunk.'

Her last assumption is correct. Of the six of us who sat down to dinner, I'm the only sober one remaining, having used the presence of my car and my need to meet Eddie

243

back at the King's Head later on as an excuse not to indulge in the tasting of tomorrow's wines that George instigated the moment we sat down to eat. 'OK,' I say, adding, 'so long as it's somewhere private. I don't want anyone walking in on us.'

'No problem,' she says with a grin, before hurrying up the stairs without another word.

I follow the intricate floral design of her dress to the second landing and then on down a corridor with which I'm unfamiliar. As I traipse along behind her, it strikes me that she's had her hair cut shorter than I've ever seen it before and the soft skin of her neck is now clearly visible at the back.

She stumbles round a corner and then comes to a halt at a closed door. Turning, she grins drunkenly at me. 'Daddy's study,' she says. 'With a nice big desk ... What a naughty girl I am ...'

'But mightn't he –' I start to ask.

She shakes her head with exaggerated movement, swinging her fringe back and forth across her forehead. 'Too drunk,' she tells me. 'And too excited. Believe me, the last thing that's going to be on his mind at the moment is work ...'

She opens the door and I follow her inside. The smell of cigar smoke hangs heavy in the air. The room is of modest proportions and bookcases are lined along its walls. Opposite the door, which I close behind me as Rebecca walks over to the desk and switches on the lamp there, is a window which overlooks the gardens. I think of my unpacked bag lying there on Eddie's bed in the King's Head. Rebecca turns to face me and, hitching up her dress, she starts to pull her knickers down.

'No,' I say, making no move to join her.

'What do you mean?' she asks, glancing up in agitation.

I lean back against the door. 'There's something I need to talk to you about,' I say.

Straightening, she pulls up her knickers and lets her dress fall back down over her legs. 'Well?' she asks, folding her arms across her chest. 'I'm listening.'

'It's about us. It's about us as a couple.'

I pause, searching for the right words, and she prompts, 'What about us?'

'It's about the fact that we're going to be getting married tomorrow,' I say, 'and we're going to be making vows to each other in front of our friends and families. And if we don't mean what we're saying, then we shouldn't be there saying it in the first place.' My face is beginning to burn as the torment inside searches for an outlet. I lift my hand to my face and slowly massage my brow. 'It's about the truth, Rebecca. It's about being honest with one another. And it's about being honest with ourselves.'

She says something which I don't catch and, looking up, I see her face, always so confident, suddenly trembling in the low glow of the lamp.

'Sorry,' I say after a moment, 'I missed what you said.'

'I knew it,' she tells me and I see now that she's crying. 'I knew it the moment you stepped out of the car . . .'

Seeing her like this, my instinct tells me to rush up to her and to comfort her, but I resist. 'But how?' I ask, surprised as I am by what she's just told me.

'How do you think?' she spits out, her shoulders beginning to shake. 'Because I know you . . . because I can read you . . . for the same reason you guessed yourself . . .'

Before I can communicate the confusion these last words have stirred up inside me, she breathes in deeply in an effort to compose herself. 'You're right, of course, to want to talk about this now,' she says. 'I should have told you before. I'm sorry, Fred. I should've told you as soon as it happened.'

I'm about to say, '*Tell me what*?' when I stop myself. 'Go on,' I say instead.

Snivelling, Rebecca reaches for a box of tissues on the

desk beside her, pulls one out and blows her nose on it loudly. She doesn't look at me as she starts to speak. 'I didn't mean for it to happen,' she says. 'Neither of us did. We were stoned. You saw how stoned we were when you left . . .'

We?

Rebecca blows her nose again. 'And Eddie said it didn't matter . . .'

Eddie?

'. . . because', she continues, 'it was just a bit of fun and it wasn't like we were married yet, and the only reason anything happened between us at all was because we'd got so stoned in the park, and it wasn't like I'd been emotionally unfaithful or anything like that . . .'

'Eddie . . .' I say, nodding my head, as I suddenly realise how blind I've been to what's been going on behind my back.

I picture the moment that I left him and Rebecca sitting there together on the picnic rug in Hyde Park on the evening of Phil's birthday party. Then a more recent memory surfaces, that of Eddie talking to me at the front of the barge on the Thames a week ago today, telling me how difficult it sometimes was to be a good friend to someone. 'Eddie . . .' I repeat, continuing to nod my head as I stare into Rebecca's terrified eyes.

'I'm sorry, darling.' She's sobbing. 'It didn't mean anything. It was just one of those . . . I swear to God, it'll never happen again . . .'

I've heard enough. 'It doesn't matter,' I tell her softly.

Dropping the tissue that she's holding on to the floor, she takes a tentative step forward. 'Do you really mean that?' she asks.

I don't hesitate for even a second. 'Yes.'

'Only I'd understand it if you were angry –'

'No,' I reassure her, 'I'm not angry, not in the least.'

The noise of a muffled voice comes from somewhere

along the corridor and we both fall silent. Then the noise comes again.

'It's your father,' I say, recognising it this time as his. 'He's calling for us.'

She reaches out to touch my face. Relief and disbelief are combined in hers in equal measure. 'And you're sure you're . . .?'

'Yes,' I tell her again, 'but while we're on the subject of honesty, there's something I've got to tell you, too . . .'

'What?' she asks, staring up into my eyes, suddenly startled.

I look away, ignoring her question. 'Go and deal with your father,' I tell her, stepping aside and opening the door. 'And when you've done that, come and find me. I'll be waiting for you in the kitchen garden.'

Outside, I walk along the meandering garden path and wait for Rebecca to arrive. The heavy scent of wisteria and night-time stocks fill my nostrils, and the air is warm and welcoming. Feeling very much alive, I think of tomorrow. I meant what I said to Rebecca just now. It really doesn't matter about what happened between her and Eddie. What I'm about to tell her I would have told her anyway, regardless, whether she'd told me about Eddie or not.

Reaching a corner in the path, I stop and gaze across the darkened garden. Then, without wishing it, I find my mind sifting back through my memory to another summer night, and another place, and another girl.

Eventually, the sound of whispering voices trailed off one by one and silence descended on the dormitory. I was lucky that exams were imminent or I could have ended up waiting for hours before it was safe to make my move.

I slipped out from under my duvet and, sitting on the edge of my bed, reached beneath it for the gym bag I'd packed before lights-out time some three-quarters of an hour before. I remained motionless, listening intently to the sounds of breathing around me, straining through the darkness for signs of wakefulness. I heard none.

Standing, my senses seemed heightened. It felt like my body had been connected to an amplifier. I could hear the rush of my breath and the creak of my joints, but above all this came the erratic thudding of my heart. Fear filled me as the obstacles between here and Mickey suddenly reared up as impossibilities in my mind. Being caught for breaking curfew wasn't what frightened me. Being kept from Mickey was.

The dormitory was arranged along a thin, straight corridor, with ten beds on either side, each of them separated from their neighbours' by tall wooden partitions. At one end of the corridor was a six-foot sash window, leading to a fire escape. The window's lock was connected to an alarm in Mr Pearce's study downstairs. Should the latch be lifted, a bell would start to clang and he, in turn, would be up here within minutes to see what was amiss.

The opposite end of the dormitory – the route I intended to take – stopped at a heavy swing door, which led to the washroom, lavatories and the rest of the boarding house. From there, a staircase climbed up to the junior dormitories above and led down to the sixth-formers' study-bedrooms below. Because of the alarm on the fire escape, I'd have to risk going downstairs, and hope that Mr Pearce wasn't doing his rounds and that the duty prefects were all safe behind closed doors, engrossed in their revision.

In an attempt to quell my growing paranoia, I forced myself to take comfort in the security provided by the darkness. In the dormitory, at least, I might be heard, but I wouldn't be seen. Once outside, the same rule would apply. In between these two places – downstairs – I could trust only to luck.

Turning, I arranged my pillows under my duvet, plumping them up so that the bed looked as though it were occupied. This was a token gesture, I realised even as I was performing it. It was for my own peace of mind. Anything more than a cursory inspection would reveal my deceit. But by then it would be too late; I'd already be gone.

Wearing nothing but the boxer shorts given to me by Mickey as a present at the end of the holidays, and with the gym bag gripped tightly in my hand, I crept away from my bed and along the corridor towards the swing door. To my left, someone moaned in his sleep, but other than that I heard only the sound of my own bare feet treading lightly on the worn brown carpet.

Before opening the door I hesitated, knowing that if either Pearce or a prefect were standing on the other side, the contents of my bag would be enough to incriminate me and leave me stuck in the housemaster's study, answering awkward question after awkward question, as Mickey stood, lonely and ignored, at the bottom of the school drive.

A shaft of bright light cut into the dormitory as I pulled the door open enough to allow me to slip through, but the hallway was clear, and I hurried into the lavatories and entered one of the cubicles, locking the door behind me. With the sound of the old black cistern dripping, and the glare of a bare light bulb above my head, I unzipped my bag and started to dress.

Two minutes later, with my empty bag now discarded behind the lavatory door, I was standing on the stairway landing, dressed in black school trousers, black school shoes and a thick woollen navy-blue turtleneck. A torch and a knife, which I'd liberated from the kitchens, were tucked into the belt of my trousers beneath. It was hardly what I would have wished to have worn to see Mickey, but it made sense under the circumstances. I'd have dressed up in nappies and a motorbike helmet if it would have guaranteed my safe passage.

Careful to tread only on the front of my shoes, so that my heels wouldn't click on the hard plastic surface on the stairs, I padded down the two flights to the bottom. There was a junction here, with a corridor to the left leading to the laundry, showers and changing rooms, and one to the right, which ran past the sixth-form study-bedrooms and terminated at the doorway separating Mr Pearce's living quarters from the rest of the building.

The overhead lights were out in both corridors and the only illumination came from a skylight to my left. Here, moonlight had imprinted a bright block of light on the polished white laminated floor. I shivered, a childhood memory surfacing of the opening of the spacecraft doors in *Close Encounters*. . . . Then I headed left, staring momentarily up at the square of starry sky as I passed beneath the skylight, feeling closer to Mickey, thinking that, somewhere near, she might be experiencing this same sight, too.

I met no one as I moved along the remainder of the corridor towards the laundry room. It was as if a spell had been cast over the rest of people in the house and I were a ghost moving undetected through their midst.

Then, as I reached the laundry door but had yet to open it, voices cut through the silence and I froze. Cursing my luck but refusing to panic, I slowly turned my head and looked up the corridor. There, barely fifteen feet away, standing in the open doorway of one of the study-bedrooms, talking in a hushed incomprehensible voice, was the unmistakable figure of Clarkson, the prefect whose wrath I had incurred while talking to Mickey on the phone earlier in the evening. Nothing, I knew, would please him more than to catch me now. All he had to do was turn.

Adrenalin charged through me, as I waited for him to make a move. But he didn't, not for whole seconds. Instead, he continued talking in agitated tones, repeatedly tapping a pen against the door frame, until, with an idio-syncratic gesture, he pushed back his fringe and pulled the door closed.

Darkness descended and then, with a click, I felt as if a searchlight had been swept on to my face: the corridor light was on. Blinking, my eyes unaccustomed to the brightness, I waited for the sound of my name to be shouted out. It never came. Instead, I heard footsteps and saw Clarkson walking in the opposite direction up the corridor, utterly oblivious to my presence. He pushed through the set of swing doors at the far end and strode up the three stairs to Mr Pearce's private part of the house.

Raising a silent prayer, I hurried through to the back of the laundry. Sitting there on the chipped paintwork of the windowsill, surrounded by the familiar smell of damp and drying sports kit, I began unfastening the lock. I lifted the window, gazed out into the moonlit garden and breathed in the still, warm air. Beyond the lawn, the school buildings were shrouded in darkness against the wide, wan sky, as if they'd been drawn in charcoal. I clambered out of the window and dropped down into the soft earth of the flowerbeds below. Pulling the window closed behind me and too afraid to use my torch, I set off across the lawn, into the undergrowth beyond.

It wasn't until I was a good half-mile away from my boarding house and the main school that I risked breaking from the cover of the trees and bushes, and stepping out on to the school drive. Gravel crunched beneath my feet as I made my way along it in spurts, jogging fifty yards, then stopping and listening, before jogging on once more. Whenever I moved I thought of the chaplain and the stories of his night-time forays into the nearby villages, and I saw his face in every patch of brambles that I passed. It was only when I neared the end of the drive some ten minutes later that I began to relax.

Then I saw the headlights. A car was coming round a

bend in the lane three hundred yards beyond the bottom of the drive. The twin beams oscillated like a strobe along the cast-iron fence which marked the school's boundary and, by the time I thought of moving, I could already hear the growl of the vehicle's diesel engine. Remembering where I was and what I was doing here, I dashed across the open ground of the drive and ducked down behind one of the stone pillars, which stood either side of the gateway to the school.

The car didn't pass and head on down the lane. Instead, it slowed and its headlights swept around in an arc until they pointed up the driveway towards the distant silhouettes of Greenaway. My stomach contracted with apprehension. Then I heard the car stopping and the noise of a door being opened and slammed shut. Cautiously, I inched forward from my hiding place and peered round the stonework, and then I smiled.

Mickey was standing beside the open window of the cab driver's door, basking in the moonlight like an actress on stage. Her denim jacket was draped casually over her shoulder and her hair, seeming shorter than when I'd seen her at the end of the holidays, was tied up bunches. She wore tight black trousers, ending below the knee. The cab driver handed over her change and Mickey stepped back from the door, as the car pulled away from her, turning a full circle, before starting back in the direction from which it had come.

I stayed watching, suddenly overcome by the arrival of this moment in which I'd invested so much. I looked terrible and I knew it. I'd lost weight over the past few weeks and when I'd stared at my face in the washroom mirror before lights-out time I'd seen how gaunt I'd become. It was going to be all right, wasn't it? Mickey would remember me for who I was and not the events which had engulfed me? Steeling myself, I stepped out from the pillar's shadows and cleared my throat.

'Hello,' I said, my voice inflected with a bravura I didn't feel. 'Remember me?'

'Fred!' she gasped, dropping her bag and rushing towards me.

She threw her arms round me and pulled me close. She was speaking, but I couldn't hear what it was she was saying. She was crying and kissing my face and, as she stepped slowly back and trailed her fingertips across my cheek, I realised that my eyes were filled with tears. Her being here was like a release. It was as if she held the key to all the terrible things that I'd locked away inside my mind. Everything that had happened to me in the last month was suddenly welling up inside me and flooding out. She held me tight, her face pressed against mine, catching my tears on her lips as they fell.

'I'm here,' I heard her whispering over and over again as I continued to sob. 'I'm here, my darling. I'm here.'

Eventually, I pulled away from her. 'We should hurry,' I said. 'I might have been missed by now. If they think I've run away, the drive and the lanes will be the first place they'll look.'

She nodded her head in understanding.

'I know somewhere we can go,' I continued, burying myself in the practicality of the moment.

Taking her bag from her, I led her into the trees. By necessity, we hardly spoke as we walked. We made swift progress to begin with, only slowing as we were forced to navigate our way through the bushes and bracken and brambles beyond. After fifteen minutes, we reached the wide vista of the school sports fields. Mickey stopped at my side and stared. In the distance, tiny blocks of lights delineated the windows of Greenaway's buildings.

'How big is this place?' she asked, amazed.

'You should see it the daytime,' I replied. 'You will tomorrow when we wake up.'

And it was there and then I realised that in my mind I

had already made my decision. I wouldn't be going back to my boarding house, either tonight or tomorrow. I was with Mickey now. I wouldn't allow myself to be separated from her again. I slipped my hand into hers and, together, we walked on.

Five minutes later, we were standing outside a small, ornamental white stone temple on the far side of Greenaway's playing fields, hundreds of yards from any inhabited part of the school. Rumour had it that the building had been gutted by fire over a decade before. Certainly, in the two and a half years I'd been at Greenaway, this building had been used just once, and then only as a backdrop for a school production of *A Midsummer Night's Dream*. Back then – over a year ago now – the gardeners had hacked out a temporary outdoor auditorium from the nettles and brambles which had surrounded it, but now nature had crept back and claimed the place as its own once more.

Neither of us had any idea what lay in wait beyond the smoke-blackened glass of the temple's windows. The beam of the torch Mickey was holding flickered over the lock, which I was attempting to lever free from the damp wooden door frame with my knife. Finally the lock gave and I turned to Mickey and quickly kissed her. 'Come on,' I said, taking the torch from her, 'let's check it out.'

Stepping through the doorway, I gave the place a quick once-over with the torch beam. It was a single room, with a floor space approximately the same size as that of a squash court. White sheets lay draped across as yet unknown objects. The walls were patterned by cobwebs and scorch marks and, somewhere close, something unseen scurried away and I felt myself tense up.

'Don't worry,' Mickey said, slipping her arm around my waist. 'It's probably a field mouse.'

I shone the torch up at the domed ceiling and ran the light across the remnants of a fresco. Among the patches of damp and the smudges of soot, you could still make out traces of angels riding on clouds. I heard Mickey sigh.

'It must have been amazing here once,' she said.

Without speaking, we set about clearing a space for ourselves. Finding a half-bald broom leaning against one of the walls, I swept clean a section of the dusty floor.

Mickey pulled down the dust sheets, revealing piles of broken school desks and stacks of chairs beneath. Shaking the sheets out, she arranged them on the floor. Then she took a packet of candles from her bag by the door and lit the bottom of each one, using the melted wax to cement them upright to the stone floor in a circle round the sheets. Finally, she lit the candles, stood back and surveyed her work. 'Well,' she said, 'it's hardly the Ritz, but it'll do.'

'It's perfect,' I said, sitting down cross-legged on the sheets and watching her walk to the door and collect her bag from where she'd left it. She pulled the door closed and turned back to face me.

As she walked towards me, it struck me how long we'd known one another and how far we'd come. Seeing her here in these strange surroundings made me look on her as if I were seeing her for the first time.

Prior to this moment, Mickey had always been as much a bundle of memories to me as a creature of flesh and blood. Thinking of her had always reminded me of a miracle story I'd read out in a reading competition at Rushton Primary School. In the story, Jesus had helped save a man called Legion, who'd been possessed by many devils, and Jesus had cast the devils from him into a herd of swine.

It wasn't that I'd thought there'd been devils inside Mickey, more that I'd always seen her as being a composite of the many versions of herself that I'd grown up with. Her laughter had been the laughter of a friend, who'd sat on a swing as I'd pushed her higher and higher up into the sky. Her tears had been those of a partner in crime, who'd saved me from drowning in the River Elo when I'd been nine years old. Her touch had been the touch of the first girl I'd ever kissed.

Now, though, now it was different: I saw only her. Gone was the child I'd grown up with. As Miles's death had signified the end of my childhood, so Mickey's continued involvement in my life had, to me, signified the end of hers. It was something I should probably have noticed earlier. She *had* changed . . . in so many ways. Her boyish hips, once as straight as rulers, had flexed outwards into a set of matching curves. My clumsy fumblings around her breasts in her back garden now struck me as the acts of someone who hadn't really known what he was meant to have been doing. Her eyes had taken on wisdom and confidence. Her stare was no longer one of defiance in the face of authority, but of self-assurance.

While all these alterations had been happening to her – even over these last six months that we'd been seeing one another – I'd never really taken time to step back and see quite how amazing she'd become. She was no longer just the girl next door, but the girl I loved. 'You're beautiful,' I said. I realised I was whispering, even though I knew we were safe.

She shrugged, embarrassed, her mouth breaking into a confused half-smile. 'You sound surprised,' she whispered back.

Joining me on the sheets, she emptied out her bag's contents. There were a V-neck jumper, a long T-shirt, a four-pack of lager, a packet of cigarettes and some sandwiches. On top of these a toothbrush and tube of toothpaste fell out.

'Sorry about the lack of running water,' I commented and she smiled, offering me her jumper to wear, then putting it on herself when I shook my head.

She passed me a can of beer and lit us both a cigarette.

'You didn't have any trouble,' I said, raising my beer and taking a sip, 'getting hold of this . . .'

'Girls always look older than they are,' she told me; and she was right: she did.

She leant up against me, her head on my shoulder, her hair against my cheek, and we drank and smoked in silence, warm against each other. Sitting there, just the two of us, in that strange and wondrous place, I felt as though we were astronauts in a capsule, orbiting high above the world.

But then, as had happened with almost every cigarette I'd smoked since Miles's death, as if the very scent I was inhaling formed a direct link to him, the knowledge of his death returned and I found myself plummeting straight back down to earth. 'Were you there?' I asked.

Her mouth opened, but I saved her the trouble of having to broach the subject fully herself.

'When it happened . . .' I said. 'Were you there when Miles died?'

Again, I saw the struggle in her eyes.

'Please,' I implored. 'Mum won't – *can't* talk about it. I need to know.'

Mickey told me the story of what had happened, about how she'd seen Miles as she'd been walking up the Avenue after the school bus had dropped her off, and about hearing him and Mum argue, and about the police, and about what had happened next, back on the Avenue once more, and finally about how Miles had attempted to swerve around the police car but had hit the tree instead.

'Do you think he died as quickly as they say?' I asked.

Her cigarette trembled in her mouth as she took a drag. 'Don't, Fred,' she said, putting the cigarette out and taking mine from me and doing the same. She wrapped her arms round me. 'I'm sorry it had to happen. I'm sorry Miles isn't alive and I'm sorry it's making you so unhappy.'

I looked down at my interlocked fingers and remembered that this was how my mother's had been, day after day in Scotland as we'd waited for news. 'I'm not unhappy,' I started to say, but already, my voice was quavering. I attempted to continue, hoping that speaking would stop me from feeling inside. 'These things happen. I can deal with it. You don't need to worry . . .'

But I was lying. I couldn't deal with it. Tears flowed once more and I felt Mickey's hand stroking my head. This time, though, my tears were different from the ones I'd shed as I'd sobbed into Mickey's arms by the school gate. Like blood flowing from a wound, they were painless, symptomatic only of the depth of the cut beneath.

'We can do this,' Mickey told me. 'Together we can get through this.'

Gradually the heaving in my chest subsided and I pulled myself together enough to speak. 'Miles came to see me,' I said. 'He came here . . . to tell me that something was wrong. I didn't listen to him. I sent him away . . .'

Mickey's voice came soothingly to me. 'You didn't know what was going to happen,' she said. 'No one did.'

I shook my head and pulled back from her. 'Miles did,' I told her. 'He knew he was in trouble. He knew they were going to come looking for him. That someone was . . . that someone would . . . I should've listened to him. I should've been there when he needed me.'

Mickey's eyes seemed gigantic. 'No,' she told me. 'There's nothing you could have done that would have made things any different.'

My mind dredged up another fear. 'Do you think it's –' I started. 'What the newspapers said he did . . . Do you think it's true?'

A tear trailed down her cheek and dropped on to her jumper.

'Do you think he . . . do you think Miles could have . . . ?'

Light danced in Mickey's eyes. I could see she was frightened, scared for me.

The temple air prickled like static around us, and I heaved breath into me and sighed it back out again.

Mickey had no answers for me. No one did. I rubbed at my face with my hands. 'Let's not talk about it any more,' I said.

Her hands were on my shoulders. 'But if you –'

'No.'

I was determined. I picked up my can of beer and drained it. Closing my eyes, I squeezed away the remaining tears and wiped them from my face with the back of my hand. I pushed a lopsided smile on to my face. 'Catharsis . . .' I said. 'I learnt about it in English. It means –'

'I know,' Mickey said. 'It means what we're doing now. And before you say it, you're right: it's good for you . . . for us . . .'

I gazed at her face, statuelike and burnished in the candlelight. As quickly as he'd arrived, Miles faded back into the darkness, almost as if her brightness had driven him away. 'What you said . . .' I asked her, '. . . on the phone. Did you mean it?'

She nodded her head. 'Yes,' she said, unsmiling.

I swallowed, searching for any trace of doubt in her face, but I found none. Her eyes were bright in the candlelight. They reminded me of . . . I tried to push the image away, but it kept flickering back. They reminded me of Miles's eyes when he'd come to visit me at school a month before, when he'd searched for words to tell me how he'd felt. It was only now that I recognised what it was that had burnt behind them: love. This was love I saw before me now in Mickey's eyes, that thing that Miles had been unable to express, but which I was now determined that I would.

'I love you,' I told her.

I'd never said this to anyone else, but here it was, coming so easily to me now. These were only words, after all, and the well of emotions they contained had been deepening inside me for months. Voicing them had been as natural as saying, 'I am', because that was how it truly was. Mickey was alive in me. We were joined. I never wanted us to die. I never wanted us to be broken in two and I never wanted to leave her side again.

'Come here,' she said, lying down on the sheets and reaching out her arms.

Chapter VIII

Mickey

It's Friday night and Joe wants to go to the cinema with Tyler. We've had a fractious week since we came back from Rushton and I guess he deserves a break, but I'm not in the best of moods. I'm also feeling wary of Tyler, and of his parents, Judith and Mike. They live in a big house up near the park and razz about in a large Mercedes people carrier and, while they're very nice people, in a gung-ho, bouffant sort of way, I'm worried that their mere presence in our lives is making Joe question his own lifestyle.

I know it's a great thing that Joe has a social life and that he gets on so well with Tyler, but I'm not equipped to deal with how out of control it's making me feel. When there was just Joe and me we made all our decisions together and what Joe did with his time was never questioned. Now his horizons seem to be changing. Already, this week, the subject of the impending school holidays has caused a row. Tyler and his parents are going on a fun-packed trip to America and Joe, understandably, is jealous. My worst fear is that Tyler's family, out of sympathy, are going to ask Joe along on the trip and it'll be up to me to decide whether he can go. I'm not sure I can make that kind of parental decision on my own, let alone afford it.

Adding to my stress levels is the fact that we've had a terrible week in the shop. It's been pouring with rain and there have been hardly any customers. I've paid Lisa and Marge, my other assistant, and given Lisa a cash loan, which doesn't exactly leave very much for me.

Joe stands in the shop, kicking his school bag, as we discuss his trip to the cinema, which will involve me handing over my last ten-pound note, not that I've told Joe this.

'But it's a twelve certificate,' I protest.

'So?' he counters.

'So, you're nine,' I remind him.

'Tyler's mum doesn't have a problem,' he says petulantly.

'Joe, I don't care what Tyler's mother says.' I suddenly feel very weary. 'It's you I'm concerned about.'

'But I've watched loads of fifteen certificates and a bit of an eighteen once.'

'Well, that's not the point,' I mumble, knowing that it is. 'It's about parental guidance.'

'So parentally guide me,' says Joe, fixing me with a beady stare.

I sigh, exasperated.

'It's not as if it's really bad,' Joe continues. He knows me well enough to see a chink in my armour and he goes for the kill. 'It's only a cartoon and everyone else at school has seen it. I'm going to look really stupid if I tell Tyler I can't go.'

He doesn't add 'because of you' to the end of his sentence, but it's implicit nevertheless. I look at him, seeing my own defiant stare in his face. There's a part of me that longs to find the words to explain to Joe that I don't want him to grow up, but it's pointless. He wouldn't understand, and it would make me a horrible old curmudgeon if I told him that being a grown-up is not all it's cracked up to be and he should, if he has any sense, hang in there being a child for as long as possible. Besides, it would make me the biggest hypocrite on the planet. I always wanted to grow up faster, to be older than my age, to defy the age labels set by governments and parents, so I can't tell Joe to be any different. Anyway, I suppose these things aren't about age, but maturity and if Joe is mature enough to run rings round me then he can probably handle a twelve-certificate film without being scarred for life.

'OK, OK, you can go,' I relent finally. 'But don't come running to me for sympathy when they won't let you in.'

'Oh, don't worry about that.' Joe smiles. 'Tyler's mum has already pre-booked the tickets.'

I watch him swing his school bag over his shoulder, and walk to the door and up to the flat. When he's out of sight, I rub my hands over my face and try to control my frustration.

A minute later Lisa walks through the door and shakes out her umbrella.

I breathe out deeply and find a smile for her. 'Any joy?' I ask. She's going on a date tonight and I let her have a few hours off to go shopping this afternoon.

'Barkers came up trumps,' she says, her eyes bright with excitement. 'I'm going to knock his socks off, even though I say so myself.'

The lucky gentleman in question is Spike, who works in the reggae record shop down the road. He's had his eye on Lisa for a while, but he's so laid-back that she hasn't twigged that their accidental meetings have not been entirely the amazing coincidences she thinks they have. Tonight's date is at a reggae club and sent Lisa into a frenzy about finding just the right image. I did point out that she'd look great in a bin bag, but she didn't agree.

She bustles over to me and opens the large carrier bag. 'These,' she says, pulling out a pair of black trousers and holding them against her. Her corkscrew curls fall across her face.

'Lovely,' I confirm.

'And this,' she goes on, pulling out a tight-fitting top, which she holds under her chin so that I see the overall effect. 'Far too expensive, but what the hell.'

'Well done.' I say, smiling encouragingly, trying not to mind that my cash advance has been so well spent.

Lisa folds her new clothes carefully and puts them back in the bag. 'Got any plans for tonight?' she asks.

'Joe's going to the cinema, so I'll probably just have a bath, or something.'

'Use some of my rose oil. It works wonders.'

'Thanks.'

There's a pause and Lisa looks at me. 'Are you OK?' she asks.

I shrug wearily. 'Just tired.'

She nods and cocks her head sympathetically. 'No word?' she asks gently.

I told Lisa edited highlights of Fred's trip to Rushton late last Sunday night when Joe and I got back. Her advice was that Fred would be bound to get in touch this week and she gave me a reassuring hug and told me to have faith, but I felt uptight and drew our conversation to a close. I was too confused either to tell her how I was feeling or to take her advice on board. There was so much I hadn't told her, too much history that had become tangled into the present, that making sense of it all in order to recount it to her was impossible.

As a result, we've barely mentioned Fred all week, but I know Lisa's been watching me, sensing, correctly, that I've been counting down the days until tomorrow when Fred gets married.

I shake my head. 'I guess that's that.'

She touches my arm. 'I'm sorry,' she says and I know she means it.

'Don't be. I'm fine, honestly,' I lie. I walk over to the door, not trusting myself to be brave. 'You go up and get ready,' I tell her. 'I'll finish up down here.'

When she's gone, I lean against the door for a moment, looking at the bus drawing up outside. The doors hiss open and I watch the queue of people getting in. It seems as if the whole world is moving on. It's only me who's stuck.

I can't bear that Fred might be near. It makes me feel crowded in and trapped. He's here, behind every car window, in every shop, living in my telephone receiver. Without knowing it, seeing Fred in my world has attached mine to his. I feel as if he's hooked tendrils around everything that's precious to me, and lifted me out of the safe world I've built and left me dangling, looking down at a deep, dark void. I watch the tired faces of the passengers on the bus and feel the weight of their exhaustion.

I close my eyes for a second, reliving the conversation I had with Fred in Rushton. I've gone over and over it all week, trying to find just a tiny bit of the resolve I had when I told Fred that I couldn't see him again. I was right. I know I was right, but somehow that doesn't make me feel any better. Maybe I should have slept with him and got it all over and done with. Maybe if we'd finally made love I'd feel better, as if we'd rounded off the past properly.

I knew at the time I was protecting myself and Joe, but now I can't find any pay-off in my bravery. I gave Fred all the reasons why it wouldn't work between us and none of the reasons why it would. I backed myself into a corner and instead of being strong, I gave Fred all my power. Since the moment I woke up last Sunday and crept downstairs to find the blankets on my parents' sofa folded, with no sign of Fred, I've been feeling empty, as if something has been ripped out of me.

It's my fault. I left it up to him to change things and despite everything I said to him, I've half expected him to turn up, or at least call. But there's been nothing. I've rejected him and he's gone: it's as simple as that. In less than twenty-four hours' time he'll be married to Rebecca who, as I pointed out (stupidly), loves him very much and will make him very happy. And that will be that. I take a deep breath, turn the 'Open' sign to 'Closed' and pull down the shutters. By the time I've cleared up the shop and made my way upstairs, Joe's ready to go out.

He's changed into the T-shirt he won at Fred's games launch, which I know for a fact smells, but I don't have the energy to make an issue of it. He's standing in the kitchen cutting up a banana with the penknife Fred gave him. 'Can we have Fred over tomorrow?' he asks.

'No, darling.' I sigh. 'He's busy.'

'We could ring him,' Joe says hopefully. 'Get him to come over and fly the kite.'

I turn to face Joe, amazed at how thick-skinned he is. 'I don't think we'll be seeing much more of Fred,' I say cautiously. 'You know that he's getting married tomorrow?'

Joe frowns. 'To that woman?'

I nod.

'She's horrible.' He screws up his nose.

'Well, Joe, we don't know that,' I say reasonably. 'And whether she's horrible or not doesn't matter. Fred loves her.'

'I don't see how –'

'It's not up for debate,' I say shakily. 'The thing is that Fred's got a new life now. One that doesn't involve us.'

'Oh.' Joe sounds crestfallen as this finally sinks in.

He puts the penknife down and seems to shrink as he puts his hands in his pockets and, for a moment, I hate Fred. I hate him for coming into our lives and then vanishing again. I hate him for making me feel like such a fool. And I hate him for letting Joe down. I knew all along he was dangerous, yet here I am floundering once more, scuppered on the same rocky emotions, only the second time around it feels much, much worse. I'm responsible for shipwrecking myself *and* Joe this time.

I turn away to the sink, looking up, so that my tears don't fall. Joe doesn't take the hint. I hear him coming up behind me.

'Mum?' he asks. 'Would *you* get married again?'

I turn back round and attempt to smile. 'What a ridiculous question,' I bluff, but Joe's not put off.

'Would you?'

'Well, nobody's asked me, Joe. You can't just decide to get married. You have to find someone to get married to.'

'But say there was someone. Someone like Fred . . .'

I swallow hard. 'I don't know. It would change everything. I mean, we're all right as we are, aren't we?'

To my surprise, Joe smiles sympathetically at me and it's obvious that it's useless trying to hide how I feel from him. He walks towards me, looking so confident and wise that I feel like crumpling, as if I'm the child and he's the grown-up.

'I wouldn't mind, you know,' he says, giving me a hug. I lower my lips to the crown of his head as he rests his cheek against the front of my jumper. 'I just want you to be happy, Mum, that's all.'

I want to reply that I am, except that I can't because my tears are falling into his hair.

My heart felt as if it were going to burst. I didn't care that it was cold, or dusty, or that we were on the hard ground. As far as I was concerned this was the most perfect place in the world and we were floating on the softest feather mattress. As Fred lay gently on top of me and I wrapped my arms round his neck, overwhelming relief flooded through me and I closed my eyes for a second, savouring the feeling of being safe, of being held by the one person who meant more than everything. I was here, finally, and nothing else mattered.

I'd spent so long imagining this moment, but now that it was here, it was nothing like the picture I'd had in my mind. I'd been terrified that my plan to meet Fred wasn't going to work out, that I'd get caught on the way out of

Rushton, that Pippa wouldn't be a safe alibi, or that Fred wouldn't be able to get out to meet me.

Then there'd been the problem of what it'd be like when we saw each other. I'd been worried that I wouldn't know what to say, never having been near someone whose dad had died. I'd thought in my worst moments that Fred would be distant and cold, that maybe he'd have gone off me, or simply withdrawn and wouldn't want to be close. But now all my fears seemed ridiculous in retrospect and the angst I'd felt for the past few weeks lifted off me.

I'd been going out my head worrying about Fred. All I needed to know was where he was. I'd guessed Louisa would probably have sent him back to school and I longed to know that he was all right. Without being able to talk to him, Miles's death had seemed a thousand times worse. Every emotion I felt seemed to be multiplied by two, as if I were experiencing the shock, anger and fear for Fred, too. In his absence I'd felt each remark from people at my school and the outrage of my parents like a body blow, as if Miles had been my father and it'd all been personally directed at me. Now that we'd talked about it, I felt as if I'd come off the tightrope I'd been teetering on and fallen down into a safety net. It didn't make things normal, but at least in telling Fred what had happened, the facts – however horrific – had lost some of their terrifying edge.

The rumours that Miles was a murderer had made living at home terrible. It hadn't seemed to matter that there'd been a horrific death on our doorstep. All people had been concerned about was the discovery of a body at Clan. In an attempt to come to terms with having known and lived in proximity to someone who could have done such a terrible thing as murder, Miles's supposed crime had become more brutal than even the newspapers would have had us believe and his victim, an unknown stranger, had been endowed with more fictitious qualities than he could ever have possessed in reality.

The thing I hated most was the way everyone had taken Miles's death as an opportunity to plump up their own egos, to prove how non-murderous, non-cowardly and non-deceitful they were compared with him. Scott had told me that in the Gordon Arms, people had avoided the seat that Miles had used to sit in. They'd talked in whispers, embellishing the times that they, themselves, had got an inkling of his violent, uncontrollable temper. Instead of remembering his good qualities and – however sporadically – that he'd been a member of our community, everyone had taken to talking about him as an outcast, a bad sort who, with his flash car and fashionable clothes, had never fitted in. Even Louisa's Bible meetings were now seen as a superstitious plan to notch up celestial Brownie points in her attempt to protect herself against her tyrannical husband.

I'd felt sorry for Miles and it had seemed as if I was the only person in the whole world who mourned for him. I'd seen with my own eyes how scared he'd been, how he'd nearly outwitted the police. I'd wanted nothing more than for him to come back and stick up for himself, and tell the inhabitants of Rushton to go to hell. Loops of sagging police tape still hung around the charred oak tree at the bottom of the Avenue where Miles had crashed, and every time I'd passed I'd wanted to cry. I'd never known anyone who'd died before and my dreams had been haunted by the sight of his Porsche, crumpling like tin foil against the solid tree. The smell of burning had seemed to be inside my nostrils and I'd felt on edge the whole time. Every day I'd woken up panicked that the feeling of being alive would drain away from me at any moment if I wasn't vigilant enough.

Whether Louisa felt the shame her old neighbours assumed she must I didn't know. All I'd seen was that the house next door had gone up for sale. The place that had once been my home from home had taken on a deserted, ghostly aura; a place that kids in the village now told spook stories about, and dared each other to run up to the windows. I'd woken up a few days previously to discover that someone had spray-painted the word 'murderer' on the front porch and I'd felt outraged, as if I'd personally been tattooed in my sleep.

But worse than all of this, for me, had been that in the aftermath of Miles's death, Fred had never been mentioned. He hadn't fitted conveniently into the scandalous saga of Miles's demise, the popular myth which had been talked about so much, that it'd been moulded and carved into a thing, almost as tangible as a totem pole. Fred had been lopped off the side, as if he hadn't belonged to the story.

If that hadn't been bad enough, the reality that Fred and I had ever been together had vanished overnight. My parents, who'd never really acknowledged the feelings I'd had for Fred, now blankly denied that there'd ever been any. Even at school, Fred and I – the 'us' that everyone had previously been so interested in – had become erased by the 'them' – the scandalous Ropers.

That was why, since I'd seen Miles crash in the car, I'd needed to show Fred that I still loved him. I'd needed to tell him that I didn't judge him, that to me he was still my Fred, whatever had happened. But above all, I'd needed to be physical with him. I'd felt so contact-starved, so in need of a hug, that now, as we lay on the ground, I was insatiable.

Fred's face flickered in the shadows. 'Am I squashing you?' he whispered, shifting to take more weight on his elbows.

'No,' I whispered back, wrapping my legs round his as tightly as I could. 'I want all of you.'

'I want you too . . .' he murmured.

I pulled back, holding his face in my hands, his nose almost touching mine. 'Fred . . . I want to do it . . .'

Fred looked startled for a moment. 'Are you sure? I mean, don't you want to wait?'

I pulled away from him, to get a better look at his face, worried that he didn't share my feelings. 'Wait until when?' I asked.

Fred looked deep into my eyes, stroking my hair. 'Oh, Mickey?' He sighed. 'Everything we planned . . .'

'It doesn't matter. Nothing matters. Only now,' I whispered, nuzzling my face into his neck, letting my nostrils delight in the smell of his skin. 'I don't want to wait any longer. Do you?'

'Of course I don't. God, Mickey –' he said, reaching round to hold me even tighter. I closed my eyes, feeling my body respond to his, as we started kissing again. I eased his jumper up, as we rolled on to our sides until Fred pulled away, smiling.

'We've got too many clothes on,' he panted.

'I know.' I giggled. 'I'll race you.'

Frantically we knelt up, ripping off our clothes, flinging them away from us. I could feel the chill air on my skin, but inside I was burning up. Naked, we knelt up opposite each other.

Fred's face was soft in the candlelight, his skin pale, almost luminous. 'Look at you . . .' He sighed, his hand reaching out to stroke my breast.

I couldn't believe how amazing he looked naked. I'd known his body all my life, but now it was like seeing him as a real man for the first time. I reached out and touched the firm muscles in his arms, letting my eyes roam over the smooth skin on his hard stomach.

Any embarrassment I thought I'd feel simply wasn't there. Instead, it felt as if we were the only people on the whole planet, as if what we were doing had never been done before. Kneeling before Fred, under the angels, I felt impossibly romantic, overwhelmingly primeval. This was nothing like anyone had ever described at school. This wasn't like I'd even imagined it to be on holiday in France in a sleeping bag. 'You're gorgeous,' I whispered. 'Oh, Fred, Fred, I've missed you so much.'

He silenced me with a kiss and we pressed our bodies together, kissing each other's skin, our fingers exploring, tentatively at first, then with more confidence as our bodies found each other. Fred wrapped his arms round me and laid me back down, and planted kisses on every inch of my skin. I arched towards him, my fingers grabbing his hair.

'You're beautiful, Mickey,' he murmured, between kisses.

Eventually, I pulled him up towards me and we stared into each other's eyes. My heart was pounding more than ever.

'Will you love me in the morning, Fred Roper?' I asked with a smile.

'I'll love you in the morning and every morning for the rest of your life. Whatever happens, I'll always be yours, Mickey, I swear it.'

Then I felt him press against me and into me. My eyes opened. 'I love you, I love you, I love you,' I sobbed repeatedly, kissing his face.

'You're perfect,' he gasped. 'Oh, Mickey –'

'Roper!'

The gruff sound of a man's angry voice fell like an axe blow. Yelping, I jerked my head away, protecting my face from the unrelenting beam of light, freezing like a convict on a fence. I felt Fred rip away from me as, frantically, he grabbed the dust sheets and pulled them round us.

'I told you,' I heard another voice say, laughing.

'Clarkson!' said Fred.

I squinted over the top of the sheet and saw a boy with a long dark fringe, folding his arms and leaning on the doorway.

'That's enough, Phillip,' said an older man, as he patted

Clarkson on the shoulder. Clarkson pointed his finger at Fred, a horrible taunting expression on his face, before pulling himself away and sloping back out of the door, flicking his fingers through his fringe.

I curled up in a ball, as the older man spoke again. 'Make yourself decent, Roper,' he told Fred. 'I'll see you and your . . . friend . . . outside. Immediately.'

The door slammed behind him and the draft blew out half our candles.

Fred's face was a mask of anguish. He clawed at his hair as he knelt up. 'Oh, God.'

I sat up and scrambled for my clothes. I felt humiliation freeze me to my bones and my teeth started chattering.

'Oh, Mickey,' Fred said desperately. 'I'm so sorry. I'm so fucking sorry.'

'Is there another way out of here?' I asked, frantically pulling on my pedal pushers. 'Surely –'

'No. That's the only door. We're trapped.'

I stared at him as we got dressed, biting my lips together, feeling the intimacy we'd shared only moments ago shatter and evaporate into the cloud of dust around us. My knees were shaking as I pulled on my trainers, my body still in shock. Without saying anything, I watched as Fred stamped out the candles angrily before holding out his hand to pull me up. He stood for a moment, squeezing my hand in the darkness, neither of us able to find words. I closed my eyes, wishing I could beam us away, but it was too late.

The door opened again and the torch filled the room with cold light. 'Come on. Get on with it,' commanded the older man, who was obviously a teacher. I stumbled after Fred into the sterile light that lead us to the door and to our fate.

The journey back to the boarding house was horrible. The housemaster, who told me his name was Mr Pearce, had his car parked on the driveway near the gate. There

273

was another master waiting there. Fred was told to get into the other master's car and then I was told to get into the back of Mr Pearce's car with Clarkson. I shrank away from him into the corner of the seat as the car crept along the gravel drive towards the school buildings, feeling his stare boring into me.

The school was much bigger than I'd imagined and looked eerily dark. A large clock in a tower above the imposing entrance chimed midnight as the two cars came to a halt on the edge of the drive.

Mr Pearce got out and opened the door next to me, but I sat, rigid, not daring to move. 'Come on,' he said.

Without looking at him, I stepped out on to the drive.

I could hear the other car stop and looked up to see Fred getting out of the passenger seat. His eyes locked with mine, but we couldn't speak as he walked towards me.

'We'll go to my house, Jerry,' Mr Pearce said to the other master, who nodded.

Clarkson slammed the passenger door and came round the back of Mr Pearce's car, as Fred and the other master walked towards us. 'I'm impressed, Roper,' he said to Fred, before whistling through his teeth. 'She's not bad –'

Fred let out a guttural yell, lunging at Clarkson, his fists raised.

'Whoa! Big fella.' Clarkson laughed, ducking out of the way, mimicking Fred's flailing fists as Fred was pulled back by the other master.

'I'll kill you!' snarled Fred, as the master yanked him away, pulling angrily at the shoulder of his jumper.

'Tut, tut,' sneered Clarkson. 'I'd have thought what happened to your father would have put you off that sort of thing.'

'Enough!' said Mr Pearce to Clarkson. 'That will be all. Now go to your room.'

Clarkson smiled and winked at me, before walking off to the large building, putting his hands casually in his pockets as he whistled. I could see Fred shaking as he watched him go and I felt my pulse racing. I wanted to pound Clarkson into the ground.

'Let's go and sort this out,' said Mr Pearce, nodding his head towards the other master who stood close to Fred. For a second, I contemplated making a run for it and I knew that Fred would follow, but Mr Pearce seemed to read my thoughts and steered me towards the door of a large house.

Desperately, I looked over my shoulder at Fred, biting back my tears.

I followed Mr Pearce through the front door into a warm, panelled hallway. There was a large wooden rack with umbrellas and coats, and several pairs of boots. A Labrador raised its head sleepily from where it was lying on a rug at the bottom of the stairs.

'If you'll come this way . . .' Mr Pearce said firmly, leading me by the elbow towards a door on the left. He opened it and directed me into a small study.

'But –' I said, as I realised Fred wasn't following.

Mr Pearce nodded at the other housemaster who lead Fred up the hallway and before I had a chance to say anything else, Mr Pearce walked into the study after me and closed the door. He was tall, with a bushy brown beard and alert blue eyes, and younger than I'd thought, probably even younger than my parents. 'You can sit down,' he said, walking behind the large, leather-topped desk.

I stood defiantly where I was, looking around the room. Most of one wall was covered in framed photos of school sports teams, the other two in floor-to-ceiling bookcases. There was a green glass reading lamp on the large leather-topped desk, which Mr Pearce clicked on.

'Where's Fred going? I want to see Fred,' I demanded, trying to stop my chin quivering as I narrowed my eyes at him.

'I'm afraid that's out of the question,' he said, throwing his keys down on to the desk.

'You can't stop me,' I raised my voice, choking.

Mr Pearce exhaled deeply, before fixing me with a serious stare. 'I'm afraid I can,' he said and I felt rage rear up in me.

'No!' I shouted, lunging for the door.

In a second Mr Pearce was round the desk and his arm slapped high on the door, holding it closed.

I pulled desperately at the porcelain door handle. 'Let me go!' I shouted. 'Let me go!'

Mr Pearce increased his force on the door and I couldn't make it budge. Hot, angry tears burnt down my face.

'Please . . . just stop it,' he said, pulling my shoulder. 'It won't do any good.' He turned me round, held my shoulders and bent to look in my face. 'Just calm down, OK?'

'But . . . what are you going to do to him?' I cried desperately.

Mr Pearce drew me away from the door and made me sit in the red leather chair. He leant on its back next to me. 'Look, er . . .?' he said calmly, leaning forward.

'Mickey,' I mumbled, swiping angrily at my tears.

'Mickey. OK . . . well, Mickey, we have a thing here called *in loco parentis*. Do you know what that means?'

I shook my head.

'It means', he continued infuriatingly calmly, 'that I am responsible for all the boys here. In this house they fall under my care. By law I have to act as their parents would if they were here.'

'Fred doesn't need you. He's old enough to do what he wants,' I spat back.

'He's not. Not according to the law and not according to the rules of this school.'

'Well, I think your rules are stupid,' I blurted out. 'You lock people up here like animals –'

276

'This is an educational establishment, Mickey, not a zoo. The rules are here for a purpose. They are here for the boys' own protection.'

'Fred doesn't need protecting.'

'I'll have to disagree with you there. How old are you?'

'Seventeen,' I lied.

Mr Pearce looked unimpressed and raised his eyebrows at me. 'I'm going to need your parents' number. I take it they don't know you're here?'

I sat silently, feeling trapped, my hands curled into tight fists. I hated this man and everything he stood for.

'Can you tell me your home number?' asked Mr Pearce, walking behind his desk and picking up the telephone receiver.

'Go to hell,' I snarled.

Mr Pearce put the phone down slowly. 'Look, Mickey,' he said reasonably, ignoring my last remark. 'I appreciate that you're angry and this situation is rather delicate, but let's not make it any worse than it already is. I think it's best if you stay the night here and your parents can come and collect you in the morning.' He looked at me, but I still refused to relent. 'If it makes you feel any better, I won't tell them about . . . well, you know.' He cleared his throat.

I bit my lips together and looked up at the ceiling. I could see a cobweb hanging from the light. I was determined not to speak, but Mr Pearce wasn't letting me off the hook.

'I've got all night,' he said, picking up the receiver again. 'I can find out your home number from Fred's mother, if you would prefer?'

The last thing I wanted was for Louisa to get involved. I had no choice but to tell him and I watched as he dialled. I could tell it was Dad who answered and I felt myself cringing, as Mr Pearce talked to him.

'Hello, it's Andrew Pearce here from Greenaway

College,' he introduced himself, scratching a tuft of his beard. 'You've no doubt been wondering where your daughter, Mickey, is?'

He glanced at me. 'Yes, that's right . . . her friend Frederick Roper . . .'

I tuned out, staring towards the wall, my eyes blurring with tears.

Eventually Mr Pearce put down the phone. 'Come on,' he said, standing up and ushering me out of the door. 'My wife will look after you. 'Sue?' he called, stepping out into the corridor, his voice jovial, as if nothing had happened. I stared at him, astounded that he could have detonated my world and yet sound so cheerful. A short woman with frizzy hair appeared from a door near the stairs. She was wearing a pink and white tracksuit and she smiled at me as she walked towards us, gently shooing the dog out of the way. 'If you can fix Mickey here up in the box room . . .'

The room was up two flights of stairs at the back of the house. It was decorated with frilly blue curtains and had speckled blue and purple wallpaper. I sat on the soft bed feeling more alone than ever. I'd already tried the window, but it was locked and I knew that Mr and Mrs Pearce would be listening out for my every move. Fred was somewhere on the other side of that wall, he could only be feet away, but he might as well have been in Australia.

The blue carpet was a blur, as tears fell on to my lap. Only half an hour ago I'd been lying naked with Fred, but it seemed like a lifetime away and, even though I was fully clothed now, I felt more exposed than ever. I was swamped by the humiliation of having been caught in the act. I supposed it would be the kind of thing that was funny, if it had happened to someone else. I could imagine Annabel and Pippa gasping with delighted horror, if they were ever to find out. But to me it felt desperate. I simply couldn't get my head past the shame of Mr Pearce, and that vile Clarkson, seeing Fred and me. It had made it all so sordid. However hard I tried to remember how beautiful and amazing it had been making love, it had been soiled and ruined by other people, and I wanted to kill them all.

Everything had been perfect. Or at least as perfect as possible, given the circumstances. But now, having been ripped away from Fred, I felt worse than I did when I hadn't been able to see him at all. I couldn't bear to think about what was happening to him, or how bad he must be feeling. At least I was on my own. Poor Fred would be back in his dormitory and everyone would know about us.

I don't know how long I sat on the bed, but eventually I heard the door open. Mrs Pearce walked into the room and put a steaming mug on the bedside table. 'I made you some hot chocolate,' she said and I glanced at the mug out of the corner of my eye, but didn't say anything.

'Mickey?' Mrs Pearce, put her hand on my shoulder and sat down next to me on the bed. The springs underneath creaked with her weight. 'Are you OK?' she asked gently.

'It's not fair,' I whispered. 'It's not fair.'

'Come on, now. It'll all seem better in the morning,' she said.

I looked up at her, my eyes narrowed with loathing. 'It won't. It won't. You don't understand. It's not Fred's fault –'

'Look, if it makes you feel any better, Fred isn't going to be expelled. He's leaving anyway after his exams in two weeks. The poor boy, he's been through quite enough.'

Her words didn't make me feel better. They were the last thing I wanted to hear, but something in her tone made me feel less bitter. I turned to her, hoping to appeal to her. 'Can't I see him? Just for a minute,' I begged.

'I don't think that's going to be possible,' she said, reaching behind me and pulling back the cover. 'Certainly not tonight. Look, the best thing you can do is get some rest. We'll see what we can do in the morning.'

Reluctantly, I shifted backwards and pulled my feet up, hugging my knees.

'There. That's right,' said Mrs Pearce, handing me a tissue.

I blew my nose. 'Thanks,' I mumbled.

'Just get some sleep now. I expect you're very tired.' She smiled at me, her eyes kind. 'It'll all be better in the morning.'

I nodded dumbly as she stood up and left the room, throwing me a worried look before closing the door. Then I buried my head in my knees and sobbed myself to sleep.

It wasn't better in the morning. I was jarred out of fitful dreams by a piercing electric bell. I could hear shouting and I leapt out of bed, pulling aside the curtain. Fifteen minutes or so later there were more bells. I looked through the window. The doors in the main part of the building burst open and a whole gang of boys in school uniform spilt out on to the drive, running against the rain. I leant up towards the glass window-pane, wiping my condensed breath off with my sleeve, hoping to find Fred's face in the crowd, but he wasn't there.

Predictably, my dad turned up early. It was odd seeing him at Fred's school. Dressed in his best, most sombre suit, he still seemed out of his depth and stuttered uncomfortably. I said nothing as he thanked Mr and Mrs Pearce, assuring them that I would be punished in the way he saw fit. I felt an icy detachment descend on me as I walked to Dad's car. I didn't look back as I left the school grounds.

Dad and I didn't speak all the way back to Rushton. I sat, fixating on the windscreen wipers, watching the blades lash back and forth, feeling as if I were being whipped. I didn't care what my parents did to me. The worst punishment in the world had already happened.

When we got home, Mum was waiting in the dining

room, angrily smoking a cigarette. I noticed the ashtray on the table was already full. 'I can't believe you,' she started, her head wobbling with fury. 'The humiliation of it all. You have no idea –'

'What made you do it?' asked Dad, finding his voice at last. 'What made you run away?'

I looked at him, astounded that he could ask such a question. How could I begin to make him understand that Fred and I were in love and that seeing Fred was the only thing that mattered to me?

Mum stood with her hands on her hips, her face set in an angry scowl. 'Answer your father,' she commanded.

I ignored her, squeezing my lips together as I looked at the light hanging over the table. From the corner of my eye I could see Dad glancing at Mum and I sensed a change of tack.

Dad cleared his throat. 'Did Fred? Did he . . . you know . . . touch you?' he asked.

I felt something inside me snap. I looked between my parents, feeling hatred surge through me. 'We were having sex,' I sneered. 'Of course he touched me.'

My mother let out a whimper and turned away. 'Oh, Geoffrey!' she said, clutching her hand to her mouth.

'Don't treat me like a child,' I shouted.

'But you *are* a child,' said Dad icily.

'You can't stop me doing what I want,' I yelled, rearing towards him. For a moment I thought he was going to slap my face, but he didn't.

'We can and we will. You're not going to see Fred again. Not ever. Do you hear me?'

'I'm going to see him. I don't care what you say. We love each other and we're going to be together.'

'No, you're not,' said Dad. 'You're going to do your exams and start showing some respect around here.'

'I hate you!' I screamed at him. 'I hate you both. You don't care about me.'

'That's it!' shouted my mother, incensed. 'Can't you understand? There'll be no more of this nonsense.' She started towards me, but Dad held her back.

I glared at her, willing every ounce of spite I could muster at her, before turning on my heel and running up the stairs to my bedroom, where I slammed the door as hard as I possibly could.

The flat feels unusually quiet when Lisa and Joe have gone out. I zap through the TV channels, feeling at a loose end. There's nothing on that's worth watching, so I turn it off and run a bath. I dig through Lisa's wooden box of aromatherapy oils and pull out the rose oil. Unscrewing the lid, I breathe in the heady scent and wonder if it really can solve all my stress.

It takes thirty roses to make just one drop of essential oil. Being in love back then was like dousing myself in a whole bottle of the stuff. It was overpowering, heady and dangerous, and every emotion since has seemed vastly diluted. It strikes me now, as I carefully tip a few drops under the gushing water, that ever since Fred, I've lived half my life in a pretty much constant state of anticlimax.

I kept a diary after we were split up that fateful night. Writing down how I felt seemed to be the only way of ordering my thoughts. For a year, I wrote daily, like a prisoner bursting with impotent outrage, as I hurled myself against the infuriating wall of parental authority. At first my lengthy outpourings were tear-stained and grief-ridden, long passages of which I duplicated in my letters to Fred. But when I heard nothing back from him my diary entries became an embittered tirade, giving way to confusion and, lastly, depression.

Then I wrote to keep my feelings alive, recording mundane events of my lonely existence with added pathos, hoping that one day those pages would be my evidence.

That if, by some miracle, I ever did see Fred again, I could show him the tomes to make him experience the misery I'd felt. Or, if the worst came to the worst and I died, my parents would be able to read and weep at the unhappiness they'd inflicted on me.

For most of my childhood I'd been chasing adulthood, willing it to be official, seeing the age of independence burning like a beacon on my horizon, but without Fred I felt robbed of any glory and I barely had the energy to blow out the candles on the cake Grandma Richie made for my sixteenth birthday. Of course, I failed my O levels, more out of protest than anything else. Since the world wanted to treat me like an imbecilic child, I decided I'd behave like one. I had nothing to live for and where there had been a future vibrant with dreams, without Fred there was just a blank.

Thinking back, it seems ironic that it wasn't the moment I lost my virginity to Fred that marked the end of my childhood, but when I slammed my bedroom door on my parents. I was more petulant and childish than ever, but as I wept into the dressing gown hanging on the inside of my door, beating my fists with muffled frustration, I became aware that I'd lost and for the first time I was defeated.

I can't blame my parents for the way they acted. They were frightened that I was growing up too quickly. And I can't blame Mr Pearce, Fred's housemaster, for splitting us up because he also acted out of fear. His hands were tied by responsibility and the possible consequences of allowing his dependants to live outside the rules. And so it was that between them, their fear seeped under my barricaded bedroom door and I became an adult.

From that moment on I never had the same view of the world. Where once my parents had had to stop me, I now stopped myself. I changed from being self-centred to being self-censored. The world ceased to be a place of wonder, a place to go and grab. I never opened an atlas after that and shouted 'stop'. I never built elaborate fantasies again. Even when I met Dan and moved to London, there was a part of my heart that was always cautious.

If Fred and I had been able to stay in touch, perhaps things would have been different. Inevitably, though, fury turned to apathy and the pain hardened into numbness. The diary writing waned and then stopped. I'd relived our passion in the temple over and over in my mind, until I'd regurgitated the memory so many times that it stopped being tangible. Eventually my whole relationship with Fred no longer felt real. We were old news. Everyone and everything moved on. Even the newspaper articles about Miles, which had seemed so important at the time, were consigned to kitty litter.

I tip my head back and let the water seep into my hair. I feel it float like seaweed around my head and wonder what life would be like if I weren't cautious. Last weekend flashes into my head. I feel the sunshine up on Jimmy Dughead's field and see myself standing with Joe and Fred looking out over the rooftops of Rushton. Could life really be like that all the time?

I sit up abruptly and smooth the water from my hair, angry with myself. I can't do this. Last weekend wasn't a promise of things to come, it was a pleasant aftertaste of things that have gone and I'm a fool to think there's any reality in it. It was no more real than a television advert showing a happily family. Life isn't like that: the parents are actors and the children have make-up on to make them look rosy.

I hug my knees up in the bath and face facts. The truth is that Fred isn't mine, he's Rebecca's. Tomorrow, he'll walk up an aisle towards her, looking impossibly handsome and the snapshot image of a happy couple full of hope will have her face in it, not mine.

It's wrong to feel jealous, but I feel sick with it. I don't think the rose oil has helped. I feel as if I've got pure green loathing pumping through my veins.

For a second I fantasise about calling Rebecca. 'Hi, Rebecca, it's Mickey here,' I say aloud. 'Fred doesn't love you. He loves me.'

As soon as I've said it, I let out a deep sigh. How can I think such a thing? What kind of a person would it make me if I did that? Why ruin her life? She hasn't done anything wrong. It's not Rebecca's fault, it's Fred's.

Of course, I could take matters into my own hands. I could, if I had the nerve, split Fred and Rebecca up. I could be the one to stand up in the church and spell out the just cause and impediment *exactly* why it is that they shouldn't be joined in holy matrimony, but what would it prove? I wouldn't be the girl Fred ran off with, I'd be the person who'd ruined everyone's day.

I know I'm being unfair because, by anyone else's standards, Fred's done nothing wrong, but I still despise him for taking the easy path. He's spent his adult life treading so carefully that he's become highly skilled at it, but I suppose he's an exemplary model of the way we're all supposed to behave. I should applaud his maturity, not denounce it.

Of course he's not going to run out on Rebecca. Why would he? He's adapted to being a Wilson and built a highly successful life around the person he is now. Why should I set such great store by the past that we once shared, or the person I loved all those years ago? Is that honestly enough to expect him to change his whole life?

After all, it's not as if I've offered him anything but a whole load of doubts. Even when we were on the brink of being reckless, even when he was right there in front of me, I still backed away and wouldn't risk my security for him. If I didn't act then, why should Fred act now?

But being adult about our situation doesn't solve it. The

reason I'm feeling so churned up is because seeing Fred again has reminded me of something. Of a girl who wasn't afraid to take action and sitting here, shivering, even though the bath is hot, I feel ashamed when I compare myself with the person I used to be.

I get out of the bath, fling on some old jeans and start a hunt for my hairdryer. I find it in Joe's room and sit on his bed. Under the bottom of the duvet is a lump and I reach under and pull out Joe's toy turtle. He's had it for a few years and I tweak the ears of the familiar friend. I press down on its head, trying to find the hard lump inside that, when pressed, activates an electronic voice.

'Make a wish,' says the turtle's voice and I smile.

'Well, turtle,' I say aloud, 'I wish I was young again.' I look up and catch my reflection in Joe's small mirror, and feel tears welling up, as I dare myself to say what I'm thinking. 'And I wish,' I say hoarsely, looking at my bedraggled, tangled hair and tired face, 'I wish . . .'

The next morning I wake up early and can't get back to sleep. I lie in bed, a strange sense of calm descending. This is Saturday, the day that Fred's getting married. All week I've been dreading going to pieces, but actually I feel fine. Fred's made his decision. For whatever reason, he came back into my life after all these years and has gone again, and I have to take what I can from it.

I check to see that Lisa is in, before deciding to do a quick dash to the flower market to pick up a few supplies. I'll be back before either Joe or Lisa is awake and it'll be more useful than sitting in bed waiting for the day to start. I leave a note for Joe, just in case.

I love driving through London in the hour before dawn. It's wonderful zipping through the streets without any traffic. As I drive down Ladbroke Grove and past Holland Park to Shepherd's Bush, apart from the odd street-cleaning truck and milk float, there's hardly anyone about.

The street lamps hang over the road, as if they've been put there to ease my journey, and I play my usual game of trying to up my record of fourteen green traffic lights in a row.

I nearly make it, but as I get down to Earls Court I'm stopped by a red light at number thirteen. I wind down the window to smell the fresh air. A bakery lorry is parked and as a man unloads the large crates, I get a whiff of fresh baguettes.

I like the sense of other people dealing with life at this time of day. Ahead of me the bright neon sign on the twenty-four-hour chemist whizzes round and, opposite, the news-stand guy is arranging the first editions of the Saturday papers. He tuts as a couple of boys stumble across the road. They're wearing sweatshirts, and look chilly and disorientated, as if they've just come out of a club. One of them throws his arm round the other's shoulder as they stumble down the road. On the other side of the road, behind the dark windows of a pub, the illuminated logos of the beer manufacturers glare out from the pumps and a tramp looks in at the window.

I drive on down to the Embankment as the sky starts to lighten and I can see the dark tips of the trees in Battersea Park becoming distinct. The lights on Albert Bridge twinkle as I approach and a large barge blasts its horn as it passes underneath along the slick stretch of water.

I turn right into New Covent Garden market just past the Battersea Dogs Home. I drive through the barriers and follow the filter road through to the car park.

Saturday is a quiet day at the flower market. I usually come on a Monday when, from 3 a.m., it's manic. But on a Saturday it's much more peaceful and I like being able to have the space and time to chat to some of the traders.

I park in my usual spot, watching the lorry drivers sipping coffee from polystyrene cups, and reach behind the seat in the van. Inside the market the temperature is always chilled to keep the flowers fresh and I pull out the padded jacket I keep especially for my visits here.

It's quiet in the car park and, with only the occasional van driving round the outer road, it still feels like the middle of the night. But as I walk towards the large warehouse and through the automatic swing doors everything changes.

Inside, the lighting is colour-corrected and it could be the middle of the day. The large floor space is packed with stalls and people, and there's a sound system that plays chirpy music, only just audible over the crowd. As usual, I stop and take the time to let my nostrils fill with the heady scent of a million flowers. I feel my spirits lifting as I survey the wall of colour. It always amazes me how these beautiful blooms make it from all over the world. There are suppliers here who bring stock in from Holland, Columbia, Israel, Italy and Africa. As well as the usual florists' staples of roses, carnations and chrysanthemums in every conceivable shape and shade, there are also the exotic and weird blooms that I love from Asia and the Caribbean, and every time I come I find something new.

The units around the perimeter of the vast hall are reserved for sundriesmen and foliage suppliers. I make my way over to Miranda's stall, where ribbons, baskets, dried and silk flowers, oasis and wire are jammed so tightly together that it's amazing she has room for herself. I find her behind a menagerie of dried moss animals. She supplies them to all the big hotels for more exotic flower arrangements and I have to duck under a huge camel to get to her. I chat for a while as she puts a big block of oasis into a bag for me, which, fortunately, she's agreed to give me on credit.

I duck out past the camel and say hello to Hilary, my lily supplier. She's surrounded by boxes and I look down into them. The long-stemmed white flowers look flawless and so velvety that I want to reach out and stroke them.

Harry, at the Hargreaves stand, is thigh deep in peonies and roses of every shade. He's a salt-of-the-earth East Ender who's been in the flower business all his life. He smiles when he sees me. 'Watcha, Mickey,' he says, with his usual grin. 'Looking lovely this morning.'

'Hi, Harry,' I reply, flipping my hand to bat away his misplaced compliment. 'Busy?'

'No,' he says. 'It's been quiet all morning. Nice to have a breather, mind.'

Harry sets up at midnight and is often here until midday the next day. We don't usually have a chance to talk much.

'What can I get you?'

'Nothing today, I'm afraid. I'm out of cash. Just browsing, really.'

'Have you seen Jimmy this morning?' he asks suddenly, as if he's remembered something.

'No.' I shrug. 'Why?'

'He was looking for you.'

'Me?' I ask, alarmed. Jimmy is one of the managers here. I usually arrange payment with him and I feel my cheeks start to burn as I realise that my credit must have run out.

'Says he's got a message for you.'

Immediately, my money worries are put to one side as I think of Joe. My mobile phone is on the blink, so maybe he's rung here, but I can't think what could be wrong.

I thank Harry and hurry towards the stairs that lead to the mezzanine floor where all the offices are, bumping into Vince, one of the porters, on the way.

'Jimmy's looking for you,' he says.

'I know. Have you seen him?'

'He's up there, I think.' He nods towards the office windows.

'Do you know what it's about?'

'There was a phone call,' he says and my heart starts to beat faster.

I find Jimmy by the door. He's in his late thirties and is completely bald. He's holding a tray full of bedding plants and I have to wait for him to put them down.

'There you are. Hang on,' he says, putting the pansies down. He digs into the pocket of his jeans. 'I got this for you.' He pulls out a piece of paper and reads it. 'This bloke . . . called about half an hour ago. Fred something or other . . .'

'Fred?' I ask, feeling like my heart has jumped into my throat. 'What did he say?'

'Said it was important. He said to tell you to meet him,' says Jimmy handing over the paper. I take it from him and look at the scribbled writing.

'Just meet him? Is that all?' I ask. 'I mean, did he say where, or when?'

'He said if you wanted to, you'd know where.'

I stare at Jimmy for a second, my brain speeding ahead into overdrive.

'You're sure that's all?' I repeat.

'The line was bad, I think he was on a mobile, but those were his exact words. If she wants to, she'll know where. That was all.'

'Oh,' I mumble.

'What is this guy? Some kind of secret agent?' asks Jimmy.

'Something like that.'

'Sorry I can't be more help,' Jimmy says with a shrug.

'It's OK. Thanks,' I mumble, clutching the piece of paper.

It's turned into a bright, sunny morning by the time I get to Rushton. I don't go to my parents, but instead park the van by the church and turn off the engine. I feel sick with apprehension. It's ridiculous coming here. Fred's not going to be here, I'm just following a foolish whim. Yet I'm still shaking with an emotion I can't name, as I put my arms on the steering wheel and take a deep breath.

I called Joe from the flower market to see whether he could shed some light on Fred's message, but he was just as vague as Jimmy.

'Did you speak to Fred?' I asked deliberately, trying to keep the excitement out of my voice

'Yes.' He yawned. 'I saw your note and told him you were at the flower market.'

'He didn't say anything else?'

'No. Is everything OK?'

'I'm not sure, darling. Can you tell Lisa to open up for me? I'm going to have to do something.'

'What?'

'I don't know yet,' I answered honestly.

And still I don't know. I step out of the van and look around me. There's not a soul in sight and the silence is only broken by the chirruping of sparrows in the large willow trees. Above me, the sky is a clear, pale blue.

Slowly I walk towards the gate. I've been racking my brains, trying to think where Fred would know I'd find him and the only place I could think of was where we first kissed. But even as I approach, I know he's not here.

Hugging my arms round me, memories seem to crowd my head, like film footage. In the silence I can hear our shrieks of delight as we raced sticks under the bridge, the crackle of our worn-out tapes as we played air guitar, the tinkle of the nursery rhymes from the old ice-cream van. I run my finger along the old wood of the church gate, feeling in its roughness the long summer days that we whiled away, as if they'd never end.

I turn and lean back against the gate, scanning the road for Fred's car, but the road remains clear. As the minutes tick by I feel tears of disappointment swelling in my chest. Fred's not coming. Either that, or I've missed him, or guessed the wrong place. In the age of communication, we've failed each other yet again. I bite my lips together, feeling totally lost.

Then I hear the long, slow sound of a car horn. It's coming from the direction of the bridge.

Then I'm running, running until I'm out of breath. I look up as I approach the bridge and stop in my tracks. Fred's sitting on the low wall next to his car, looking across at me. For a second I'm stunned by how old he looks. Where did the time go? How did he stop being a child so quickly?

I make it on to the bridge and stop a few metres from him. As he stands up, all the maturity I saw when he was sitting has gone. Instead, in the angle of his head, all I can see is a little boy, waiting for me to take the lead, not realising that he was the one who always gave me my strength.

'I hoped you'd come,' he says. He looks tired, but even so, his eyes are shining as they lock with mine.

'What's going on?' I gulp, trying to read his expression. 'Aren't you getting married?'

He shakes his head and his shoulders slump, as he runs his toe over the shiny cobbles of the bridge road. 'No. Not any more.'

I stare at him, realising the enormity of what he's saying. 'You mean –'

'It's over. I mean, Rebecca . . . it's . . . gone.'

My eyes widen and I want to reach out and hold him. 'Was it terrible?' I ask.

He nods and there's a long pause.

I can hear the birds singing and the river bubbling below us, as we stare at each other. It's as if we're kids again and we're taking on the world, making pacts and keeping secrets that are just ours. All of a sudden life seems so incredibly precious and so unbelievably short. The future that had seemed so mundane and inevitable is now blasted open with endless possibilities and I'm grinning so hard my face hurts.

We take the last step towards each other and we're just inches apart. There are so many questions, but it doesn't matter: the answer to them all is yes.

'Looks like you've saved my life,' I say.

'Well, I owed you,' Fred says, reaching out his hands.

I grab them, looking at how our fingers fold together and I know that, whatever it takes, I'll never let go.

Meet Jack

Jack Rossiter. I'm twenty-seven years old, single, live with my best mate, Matt. Matt and I started hanging out when we were eight. Life was simpler then. Our idea of fashion was polyester. I told him I wanted to be a spy and he asked me who I'd marry. I imagined falling in love with a girl so perfect I couldn't even guess her name. Things have changed since then. I did fall in love for a while but it didn't work out. And single is good, single is fun.

Meet Amy

Sometimes in my darker moments I've thought about applying to go on Blind Date. 'She's gorgeous, she's from London, come in Amy Crosbie!' (Wolf whistling and applause). Actually it's a bit of a worry. I think it's my warped way of telling myself something's got to change. It's been six months since I last had sex. Six months! I mean, I've got my own flat, I've got A levels – so come down Mr Right. At least it would get my mother off my back.

Now find out what happens when they meet each other in the first novel to tell both sides of the story.

COME AGAIN

Friends. You can't live with them – and you can't live without them.

Or so Matt is discovering. His mate is getting married, leaving him high and dry. No flatmate – and no girlfriend. Then he remembers Helen (H) to her friends. H has no life outside her brilliant career – and all her best friend Amy wants to talk about is her wedding. Which suits Stringer, because catering the wedding is his first real chance to prove himself. The last thing he needs is to fall for one of the bride's friends, Susie, particularly because she's sworn off men while she sorts out her life . . .

Friendship, commitment, work, lust and loyalty all come under the spotlight as Matt, H, Stringer and Susie relate – in their own voices – events in the run up to the big day.

ALSO AVAILABLE IN PAPERBACK

☐ Come Together	Josie Lloyd & Emlyn Rees	£5.99
☐ Come Again	Josie Lloyd & Emlyn Rees	£5.99
☐ Running in Heels	Anna Maxted	£6.99
☐ Getting Over It	Anna Maxted	£5.99
☐ Polly	Freya North	£5.99
☐ Cat	Freya North	£5.99
☐ Tunnel Vision	Keith Lowe	£6.99
☐ T-Shirt and Genes	Richard Asplin	£5.99
☐ Rising to the Occasion	Linda Taylor	£5.99
☐ Lucy Sullivan is Getting Married	Marian Keyes	£6.99
☐ Watermelon	Marian Keyes	£6.99
☐ Maddy Goes to Hollywood	Maureen Martella	£5.99
☐ Animal Husbandry	Laura Zigman	£6.99

ALL ARROW BOOKS ARE AVAILABLE THROUGH MAIL ORDER OR FROM YOUR LOCAL BOOKSHOP.

PAYMENT MAY BE MADE USING ACCESS, VISA, MASTERCARD, DINERS CLUB, SWITCH AND AMEX, OR CHEQUE, EUROCHEQUE AND POSTAL ORDER (STERLING ONLY).

EXPIRY DATE .... SWITCH ISSUE NO.

SIGNATURE ....

PLEASE ALLOW £2.50 FOR POST AND PACKING FOR THE FIRST BOOK AND £1.00 PER BOOK THEREAFTER.

ORDER TOTAL: £................................. (INCLUDING P&P)

ALL ORDERS TO:
ARROW BOOKS, BOOKS BY POST, TBS LIMITED, THE BOOK SERVICE, COLCHESTER ROAD, FRATING GREEN, COLCHESTER, ESSEX, CO7 7DW, UK.

TELEPHONE: (01206) 256 000
FAX: (01206) 255 914

NAME ....

ADDRESS..

....

Please allow 28 days for delivery. Please tick box if you do not wish to receive any additional information. ☐

Prices and availability subject to change without notice.